Praise for Kelly Meding's
THREE DAYS TO DEAD

"Dark, dangerous and delectable. A fantastic debut, impossible to put down!"

—GENA SHOWALTER,
New York Times bestselling author of
Seduce the Darkness

"Action-packed, edgy, and thrilling, *Three Days to Dead* is a fabulous debut! Kelly Meding's world and characters will grab you from the first page. You won't want to miss this one."

—JEANIENE FROST,
New York Times bestselling author of
the Night Huntress series

"*Three Days to Dead* is gritty, imaginative, and a terrific read. Debut author Kelly Meding is a real storyteller and I look forward to reading more of her work."

—PATRICIA BRIGGS,
New York Times bestselling author of *Bone Crossed*

"*Three Days to Dead* is one of the best books I've read. *Ever.* Evy Stone is a heroine's heroine, and I rooted for her from the moment I met her. Kelly Meding has written a phenomenal story, one that's fast-paced, gritty, and utterly addictive. Brava! More! More! *More!*"

—JACKIE KESSLER, co-author of *Black and White*

"Meding delivers a thrilling urban fantasy full of desperate humans and menacing evil. Especially impressive are her worldbuilding skills, which she uses to deftly paint a portrait of a city on the edge of disaster."

—*Romantic Times* (four and a half stars)

"A fun, fast-paced book, with a likable lead and a lot of energy."
—CHARLES deLINT, *F&SF*

"I read *Three Days to Dead* in about four hours because it was just that good [and] Meding has shown that she isn't afraid of breaking her readers' hearts."
—The Good, The Bad and The Unread

"A fast-paced, immensely readable novel. . . . There's a lot of potential for a great series here."
—The Book Smugglers

"A fabulous read and a great addition to the urban fantasy genre."
—Literary Escapism

"From beginning to end, I was completely absorbed in Evy's story. . . . I wanted to savor each word. . . . Everything, from the plot to the description and fabulous action scenes, is sharp and original. . . . *Three Days to Dead* is a gritty, action-packed, fabulous urban fantasy novel by an author that has become an absolutely autobuy for me!"
—The Book Lush

Praise for AS LIE THE DEAD

"Rising star Meding returns to the ominous world and gutsy heroine first introduced in her exceptional debut. . . . Evy is an unforgettable heroine and Meding an author to watch!"
—*Romantic Times* (four stars)

"Fabulous . . . One outstanding feature of this excellent series is the author's ability to mix her fantastical, astounding paranormal world with the grime and typical troubles we all experience in our everyday mundane lives—and both feel completely real. . . . The Dreg City series remains a must for all urban fantasy fans."

—Bitten by Books

"After reading *Three Days to Dead* my expectations for *As Lie the Dead* were really high and I'm happy to say that I was not disappointed at all. *As Lie the Dead* is an action-packed read with a thrilling story and a heart-breakingly sweet romance."

—Book Lovers, Inc.

"After reading the first book in this new series, *Three Days to Dead,* I was in awe of the author and I was glad to have found a book that I had *really* enjoyed reading. After reading *As Lie the Dead,* I am again in awe of the author and now I know for sure that I have found a series that has me hooked."

—Yummy Men and Kick Ass Chicks

"Wow! I LOVED Kelly's debut novel, *Three Days to Dead. . . . As Lie the Dead* is even better."

—Hoosblog

"Meding is definitely an author to add to your must-read piles."

—The Phantom Paragrapher

"Great non-stop action with fun characters and twists you won't see coming. . . . This is a great book."

—My World . . . in words and pages

"Kelly Meding continues to make me a happy reader, and once again I couldn't put her book down until I finished it."

—The Good, The Bad and The Unread

By KELLY MEDING

Another Kind of Dead
As Lie the Dead
Three Days to Dead

ANOTHER KIND OF DEAD

KELLY MEDING

BANTAM BOOKS
NEW YORK

A Bantam Books Mass Market Original

Copyright © 2011 by Kelly Meding

Excerpt of *Wrong Side of Dead* copyright © 2011 by Kelly Meding

Published in the United States by Bantam Books, an imprint of The Random House Publishing Group, a division of Random House, Inc., New York.

BANTAM BOOKS and the rooster colophon are registered trademarks of Random House, Inc.

This book contains an excerpt from the forthcoming book *Wrong Side of Dead* by Kelly Meding. This excerpt has been set for this edition only and may not reflect the final content of the forthcoming edition.

ISBN 978-0-345-52577-2
eBook ISBN 978-345-52578-9

Cover illustration: Cliff Nielsen

Printed in the United States of America

www.bantamdell.com

9 8 7 6 5 4 3 2 1

Books mass market edition: August 2011

For Mom and Dad—
there aren't enough ways to say "thank you"

Acknowledgments

As always, special thanks to the usual suspects who've helped shape this series into what it's become—my fabulous agent, Jonathan Lyons; my equally fabulous editor, Anne Groell; the awesome David Pomerico and the amazing and patient folks at Bantam/Random House and Suvudu.

Lots of love to Nancy and Melissa for listening to my rants, frustrations, and shrieks of joy when something goes right, and for being terrific friends. Thanks to my family for loving me no matter what, ignoring my mood swings, and for being my biggest fans.

A shout-out to Wendy and the Newark crew—because you didn't think I would! Your support has meant the world to me.

And of course, hugs and kisses to my readers, I wouldn't be here without you. Thank you for exploring Dreg City with me.

Chapter One

On the day of Alex Forrester's funeral, the sun gleamed high in the sky. I wanted it to rain, if only to prove that the heavens really opened to mourn our tragedies and the friends we lost. Instead, the sunshine mocked our grief from on high, watchful and seeing nothing.

It was a simple affair in a small cemetery five miles outside the city, orchestrated within a day of the official death declaration. We had no body, so there was no casket—it's damned hard to find the ashes of a half-Blood vampire amid the rubble of an apartment fire. But his father, Leo Forrester, wanted a small memorial. He needed to believe his son was at peace, even though Alex had died at war with himself. And what better way to offer postmortem peace to the dead than with an ancient burial ritual meant to comfort the living?

I wanted the comforting commiseration of rain as I followed Leo through the cemetery, but rain would have revealed me to the prying eyes of people who still thought me dead. We were all safer for the deception, Wyatt had insisted, and I agreed.

A sleepy minister already hovered next to the simple marble marker, laid flat on the earth. "Alexander Forrester, Beloved Son, Best Friend," above the years in which he was born and died. It was all we could afford. Part of me wanted something grander to show he'd been here and touched our lives. The other part of me knew this was enough, maybe more than was necessary, and not to waste good money on sentimentality.

Especially with me and Wyatt both out of jobs.

Leo stopped across the marker from the minister. Wyatt Truman, my partner and constant companion, flanked his left side as we had agreed. I shifted to Leo's right and brushed his elbow to indicate my presence. The minister acknowledged the two men with a nod and began to recite a prayer. He wasn't ignoring me. Thanks to an orange crystal shard and a bargained favor from a human mage named Brutus, the minister couldn't see me. No one could, due to the invisibility spell contained in the crystal.

I tuned out the words of the prayer and closed my eyes. I reached up and held the plain silver cross looped around my neck on a thin chain—a gift Alex had once given to his best friend Chalice. I tried to picture Alex's face in the short time I'd known him—friendly blue eyes, broad shoulders, an innocent smile that didn't belong on a twenty-eight-year-old medical student. I caught the memory and enjoyed it briefly until another superimposed itself. Hair mottled with silver and irides-cent eyes, baby fangs that had punctured his lower lip. Sniveling and crying and begging me to kill him.

And I had, a little over a week ago. I'd shot him in the back of the head. Just another on the long list of sins I'd never atone for.

I wanted to cry, but I had no tears left to shed.

No, that was a lie. I'd mourned Alex as best I could, and I was sick of crying. It was time to stop punishing myself for Alex and move on with my life. The life I wanted to start with Wyatt. Burying Alex, putting this chapter of my afterlife behind me, was the first step.

I hoped.

". . . and I will dwell in the house of the Lord. Amen," the minister said.

I opened my eyes and stepped back, barely missing Leo's elbow as he reached out to shake the minister's hand. It was over that quickly. A few mourners, a smattering of words, and the well-wishes of a man who didn't know us or the dead man he'd just prayed over.

Rituals were so odd.

The minister hustled off, probably racing away to his next gig of offering empty comfort to those willing to pay him for it. Once he was out of earshot, I said, "That was nice," and could have smacked myself for it. It was a stupid thing to say.

"It was," Leo said. He turned, seeking a face he couldn't see, and fixed his attention on Wyatt instead. It was probably easier to have a conversation with an invisible person when you had a visible one to look at. "That's it, then."

"What do you mean?" I asked.

Leo removed his wire-rimmed glasses and wiped the lenses on the corner of a wadded tissue. His eyes were red. He seemed to be choosing his words as he cleaned the glasses, then returned them to the bridge of his nose. "Simple words for a simple fact, Evy," he said. "I've buried the last of my family. I have no home. That's it for me."

I put my hand on his shoulder. He jumped under the unexpected touch but didn't pull away. He seemed to easily accept the notion that I was invisible and yet standing right next to him. We'd talked yesterday for hours. Well, I'd talked for hours, feeding him details of my old life as a Dreg Bounty Hunter, the circumstances of my death and resurrection into the body of a woman who happened to have magical teleporting powers, and Alex's brave and tragic desire to help me, all the way through my second "death" in a factory fire last Saturday. All in all, he was handling his newfound education with amazing aplomb.

"Those of us who survive owe it to our loved ones to make our lives count," I said. Words I'd come to believe in more and more since the violent deaths of my former Triad partners, Jesse and Ash, two weeks ago.

But my disembodied words didn't sink in. I considered removing the crystal from my jeans pocket and speaking the phrase meant to reverse the magic early, before its six-hour time limit wore off. I could force Leo to look me in the eye, get him to understand why he had to keep going.

But training won out over emotion. All but five people in the world thought I was dead—burned to death in a factory fire started, on purpose, to kill me—and I couldn't risk exposing myself. I had more enemies than allies now, and that meant preserving every advantage I could find. Being dead had worked in my favor once before.

Besides, I couldn't possibly hope to understand Leo's perspective. I knew much of his story—enough to realize he would never get to ask Alex's forgiveness for past sins, and that was eating him up inside. A son had died blaming his father. No, I couldn't relate—not to that—but perhaps Wyatt could.

Wyatt had, after all, been the unwitting pawn in the game that had killed my partners, killed me, then brought me back only to further a plot to unleash an ancient demon on the world. He'd once destroyed the life of one of his former Hunters in a misguided effort to save it, and that Hunter had returned with a vendetta that led to the deaths of sixty-four people. So many unforgiven sins.

"I'm fifty-six years old," Leo said. "I can't see making my life count for much of anything now."

"You can stay in the city and help us." I ignored the strangled sound Wyatt made from somewhere behind me. "I can use all the allies I can get."

Leo shook his head, the lines around his mouth deepening in a frown. "No, I don't think I can do that. I've accepted what you've both told me about the things in this city, but I don't want any part of it."

I guess he still wasn't over shooting a jaguar that had morphed into a naked man. I had mental images of him ending up drunk in a gutter, dead of alcohol poisoning, gnawed on by stray animals. I wanted more for him than I'd been able to do for his son.

"Your motel is paid up for another couple of days," Wyatt said.

Leo nodded. "I appreciate that, but—"

"Someone's coming," Wyatt said. He'd twisted his head around to look behind him. From the direction of the cemetery's narrow road, a man strode toward us. He was lean, of average height and looks, with a narrow nose and wild, curly hair sporting more gray than brown. Older, in his mid-forties by the looks of him, he walked with the tired gait of someone who'd seen too much. Probably a cop.

"I'm on your right, Leo," I said softly. I maintained proximity while staying out of his way if he turned suddenly. I didn't want to try to explain Leo's elbowing an invisible obstacle, or the splat in the grass I'd make if I fell.

The stranger smiled pleasantly as he approached, both hands tucked into the pockets of his khaki trousers. He wore a blue collared shirt without a jacket, sleeves rolled up in the day's heat. Wyatt tensed and took up a defensive position between the stranger and Leo, hands loose at his sides.

"Mr. Leo Forrester?" the man asked, looking right past Wyatt. His voice was pleasant enough, nondescript and polite.

"Yeah," Leo said. "Why?"

The stranger's already gentle expression softened further, as though Leo's gruffness demanded he pour on the honey, only it didn't seem to be an act. "I'm truly sorry for your loss, Mr. Forrester."

Leo grunted. I smiled and could almost hear Wyatt's internal monologue—wondering who had the potential to be ruder, me or Leo.

"And you are?" Wyatt said, asking the question on all our minds.

"Apologies," the man said. "My name's James Reilly. I'm a private investigator, Mister . . . ?"

"Truman."

"Mr. Truman." Reilly offered his hand, the same affable smile firmly in place.

Wyatt observed Reilly's hand. I couldn't see his face, but the tilt of Wyatt's head hinted at what was probably his own special brand of distrust mixed with interest. "A P.I., huh?" he said, giving Reilly's hand a brief, loose shake. "What are you investigating, Mr. Reilly?"

"Real estate, mostly."

"Looking into a plot of your own?"

"Oh no, not that sort of real estate. I'm more interested in apartment buildings."

And he'd come here on the day of Alex's funeral. Alarms clanged in my head. This guy had to be investigating the building where Alex had "officially" died. The fire that had consumed the entire fifth floor of a low-rent apartment building had been ruled an accident, or so all the official reports said. But that never squelched speculation. Especially when the fire had actually been set by a were-osprey intent on revenge for his slaughtered Clan, and Alex had been long dead by the time the blaze began.

"I haven't got one to sell you," Leo snapped. He stepped forward, across the marker, and stood shoulder to shoulder with Wyatt. "If you don't mind, I just buried my son."

"I realize this is bad timing, Mr. Forrester, and I apologize," Reilly said. The words were scripted, but the delivery was genuine. Annoying. "But police were called to your son's own apartment three times in the last nine days, with one of those calls coming a day after he died. I'm sure you agree that those facts are a bit strange—especially the third call."

"He had a roo—"

I kicked Leo in the calf before he could blurt out the word "roommate." His right leg buckled, and he stumbled a bit before catching himself. Reilly's eyebrows arched into twin peaks.

"Are you all right, Mr. Forrester?" he asked.

"Leg cramp is all. Old injury, it's nothing."

"You were saying he had a what?"

Leo stayed silent. He was smart enough to recognize when discretion was needed, but not a good enough actor to come up with a better lie on the spot. He chose a blank stare.

"Do you have to ask your questions now?" Wyatt asked, affecting a nice snarl. It was almost protective.

"Again, I do apologize for the venue," Reilly said, "but Mr. Forrester is a difficult man to find."

"Side effect of being homeless," Leo said.

Reilly's genuine sympathy and nice-guy attitude were starting to grate on my nerves. People just weren't that kind. "I'll be brief, I promise," he said. "You see, I spoke to the leasing agent at your son's building, and the very helpful Ms. Young said she was sure that two names were on the lease. However, computer records only showed Alexander's name, and the hard copy was missing several pages. The ones with the signatures on them, as a matter of fact."

Leo didn't have to fake his confusion. "So? Maybe this mysterious second name moved out?"

"Perhaps. But, you see, I also spoke with the young

couple next door in 505. They'd been neighbors the entire two years Alexander lived in the apartment, and Mrs. Gates told me he lived there with a pretty brunette named Chalice."

"Probably his girlfriend," Wyatt said.

"Mrs. Gates didn't think so. Her daughter, Angie, claimed to be good friends with Chalice Frost. She said they shared secrets."

Angie was the little girl I'd met in the elevator. The inquisitive child had given me a spare key and let me into a strange woman's apartment on my first day of resurrection. A meeting that was coming back around to bite us in the ass, and I was helpless to direct the conversation.

"What sort of secrets does a child have?" Leo asked.

"You know, I asked Angie the same question in slightly different words. She said girl secrets."

"Fascinating," Wyatt drawled.

"Yes, it was, actually," Reilly said, completely missing Wyatt's sarcasm. He was either doing it on purpose or was denser than he looked. My money was on the former. "I asked Angie when was the last time she spoke to Chalice, and she said Tuesday last week, around dinnertime. She said Chalice was wearing funny clothes and had forgotten her keys somewhere, so Angie gave her a spare."

"A lot of things can explain a woman coming home wearing strange clothes."

"Yes, they can." Reilly seemed pleased with himself, and I realized Wyatt's verbal flub. "It also seems to confirm that Chalice did indeed live there with Alexander, which is why I'm here. I'm trying to find Chalice, so I can ask her a few questions."

"Have you tried the phone book?"

"I have, but the apartment number was listed under Forrester. And as I said, computer searches bring up nothing. Mrs. Gates wasn't sure where Chalice worked, so I dead-ended there."

"Why don't you ask one of your cop friends to let you into the apartment to sniff around?"

Wyatt and I both knew the answer to that one. The Triads had gone in not long after the were-cats attacked me and Leo there and cleaned house. Removed belongings, furniture, carpet, scrubbed the place down, and done it efficiently to remove all traces of what had happened. Nothing remained for Reilly to find.

He gave an answer, though, that I didn't expect. "I would have, Mr. Truman, but I'm new to the city. I'm still making connections here."

Someone from the outside brought in to investigate the fire?

Terrific.

Reilly switched his attention to Leo. "Is there anything you can tell me about Chalice, Mr. Forrester? Anything your son might have mentioned?"

Leo paused—a perfect tell for anyone who knew how to spot them. And Reilly struck me as much brighter than he let on. I considered becoming visible and scaring the shit out of him—an amusing fantasy I had no real inclination to enact. Keeping my cover was more important.

"I never met Chalice," Leo finally said. "Alex and I . . . we didn't talk much. I came to the city hoping to fix things, but I was too late. Missed my chance."

"But you're still here."

"Like I said, I've got nowhere to go."

Reilly nodded, then shifted his attention. "And you were a friend of the deceased, Mr. Truman?"

Wyatt didn't even blink; he'd probably been rehearsing his story from the moment Reilly walked over. "Alex and I were pals in elementary school. We even liked the same girl on the playground once."

"Which school was that?"

A deep frown creased Wyatt's forehead. "It was twenty years ago, halfway across the state," he said, doing a great job of appearing deep in thought.

"Mancini Elementary, wasn't it?" Leo asked.

"Yeah, that was it."

"Of course," Reilly said. "I'm sorry, Mr. Truman, but I didn't catch your first name."

"That's because I didn't give it to you." He said it matter-of-factly, no hint of confrontation or ire. It could have been a joke between friends, and Reilly seemed to take it as such. The man was inscrutable.

"Right. I don't suppose you can shed any light on this mystery girlfriend, or where I might find her?"

I bit down on my lower lip, mostly to keep in an amused snort. If he only knew how close he stood to the mystery girl, he'd shit his shorts. I hated snooping into a conversation in which I couldn't participate.

"Like I said," Wyatt replied in a mimic of Leo's earlier comment, "I hadn't seen Alex in twenty years. I heard he died, so I came to support his dad."

Reilly reached into his jacket. I tensed, but instead of a weapon, he produced a well-thumbed notebook and nub of a pencil. He flipped through scribbled-on, dog-eared pages until he found a clean one near the end, then wrote what looked like gibberish. I couldn't scoot around to read over his shoulder—I might be invisible, but my feet would still imprint on the grass, and my jeans would whisper my presence. Couldn't risk it around someone so used to noticing tiny details.

"I apologize for taking your time," Reilly said for the umpteenth time. Someone who apologized so much needed to work in a confessional. He tucked the pencil nub behind his ear, then thumbed back a few pages. "Just one more question, and I'll leave you be."

"Which is?" Leo asked.

"I've been equally unsuccessful at locating someone else involved in the fire that killed your son, Mr. Forrester. The man whose apartment was the source of the blaze—a man named Rufus St. James."

I grunted before I could stop myself. Reilly's head snapped to the space between Wyatt and Leo, right where I stood. He seemed to look me directly in the throat for a moment, then down. At my feet. I followed his gaze.

The creepy thing about the invisibility spell was that I was not only cloaked from other people, I couldn't even see my own damned self. Not my own hands or legs or feet. Just the four vaguely flat patches of grass where my boots' heels and soles pressed down. I kept still and held my breath.

"Don't know him," Leo said.

Reilly pulled himself out of it and looked up. "And you, Mr. Truman?"

Wyatt shook his head. "I wish I could help you out. Have you tried the hospitals, or local motels?"

"Yes, I have, actually, but thank you for the suggestions." Reilly shook both of their hands briefly, then turned and strolled back toward the narrow road where his car was likely parked.

No one spoke until he was well out of earshot.

"That was bizarre," I said.

Leo jumped a mile, hand flying to his heart. "Christ, I forgot you were there."

"This is just what we don't need," Wyatt said. "Some glory-hungry P.I. poking around, asking questions."

"We've dealt with them before," I said. With all the strange events that happened in the city on a daily basis, someone was always asking the wrong questions. Trying to dig up an explanation for misshapen, rotting bodies that didn't look human. Rag reporters looking for answers to questions they were better off not asking, until the Triads politely instructed them to shut the hell up.

I'd always hated threatening civilians, but the alternative was allowing them to ask the wrong question of the wrong person and end up dead. Or worse. And contrary to popular opinion, there are things worse than death.

"Yeah, but back then we weren't freelance, remember?" he said.

"He seems harmless enough," Leo said.

"Yeah," I replied, "and so does a rose until it stabs you with a thorn."

"People stab themselves on thorns."

I started to retort, but words failed me. Good thing he couldn't see my expression. I imagined it was full of priceless confusion.

"Regardless," Wyatt said, "I don't like that he's asking around about Chalice or Rufus."

"So report him to the Triads and be done with it," I said, not much liking the idea but unable to offer an alternative. Investigating private investigators wasn't my idea of a fun afterlife.

He sighed and dug his hands into the pockets of his jeans. "Guess we should go."

Leo gave his son's marker another look, then turned awkwardly and walked back to the cars; his was parked in the lane in front of Wyatt's. We didn't speak, which suited me fine. Dozens of thoughts whirled through my mind—questions about what was next for us, with Wyatt stuck in some sort of limbo with the Triads, not really fired but not allowed to just quit, and me dead (again). The city was still picking up the pieces after the Parker's Palace massacre, and people were asking questions. Headlines reported everything from a massive gang initiation to a gas leak that made everyone inside the theater go mass-murder crazy.

Everything we'd dedicated our lives to protecting was starting to crumble.

A tremor vibrated through my feet, into my legs, all the way to my chest. I faltered. Stopped walking. The vibration was so faint, I was certain I'd imagined it. Like the gentlest of earthquakes, it was there and gone in seconds.

"Whoa," I muttered.

"Did you feel that?" Wyatt asked. He'd stopped an arm's reach from his car and was looking at a point just past my head, but close enough.

"Yeah, I felt it."

"Felt what?" Leo asked.

"Small earthquake, just now. You didn't feel it?"

"No."

He wasn't lying. I saw it in his face. So why had Wyatt and I felt it?

"Probably nothing, then," Wyatt said.

I scowled but didn't press. It wasn't something to discuss in front of Leo.

"I suppose I should get going," Leo said. "No use in hanging around here all day when I've got miles to make."

My heart sped up. As much as I didn't want Leo to stay so I would worry about his safety, I also didn't want him to leave. He'd saved my life and kept my bizarre secret. I'd never known my own father, and while Leo had a truckload of faults, in the end he'd loved his children.

He'd also never be safe in my world. We'd talked about it for long hours and, finally, agreed that leaving the city was the lesser of two evils.

"Wish I could see your face to say good-bye."

"It's not safe," Wyatt said.

I could have punched him in the arm for that, but refrained. "You don't have to go," I said. But we all knew he did.

Leo looked in my direction. I shifted so at least I knew he was looking me in the eye. "Thanks for being his friend," he said. "You did more for him than I ever could."

The irony in his statement struck like a fist. As his father, Leo had given Alex life. As his friend, all I'd done was take it away from him. I'd introduced him to my horrifying, painful world, then to death.

I touched his face. Leo flinched from the unexpected contact, then relaxed. I wanted to hug him but didn't. I had to let him go, and quickly. "Good-bye, Leo. Take care of yourself."

"You, too, Evy Stone." He gave my invisible form a wide berth, then shook Wyatt's hand. "You take good care of her."

"I will if she lets me," Wyatt said.

This time I did swat him on the shoulder. The blow rustled the fabric of his shirt. Somehow he caught my hand in his and gave it a gentle squeeze. The way his fingers curled around air, even though I felt the warmth of his touch, looked a bit ridiculous.

Leo's mouth quirked in a wistful smile. His plan was to leave the city and drive north, past the mountains. There were some nice towns up there. I hoped he found the fresh start he wanted. He climbed into his car. The engine gurgled to life a moment later. We watched him navigate the narrow road that wound through the cemetery, until his car was out of sight.

"That wasn't an earthquake, was it?" I asked.

"Not a normal one, no." Wyatt squeezed my hand again, let it go, and then unlocked the car door. "That wasn't from the ground, Evy, not the tremor I felt. It came from deeper than that."

"What do you mean?" I slid across the bench into the passenger seat.

He climbed in and slammed the door shut, mouth drawn and face pinched. I hated that look. "It wasn't external. It was an internal tremor that only you and I felt—two Gifted people, Evy. I think something's happening at First Break."

Chapter Two

Besides being an enormous underground community of faeries, sprites, gnomes, pixies, dryads, and sylphs—creatures more commonly referred to as Fey or Fair Ones—First Break is also a doorway of sorts. I don't know exactly what's on the other side, besides banished demons and the source of magic in our world, but I do know that the Fair Ones protect it. They keep the demons—the Tainted Ones—from crossing over, and have been human allies for . . . well, at least for the ten years the Triads have been in operation.

Wyatt and I had both felt the tremor, which meant it had something to do with the Break and our connection to its magic. Only we had no way of contacting First Break to find out what was going on. It was miles outside the city and deep underground; I knew of only one way in that didn't include being swallowed by a troll, and we didn't have time to make that trek. It wasn't like Amalie, the sprite Queen, had installed a phone after our last visit. She appeared when she wished, via her human avatar, then disappeared when her task was finished.

As soon as we returned to our shared apartment in Mercy's Lot, Wyatt was on his cell phone. It was the same apartment I'd once shared with my old Triad partners and as close to a real home as I'd ever known, even if it was kind of a hole.

I realized I was still very invisible and pulled the slim

crystal out of my pocket. It was due to lose its potency in a few hours anyway, so there was no sense sitting around like a ghost. I repeated the foreign words I'd used to activate the crystal and its spell—spells are cast in the native language of the person creating them—and felt the same stomach-churning sense of being flipped inside out. It wasn't painful, just uncomfortable.

I blinked back into existence, once again able to see flesh and fingernails and clothing. Part of me expected something to go wrong—because, seriously, how often had things gone my way lately?—and for there to be a hole left someplace. But, no, a quick inspection showed everything was visible.

Wyatt was pacing in and out of the narrow kitchenette, lips pressed together, eyebrows furrowed. He dialed another number, then listened. He had to be getting a lot of voice mails, but he wasn't leaving messages. Unless they were ignoring him, which was also entirely possible. Apparently, while I was unconscious and recovering from my dive out a four-story window, Wyatt had said some pretty cruel things to both of his former fellow Handlers Gina Kismet and Adrian Baylor.

I perched on the arm of the apartment's faded sofa and watched him dial again.

His face brightened. "Morgan, it's Truman. Look, has anyone else reported a minor earthquake this morning?" He listened. "Claudia's Gifted, right? Yeah, thought so. I felt it, too." Another pause. "No idea what it could be, but I wanted to make sure I wasn't imagining things. If you hear anything . . . Yeah, thanks."

He snapped his cell phone shut and dropped it on the narrow counter.

"What are you thinking?" I asked.

He started, gazing at me with surprise. As if he'd forgotten he *should* be able to see me. "I'm thinking I started out the day hoping to relax after the memorial, and now that hope has been shattered."

"How do you figure?"

"Come on, Evy. Anything strong enough to affect the entirety of the Break like that isn't going to just go away."

"Doesn't mean we'll automatically get swept up into it." But even as I said the words, I knew how ridiculous they sounded. Ever since my resurrection, I'd been at the center of every major event affecting the city and its nonhuman inhabitants. Factor in my training-born need to protect the innocents of the city, and I'd probably get myself sucked into it anyway. "Dead" or alive.

"We've put up with so much these last few weeks," he said, almost sulking. "I just want a couple of days of peace and quiet." He didn't have to say "with you." The words were in his tone and in the way he was looking at me.

Three days ago, after waking up from a brief coma, I'd finally told him I loved him and hadn't repeated it since. He didn't push. I didn't want the inevitable discussion that would come with a revelation of feelings. I didn't want to talk about it or us, or anything else. Avoiding it meant avoiding any potential "next steps" in our burgeoning relationship.

It wasn't like we'd never had sex. Well, that was half-true. We'd slept together once, two weeks ago, right before I died and left my old body behind. We hadn't had sex since my resurrection—although we'd come close once—mostly due to my inability to figure out my own emotional chaos.

Before I'd died, I hadn't been in love with Wyatt. I'd loved him, sure, as a coworker and a man I respected. But being born again into the body of Chalice Frost came not only with handy teleporting powers but also with a powerful physical attraction to Wyatt. My head and my heart were on two different wavelengths, and I just didn't know how to reconcile them.

Sex with Wyatt now, as the people we'd both become, was a step I both craved and feared. I wanted him; I also didn't think I deserved him.

"Peace and quiet don't come with the job description," I said.

"Need I remind you we're both unemployed?"

I slid off the arm of the sofa and sank into the springy cushions. It was the same sofa from when I'd lived here before; nothing had changed except the inhabitants. The apartment had always been a haven of sorts, a place away from the chaos and bloodshed of our daily (and nightly) lives. It still felt like that sanctuary. But with the ghosts of my old life so firmly entrenched in each piece of furniture and carpet stain, it also felt like a prison.

Wyatt sat next to me, sinking the old cushions toward the middle. I let gravity tilt me sideways and rested my head on his chest. He draped his right arm over my shoulders in a gentle embrace. His familiar scent—spice and cinnamon and male musk—filled my senses. Relaxing and safe.

"Five gets you twenty your phone rings in the next ten minutes," I said, "and shatters the mood."

He chuckled, the sound rumbling through his chest, against my ear. He didn't laugh nearly enough. Neither of us did. "You do realize you've jinxed us by saying that?"

"Oops." I picked at a lint pill on the front of his shirt. "So about that earthquake—"

"It wasn't an earthquake."

"Yeah, okay, so about that Break-quake . . . any thoughts? You've been Gifted a hell of a lot longer than me." Over a decade longer; he'd discovered his Gift as a teenager. Mine had technically belonged to Chalice, the woman whose body I'd inherited and who was also a part of me now. Even my healing ability was new, cleverly gifted to me by a gnome name Horzt. "Has it happened before?"

"I've never felt anything like it, so I don't think it's happened recently. Not in the dozen years or so I've been aware of my Gift."

"Which rules out only the recent past."

"Right."

Terrific. "Too bad we can't just call up Amalie and ask her."

"Where's the fun in that?"

I snorted and poked him in the ribs. "Sitting around and wondering why we both felt a magical earthquake, and if it's leading up to something bigger, is not my idea of fun, Truman."

"Maybe you aren't sitting right."

I was in no mood for his teasing. I started to stand, but he snagged my left wrist. A week ago, I probably would have fought tooth and nail to get free of his grip, spurred on by fear of capture and the memory of my wrists being bound by cold, biting handcuffs. I probably would have kicked and punched, maybe drawn blood. Overreacted in the worst way to a simple attempt to keep me from walking away.

I guess I'd grown some since last week, because I simply froze in place, not fighting but also not sitting back down. He didn't say anything until I turned and looked at him. Down at his concerned black eyes, strong jaw, narrow nose—a face I knew so damned well.

He asked, "What, Evy?"

I had no good answer, so I didn't give him one. He tugged gently; I gave in and sat back down. He caught me around the waist and pulled me closer, practically into his lap. It was both a ridiculous and an alluring position to be in. I pressed my hands against his chest.

Felt his heart thrumming steadily as his arms snaked around me.

"I'm sorry," he said. "I'm not making light of this Break-quake, but there's not much we can do at the moment. I reported it to the Triads. I still feel my tap to the Break, and I'm guessing you do, too. There's just nothing left to be done, and I know that makes you crazy."

The corners of my mouth twitched. He had me there. "I hate waiting," I said, "about as much as I hate being on the outside of this."

"I know. Your drive is one of the things I love about you."

Oh God, he said the L-word. I swallowed back a tiny, blinding moment of panic. Irrational panic. Something I needed to get a fucking handle on before it drove me insane. His eyes flickered back and forth, searching mine for something—some sort of reaction. Very few people had the ability to render me speechless the way Wyatt did.

Actions speak louder than words, though. I skated my fingertips up his shoulders and around to the back of his neck, tilted my head, and brushed my lips across his. The gentle kiss worked wonders as a distraction, and, like a moth to a flame, his mouth sought mine.

The second kiss was more insistent. I parted my lips, enjoying the heady taste of him. The way he lazily drew his tongue across my teeth before probing more deeply. The sensation of his fingers running through my long hair, tangling and touching. The way my stomach quivered, and the heat that went straight to my core when he pulled me closer.

My hips ached from the awkward position on the too-soft sofa. I shifted around until I was kneeling on both sides of his hips, butt resting on his thighs, in a more dominant position now. More comfortable, too. He squeezed my waist, just above my hips, and I yelped.

"That tickles," I said, swatting his shoulder.

"Sorry about that." He did it again.

I giggled. As I plotted my revenge, he captured my mouth in another, more dizzying kiss. Thoughts of the Break fell away. The rasp of his unshaven skin against mine, the taste of him I knew so well, the heat of his hands splayed across my lower back. He was pushing me forward, harder against him. I teased his tongue with mine, stroking and probing. Exploring depths I'd grown to know by heart.

The kissing I could handle. The touching and holding—no sweat. Hell, we'd shared the same bed the last two nights, finding comfort in our fully clothed selves, and I'd never felt exposed or out of control. I felt out of control only when we started to move past kissing. When my body started taking over for my conscious mind, and when pleasure started mixing with memories of pain. That's when I'd start to panic.

Only I was determined not to today. Wyatt was patient and supportive. He knew what I'd gone through— he'd seen the results with his own eyes and held me when I died the first time, raped and tortured to death by goblins. The psychological scars didn't heal as quickly as the rest of me, but I was getting damned tired of waiting.

I raked my fingers down his chest, the cotton shirt soft and pliant and warmed by his skin. He moaned softly. I broke our kiss and pressed my forehead to his. Gazed into his eyes, his breath puffing hot and sweet in my face.

"What do you really think," I asked, "the odds of that phone ringing in the near future are?"

He blinked. Then understanding dawned. It was quickly tempered by surprise and, deeper still, desire. Desire meant for me and no one else. One of his hands drew a lazy circle in the small of my back. "I'll break the phone if you want me to," he whispered.

"Nah, that requires getting up. I like you right here."

His eyes asked the question: are you sure? I wanted to tell him I wasn't sure, but I was hell-bent and determined. We'd bared our souls a few days ago, revealing to each other the darkest of our kept secrets. Wyatt's had been blacker than mine, more damaging, and I was still processing some of the things he'd told me. Some of the horrible things he'd done. I should have hated him for them. Instead, they had deepened my understanding of the complex, haunted man I'd known for four years, and still barely knew at all.

I crushed my mouth to his. His response was nearly instantaneous and impossible not to feel. I urged him on by rocking my hips, adding a bit of friction, and he groaned. His hips jerked hard against me. My stomach quaked, and I matched his groan. His hands cupped my ass and held me there, pressed to him.

His lips left mine, trailing nips and licks across my cheek to my chin, then down to my throat. He found the sensitive spot, just below my ear and behind my jaw. I gasped and rocked into him. He growled, pleased with himself, and did it again. I shifted, pressed forward, hands on his chest. He groaned.

Not a happy groan. It was definitely a pained groan. I jerked back, hands off. He tried to wipe away the grimace; I saw the last edges before it disappeared. It had been barely over a week since he'd had a sliver of metal removed from his back, three inches from his spine. The wound was small but deep, and had proved quite painful as it healed.

"Did I hurt you?" I asked.

"It'll pass."

"The way my mood always passes?"

My intended humor hit rock bottom. His expression darkened.

"Sorry," I said.

"Maybe we should stop."

Mood Killer 101—your instructor today is Evy Stone. No, I wasn't doing that again. I didn't run from things, dammit; I chased them down, tackled them, and slammed their noses into the pavement. It wasn't about proving anything to Wyatt. As frustrated as he got on occasion, he *knew*; therefore, he forgave. But just once I wanted him to get mad at me. To tell me he didn't want to entertain himself with Mr. Righty again.

Only he'd never do that. In this new thing we were trying, we were no longer Hunter and Handler. He wasn't my boss. He wouldn't push me or cajole me or embarrass me into positive results. We were partners now and on even footing. He didn't have to coax what I wished to give freely.

If only the damaged part of my psyche would let me.

"I think—" he started to say, and I silenced him by pressing a finger to his lips.

"You think too much," I said. "*I* think too much."

He nipped at the tip of my finger. I dropped my hand to his chest. He searched my face, long enough to make me squirm.

"If you're thinking it, say it," I said, frustrated at his stalling and inability to simply speak his damned mind.

"I'm thinking we may need to take this show on the road."

I scowled. "To the bedroom?"

"No," he said with the temerity to laugh at my confusion. Sweet laughter—amused, without condescension. "Out of the city, Evy. We need to get away for a couple of days, far from the Break, the Dregs, and all the reminders of what our lives were before this started. Maybe it will help."

I swallowed a snort. He had the best intentions, but I seriously doubted a change of venue would alter how my heart reacted to his proximity, or how my guts twisted when my mind wandered back to that tiny closet at the abandoned train station. The place where I'd been tortured and left to die.

"I don't know," I said. Nothing else came to mind.

"About leaving, or about it helping?"

"Both. Neither. Take your pick." The only thing I knew for sure was that I didn't want to stop. For a man who had frustrated me endlessly in my old life, he had become the most patient person on the planet in my new life. He didn't deserve me jerking him around like this.

I brushed my lips across his nose, a teasing kiss that made him shiver. Smiling, I grabbed the hem of my shirt and whisked it off in one smooth motion. It whispered to the floor, forgotten. His eyebrows arched.

The sofa vibrated.

Wyatt tensed. "Did you feel—?"

The second wave wasn't so subtle. I pitched off his lap and hit the floor on my back. Both elbows scraped against the rough carpet. Glass shattered somewhere in the apartment. Everything was moving, shaking. Books fell to the floor like thunderclaps. Car alarms blasted outside.

"Is it an earthquake?" I shouted.

"Stay there and curl up." Wyatt tumbled off the sofa and joined me on the floor, wrapping his body around mine from behind. We didn't fit well in the pocket between the sofa and the coffee table, but I trusted him. I'd always thought you got into the nearest doorway— I guess I was told wrong.

The shaking stopped after less than a minute. Car horns added to the mix of alarms coming from the street. Something in the kitchenette fell in a pop of noise and broke. I sat up and gazed around the apartment, taking in the fallen items. The wall by the door now sported a thin crack the length of my arm.

"Holy shit." I clenched my fists, unsure when my hands had started shaking.

"You okay?" Wyatt asked as he sat up next to me. His wide-eyed gaze was reflective of what mine probably looked like.

"Yeah. That wasn't just from the Break."

"No, that was a full-on earthquake."

The city was no stranger to earthquakes of a much smaller magnitude. Mostly they were barely felt. Earthquakes this powerful were rare and, if hidden history showed anything, usually products of troll activity. Trolls, also called Earth Guardians by the Fair Ones, were part of the Earth itself—dirt and stone and natural elements. They'd had their internal wars a hundred years ago, and the city had suffered for it.

Combined with the earlier Break-hiccup, I had no doubt something bigger was brewing belowground.

Wyatt's cell phone jangled, no longer on the counter where he'd left it. He rummaged in the mess covering the kitchenette floor. Checked the display. The surprise on his face was hard to miss as he received the call. "Truman."

I stood up and wandered closer, concerned as his surprise gave way to actual shock. My heart sped up.

"Hold on," Wyatt said. He pulled the phone away from his ear, hit a button, then said, "Say that again for me."

On speaker now, Adrian Baylor's voice came over loud and clear. "I said Boot Camp was attacked, Truman. Unplug your ears."

A chill wormed down my spine and spread gooseflesh across the backs of my legs. This was so not what I expected to hear. The start of a question squeaked out of my mouth. I clamped a hand over it to silence myself. Baylor was a Handler and a former colleague of Wyatt's, and among those people who thought me dead. Again.

"That's what caused the earthquake," Baylor continued. "At least three trolls were systematically testing the underground security measures for about five minutes before the quake. A couple of their friends must have come along to stop them, because their fight? That's what shook the city."

Troll wars. Holy shit. My mind raced. Boot Camp was a secret, supersecure facility in the mountains south of the city. It was where new Hunters were trained to kill, and it was a place where only one in two people came out alive. Four years ago, I'd been one of the lucky ones.

I couldn't imagine why a bunch of trolls would want to get at those kids and their trainers. But they weren't the only secrets hiding behind the high, magically secured walls or the deep, oil-slicked, electricity-bound barrier beneath. After the discovery of a macabre lab of science experiments in an abandoned nature preserve a week ago, the contents of that lab had been moved to Boot Camp. Contents including scientific research notes, vials of liquids no one could identify, lab equipment and technology beyond anything I'd ever seen in person, and fourteen living, breathing creatures that had been tortured in the name of science.

Creatures that ran the spectrum from docile and harmless to vicious hellhounds created with the worst intentions. Creatures that could terrorize the public and kill without remorse if set loose.

"Has anyone heard from the Fey Council about this?" Wyatt asked.

"Feelers are out, but the brass says no word yet. We've got teams coming in to keep the place locked up tight, but we aren't making the same mistake we made at Parker's Palace."

The mistake of thinning out our ranks to chase after minor incidents while those closest to the imminent slaughter didn't believe it would happen. Sixty-four people were dead because of that mistake.

Wyatt puckered his eyebrows. "What do you want me to do?"

"Stay by your phone for now, at least until we have a plan."

"Fine."

As he snapped his phone shut, I said, "Fortunately, with the advent of mobiles, asking someone to stay by the phone no longer requires them to sit around at home and fidget."

Wyatt gave a tolerant sigh. "You want to go out there."

"You'd rather sit around and hope Baylor gives you an assignment? If trolls are attacking, then something's wrong. They've been one of the most neutral species in this city for years."

"Neutral or not, they seem to take direction from the Fey."

His accusation struck me dumb. A chill settled in my stomach. True, at Amalie's request, a troll named Smedge had once rescued Wyatt and me from a group of Halfies. The Earth-bound trolls had some sort of partnership with the Fey, but that didn't preclude trolls from working for others given the right incentive. Or they had attacked on their own, for reasons beyond my present understanding.

"So now you're accusing Amalie of turning against us?" I asked.

He scowled. "No, just making an observation based on fact. Amalie has been a staunch supporter of the Triads since the beginning, but she doesn't speak for all Fey. Just for the sprites and the decisions of the Council."

"A power play by other Fey?" Saying it aloud sounded ridiculous. The Fey seemed perfectly content to live outside the city, happily roaming the mountains and forests that surrounded us and leaving the more violent, city-dwelling species to kill one another.

"I'm just thinking out loud, Evy," he said. "I'm not accusing anyone of anything, because I really don't have a damned clue what's going on."

I nodded, knowing exactly how he felt. "Too bad I have no idea where Smedge went to ground. He'd probably know what's happening."

A smile tugged at the corners of his mouth. "That would make things too easy."

"Yeah, and God forbid anything ever be—" A heavy thud rattled our front door. For a brief moment, I expected the world to start shaking. Instead, whatever had thudded slid down the length of the door until it hit the ground.

I reached under the coffee table and pulled a knife from its hiding place. Weapons were stashed all over the apartment, and this one was the most immediately accessible. Wyatt didn't try to stop me; he didn't tell me to be careful. I approached the door on silent feet, glad for the cement floor, and checked the peephole first—nothing in sight except the opposite wall.

Pressing my ear to the door, I listened. Heard the faint, muffled sound of heavy breathing. By my feet, something dark red caught my attention. It glistened on the floor, just under the door's edge. Blood. I curled my fingers around the knob and snicked the lock back. Twisted. Yanked.

And leapt backward as a man's body tumbled halfway into the apartment, landing flat on his back. Blood oozed from multiple wounds in his abdomen and had soaked through his once white shirt.

"She knew you were alive," the man croaked, and I finally took a good look at his upside-down face.

It was Jaron, another sprite and Amalie's most trusted bodyguard. And s/he was dying.

Chapter Three

Sprite-Jaron was an orange crystal-encrusted woman who barely came up to my waist. Jaron's human avatar, besides being male, had the height and bulk of a professional wrestler, which made him an ideal bodyguard for Amalie's avatar. It did not make him ideal for being dragged across the floor to the sofa. Even with Wyatt and me, it took several minutes to get him there. Jaron stayed quiet, grimacing but making no noise, even though he had to be in agony.

We finally gave up on the couch and left him on the rag rug that covered the area nearest the sofa. While Wyatt closed and locked the door, I fetched a couple of towels from the bathroom. I put one beneath his head and pressed another over his wounds. That's when he cried out.

"Who did this?" I asked, trying to ignore the streak of blood that stretched from his feet to the door.

"Goblin," he rasped. "I think."

He thinks? Goblins were pretty damned easy to pick out of a crowd. "Why did it attack?"

"Don't know." Sweat beaded on his forehead. His brown eyes were wide, pained, unfocused. "Earth Guardians attacked. I left First Break. Situated myself here. Left my apartment. It stabbed me with . . . its hand."

"Its hand?" Goblins had sharp claws, but not long

enough to inflict the kind of damage done to Jaron's abdomen.

"Fingernails, like small knives. Too long."

Just the mental image of that made my stomach roil.

"Why come here?" Wyatt asked, kneeling on the
other side of Jaron. "How did you know Evy was
alive?"

Jaron rolled his eyes toward Wyatt. "Amalie knew.
Gifted who are in her true presence . . . she can sense
their aura. Their tether to the Break. She can sense you
both."

Creepy and cool. Wyatt and I had both spent time in
Amalie's true presence, seen her as she really was and
not just in her human avatar. The aura thing was new information, but I really knew little about sprites and their
ways with the Break. She knew I hadn't died last Saturday, and she also, apparently, hadn't shared that intel
with the Triads. Interesting.

"But why here?" Wyatt persisted.

Jaron groaned. Blood gurgled up his throat, into his
mouth, and down his cheeks. He coughed, dim eyes
searching. I squeezed his shoulder and leaned in, desperate to know what had driven the sprite to drag a dying
man to our little corner of Hell. His head listed toward
me, but he didn't seem to see.

"Jaron, please, tell us," I said.

He shook his head. "Not . . . betrayal." The words
were barely intelligible. I leaned closer, missing most of
his whispers. "Don't . . . trust . . ." His eyes flared
white, the briefest flash of the power of the Fey possess-
ing his body. Then the light went out. His body stilled.

"Jaron? Fuck." I rocked back on my heels, stunned.
Why did they always die before they finished saying
what needed to be said?

Wyatt checked his pulse and found none. We didn't
even know the man's real name—the man who gave his

body over to the will of a powerful sprite whenever she needed to walk among humans and was none the wiser. The man who died because someone had been sent to kill Jaron in her most vulnerable state.

"Betrayal," Wyatt said. "But who's betraying who?"

"She said she came here after the trolls attacked." Or were attacked—either way, she had to be referencing the earlier earthquake. "Could they have turned on the other Fey? Maybe she was going to give that information to the Triads."

He shook his head. "Then why come to us after being stabbed? Why not call the brass or one of the Handlers?"

"I don't know." I thought of how the avatar's eyes had flashed, glowed that brilliant white at the moment of death. Just the avatar's death, or . . . "Wyatt, if a sprite's avatar dies while the sprite still possesses it, what does that do to the sprite?"

His eyes widened. "I have no idea. I don't know enough about avatars to even guess."

My stomach twisted as the implications caught up with me. Had Jaron come to the city to tell us something important about a betrayal? One so big she'd dragged her wounded avatar across town to find us, only to die before giving up anything useful? Possible. Horrifying, but possible. And who the hell was the man/goblin/thing with the clawed hands? Except for certain shapeshifters, I didn't know of any other nonhuman species capable of manipulating their bodies like that.

"Amalie knows I'm alive," I said. "She must have sent Jaron to contact us, which means that whether Jaron's alive or dead, Amalie will know something went wrong. Maybe she'll try to contact us again, some other way."

"Let's hope." He dug beneath the dead man's behind and retrieved a billfold. Some cash fell out when he

flipped it open. "Jed Peters is the name on the driver's license. He lives five blocks from here."

"I would have pegged Jaron for picking a Parkside
East type for her avatar."

"They need humans with open minds, who willingly
believe. They're probably a lot more cynical on the other
side of the river."

"Good point." I pulled the folded towel from beneath
Jed Peters's head and draped it over his face, then stood
up. "So a dead body decorating the living room certainly adds a new wrinkle to today's plans."

"I'd say it's less a wrinkle than a big damned bump."
He snagged one of the other towels and started wiping
the blood off the floor, cleaning up the smear that led
to the door. There'd be blood in the hall, too. Peters/
Jaron had probably left a trail of it all the way from his
apartment. Five blocks to here.

Wyatt mopped closer to the door. I watched him, uneasy, instinct telling me what my mind wouldn't.

"The goblin with the claws he told us attacked him,"
I said, trying to process it out loud. Hoping for a clue.

"What about it?" He reached up from his half crouch
and flicked the door lock open.

"Jaron didn't say she fought it off, just that it stabbed
her and she came to us."

He paused, turned his head, and looked at me. Understanding bloomed like a deadly flower. The knob turned
under his hand. Wyatt slammed his shoulder into the
door, but someone pushed from the other side. Someone
a lot stronger. Wyatt went sprawling onto his left hip
and continued to roll, clearing the door, which had just
been kicked completely open. Jaron hadn't managed to
describe her attacker beyond the claws and *thinking* it
was a goblin, but what stood in the open doorway
wasn't what I expected.

It was a goblin—or had been, at one time. Maybe four

and a half feet tall, it stood up straight rather than hunched as other goblin males did. Skin that should have been slick and oily was dull, as if powdered with starch. Black hair tufted out from in and around its ears—ears that should have been wide and pointed but instead were round like a human's.

I looked in its eyes, and my stomach lurched. Not the lusty red eyes I'd grown to know, but watchful brown that were completely human. The mismatched features, combined with the clothes—jeans and a black T-shirt, for Christ's sake!—sent a shock wave of cold through my body. My insides quaked. This wasn't right. I couldn't possibly be seeing it.

Until it stretched out a decidedly goblinesque arm in my direction, as though pointing with its entire hand. Goblins had long, sharp fingernails, good for rending flesh and getting a grip. This creature had them, too, and before my very eyes, they grew to the length of four inches each. Tiny daggers, four in a row. Only the thumbnail didn't grow.

It looked past me, at the body by my feet, and snarled. Dry lips pulled back, showing off a single row of sharp, jagged teeth. Bile scorched the back of my throat. It still didn't attack. Good for us.

I had a small knife strapped to the side of my right boot, an easy grab, but the goblin-thing would be on me the instant I reached. The knife I'd taken from beneath the coffee table was still on the floor where I'd dropped it minutes ago, halfway between me and the monster. More weapons were in the kitchenette, another beneath the sofa, others in the bedrooms. If I went for any of them, it could attack and kill Wyatt.

Its too-human eyes flickered around the apartment, as though calculating its surroundings and various threats. It was a predatory thing to do, a hunter's trait. But goblins were scavengers. The males didn't assess threats; they followed orders given to them by their queens.

What are you?

That observant gaze swung back to me, and I realized I'd whispered out loud. Our gazes locked. I thought I saw a spark of emotion, some distant cousin to regret—which was impossible in a goblin, so it had to be something else—then it snarled again.

"Kill," it growled.

My brain stuttered to a halt as the full implications of that single word sank in. I gaped, my chest tight, breath frozen in my lungs. Goblin males didn't speak English. Females can barely manage the language in their harsh, guttural voices. It couldn't have spoken.

"Kill who?" Wyatt asked.

It pointed one sharply clawed finger at Peters's body. "Whoever . . . went to."

Oh God, it's talking. I was in the middle of a nightmare and I couldn't wake up. Not an unusual state for me of late, but unsettling nonetheless. Downright nauseating. Almost terrifying, in so many ways.

This wasn't the first time I'd faced down a creature that had traits of more than one species. The first had been right after my resurrection, when I was attacked by a monster from a horror movie. Part vampire and part beast, the thing had been one hundred percent predator. Engineered by whoever had been helping Tovin, it was a prototype to house the other demons the mad elf hoped to bring across First Break. We'd found even more hybrid monstrosities in Tovin's underground lab.

Only this one seemed mildly intelligent.

"Why?" I asked.

It swung its hateful stare back at me. Mixed with its need to attack and kill was a bit of confusion. I latched onto that as its best weakness. "Master . . . said," it ground out.

"Who's your master?"

Wrong question. It moved at a speed I didn't expect, in a direct line for my guts, clawed hand slashing and hoping to spill them all over the floor. I dropped at the last possible moment, hips twisting, and brought my right heel up to crack it in the chest. It tumbled sideways, stunned by the blow. Claws ripped the hem of my pant leg, missing skin.

I rolled out of its way, already reaching for the knife at my ankle. My fingers closed around the handle just as a body slammed me sideways into the sofa—thing was fucking fast. The knife clattered to the floor, out of reach. Dammit. I jerked to my right, throwing all my weight down, smashing the creature against the cement floor. Its claws ghosted the skin on my neck, too damned close.

"Evy, left," Wyatt shouted.

I moved without thinking, tumbling to my left, barely missing the couch a second time. A dark blur passed—it had to be Wyatt. His target let out some sort of grunt. I twisted around, rolled to my feet, and sought the nearest weapon handy, which just happened to be a ten-dollar thrift store table lamp. I yanked off the shade, ripped the cord out of the wall, and pulled it back like a baseball bat.

Wyatt and the goblin-thing were tangled together on the floor, wrestling for dominance. Both of Wyatt's hands were wrapped around the creature's wrists, keeping those claws at a distance, but what Wyatt had in bulk, the goblin had in speed. It wriggled like an eel on a fishing line. I looked for an opportunity to hit it with my lamp, but it just wouldn't stop moving.

Screw this. I shifted the lamp into my left hand and scooped up my discarded knife in my right. I turned back to the flailing pair and took aim, ready to drive my knife straight into the middle of the goblin-thing's back.

"Don't kill it," Wyatt said.

"Why not?" But I stabbed it in the back of the thigh instead—no easy feat with a moving target—and for a brief moment of panic, I thought I'd missed and hit Wyatt.

Then the goblin shrieked and lurched away, tugging at the knife stuck in its leg. Wyatt sat up quickly. The front of his shirt was torn, four equally wide slash marks. "We need to question it."

Oh, right, a talking goblin-hybrid. As much as we needed to pick answers out of its brain, killing was so much simpler than taking prisoners.

The creature was crouched near the kitchenette counter, blood running down its leg. It looked at the knife I'd stuck it with, then tossed it over its shoulder. It snarled at us, this time less angry and more . . . fearful?

"Don't like being ganged up on?" I asked.

It bared its teeth.

"You're not as impressive as your big brothers." Taunting an unknown element wasn't the smartest trick in my arsenal, and Wyatt gave me a withering stare.

It growled something that could have been any number of garbled cuss words and lunged—*okay, so stupid question*—at my throat. I swung hard with the lamp, aiming for its slashing hand, and heard bone crunch as I connected. Its body slammed into mine and knocked us both sideways. I tripped over the lamp cord, hit the floor on my ass, and kept rolling. Momentum threw the goblin-hybrid over my head and into the far wall.

The splat was punctuated by a pained roar. Wyatt bolted past me. I curled onto my knees and pulled up in a crouch just in time to see Wyatt spear the critter's left hand to the wall with a knife. It squealed and slapped at the knife's hilt with its useless, broken right hand. It tried its teeth, but Wyatt kicked it in its jeans-clad groin. The thing shrieked.

"I think that was a two-base hit," Wyatt said without looking away from our quarry.

"Three at least," I said. "Maybe even a homer." I dropped the lamp on the sofa and circled, giving the wriggling creature a wide berth. Actual tears streaked its cheeks. Amazing.

I took the brief respite from attack to remove the knife from my ankle sheath. As soon as I got what I needed, I intended to kill it quickly—which was an odd realization. I should have wanted to take my time, use the captured goblin for a little therapeutic payback for all the hell I'd been put through by one of its queens, but I didn't. Something in its too-human eyes, as brown as my own, quelled that need. Produced just a little bit of mercy.

And let's face it—mercy and I were not good friends.

The hybrid kicked out with one foot, slipped on its own blood, and fell. Its hand was knifed to the wall above its head, and the jerking stop produced another bellow of anguish. Wyatt had the sense to dash back across the apartment and shut the door. No need to arouse the neighbors any more than we already had.

"Who sent you here?" I asked, staying out of the wailing creature's reach.

"Master," it snarled.

I rolled my eyes. "Yeah, we've been over that. Who is your master?"

"He."

Okay, that narrowed my suspect list down to the entire male population of the city, maybe even the state. "Do you know his name?"

It snarled and tried to stand. I kicked its legs out from under it, eliciting another shriek as its hand ripped against the knife. Blood ran down its arm and pitter-pattered to the floor. The color was off—some dusky shade of mauve that wasn't goblin-fuchsia or human-

red. I sniffed the air. Goblin blood had a very distinct
seawater odor. All I smelled was sweat and, from the
dead body behind me, the faint metallic scent of Peters's
blood.

"What is your master's name?" I asked again. It didn't
reply. I dangled my knife in front of its face. "Want me
to nail your other hand to the wall?"

A whimper hid behind its growl; it understood my
threat. "For . . . forbid . . . den."

"You're forbidden from saying his name?"

Nod.

Fabric whispered behind me. I twisted my neck to
look at Wyatt. Intense concentration creased his forehead and deepened the lines around his mouth. The
look was similar to when he was summoning something
difficult—far away or too large to move without serious
effort. Energy crackled around us. I started to ask what
he was doing but didn't want to break his focus.

The hybrid shrieked. A dark bruise appeared on its
neck, to the left of where its Adam's apple should be. I
blinked. Wyatt grunted. On his outstretched palm was a
tiny square of metal, barely half an inch wide.

"What is that?" I asked.

"Tracking device, I think," Wyatt said.

I watched, flummoxed, while Wyatt dropped the device into the sink, turned on the water, and then flipped
the switch on the disposal. Metal gears ground it with a
sound like nails on a chalkboard. When he turned it off,
I asked, "How did you know?"

"I guessed. I couldn't see it, but I felt something inside
its body that could be summoned, something small. I
wasn't sure what it was until I had it in my hand."

"I thought you needed line of sight to summon something."

He blinked. "I always have before," he said slowly,

speaking while turning the realization over in his mind. "But it was just under the skin. Practically line of sight."

Neither one of us said it, but we had to both be thinking it—had Wyatt's death and resurrection-via-magic last week altered his Gift?

"Guess this master likes to keep track of his toys," I said, dragging the conversation back to our prisoner.

"Looks that way."

Still out of reach, I squatted eye level with the sobbing creature. It seemed to know it had lost its last advantage. "So," I said, drawing the single syllable out into three, "now that backup isn't going to find you, how about you make a choice? Long, slow death, or fast and mostly painless?" Part of me begged it to say long and slow.

Too-human eyes gazed at me, full of very human tears. How did a goblin get eyes so human, ears so much like mine? Its skin was smooth, unmarred by age, almost young. Colored oddly, but not slick and oily like a goblin's normally was.

My stomach twisted as a frightening idea burrowed into my brain and didn't let go. This hybrid was not, as I first assumed, a goblin with human traits. Worse than that, it had once been human, and a very young human, given its size. I was certain of it, and grew more certain as the seconds passed—so certain I nearly vomited. I did drop the knife.

"Evy?" Wyatt was beside me instantly. I couldn't look away from the creature, but he must have seen something in my expression. "Evy, what is it?"

Ignoring him, I pierced the hybrid with a stare. "You were human once."

The creature cocked its head, a picture of perfect agony. It wetted its lips with a pink tongue—not the thin sandpaper strip of a goblin. "Toe . . . kin," it said. Raised its broken hand toward its chest. "Token."

"Your name is Token?" Wyatt asked.

No, no, no. I didn't want to know the thing's name. Not when I was about to put it out of its misery. We weren't friends, or allies. It was an abomination of nature. A creature that had no business existing, much less having a name.

"Name," it tried out the word. "Yes."

"Okay, great," I said, snarl indicating it was anything but. "So, Token, what's your master's name?"

Token crunched up his face. "Token . . . good."

I snorted. "Good? You murdered a man!"

Wyatt wrapped his hand around my forearm, a silent comfort and an attempt to control me. My temper was spiking, and he knew it.

"Master told . . . me."

"Your master was wrong."

Token's face reflected utter disbelief. He'd stopped crying, but a river of clear snot trailed from nose to chin. He looked like a chastised child who'd been told Santa Claus was dead. "Can't be," he said. "Is master."

"Even masters can fuck up."

Wyatt made a sound—something between a grunt and a snort. We knew all too well how people in charge could make blind, dumbass decisions that got people under them killed. Me, for example.

Token stared at me, long seconds ticking away while his childlike mind tried to puzzle things out. Something sparked in his brown eyes. I braced for an attack. He surprised me with "You . . . master?"

I shuddered. "No, I'm no one's master."

"Token's master."

"Fuck you, you piece of shit." I shot to my feet too damned fast and my left knee buckled. Wyatt caught me before I fell. I pushed him away, harder than I intended, and he almost tipped backward over the sofa.

I wheeled around and stormed into the kitchenette,

hands fisted, fuming. Angrier for the uncontrolled out-burst than at Token's actual statement. "Hate" wasn't a strong enough word for how I felt about goblins. Experience had taught me everything that training hadn't, and I'd put all that information to good use over the last four years, hunting and killing any I could find. Enjoying it when I knew they'd broken the law and harmed a human. And I'd done my job well.

If I'd done it too well, I had paid for it and more ten days ago, when a goblin queen had kidnapped me and tortured me to death. She'd enjoyed it, returning every injury I'd inflicted on her kind and then some over the course of two and a half days. I'd hated goblins before that; now my gut desire (right or wrong) was to see the entire race wiped off the face of the Earth.

Genocide wouldn't make the pain go away, but the illusion did tend to brighten my day.

I slapped my open palms flat against the counter, frustrated at my inability to control myself. My former partners, Jesse and Ash, had taught me what Boot Camp never could—how to put a safety on my hair-trigger temper. How and when to unleash that anger upon the Dregs I hunted. All that training had been destroyed by my first death, and I was constantly struggling to keep it in check. I'd be ineffective if every goblin I stumbled across set me off into a rage.

Wyatt appeared on the opposite side of the counter. He slid his hands over mine. I looked up, into warm black eyes. No sympathy, no annoyance—just understanding, colored with an unspoken command to get ahold of myself.

"We should have suspected this," he said.

I quirked an eyebrow. "What? Me blowing up?"

"No." The corner of his mouth pulled into a half smile. "We should have expected more hybrids. The lab we found at Olsmill probably wasn't the only one. It was just the only one we found."

The horror movie laboratory I'd discovered in the basement of a defunct nature preserve had held monsters from nightmares—genetic mutations of all sorts, caged in cinder block and steel. Things that shouldn't have existed, much like the boy-monster impaled to my apartment wall.

"If there was another lab," I said, "then who turned Token loose?" A chill niggled its way down my spine. "A third partner?"

"Possibly. We know that Tovin was the brains of the operation, and we know that Leonard Call provided the muscle to get it all done."

"But neither one of them were scientists, capable of combining and manipulating the DNA of such disparate species." I tried to recall my conversation (if it could be termed that) with Call the night I'd put him into a coma. He'd admitted to working with Tovin, to providing brawn in the form of cooperative goblins and Halfies, in return for Tovin's help in his own personal quest for vengeance. Vengeance against Wyatt specifically, and humanity in general, for the murder of Call's lover.

Motives that I understood but couldn't support—for obvious reasons.

"Following that train of thought," Wyatt said, "we could also assume that whoever organized the attack on Boot Camp wants their science projects back."

I closed my eyes and thought about the creatures we'd found at Olsmill. I'd only gotten a good look at three of them. One had been a teenage boy. Half his body was stone, as though he'd been split down the middle and sprayed with cement coating. At the time, I had assumed some sort of cross with a gargoyle. Now I wasn't so sure. This mysterious third party had creatures who could attack via the ground, moving through the earth as easily as trolls. That was bad on so many new levels. . . .

Wyatt's face remained annoyingly neutral when I shared my thoughts. "I can see the goblin queens donating a few of their weaker warriors to experimentation if it meant gaining an advantage," he said.

"Some advantage. The goblins have all but disappeared since we kicked their asses at Olsmill." I said it lightly, but the truth of my statement was worrisome. Goblins were a matriarchal society, and while we'd killed one of their rare queens, she wasn't the only one they had. The fact that most of the goblins had withdrawn from the city, or were at least hiding underground where we couldn't find them, hinted at something big on the horizon. And I hated surprises.

"Yeah," Wyatt said. "Which means they probably have a plan we won't see coming."

So what else is new?

"We need concrete information to give to the Triads," he continued. "Something they can look into that's more tangible than our leaps of logic."

"I know." I shot him a determined look. "So let's get it."

Chapter Four

I rummaged around in one of the drawers until I found a butter knife and a barbecue lighter, then returned to Token. He'd stopped crying. Blood still dripped from his wounded hand. He watched me squat in front of him, flick on the lighter, and heat the tip of the knife.

"Do you hurt?" I asked, choosing the simplest words I could manage.

"Yes," Token replied. "Hurt."

"Do you like to hurt?"

"No. Hate . . . to hurt."

"Who's your master?" Silence. I held up the heated knife. "Do you think this will hurt?" His too-human eyes flickered to the blade. Like a child who doesn't understand about a hot stove, he just stared.

I swallowed, then pressed the tip to the skin on the back of his broken hand. He screamed. I jerked out of reach, wincing. Cruel, perhaps, but now he understood my threat.

"Hurts," he said, betrayal in his eyes. "Why?"

"Who is your master?" After another pained, sulky glare, I started heating the blade again. "I will keep hurting you until you tell me. Do you want me to hurt you again?"

"No." Such a human whine; it turned my stomach.

"Who is your master?"

He fidgeted, wriggled, whined, did everything except

answer my question. I had no real desire to torture the thing further, but I needed this answer.

"Ask him differently," Wyatt said. "I don't think he understands what you want."

Okay, fine. I waved the heated knife in front of him. "Token, what is your master's name?"

Understanding dawned. "The . . . cur . . . ee," he said, forcing out each sound.

I looked up at Wyatt; he shrugged, not recognizing the combination, either. To Token, I repeated it back. "The cur ee. This is your master's name?"

"All name."

"Come again?" No response. "What the hell does—?"

"Thackery," Wyatt said. "Walter Thackery."

"Yes," Token said.

"Who's he?" I asked.

"Master."

"Not you." I stood up and abandoned the knife and lighter on the back of the sofa. "Wyatt, who's Walter Thackery?"

He held up his index finger in a "wait" gesture, dashed into my bedroom, and returned moments later with my laptop already open and booting up. He put it on the scarred table that served as our eating area. As soon as it was ready, he opened an Internet search engine and typed in the name.

"Thackery was a molecular biologist who worked and taught at the university, up until five years ago," he said as news articles began to scroll across the computer screen. "He wasn't even on the Triads' radar until August of that year. Three days before classes were to resume, he cashed out all his stocks, liquidated his assets, issued his resignation, then disappeared with his wife and a boatload of cash. At the same time, the labs at the university were broken into and ransacked. A quarter-million dollars in equipment was stolen. The regular police never connected the two, but we did."

"Why?" I asked, not sure I wanted to know.

"Six months after the disappearance, Morgan's team found Thackery's wife in an alley, sucking a teenage boy dry, and killed them both."

"His wife was a Halfie?"

"There was no way to know for how long, but Morgan reported she had a completely developed set of fangs, so she wasn't new. Probably turned right before Thackery quit and dropped off the radar. We had no luck tracking him down."

I reached around Wyatt, keenly aware of the slim pocket of air between us, and fingered the mouse pad. I clicked on a photo from a university benefit; the date put it at a few weeks before the disappearance. In the image, a beaming couple radiated their love for each other. Walter Thackery was tall, lean, with close-cut dark hair and dark eyes, a sharply chiseled jaw, and ear-to-ear grin. His wife (the caption named her Anne) glowed, even in the black-and-white image. Her dress was tasteful, her makeup and jewelry simple. She held one arm loosely around her tuxedo-clad husband's waist. The other hand was draped across her flat belly, almost protectively. Poor woman.

"So that's our bad guy?" I poked the screen right above Thackery's too-handsome face. "Doesn't really look like the sort to turn humans into goblins, does he?"

"Few people seem capable of murder until they actually pull the trigger. As far as I know, he's been completely off the grid since his disappearance, but given those circumstances, and his scientific background, he's a damned likely candidate."

"Not to mention the admission of our hostage over there." I fought against quick acceptance of this information. It was too easy, having the name of the bad guy in front of me, along with an identifying photograph. I was used to struggling for info, getting frustrated when I didn't get it, and using that frustration to drive me even harder. This was weird.

"Thackery had the money and the means, not to mention the professional experience, to set up his own lab." Wyatt shifted, facing me more directly. His eyebrows were furrowed, but he seemed more determined than annoyed. "This is something we can give the Triads."

"But Rhys Willemy's been researching Olsmill since we found it. Wouldn't someone have made the connection by now?"

"Not necessarily. Memory's a tricky thing, and like I said, no one's had contact with Thackery for five years. The file probably hasn't been looked at since his wife was neutralized. I might never have thought of it without Token."

"Which brings us to problem number one with telling the Triads anything. How are you going to explain Jaron and Token to them?" I did not want to be the one to tell Amalie her personal bodyguard was dead, and that the killer was stuck to my wall.

"Lying by omission, I suppose. Amalie knows you're alive, but I don't have to tell them that's why Jaron came to us. And I'm not exactly helpless, so they'll believe that I subdued Token by myself."

I grinned and poked him in the ribs. "They'll probably be amazed you didn't kill him yet, Mr. Not Helpless."

"Part of me's amazed you haven't killed him yet."

That sobered me right up. "He was human, Wyatt. He's a killer and I want to put him out of his misery, but I can't. He's being helpful." The last was tacked on to avoid expressing just what I was feeling—sympathy. Sympathy for his being manipulated against his will. I knew exactly how that felt.

"He was, but the Triads will want him for questioning."

I nodded. They'd do a lot worse than a tiny burn on his hand. In the past, I would have done much worse myself, and with sharper instruments. "Then let's call them and get this thing started."

Wyatt reached for his phone.

"This really isn't healthy, Truman," Gina Kismet said.

Wyatt snorted but didn't reply.

I didn't need to see him to know he was glaring. After hiding all traces of my existence in the oven—my meager collection of clothing, a photograph, and a handful of books was sort of pathetic when lumped together—I'd taken refuge in the dark bathroom. Even with the door slightly ajar, I had a minuscule view into the living room. Just a slice of the sofa, far enough out to see Jaron's foot and the opposite wall near the door. Wyatt and Kismet were somewhere on my right, near the kitchenette. She'd brought over two of her Hunters, Milo Gant and Felix Diggory. The third member of her Triad, Tybalt Monahan, had lost half his forearm a week ago, but she'd yet to replace him with a rookie from Boot Camp.

Kismet had been commenting on Wyatt's choice to live in this particular apartment. I was amazed she would get within twenty feet of Wyatt, considering she still thought she'd killed me. The tiny part of me that liked and respected Gina Kismet, the only female Handler in the Triads, hated that I hadn't yet come out of the closet (or the bathroom, in this case) and told her the truth.

My logic and her inability to be flexible and give someone the benefit of the doubt kept me silent and still.

"How did Jaron know you were here?" she asked.

"Because I met her while she was in her true sprite form," he explained. "Apparently, sprites can sense auras of those people, so she was able to track me down."

"But why you? Jaron knew how to contact the Triads."

"I don't know. Protection from that thing, maybe?" I imagined him jacking a thumb at Token, still knifed to the wall where I'd left him with firm instructions to tell no one about me. He'd seemed to understand the order. "I checked the avatar's license, and he lived only a few blocks from here."

"I wonder if Amalie knows."

"You haven't heard anything from her yet?"

"No, and nothing's been communicated to me by the brass, if she's contacted them at all."

"Has anyone checked on her avatar?" Wyatt asked exactly what was on my mind.

"No one knows where she lives, remember?" She exhaled hard. "I frigging hate not knowing what's going on."

"That makes two of us."

"Three of us," Felix said, piping up close to the bathroom door. "So did you get anything useful from that thing?"

"Just that it was sent to kill Jaron by its master, and what I told you about its possible connection to Walter Thackery." The only thing we'd agreed to keep to ourselves was Jaron's dying declaration of betrayal. We didn't know who had been betrayed, or if someone was going to be betrayed, or who any of the players were. It was a lead we could follow better on our own. We weren't strangers to betrayal, and it was easier to work with someone you knew wouldn't betray you than with people you just weren't sure about.

"We'll have to do a little old-fashioned detective work on that," Kismet said. "Looking into who's been ordering lab supplies, renting space, getting large shipments of unusual product. Anything like that is bound to leave a paper trail."

"Do you have an inventory of everything that was taken from Olsmill and stored at Boot Camp?"

"Of course."

"I'd like to get a look at it."

"Why?"

"Because if the perimeter was tested because of what's stored there, I want to know what's so valuable he'd send creatures to attack an impenetrable fortress in broad daylight."

"I'll get it to you."

"Thank you." After a moment's pause, he asked, "How's Tybalt?"

"Out of the hospital and researching prosthetics. He's already talking about going back to Boot Camp and learning how to fight with one good hand. He won't quit."

"Good." Feet shuffled, and when Wyatt spoke again, his voice was closer. "It takes balls of brass to cut off a friend's arm when he asks you."

"He didn't want to die," Milo said, a small tremor in his voice. "And he sure as hell didn't want to turn. He would have done the same for any of us."

"I don't doubt it."

I could only imagine the volley of meaningful glances being thrown around the room. Felix had tried to kidnap me. Milo and Tybalt were with Kismet when she "killed" me. And yet they had all acted with the best interests of humanity at heart. That made it impossible to hate them, but I bet Wyatt's outward calm in their presence had the trio thoroughly flummoxed. Probably a tiny bit terrified.

A knock at the door drew their attention. Minutes later, Jed Peters had been carted away, his body headed for the Triads' private morgue until we heard from Amalie. We knew nothing about the sprite's chosen avatar. Did he have family? Friends? Was he alone? Was Jaron even still alive?

"We'll take the goblin to Boot Camp," Kismet said, once the other team was gone. "Interrogate it, then lock it away with its friends."

I took small comfort that she hadn't said they'd execute it once they were finished. Maybe she saw what I saw in its eyes. Though I did wonder at Token's ability to switch loyalties—enough interrogation and Kismet would be looking for the woman who'd helped capture him.

"Do you need me to do anything?" Wyatt asked.

"You've already been a huge help, Truman." Absolute sincerity colored her words. "When I have something you can do without leading a team, I'll let you know. Bathroom's in there, right?"

"Uh, yeah."

It took my brain a few seconds to catch up. I leapt into the claw-foot tub, hoping to manage both quick and quiet, and gently drew the curtain the rest of the way closed. Light flooded the room; the door clicked shut. I tensed, breathing slow and deep. She had no reason to look in the tub.

I expected to hear a zipper and familiar tinkle of liquid. Instead, the faucet ran for a few seconds. Numerous small items rattled. I hazarded a peek through the curtain slit. Kismet palmed two blue capsules from a bottle I couldn't see, then chased them down with tap water from a plastic cup. She gripped the sides of the sink and bowed her head. Tension thrummed from her slight frame, every toned muscle clenched and tight. Shoulder-length red hair curtained her face from me.

I backed away, ashamed at intruding on this private moment of weakness from the experienced Handler. I'd never seen Kismet as anything other than a woman in charge of her situation, barking orders, sure of herself and her command. We weren't friends, and hadn't been even before my deaths. I'd interacted with her more in the last ten days than I ever had in my old life, and we'd even come close to having a friendly conversation once. A conversation about relationships with coworkers and how they never panned out. She'd spoken from experience and I'd been curious. I still was.

I harbored no illusions that my "not dead" status would remain a secret for long, so perhaps, one day, I'd get to ask her about it.

She took several deep breaths, working to get something under control. Migraine, maybe? Her phone rang—a shrill buzzing sound that hurt my ears.

"Kismet," she said, all business. After a pause, she said, "I'm already with Truman." She gave someone our street address. I tensed. "Yes, I'll wait until you arrive. Five minutes."

She snapped the phone shut, flicked off the light, and left. The door stayed wide open, a shaft of light hitting the floor near the tub. I couldn't get out, but I could hear their voices clearly from the living room.

"Amalie is coming here," Kismet announced. I wouldn't have been more surprised if she'd said a meteor was going to crash into the city. "In about five minutes."

"Does she know about Jaron's avatar?" Wyatt asked.

"She didn't mention it. She just said to stay put. She wants to talk to us, and it's urgent."

"Too urgent to say over the phone?"

"Apparently."

The conversation waned. My legs ached from standing still. I shifted my weight but had little room in the small tub. Getting out would make a lot of noise, too noticeable with the door wide open. My trouble could be for naught anyway if Amalie showed up and mentioned me. I had a funny feeling all our work to keep my current "alive" state under wraps was about to be undone.

I stayed put anyway until a sharp crack on the apartment door preceded the familiar squeal of old hinges. Hazarding a peek through the curtain slit, I could see part of the sofa and the wall behind it. No one was in view.

"This is Deaem," Amalie said, her voice clear as a bell. "She accompanies me now as my second."

My stomach bottomed out as the simple statement confirmed my fear. Wyatt further clarified it by saying, "Jaron is really dead, then."

If Amalie nodded, I couldn't see it. "I do not understand." The confusion in her words broke my heart. "The moment an avatar is wounded, the sprite returns. Instead, she chose to stay and so died trapped within the human host. I wish to know the reason for my loss."

I imagined the icy look her avatar had directed at Wyatt. As a human, Amalie was a striking figure—tall and curvy and feminine, with tight red ringlets of hair and the beauty of a fashion model. She had the body most women wanted, and it often amazed me the owner of it never realized she got hijacked a couple of times a week.

"She had a message for me," Wyatt said. "It must have been important enough to die for, but she was gone before she really said anything."

"You are certain?"

"She said the word 'betrayal,' but not who or what specifically."

Kismet made a choking sound as she was fed this tidbit of withheld information.

"I can only guess at the meaning," Amalie said. "However, I have further news to report. News I felt must be shared in person. Where is she?"

Fuck. I was about to be outed.

"She who?" Kismet asked.

"This concerns her more than anyone else, Wyatt Truman," Amalie said. "Produce her."

I produced myself. Three jaws hit the floor when I stepped out of the bathroom. Felix and Milo were standing guard around Token, who'd been uncoupled from the wall and was bound at wrists and ankles. Their expressions were nearly identical and quite comical.

Kismet recovered from her shock first and coiled tight. A thundercloud hovered around her. I could well imagine her roiling cauldron of emotions—surprise, anger, betrayal, suspicion. She was standing an arm's reach from Wyatt, and as I stepped closer, she retreated from him, toward the safety of the sofa. Never taking her eyes off me.

Amalie and her new guard—a small Asian man—hovered by the closed door. Her expression was grim, her manner disheveled. Not as together and in control as the few other times I'd seen her in this human body.

"How?" Kismet asked, the single word practically a growl.

I forced a quasi-sheepish smile, more for her benefit than because I was embarrassed by being alive. "Handy-dandy healing powers, plus a little help from some friends. If it makes you feel any better, the fire nearly did kill me."

She grunted.

"Boss?" Felix asked. His right hand had inched beneath the hem of his sweatshirt, probably close to a sheathed knife or holstered gun. He looked past me, right at Kismet, waiting for orders.

I held my breath. Kismet had wanted me neutralized

because I had posed a serious threat to the established order of the Triads. While I no longer had the same goals as a week ago, her opinion of me might not have changed. And Kismet knew how to hold a grudge.

"Please," Amalie said. "There are more urgent matters at hand."

Felix relaxed his stance, hand going back to his hip. Empty.

Good. Giving Amalie my undivided attention, I asked, "What's going on that concerns me so much?"

"Something valuable has gone missing," she said.

"Gone missing?"

"Stolen."

Alarm bells clanged in my head, telling me I really didn't want to know the answer to my next question. "What's been stolen?"

"The crystal in which we sealed the Tainted One."

Wyatt made a soft choking sound. I couldn't tear my attention off Amalie, too mesmerized by what I saw in her face—fear. Never in my life had I thought to see a frightened sprite. They could manipulate so much power because of their direct ties to the Break. It was the reason sprites, and no other race, held the most sway over the Fey Council, and why we needed to keep them as our allies.

But more than that, my ears had filled with a dull roar, and even above the fear I saw in her, I didn't believe what I'd just heard. Heart jackhammering, I asked, "Say that again?"

She didn't. Instead, she started in on a story. "After your initial entrapment, we devised a method to more permanently seal the Tainted One's essence into a crystal. When the spell was cast, we sought a safe place for it elsewhere. We gave it to our brethren in the forest west of here, an expanse of mountains few humans ever hike into. They could cloak the Tainted's draw. I believed it was safe there."

I snorted, red fury creeping into the corners of my vision. "Why the hell did you take it out of First Break?"

"The power of the Tainted affects not only humans, Evangeline, but many of my kind as well. Having its evil so near was . . . unsettling. I feared its effects on our well-being. One does not allow disease to remain in one's orchard to infect all around it."

"So you let someone steal it?" I seethed, in no mood to understand her reasons. Only one thing was crystal clear to me. "The fucking Tainted is loose?"

She shook her head, red ringlets flying. "No, I do not believe it is. Not yet. The person who stole the crystal would need to have knowledge of our magic and the spell used to encase the Tainted within the crystal. Few outside my people can manage such a feat."

My stomach flipped. "That doesn't make me feel better, dammit." We'd sacrificed so much to contain the Tainted the first time and nearly lost. I'd seen the entity take over the body of an elf, growing to horrifying and grotesque proportions, becoming a black-skinned creature of nightmares.

I'll put my wife into you, girl, it had said. *I look forward to getting to know her again.*

I swallowed hard, pressed my lips together, determined not to be sick. Wyatt moved into my line of sight. He grasped my shoulders and squeezed. I stared at his throat, unwilling to meet his gaze.

"Stay here, Evy," he whispered.

"I'm fine," I ground out, anything but. Leaning sideways far enough to see past his shoulder, I reaffixed my glare on Amalie. "What happened to seeking out other elves who could send the damned thing back across the Break?"

"We have tried and been unsuccessful," she replied. "I

told you once that very few elves still walk this world. They are difficult to find at the best of times."

Wyatt shifted to my right side, probably sensing I wasn't going to fall apart or leap across the room and throttle anyone. He stayed close, though, his left hand still lingering on my hip. I was grateful for his touch.

"Who did you give this crystal to?" Kismet asked, finding her voice. She'd been there the night we'd contained the Tainted, and had seen the things we'd removed from Olsmill. She'd spilled blood with the rest of us.

"The Nerei," Amalie said. "You would call them nymphs, or more to your specificity, wood nymphs."

"Dryads?"

A nod. "Yes. They were the guardians of a grove of ash trees." Her complexion darkened, cheeks glowing rosy red. "By now your people will have learned of a forest fire many miles from the nearest hiking trail. That is where my people died protecting this crystal."

"Do you have any idea who took it?" I asked, at the same time as Wyatt asked, "When did this happen?"

Amalie blinked, her electric-blue gaze shifting between us. "Moments after the earthquake that shook the city, and no, we do not know who took it. We sent two of our Earth Guardians to investigate the earth, but there are so many conflicting auras they are unable to sort it. I will go myself in an hour's time."

I balked. "Alone."

She tilted her head toward the silent Asian man. "Deaem will accompany me. It is imperative that we learn who has done this before the crystal is compromised."

"You think?" Okay, so sarcasm isn't the best tactic to use with a sprite. "Well, now that my not-really-dead cover is blown wide open, what do you need me to do?"

"Be wary, Evangeline. For your assistance in defeating Tovin, I believe I owed you this information in person. I cannot begin to guess if this is somehow linked to the cry of betrayal."

"Yeah, well, things like this always have a habit of ending up connected." Jaron may have discovered the person responsible for leaking the crystal's location to whoever stole it. The tiny fact still bothering me was why not share the info with Amalie? Why seek me out first? It didn't make sense. "Do you think the attack on Boot Camp was just a diversion, then? Get our attention south of town while this mystery baddie steals in the north?"

"It is probable."

"Well, it worked like a charm." I eyed the crack in the apartment wall. "Now we just have to wait until the crystal thief reveals his master plan or we're suddenly overrun by demons."

Amalie shuddered visibly.

A phone buzzed. Kismet fished her cell out of her pocket and snapped it open. Announced herself. Went absolutely still as the voice on the line spoke, a scratchy hiss barely audible in the room's newfound silence. Already pale skin accrued a deathly pallor. Her eyes widened, glimmered, as though on the verge of tears.

I reached over and twined my fingers with Wyatt's, holding tight. We knew it without saying it: not good news.

"We'll be there in fifteen minutes," Kismet said, and snapped her phone shut. Her voice was mechanical, distant.

"Boss?" Felix asked, the one-word question coated with worry.

She ignored him; instead, her fiery gaze landed on me, as forceful as a fist. "You two are coming with us."

"Where?" I asked.

"East Side."

It was on the tip of my tongue to ask why, but she'd

redirected her attention. To Amalie, she said, "You may want to see this as well."

Three Hunters, two Handlers, and two sprite avatars were going on a road trip to an unknown destination. I hoped she had a big car.

Chapter Five

Kismet's seven-seat SUV was the perfect size for our mismatched band of travelers. Amalie got shotgun by default of status. The man she called Deaem sat directly behind her, stiff as a board and wary as a pit bull. Milo took the other single seat, which left me in the rear, uncomfortably sandwiched between Felix and Wyatt, who'd changed his ripped shirt before we left. I was practically in Wyatt's lap, repelled by the poisonous glare Felix couldn't seem to lose—as though I caused him great pain by my proximity. Kismet had yet to retract her death sentence on me, but she also hadn't ordered them to accost me.

Small favors.

East Side encompassed a large portion of the city, south and east of the point where its two rivers connected into one. Kismet crossed at the Lincoln Street Bridge, and I felt a slight twinge of loss. A not-quite-friend had once made his home beneath that bridge—a troll named Smedge, who'd helped me out on assignments and been a good source of intel on various Dreg activities. I hadn't spoken to him in nearly two weeks.

Amalie might know where he was, but it was definitely not the right time to ask. No one had spoken a word since we'd begun the trip, and I wasn't about to break the silence first.

The familiarity of Kismet's route startled me, and it wasn't lost on Wyatt, either. We stared out his window at the length of train tracks running along our chosen street, taking us away from the busier portion of the neighborhood and into a section of empty lots and cracked pavement.

Ice settled in my chest as Kismet slowed and turned toward an open gate. Wyatt clasped my hand; I squeezed back. Through the gate, into a large, overgrown parking lot that was surrounded by a chain-link fence. Ahead of us was our destination. I shuddered just looking at it. A run-down, paint-peeling, gabled train station that hadn't seen regular use in over a decade stood near a swath of crisscrossing tracks. The trains no longer stopped at the passenger station, but that didn't prevent people from coming here.

Three other cars were parked near the building, including the stripped and tire-less car Alex and I had driven and left there once upon a time. One person paced around outside, a pistol steady in one hand. Dark clothes, tense stance—a Hunter I didn't know. My chest ached.

"Evy, breathe," Wyatt said.

I exhaled hard, unaware I'd been holding my breath. I tasted bile in the back of my throat. Heat flushed my cheeks, even though my entire body was numb. Cold.

This was where I'd died. What the hell were we doing here?

Kismet parked near the other cars and got out without a word. The rest of us followed. My limbs didn't want to cooperate. I forced my feet to move forward, past the sullen glare of the Hunter standing watch by the vehicles. He barely gave me a look but had acknowledging nods for Felix and Milo. I hadn't known every Hunter during my tenure (no one did), but those three were acquainted.

Up the steps and onto the porch went everyone except me and Wyatt. My feet just wouldn't move. Wyatt hadn't let go of my hand, and I concentrated on him—his warmth and stability. It was the only thing keeping me from freaking out.

"Why are we here?" I asked, finally finding my voice. Alarmed at its shakiness.

Kismet turned, and her glare softened a fraction when she looked at me. "Someone left a message here," she said icily. "Given the location, it seemed like a message meant as much for you as the rest of the Triads."

Oh God. I don't want to see this. Nothing good was waiting for me inside. All signs pointed toward someone having been killed, or worse. And it was the "or worse" that nearly rooted me to the pavement. I'd been "or worse" once; I didn't think I could witness that sort of suffering again.

Wyatt took the first step and tugged at my hand. I swallowed, gathered the last tattered remnants of my courage, and followed. One foot in front of the other, across the warped and rotting platform. Through the door and into the dusty ticket office. Following a familiar path of footsteps through grime that led toward a door marked "Stairs."

This was the third time I'd come to this damnable place and had gone down these creaky stairs into the dank basement corridor. The first time was as a hostage, and I'd been taken out in a body bag. The second time I'd entered alone, with no memory of having been there before, seeking answers. Now I was here with the full weight of what I'd experienced. Clarity of detail had lessened a bit with time, as violent trauma often does, the sharp edges taking on a fuzzy hue like a sepia-toned photograph. Dulled, but not gone.

Another Hunter stood down the corridor, across from an open door. I didn't have to look to know which door—the one marked with a black "X," painted in my old body's blood. He looked up, ebony face as blank as a coma patient, dark eyes devoid of emotion. He just stared, glazed. I'd seen him around—he'd been at the Olsmill battle, but I couldn't remember his name.

"Perimeter's been set," he said to Kismet as she approached. Even his voice was detached, and I realized it wasn't apathy—it was shock. "No one else has been inside."

She turned with visible effort and looked into the room (although "room" was generous, as it was barely larger than a linen closet). Blood rushed from her face; her hands shook, and she couldn't help releasing a startled cry. Felix and Milo scrambled to her. They looked in as they moved her away, protective of their Handler, and as visibly sickened by what they saw as she.

Deaem glanced at the room—probably doing his duty to check for danger—then let Amalie go in. I couldn't go farther. Ten feet from the door, I was still too damned close. The humid basement air tickled my nose. The odor made me want to retch. Memory was trying to overcome common sense, and I had half a mind to let the former win.

Amalie emerged moments later and waved me forward. I swallowed, certain the lump in my throat would choke me before I made it to her side. Wyatt stuck close. I squeezed his hand so hard I was sure I'd break it. As expected, the telltale "X" was still on the door. Lingering odors of blood and rot and death wafted out like black fingers, caressing my skin with their awful touch. I wanted to run, as much from what I remembered about this room as from what was waiting inside for me now.

I looked.

Past did not superimpose on the present as I thought it might. The mattress I'd died on and the shackles I'd been bound with were gone. Old splatters and sprays of my blood were washed away, the cement floor scrubbed clean. The odor of old bleach made me want to sneeze. Yesterday's gore was gone—but today's was nailed to the far wall.

At first, I couldn't tell who it was. He was bare-chested, stripped down to his boxer shorts. Long metal spikes had been pushed through his shoulders, chest, abdomen, and upper thighs, but very little blood had fallen. No, the majority of his blood had come from the wide gash in his throat and was collected in a metal bucket near his feet.

"Fuck," Wyatt snarled.

I squinted at the man's face, hard to see from its downward angle. It dawned on me moments later—Rhys Willemy. I'd only ever seen the Handler in fancy, pressed suits and polished shoes—an odd wardrobe choice, given his profession. I also realized that the stricken Hunter outside was one of his. Or had been.

I stared, dumbfounded and sickened by the dead man displayed in front of me. Why here, of all places to leave a body? The location by itself wasn't much of a message. There had to be something else. I took a step closer. Wyatt made a noise but didn't try to stop me.

If the blood drips were any indication, he'd been killed and drained elsewhere, then hung up on the wall. One person alone couldn't have done it. At least two were needed, maybe three, and strong. Willemy wasn't a defensive linebacker, but he wasn't a small man, either. Even dead, nailing him to the wall couldn't have been easy.

"This doesn't make sense," I muttered.

"Evy?" Wyatt asked.

"What?"

"Turn around."

I did. On the wall by the door, painted in blood, was a message: *Give me back what's mine.*

An icy hand twisted my guts. I fled the room, panting,

and didn't stop until I'd reached the bottom of the stairs. Above the lingering odor of bleach was the tangy stink of blood. All around me now, in my nose and hair and clothes. I bent over, hands on the third-from-bottom stair and sucked in great lungfuls of air. Tamping down panic and overwhelming disgust.

Near the base of the stairs was a pile of what looked like dried oatmeal. As I stared at it, I remembered Alex vomiting after seeing the room in which I'd been tortured to death. He'd been here a week ago. I saw his sweet, smiling face and wanted to cry for him all over again.

"You okay?" Not Wyatt's voice, as expected. I turned my head and looked into the concerned chocolate eyes of the familiar Hunter. His Handler was stuck to the wall like artwork and he was asking if I was okay?

"Yeah, I'm okay." His sensitivity shamed me into standing upright. "I'm sorry. I don't remember your name."

"David Moreau. Stone, right? Someone said you were dead."

"Only on paper."

"Guess I kind of know how you feel now."

"How's that?"

"Being the last of your Triad." The quiet despair in his voice made my heart ache. "I lost my partners at Olsmill, and now I lost my Handler to some friggin' psychopath."

"I'm sorry" was all I could think to say. At least it was the truth.

"What kind of message is that?" Wyatt asked, his voice booming down the corridor for all to hear.

Kismet had gathered herself back together, and she stepped forward. "I don't know, but I don't like cryptic notes from fuck-jobs who turn my friends into wall décor. Thoughts?"

"Who found him?" I asked, wandering toward the group. David stuck close.

"Anonymous tip," she replied.

"So it's down to who and what. Who did it and what do we have that they want back?"

"That's why the perimeter. I figure if our killer is going to make a move, it'll be while we're here."

I scrubbed both hands over my face. "And you think it's connected to me somehow, because of where we are?"

Kismet nodded. "It can't possibly be a coincidence."

"Agreed," Wyatt said.

"Trouble with that theory," Felix said, "is everyone thought Stone was dead this past week. Longer than that, if they didn't know she'd been brought back in the first place." He didn't seem happy about either piece of information, and the attitude was starting to grate.

"Then maybe it isn't me specifically," I said. "Maybe it's just me tangentially, and it only has something minor to do with me. Maybe it isn't— Wait. 'Give me back what's mine.'" It struck so fast my mental brakes left skid marks. "No way."

"What no way?" Wyatt asked, alarmed.

"Token's master, the one we took those hybrids and science projects from. It has to be him, Wyatt. He already sent his . . . whatevers out there to attack Boot Camp."

Wyatt's eyebrows arched, mouth forming a surprised O. He was finally on track with my train of thought. Then Kismet jumped on board and said, "You mean the name you gave me back at the apartment?"

"Walter Fucking Thackery," I said.

As if on cue, a phone rang somewhere inside the little closet of death.

Everyone in the hall who still possessed a phone checked, but I was already making tracks toward the sound. Willemy had been stripped to his boxers, leaving few other places to hide a cell phone. The muffled ringtone grew no louder when I stepped inside. Breathing carefully through my mouth, I approached the body—it seemed to be the source of the sound.

No, not the body.

"Tell me it's not in there," Kismet said.

Another ring confirmed it. The phone was submerged inside the bucket of blood.

"That's fucking sick," Felix said.

The person who'd killed Willemy was on the other end of that line, and I had every intention of answering. I crouched in front of the bucket. The thick, metallic tang of blood invaded my mouth. I could taste it, smell it even without using my nose.

"We need to get it," I said. I reached toward the shiny crimson surface, pulled back, then tried again.

"I'll do it," David said. Rolling up his sleeve, he squatted across from me and reached right in. His lips pulled back from his teeth. Blood swished over the edge of the bucket and splattered on the floor. I couldn't begin to pretend I knew how he felt, feeling around in a bucket of his Handler's blood for a ringing phone.

He withdrew his arm. Clasped in his hand was a dripping, sealed plastic bag. He stood, careful to keep his arm over the bucket, and held the bag out toward me. I swallowed, grasped one edge of the seal with the tips of my fingers and pulled. David pulled opposite me. The seal hissed open. I plucked out the still-ringing phone, and the bag splashed back into the bucket.

A generic phone, nothing special. The I.D. said "Willemy, R." I grunted. Bastard.

"You gonna answer?" David asked.

I found the Speaker button, turned toward the waiting crowd that had spilled halfway into the tiny room, and accepted the call. "This isn't Rhys Willemy, so who the fuck are you?"

Wyatt flinched. My greeting could have been more polite. I wasn't in the mood for false pleasantries.

A deep chuckle answered me first, and then a male voice spoke. "I was hoping they would scare you up, Ms. Stone. I've heard so much about you, and yet we've never managed to meet." His cadence was a little too precise, like a man trying hard to affect a nondescript accent and not quite succeeding.

"How about you turn yourself in so we can get better acquainted, Thackery?"

"I see you've done your homework."

"It's easy when you know how to get answers from people. You fond of turning humans into goblins?"

David blanched—the only one listening who hadn't met Token.

"I have a fondness for a great many things," Thackery said. "Not the least of which being the things you confiscated from Olsmill."

I glanced at the painted message. "If you wanted your toys back, you could have just asked. Murdering people to make a point is a sure as shit way to end up on my bad side."

"Mr. Willemy's death is unfortunate. Yet you are taking me more seriously now than had I merely called you up for a chat over tea. Don't you agree?"

Bastard. If Thackery had been in the room, I would have wrapped my hands around his throat and squeezed until his eyes popped out. "Violence gets your attention, huh? I'll keep that in mind for when we meet."

"You're so certain we will."

"Well, given the location in which we found the phone and your own admission that you're glad they scared me up, I'd say it's a damned good bet." The conversation was grating on my nerves and composure. I didn't like talking; I liked pummeling. "So what is it you think we have that's yours?"

"Two things, specifically, that I would like returned to me. One of them is a sealed jar of amber liquid, marked with the designation 'X-235.' "

Kismet had produced a small notepad and miniature retractable pen, and she was scribbling notes. Prepared.

"The second thing," he continued, "is in a vial the size of an average cigar, red in color. It has no markings but was the only red vial in the lab that night."

I glanced at Kismet; she nodded, to confirm the vial or simply that she'd written it all down. Thackery wasn't getting anything back from me. "Don't suppose you're going to tell me what's in those vials?" I asked.

"I have no intention of doing so, no. Rest assured they are nontoxic as long as the seals remain unbroken."

Terrific. "And what makes you think I'm going to give them back? Because you killed a man, then asked so nicely?"

"I'm not so naïve, Ms. Stone. And I'm not a greedy man, which is why I asked for those two items and not my entire laboratory's contents."

"Still not giving them back."

"Then I'll propose a trade."

I tensed, alarmed now. "What could you possibly have that I want?"

"Ask the sprite if she lost anything today." His tenor had darkened, coated in menace and promising something terrible.

Something nasty in the form of a stolen containment crystal. My hand shook and I nearly dropped the phone. Amalie had gone pale, her human eyes glowing an eerie, incandescent blue, radiating fury and power. She glared at the phone as though its mere presence disgusted her. Energy crackled around us, whip-snapping and tingling. It danced through me like an electrical current.

I'd seen Amalie angry, but never this pissed off.

"Do you know what that crystal is?" I asked. I didn't have to ask for proof he had it. Few enough people knew it existed in the first place, never mind where it had been hidden.

"Of course I know," Thackery replied, as if I were the biggest dolt ever to utter a question. "I feel its power calling to me. It wants to be freed, Ms. Stone. It's not as stable as you might think."

Old habits had me looking to Wyatt for a plan of action. A Hunter seeking the advice of her Handler in a situation she wasn't certain how to manage. His expression was mostly blank, with only the barest hint of anger; I could see the rage boiling beneath the surface and how hard he was fighting to maintain decorum in mixed company.

"When and where?" I asked the phone.

"Four hours" was the response. "Keep the phone on you. I'll call you with a location in three and a half, and with further instructions." He hung up before I could utter another word.

Milo shouldered his way forward. "Nothing on the trace," he said. "Wherever this guy is, he's blocking us."

"So we just give this loony tune what he wants?" David asked.

"Only if we have to," I replied. "He has something far more dangerous than two vials of liquid."

"You don't know what's in those two vials."

"No, I don't, but I sure as hell know what's in that crystal. And if gets out, hunting Dregs will look like patty-cake compared to the things we'll be fighting."

"But what is it?"

I hesitated. I found no permission in Amalie's gaze, but also no demand for silence. David had fought with us at Olsmill. His Handler had just been murdered. He deserved to know, especially if he tagged along for the ride, as I suspected he would.

"It's a demon. It's what Tovin pulled over from the other side at Olsmill, and what we barely managed to contain once. It is ancient and it wants to be free."

David blinked. "Demon?"

"We hunt down half-Blood vampires for a living, David. Don't tell me this really shocks you." It had shocked the hell out of me once, but I needed him focused, not pondering the possibilities.

It worked, because he snapped to. "No, not really."

I crammed the phone into my jeans pocket and took a step toward Kismet. "All of the stuff from Olsmill is still at Boot Camp, right?" She nodded. "Great. Road trip. Amalie?"

The still-sparking sprite queen turned those awful eyes on me. "I must return and report these events to the Fey Council. I will contact you again when the hour of the exchange draws near, and will offer any assistance you may require at that time."

"David," Kismet said, "can you give them a ride back—?"

"I'd like to go with you, if it's all the same," David said.

Kismet's lips parted, but she hesitated on her answer. "All right. Felix, take David's car and drop Amalie and Deaem off wherever they need to go, then meet me back at your place."

"Sure, boss," Felix said, though his tone communicated annoyance at being dumped with chauffeur duty.

I didn't look back at Willemy as we left. I hadn't really known him, and I grieved the loss of another experienced Handler rather than a friend. But all that aside, I had every intention of ripping his death out of Thackery's ass.

* . * . *

This time around, David rode shotgun. Milo took his same single seat behind Kismet, so Wyatt and I sat together in the rear. We didn't talk—just existed in each other's pain. The city's ten Handlers knew one another— it was essential for them to work together—whereas most Hunters knew only their two Triad partners. Wyatt and Kismet had to be taking Willemy's murder hard.

I saw Wyatt's grief in the tight line of his shoulders and tension in his jaw. I swear I heard his teeth grinding. He wanted to blow up or break down, but couldn't allow himself that luxury. So I sat close, one hand on his left knee, in silent support. It was all I could do during the half-hour drive.

Boot Camp is more prison than sleepaway camp. High electrified walls bordered nearly two miles of perimeter, and deep fortified barriers ran beneath it. It was nestled in a valley almost twenty miles south of the city limits, off an unpaved mountain road that had no signs pointing it out. Fifteen yards onto the road, surrounded by dense underbrush and various booby traps, was the first checkpoint—a single gate accessible only with a PIN code. Only Handlers had them; once Hunters graduated, we were never expected to return unescorted.

As soon as Kismet stopped to enter her code, my pulse began to race. I'd not been back since completing my training four years ago. I had tried to forget about the people I'd hurt and seen hurt, forget the pain I'd suffered and inflicted.

Wyatt sat up straighter and covered my hand with his. "It might be safer if you lie low while we get the vials," he said.

David had tensed considerably since passing through the gate. His visible left hand was curled around the armrest so tightly it trembled. Even Milo was uneasy, shifting in his seat as the SUV rumbled down the dirt road toward our personal hell.

"Maybe we all should stay," I said, and Wyatt didn't have to ask who I meant. He just nodded.

The dense foliage ceased abruptly. Beyond it lay a sun-lit clearing.

Six buildings made up the main compound, and, to a stranger's eyes, it looked like a small community college. The concrete structures varied in height from single-story to six stories. They were clean and painted ivory, their simple tin roofs gleaming in the sun. Windows covered with steel bars didn't seem completely out of place, given the outlying security.

Past those six buildings—dormitories, a cafeteria, the infirmary, classrooms, an indoor gymnasium—was a line of loblolly pines. Beyond those, out of eyesight, was where we'd done most of our training. A ghost town for maneuvers and tactics, obstacle courses to test reflexes, a pool for water exercises and breath-holding games, a shooting range for guns and crossbows, and targets for knife throwing. Everything our trainers needed to churn out perfect little killing machines.

We stayed far away from the rear of the compound. Kismet parked in front of the farthest building from the entrance, a two-story job the size of half a football field—one of the only two buildings trainees were forbidden to enter. Its front doors had familiar keypad locks, bars on all windows that I could see, and it looked as quiet as a morgue. In fact, the entire compound was strangely silent.

"Truman, come with me," Kismet said, palming the keys. "The rest of you, hang out for a bit."

She didn't have to ask me twice. Wyatt gave my knee a squeeze, then climbed out with Kismet. They disappeared inside, swallowed up by the building's forbidding façade.

David twisted around to face the rear. "Anyone else not really comfortable being here?" he asked.

Milo and I raised our hands; I smiled at the comical display of solidarity.

"The day I walked out that gate," Milo said, "I swore I'd never come back. Then what happens? I get to help move the ugliest, creepiest critters I've ever seen out of a forest lab and into Research and Development."

I flinched at the sideways jab. "I never wanted to return, either. Guess I sort of kept that personal promise, since this isn't the body I trained in."

"Suffered in," David said. "They don't tell you about the suffering when they pitch the idea of coming here."

"Most of us aren't in a position to say no."

"On the bright side," Milo said with false bravado, "we're the ones who passed, so we're the lucky ones, right?"

Silence. I picked at a thread on the seam of my jeans, wishing for a swift return of our Handlers. Memory Lane was an uncomfortable place for me at the best of times, and given present company and location, this was definitely on the list of worst times.

"Your other teammate," David said to Milo, "he lost his hand last week. How's he doing?"

"Fast track to recovering," Milo replied.

"It's not an easy thing, man." He could have meant a lot of things—cutting off a friend's hand to save his life, relearning how to live with one hand—but it didn't matter. Milo didn't ask for clarification, and the comment hung there for a while in the uneasy silence.

Movement flickered in the corner of my eye. I turned toward the passenger side window. A line of six young folks, late teens at the oldest, were jogging near the edge of the tree line, led by an older man in blue sweats. Physical-conditioning time. At my peak, I'd been able to run a four-mile mountain trail in under twenty minutes. I doubted I could walk the same trail in two hours in this new body.

It wasn't that I'd inherited an out-of-shape body, just an out-of-practice one. I was curvy but trim. My muscles didn't thrum with the same taut power I'd once possessed, or the flexibility I'd acquired over six months of hard training. I didn't look forward to taking up that regime again—I kind of liked the softness of my body now. Rounder hips, fuller breasts, definitely more feminine. For the first time in my life, I felt like a woman.

"Well, I'll be damned," Milo said.

He was staring out his driver's side window. I squinted out, curious. A dozen yards away, a man had exited the cafeteria. Dressed in familiar black slacks and a white, buttoned-up shirt that seemed to weep for its missing tie, he paused on the steps and consulted a leather binder.

Light glinted off the white-blond hair of the silver-tongued recruiter who tracked down and brought trainees to Boot Camp. The man who had negotiated my release from prison with the promise of a more fulfilling life.

Bastian.

The fucker.

Chapter Six

Four and a Half Years Ago

I can survive another twenty-eight days in Hell. After all, I've lived in it for seventeen years and eleven months. One more month is nothing, and then I'll finally be free. Free of Juvie, free of adults who don't understand me, free of rules and restrictions and walls. I can do anything.

In twenty-eight days.

As quietly as I can in my thin slippers, I pad down the chilly corridor, knowing full well I'm not supposed to be here. The plain globe lights are set to nighttime levels, giving the faded blue linoleum floor a sickly tint. Not my fault I drank too much juice at dinner and have to pee after lights-out. Okay, yes it is. Still, I'm not pissing in my bed. Haven't done that since I was four.

No one stirs in the rooms I pass. Soft snores and occasional whimpers drift out through the doorless frames. Took me a long time to get used to sleeping with an open door and lots of light, not to mention three other girls in the same room. Doesn't bother me so much now, not after three-plus years here.

The bathroom is at the far end of the corridor from my room, naturally, practically next to the watch room. Blinds are shut, though, so Joanie Willis, the overnight guard on weekdays, is either watching a movie she shouldn't be or entertaining one of the night guards from the boys' block. I don't hear anything like heavy breathing or wailing as I slip past, so probably a movie.

I'm careful about the door—it likes to squeal sometimes. I know the layout by heart, so I don't bother with the lights. I just cross six steps straight ahead, then make a sharp right. My palm slaps a stall partition. I creep inside in the near-pitch, tug down my pajama bottoms, and do my business. Feels great. I've been holding that too damned long.

I don't flush. Someone will be pissed in the morning (no pun intended), but it makes too much noise. Can't risk it when the battle's half-won. I emerge from the stall at the same moment the door opens. My stomach knots. Fear roots my feet, even though common sense screams to hide. Several shadows move inward, and then a bright beam of light hits me in the eyes.

I gasp and look away, spots of color dancing behind my eyelids. The door creaks shut. Slippered feet whisper across the floor, moving toward me. Panic hits like ice, chilling me inside and setting my hands shaking. I backpedal until my ass hits the cement wall. I've been in my share of fights, sure, but never in the dark.

The light beam tilts toward my feet, and beyond it are four shapes. Girls from my hall, girls who hate me for one reason or another. The biggest girl, six inches and a good thirty pounds on me, is also the meanest. Her name is Lana. She picked a fight with me my first week here because I refused to kiss her shoes. Literally, kiss her fucking shoes. We tussled; I smashed her face into the wall and broke her nose. After that, mean or not, she liked to let her "girls" pick on me.

Those girls are with her now. Alicia hates me because I have straight blond hair, while hers is shit brown and frizzy. She cut a huge hank of my hair off once, so I put ice cubes in her bed half an hour before inspection, which got her tossed into the Thinking Room. Standing next to Alicia is Rowan—who likes to brag about the dogs she killed and skinned to get her here—and a bony corpse of a girl named Cathy. She hates me because her friends do, but we've not had it out personally. Yet.

"You aren't supposed to be here, Evil," Lana says, her voice a hoarse whisper.

I bristle. I hate the nickname. "Neither are you."

"Sure we are. We came to give you a good-bye present, since you're leaving us soon."

Alicia skirts closer to me, getting within spitting distance. Something long and thin is in her hand. "Going to be eighteen soon," she says. "Can't have you leaving us without breaking you in first."

A tremor rips down my spine. "I've had enough fucking things broken since I got here," I snarl, hands balling into fists at my sides.

"We don't mean bones." Alicia brings that thing out from behind her back and into the beam of light. It takes me a minute to understand what it is—a plunger—and what exactly she means to do with it. Holy fuck!

Irrationality strikes hard, and I bolt. Right at Cathy, who doesn't expect me. I knock her sideways into Rowan, dart left, and get past them. I'm almost at the door when Lana slams into me sideways. I shriek as we tumble to the floor, kicking and scratching. I get a handful of her hair and pull hard. A lot of it breaks and she shouts.

A foot kicks me in the head, and I see colorful lights. The flashlight beam is streaking all over the walls, making it hard to understand what's happening. I punch out, scratch at flesh, fight back against the weight pressing down on me. Someone's sitting on my chest, someone else tries to hold my legs still, but I'm kicking and flailing. I connect—I think it's Rowan from the grunt—and her body falls away.

No, no, fucking hell no! I've kept them away from me

this long. I start to scream, hoping to lure in any guard close by—*why the hell hasn't anyone heard us by now?*—but fabric is shoved into my mouth. Foul and scratchy, maybe a sock. Hands on my legs again.

I go limp, which seems to surprise them. Then I shock the shit out of them by twisting my entire body, fast enough to dislodge Lana. I keep twisting and roll until I hit a wall. A hard cylinder is by my hand—the flashlight. Someone must have dropped it in the confusion. I grab it and swing at the nearest thing to me, which just happens to be Alicia's head. She drops like a sack of stones, blood spurting from her mouth.

"Bitch!" That's Cathy, and she trips over Alicia in her haste to get to me. Falls hard and cracks her own damned head on the tile floor. Moron.

The hard wood plunger pole smacks into my belly. Didn't see that coming. I double over, gasping, tears stinging my eyes. Another blow across my spine sends me to my knees as fire blossoms in my lower back. A foot swings at my head; I react on sheer instinct. I grab the ankle and pull, tripping the owner into falling on her ample ass, then clamp my teeth down on her calf. Hard.

Lana shrieks and kicks with her other foot. She connects with my shoulder, and I bite harder. Blood floods my mouth, thick and metallic. Her next kick combines with Alicia's swing with the plunger, and I let go. Spit the blood at Alicia and somehow duck her next brutal blow, then use my entire body to bowl her over. Her shoulder strikes first with a solid crunch. The plunger skitters away.

A boy from my first foster home once called me a scrappy fighter. I guess this is what he meant.

Lana and I fling ourselves toward the plunger at the same time and nearly knock heads. We both grab for it, hissing and spitting at each other like cats. I do the only thing I can think of and slam my forehead against her nose. It hurts me like a fucking bitch, but it hurts Lana more. She scrambles away, holding her bleeding nose, crying.

Plunger in hand, I pull up to my knees and bring the handle down across her head. That sends her into never-never land with her cronies. The room falls into silence, the flashlight beam aimed at the far wall, away from the carnage. My entire body begins to tremble. I stand on shaking legs, plunger still in one unsteady hand, dazed and unsure what to do.

The decision is made for me. The door opens and lights are turned on, and I blink hard against the sudden glare. Three female guards storm the room, batons in hand. I don't have time to drop the plunger before they're on me. No time to explain as I curl into a ball, protecting myself as best I can. I'm the last person standing, and this is my punishment for winning.

The Thinking Room has a unique odor I recognize before I can peel my eyes open. It smells of urine and shit and sweat. I've been here many times, in this center's version of solitary confinement, and usually I deserve it. For starting fights, talking back to guards, generally being pissed off.

This time it isn't my fault.

Cold seeps through my back from the floor. I open my eyes to a familiar plaster ceiling and single bare bulb. Let my head loll around, too sore and achy to bother sitting up yet. Same hard plastic chair, same wall-embedded toilet that flushes once a day like clockwork. Nothing else.

I test my legs, and both move without trouble. Just lots of aches, probably lots of bruises, too. Back and stomach already hurt from the blows of the plunger, compounded times ten by additional baton hits. My ribs scream when I inhale too deeply, testing them. My left shoulder feels swollen; my left hand, too. And heavy. Maybe broken, maybe sprained. My right arm is fine, though.

My face is puffy. I can tell just by moving my cheeks a little bit. At least one black eye, I bet. My lips are cut, flecked with dried blood. My forehead is sore, too. My head is throbbing, three sizes too big. I want to curl into a ball until the pain goes away, but the idea of moving horrifies me. No, better to lie here and suffer. And not cry.

Just thinking about crying sparks tears. I bite my tongue to keep them at bay. I won't cry—not when I'm so close to getting the fuck out of here.

Time passes in never-ending pain. At some point my bowels release, and I just don't have the strength to care. I drift in and out, and when I'm on the edge of real sleep, the door squeals open. I wince away from the light and chilly air that moves in. Wait for . . . whatever.

The door closes again, and I'm glad. I don't want to be bothered. Only I'm not alone. Leather soles patter across the floor toward me. Fabric rustles as someone squats down close by. I don't look. Don't want to be hit again. Then I smell it—spicy and inviting cologne.

"Evangeline Stone?" The strange male voice is smooth as butter, lightly accented, and oddly warm. Curious.

I grunt, eyes still shut.

"I'll see that they're all fired for this."

That gets my attention. I angle my head toward him and open my eyes. The most handsome grown man I've ever seen is hovering above me. White-blond hair is cut short, the perfect accent to his dark blue eyes. High forehead, narrow nose, sharp jaw, and wide pink lips. Just . . . wow.

"Who?" I croaked.

"The guards who did this to you, of course." His eyebrows arch at my confused frown. "Oh, I apologize. My name is Bastian." He lets his navy gaze roam up and down my body, and if not for my injuries, I'd swear he was checking me out. It's uncomfortable, but I have no strength to make him stop.

"What do . . . you want?"

"To help you," he says, soothing.

I've heard that one before, motherfucker. And I want to say it so badly. Only my throat is raw, too sore to force out such a mouthful. So I settle for glaring at him.

"You've got something special in you, Evangeline. Something I could use."

My nostrils flare, and I force out, "Not gonna . . . blow you . . . fuckwad."

Slender eyebrows shoot to his hairline. "I'd never ask such a thing from you, and I hope you can learn to believe that. You find it difficult to trust people, I understand. Do you always wish to reach for suspicion first?"

What the hell is this guy's deal? Strangely, I find myself shaking my head. Suspicion is all I know, and it's my default reaction to new people. Hell, it's often my default for old people, too. But something about this man makes me want to trust him, even if just for a few seconds. Since everything good in my life seems to last only minutes, I figure a few seconds is all I'll manage.

"What do you plan on doing with your life, Evangeline, when you're free from this place?"

I can think of a lot of things I want to do, including a few nasty ones to Terry McManus, the guy in charge of this place. Maybe a few of his favorite guards, too, like the ones Bastian seems keen on firing. Won't tell Bastian that, though. "Run" is all I say.

Something flickers across his face. Sadness maybe, or understanding. "What if I offered you an opportunity? A career that would give your life meaning, give you a goal, and put you among some of the most dedicated, loyal people you'll ever meet in your life?" He is absolutely serious.

"I'd say . . . you're fucking nuts."

He smiles, those pink lips pulling back to expose perfect, pearly teeth. "I've heard worse. It isn't an easy job, especially at first. You have to train hard for this, but in the end, you'll be serving a higher purpose."

Now I know he's insane. How did he even get in here?

"Your release is in twenty-six days, and I promise you will live the rest of them in peace. Those girls and those guards will not bother you again, you have my word."

Uh-huh, yeah, and tomorrow I'll fart rainbows. I only nod, ready for him to be gone.

"On the day of your release, they'll put you on a public bus back to the city," he continues. "Get off on Wharton Street, and I'll meet you in the middle of the footbridge. Open area, plenty of witnesses, in case you think I plan on attacking you. We'll talk more then."

I haven't agreed to anything, but that doesn't faze him. He stands and leaves as quickly as he came. No further explanation, no other words of wisdom. I push him from my mind. No way in hell am I going to meet him on that bridge. No way.

The next time I wake up, I'm in the infirmary. My head feels better, my left arm is in a cast, and I even feel bathed. Clean. I stay in the infirmary for the rest of my time at Juvie, long after I should have been sent back to my block. Scuttlebutt whispered at night tells me those three guards have indeed been fired. No one bothers me, not even that bastard McManus, who runs the detention center. I don't connect it to my strange visitor. I'm convinced I dreamed him.

The cast is removed before my release, and I'm free of the remnants of my good-bye gift at long last. Except for the fear. Going to the bathroom still brings a flash of terror, a chill down my spine, bile in my throat. It will pass, as it always does. I'm a survivor after all.

Four days after I taste freedom, I'm being dumped into a holding cell in a Mercy's Lot police station. The charge is breaking and entering and assault. I have no money to hire a lawyer, so I keep my mouth shut, curl into a corner, and wait. Instead of a court-appointed lawyer, my first visitor is the man I've convinced myself I imagined.

"You didn't come to meet me," Bastian says, his voice dripping with disappointment, colored by gentle mocking. "Afraid?"

Seeing him again frightens me. Frightens me because this strange offer of a fulfilling job and hard training is real. "I told you once, I'm not blowing you."

"Well, good, because I told you I'd never ask you to. I have no interest in you as a sexual being, Evangeline, only as a fighter."

I blink, sure he's off his nut again. "I don't know how to box."

"I don't mean boxing, and you'll be taught. You'll be taught a great many things about this city. You will be shown a whole new world you never knew existed, and if you are strong enough, tough enough, and have wits enough to survive training, you'll have a career that will save lives in ways you can't imagine."

"That'll be tough to do while I'm in jail again."

He smiles, and damn, he's handsome. "If you agree to sign up for this adventure, I can help you out with that small problem."

I perk up. "Really? You can get me off the hook with the cops?"

"In a manner of speaking."

"Speak it." I unfold myself and stand, giving him my full attention.

"I can make these charges go away, but only if you willingly agree to this program. You can't run, you can't change your mind, or you'll be back in jail faster than you can spit." He's still smiling, no mirth in his eyes now.

"Blackmail?"

"Absolutely not. It's a choice you must make, but you have to make it now."

I stare at him and those lovely navy eyes. I've known enough untrustworthy bastards that I can spot them pretty quick. Bastian isn't one of those men. He is sincere, but he's also elusive. Makes hefty promises without proof of payoff.

Anything's better than jail, though, right? I hadn't really thought through the consequences of breaking into the Juvie director's house and beating him senseless. Hadn't realized it would land me right back where I'd just escaped, only in the adult version. Where my scrappy fighting won't amount to much against grown women who take what they want when they want it.

"So what is this program exactly?" I ask. "Some sort of covert military project?"

"Covert, yes; military, no. We run it ourselves, with some oversight from a private corporation. If you pass training requirements, you'll be provided with a steady paycheck and a place to live, along with coverage for medical expenses incurred while on the job."

Oka-ay. Never heard medical insurance explained quite like this. Good perks, though. And way better than the option of jail.

"All right, then," I say, planting both hands on my hips. "Where do I sign up?"

Chapter Seven

We three Hunters seemed to hold a collective breath while Bastian stood on that stoop reading his folder, as though any movement from us would draw his attention. It wasn't that he was scary—quite the opposite, given his good looks, easygoing demeanor, and slight accent. I'd learned within months of my recruitment that he was originally from the Ukraine. I could only guess at Milo and David's apprehension. Mine stemmed from the simple desire not to be seen—and, less simply, a buried resentment toward the person who'd tricked me into this life.

Hard training had been an understatement, and the final exam wasn't even mentioned until a week before our six months were up. Fulfilling life wasn't far from the truth; he'd just forgotten to mention the "short, brutal" part of that career description. He didn't comment on our projected life span of two to four years after we entered the field. And Dregs? *Ha!*

I glanced at the young men in my company. Their apprehension was etched on their faces and seemed to telegraph one thing: if Bastian came over, they'd probably beat him senseless. Justice for pain endured, lives lost, and the memories of it all. It occurred to me that in the last four years, I'd not seen Bastian once before now.

He had the covert thing down pat.

"Unbelievable," Milo whispered.

"What's that, man?" David asked.

"Just really thinking about the fact that half the people Bastian brings to this place end up dead."

"Technically, it's closer to one hundred percent," I said. Both of them turned to look at me; I shrugged one shoulder. "Most Hunters die within three years. You don't get past the mortality thing."

"Unless you're you," Milo said.

"Hey, I still technically died. The girl who went through hell here is long gone, ashes scattered to the wind. I didn't ask to be brought back, and I'm done fucking apologizing for it."

An uneasy silence settled over the car. The next time I looked, Bastian was gone, probably off to drag more uninformed teenagers into a new, brief, pain-filled life. Recruits we desperately needed, as our cache of trained Hunters was diminishing at an alarming rate.

Just as the air in the SUV started reaching unbearable stuffiness, the building door swung open. Kismet emerged first, Wyatt right behind her with a lunch bag of some sort in his hands. Blue nylon, square, nondescript. Had to have our bargaining chips in it. They were in the middle of a conversation that abruptly stopped when they yanked on their door handles.

"Took long enough," I said as Wyatt fell into the seat beside me.

He settled the bag on his lap, color high in his cheeks. "Took some time to convince Erickson to let us have what we needed."

"Erickson?"

"The guy who runs R&D." He said it as if I should know exactly who Erickson was. I replied with a blank stare that finally registered. Hunters were forbidden from entering that building, and no one told us what exactly went on in there under the broad label of Research and Development. Or who worked there. He leaned close until his cheek brushed mine and whispered, "It's where they developed the anticoag and fragging rounds we use, among other things."

Aha. Grateful for the info—and additionally curious about what else Erickson and his pals were cooking up within those walls—I turned my attention back to the rest of the van. Milo looked away too sharply; he'd been listening, probably just as curious, and annoyed that I'd gotten an answer he hadn't. Wyatt had already broken one rule by bringing an unbound fugitive onto the premises, so what was one more?

"We've still got two hours before Thackery's supposed to call," David said. "What's our next move?"

"We meet Felix at his apartment," Kismet said. "Then we sit tight until Thackery calls and we know what we're dealing with."

"We sit tight?" I echoed. "All of us?"

She didn't stop driving, even as she met my gaze in the rearview mirror, steely determination in her eyes. "Yes, all of us, because until I have some damned clue what to tell the brass about all this, I'm not letting you two out of my sight."

I made a rude noise but didn't argue further. Admittedly, it was better than reporting me right away, or telling Milo to shoot me in the head. I resigned myself to being babysat by Kismet and her team, and settled back for the long ride into the city.

The apartment Kismet's Triad shared was on the opposite side of Mercy's Lot from mine, closer to downtown and the Anjean tributary. Other low-rent apartment buildings surrounded theirs, all made of the same brick façade and cheap plaster that had sprung up fifty-odd years ago. Tiny terraces barely large enough for two people to stand on, security bars on most of the windows, untended flower boxes, and postage-stamp grassy areas for kids to play.

No one paid much attention to the six of us as we followed Milo through a space-numbered parking lot toward one of the five-story buildings. The bricks looked power-washed and the sidewalks neatly swept. No graffiti, no hookers or homeless wandering around. Definitely a step up from the place I'd once called home. Into an echoing lobby/stairwell and past a row of metal mailboxes, we marched up to the third floor, our footsteps reverberating hollowly.

Milo produced a key, but the door swung open before he could use it. The apartment seemed to face the parking lot, so Felix must have seen us coming. Kismet was behind me and the last to go inside.

The front room was an impressive disaster—clothes strewn around on the sofa and two overstuffed chairs, a trash can overflowing with takeout bags marking the entrance to the kitchen, and empty cola bottles and cans littering other available surfaces. More impressive than the disaster, though, was the enormous—and ten years outdated—television shoved into the far corner, surrounded by gaming devices. Men.

Wyatt wrinkled his nose as he looked around. Milo headed straight for one of the back bedrooms while Kismet perched on the corner of the sofa. Felix leaned against the wall near the front door, arms crossed over his chest, daring any of us to comment.

David let loose with a low whistle. "Goddamn, man, you ever heard of housekeeping?"

"Wasn't expecting houseguests today," Felix replied.

One face was conspicuously missing. "Tybalt home?" I asked.

"Yeah." Felix jacked his thumb toward the rear of the apartment. "He promised not to shoot you if you went back."

To a stranger on the street, that might sound odd, but it made me smile. I didn't wait for anyone else's permission. The door at the end of the short hall was half-open. Milo's low voice drifted out. I tapped my knuckles on the frame and waited.

Milo appeared in front of me, familiar sour expression back in place. "Don't tire him out," he whispered, then brushed past me.

I rolled my eyes, slipping through the half-open door and into a dimly lit bedroom. Curtains were drawn, casting a brown glow on the room. Two twin beds opposite each other, a single closet and dresser with clothes spilling out. I didn't see Tybalt until he stepped from the corner of the room, pulling his tall, lean frame out of a deep shadow. I scooted sideways, startled. His left arm was in a sling, the canvas flat just below his elbow—where his forearm would have been.

"Someone should nickname you the Cat Lady," he said. "You've got nine fucking lives, don't you?" There was no derision, no sarcasm. Just measured sincerity and something very close to awe. He tilted his head; I understood and closed the door.

"We were wrong, Evy."

His words struck like iron, heavy and forceful. I stared dumbfounded as he sat on one of the beds. He shuffled like an old man, aged and beaten. Seeing him like that, a warrior I'd not have wanted to go toe to toe with in the past, broke my heart a little.

"We've all been wrong about a lot of things," I said.

"We should have trusted you, though, when you asked for more time at the factory. Should have given you until noon like you asked."

"You thought I was a traitor, Tybalt, and you weren't wrong. I knew going after the brass would hang a Neutralize order around my neck, but I was so sure. . . ." I found a spot on the floor that was a lot more interesting to stare at than him.

"If we'd listened to you, maybe those people wouldn't have died at Parker's Palace."

My head snapped up. He was on the self-pity train after all. "Listen up, pal," I said, stalking toward him. "You cannot change the fact that those people died. Getting blown up in a potato chip factory hurt like fucking hell, but I lived. I still figured it out in time, and we saved a lot of lives that night."

"You could have figured it out sooner if we hadn't—"

"Snap out of it!" My voice was louder than I intended. "We did our jobs, you and me. You were ordered to stop me because I was a threat. I don't like it, but I accept it, and if you need to hear it, I forgive you. I did my job by not dying, and by stopping the asshole who set up the benefit attack in the first place. Three hundred people could have died that night instead of sixty-four. Weigh it."

He looked up, searching my face, and in his I saw just how scared he was. Scared of being kicked out of the Triads because of his injury. Scared of losing the only career he knew, the family he'd built, and the life he'd fought so hard for. I didn't know Tybalt Monahan well—hardly at all before the last few weeks—but I swore to myself I'd do what I could for him.

"You know," he said, "you sound like a Handler sometimes. Sure you aren't bucking for a promotion?"

I snorted. "Not on your life, pal. I'm grateful to the Triads for my training and my knowledge, but after this is all settled, I'm out of here." The words came out before I realized I'd made that decision. To get away from all this shit and try to be normal, even if only for a little while.

As if. Unless we found another city with a tap into the Break, we couldn't stay away long. Chalice, my host body's former owner, had been away for years, and the loss of her tap had driven her to depression, which later resulted in her suicide. I had no desire to fall into that pit, or see Wyatt do the same. We'd both died enough for a lifetime.

"Do you really think they'll let you quit?"

The question hung between us for a moment. It wasn't mocking or sarcastic, and it was a damned good question. I'd tried once, right after defeating Tovin. Letting everyone think I'd died in the factory fire had been attempt number two, and that wasn't working, either.

"What did they always tell us at Boot Camp?" I asked. "The job ends when we're dead. Seems to me I've been given the pink slip, but shit keeps happening to bring me back in to consult. The person they trained, beat the crap out of, and forced to kill another person in order to graduate? She's dead. I think Kismet and the brass just need to get their fucking heads around that concept."

His face hardened as a high flush rose in his cheeks. "Your body died, yeah, but not the things you know. Look at it from our side, Stone. It's like having a how-to manual floating around out there, full of every method of defeating the Triads and revealing Dregs to the unsuspecting world, and we can't keep track of it. When you threatened to expose the brass last week? That was cutting our legs out from under us, and you know it. You didn't give us a goddamned choice about neutralizing you."

"You're right," I said.

He stared for several long seconds, mouth flapping open, words not coming. He hadn't expected me to agree so readily.

"I've had that conversation with myself half a dozen times, Tybalt. I was looking for any possible way to save Rufus's life, and I latched onto a really bad idea. You didn't have a choice, and I get that. I also get that I have a lot of knowledge in my head, but after this mess is sorted, I meant what I said. I'm through being a hired gun for the Triads. At least, as they stand now, because if Leonard Call said anything to me I believed, it was that change is coming. We worked for ten years, but we won't work like this much longer. Especially not at the rate we're losing people."

If possible, his expression became even stonier. "Yeah, Felix told me about Willemy."

"The rookie we lost at the theater," I went on. "The six Hunters we lost at Olsmill, not to mention Rufus's entire Triad and mine. And we're another Handler down until he's fully recovered. We're bleeding out right now."

"You have some useful alternatives?" The corners of his mouth twitched. "Something more practical than resurrecting our lost friends and giving them super-powers?"

I heaved a tolerant sigh. "Not really, no. But you want to know something tragic, Tybalt? I seem to be the person all the city's shit storms center around, but there's really nothing so special about me. It's random, blind bad luck that I've got these weird abilities now."

Entirely coincidence that I'd died at all the first time. The night I was kidnapped by goblins, I'd gone to meet a gargoyle informant named Max, hoping to get any information he might have on why my Triad was set up and my partners killed. Max had always come through for me before; that night, he stepped back and let the goblins take me. If I'd arrived a few minutes later or earlier, or if Max had done something to interfere . . . No. I couldn't change it, and I was stuck with this freaky new body.

"Tovin picked me as his target for no other reason

than because he knew Wyatt loved me enough to agree to that spell," I said, completing my spiel.

"No other reason?" His high forehead wrinkled as both eyebrows arched. "Stone, someone loves you enough to trade his freedom—hell, his soul—to give you a chance to live. Most of us would kill—no pun intended—to have someone love us that much."

I felt a blush coming on and tried to redirect. "Your team loves you. It takes a hell of a friend to hack off your hand rather than let you die a monster."

"Yeah, I love 'em, too, but I'm not about to go around kissing Milo for saving my life." He didn't smile, but I saw the humor in his eyes. It flickered a moment, then died as the fierce hardness returned. "Besides, they'll have to replace me sooner or later."

"Why? Kismet said you were trying to get back—"

"Into Boot Camp?" He snorted. "That's a long shot at best. I have one fucking arm, Stone. They'd put me back in as a trainee, and I'd be dead by the end of the first three months. The shit they put us through, the obstacle course . . . I'm good, but I can't manage that anymore."

The idea of lumping a nearly four-year veteran back in with wet-nosed trainees infuriated me. Not giving him latitude because of an on-the-job disability, basically saying he was no longer worthwhile. I relaxed my hands before my fingernails broke skin. "How about we get through this current crisis?" I said. "Then we chat about alternative career options?"

He frowned. "You starting up your own freelance Triad operation?"

"Not at all, but I'm sure Milo didn't save your life just so you could be tossed out on your ass. So?"

He nodded. Figuring the conversation had run its course, I started for the door. Halfway there, the oddest thought struck. Something I'd wondered in the past but never had the conversational opportunity to question. "Okay, I have to ask just one more thing."

"Which is what?" He inclined his head, interested.

"What were your parents thinking when they named you Tybalt?"

Blankness hung on his face for a split second, then he smiled. "I chose it out of a book of Shakespeare when I was eleven. I liked that he was the Prince of Cats."

"You changed your name when you were eleven?" Why not? I knew nothing about his past. Hell, he knew nothing about mine, either. It was just the way things had always been—Triads were not supposed to fraternize.

"No, I picked my name. I didn't have one before."

My lips parted. "What were you raised by? Wolves?"

"Something like that."

I had every intention of getting more details out of him, but a soft knock preceded the door swinging open. Milo poked his head inside. "Lunchtime, kids."

Tybalt groaned. "I'm not—"

"Gina said if you don't get your ass out here and eat something, she'll tie you up, blend it, and force it down your throat with a turkey baster."

I tried to hide my laughter under a cough; Tybalt glared at me. The three of us rejoined the others. The dining table held two loaves of bread—one rye, the other wheat—a jar of mayo, lettuce, and several plastic containers of deli meat and cheese. Wyatt and Felix sat at opposite ends of the sofa, already munching on sandwiches.

Kismet handed a plate to Tybalt. On it was a neatly made sandwich, cut into four triangles, each section held together with a toothpick. The motherly way she buzzed around her injured Hunter was nothing like the ballsy, bellowing Handler she played in the field.

"I don't get a sandwich, too?" Milo asked.

"You've got two hands," Kismet shot back.

Milo looked mortified. Tybalt laughed, elbowed his friend in the ribs, and wandered toward the sofa with his lunch. I reached for the rye bread. Might as well eat something before all this went down.

Five minutes or so before the call was expected, I was in the bathroom, hands braced on either side of the porcelain sink bowl, glaring at myself in the mirror. A wave of nerves had hit, leaving me completely unsettled. I'd walked into unknown situations before, faced unknown enemies alone, and even tackled one particularly nasty hostage situation involving my late partner Ash and three Halfies. I had no reason to be so scared of this phone call.

No, that wasn't true. Thackery had something that, if released, could be truly devastating to this city. He wanted us to give him two unknown vials of liquid, for his own unknown purposes. In an unknown location, with a very uncertain outcome.

I hated the word "unknown."

I splashed cool water on my face and patted dry on a frayed towel. Compared to the rest of their apartment, the bathroom was oddly tidy. I guess they had some standards of cleanliness when it came to their throne. Even the mirror lacked water spots or toothpaste spray. I had a clear view of my face. The tension bracketing both brown eyes, lips pursed so tightly they were almost gone. Familiar and foreign—mine and hers. Sometimes I still glanced in a mirror and expected my old face—blond hair cut short and uneven, wide blue eyes, pale skin. Not the dark-haired, curvy, freckled-nose woman I'd been for nearly two weeks.

The door opened and shut. "You okay?" Wyatt asked.

He shuffled behind me, and our gazes met in the mirror's reflection.

"If I say yes, will you believe me?"

"Not while you're hunched over the sink like you want to vomit."

"What happens if we don't get the crystal back?"

"We deal with it."

"Deal with it?" I rounded in the tiny space, long hair whipping across my face. "I saw that entity in Tovin's body, Wyatt. I have never been so terrified as when I looked into its face and knew it could snap me in half before I could blink. It was the ugliest, most evil thing I've ever seen. We can't just deal with it."

Warm palms framed my cheeks. I wrapped my hands around his wrists. His outward calm helped, even though I imagined his insides quaked as hard as mine. No one else had seen the Tainted elf; my description could never do the terror justice. He couldn't understand.

"We. Will. Deal. With. It." Each word from him fell like a promise, driven home by the gentle crackle of energy around us. I tried to believe in that promise.

Then the damned cell phone rang, and my stomach clenched. We parted. I fished the phone out of my jeans pocket as I led the way back into the living room. Five expectant faces watched me.

"You're pretty prompt, aren't you?" I asked by way of greeting.

"I desire my property," Thackery replied, on speakerphone. "Do you have it?"

"What do you think?"

Kismet shot me a glare that telegraphed: Don't piss off the bad guy. I ignored her.

Thackery said, "I think you're too smart not to have it, and I would also appreciate simple answers to simple questions. Now, I'm certain you know where the Wharton Street footbridge is, yes?"

Do goblins bleed magenta? "Yes."

"Be at the center of the footbridge, overlooking the river, in half an hour. Be there alone, and when I say alone, I mean no one within half a mile of your position. I have explosives rigged to the furnace of an office building Uptown that I will not hesitate to detonate if I suspect you're being watched. Are we clear?"

"Clear," I said. My heart was pounding so hard I was certain he could hear it. I was going in very much alone and without a choice. *Shit, fuck, and dammit.*

"I don't suppose I have to remind you to bring my property?"

"I'll have it. Just don't forget my crystal."

"I'm a man of my word, Evangeline. The exchange will be made as agreed, but under my terms. Come to the bridge." And he hung up.

I could barely keep my hand from trembling as I put away the phone. "I think he's serious," I said, but the quip fell flat.

"There are several buildings west of the river with a good vantage point," Kismet said. "And they're outside his half-mile limit, so we can keep visual surveillance on you while you're on the bridge."

"What about audio?" David asked. He looked horrified, but determined.

"He'll probably search me, so I can't risk it," I said. "As long as there are eyes on me, though . . . I guess we should hit the road. I'll have to walk part of the way. David and Wyatt can drop me off, then stay back on this side of the river. Kismet, you and the boys get to those vantage points."

She nodded.

We gathered a few things from hidden places. I'd left that morning without any weapons, so I borrowed a hunting knife from Tybalt's stash and put it in my boot strap. If Thackery found it, he found it, but I needed something close to me.

On the way out, I looked back at Tybalt. He nodded curtly, and I saw the frustration in his eyes. He hated being left behind. I hated leaving him there. But for now, it was where he had to stay. I winked with more confidence than I felt and followed the others to the parking lot. Once there, I realized something with ominous clarity—Amalie had never called.

I had no time to worry about her, though. It was time to trade the devil I didn't know for the devil I did.

Chapter Eight

Wyatt drove David's car to our drop-off point, me in the passenger seat with the vinyl cooler tight in my lap. David seemed just as uncomfortable in the rear, fidgeting like a kid on a sugar high. Our destination was a small grocery store parking lot just over a half mile from the river. They had no visual, but it was a more direct route there if Kismet called.

Traffic allowed for an easy trip, and we turned into the lot too soon. I checked the time—fifteen minutes until showdown. Wyatt backed into a space near the entrance. I'd patronized this store a few times, mostly for cold sodas and snacks. It was a hole shoved between newer buildings, a line of glass windows papered over with yellowed advertisements. Three roughhousing teenage boys tumbled out of the store, snapping the tabs on their colas.

"We can be there in three minutes," Wyatt said.

Fat lot of good that would do me. I smiled anyway. "I know. And I promise to try and curb my sarcastic nature while doing this."

"Good girl."

We shared a look that said so many things: *good luck, I love you, be careful, watch your back*—and more. I grabbed his shirt collar and yanked him toward me. The kiss was brief. Not good-bye, just see you soon. I pushed him away, grabbed my bag, and leapt from the car.

Didn't look back as I walked down Wharton Street, toward the Black River.

Each step forward drove a spike of fear deeper into my gut. I tried to dislodge it with reassurances, but even in my own mind they felt hollow. All I could do was see this through. Get the crystal safely, then worry about capturing Thackery.

The bridge loomed ahead of me, all gray steel and pylons. The last time I'd walked across it was ten days ago, an hour or so after my resurrection. On this side of the river was a train yard, dozens of track lines crisscrossing the sandy ground and butting up to the river's edge. Abandoned boxcars lined a few of the unused tracks, cracked and dusty with age. I'd hunted a lot of Halfies down there. It had been a favorite feeding ground for years until Jesse, Ash, and I started patrolling it.

I kept a steady pace as the bridge arched up. Faint odors of motor oil mixed with the heavy water scent of the river. A gentle breeze tickled my cheeks, blustering hard each time a car sped past. I continued beyond the train yard, over the rushing slate water below. I reached dead center with a few minutes to spare—according to the clock on the cell phone—and stopped. Looked around in all directions. Car traffic continued at a steady pace, going east and west across the bridge. No other foot traffic, though, in either direction.

What the hell was he going to do, fly in?

The phone rang. I flipped it open, not bothering with speaker. "Running late?" I asked.

"No, you're pleasantly early. Look down toward the train yards, Evangeline, near that thatch of trees on the water's edge. Quarter mile down."

I squinted at the thick, stunted trees that had been left to grow wild on the perimeter of the train yard's northern border. Something glinted in the sunlight, flashing a signal at me. "I see it."

"Come to me."

"What?"

"I wanted to give us a bit of privacy for the exchange. I know you'll be here in mere moments. Others have seen your Gift, and now I'd like a peek."

Son of a bitch. I put the phone away, then stared at the location. I couldn't see anyone, just the trees and brown dirt. I focused on the spot, searched past my anxiety to find a bit of loneliness—my emotional tap into the power of the Break. I caught it and slipped in. The sensation of flying apart and melting back together again was familiar, but new each time I did it. A dull ache settled between my eyes as I teleported, centering me the moment I materialized in the train yard.

The stench of grease and coal was thicker here, almost nauseatingly so, and the roar of the river louder. Ten feet away, a stone wall separated me from a steep drop to its rushing water. The tangled, gnarly trees ahead mocked me with gray, leafless branches, daring me to try to enter them.

He didn't emerge from the trees as I'd expected. He came around them, as at ease as a man on a Sunday stroll, the living embodiment of his photograph. Tall and lean, he wore a navy-blue suit coat that fell to midcalf. Dust coated his leather shoes and the hem of his trousers. He smiled pleasantly, more handsome in person than he had any right to be. Boyishly so, with glittering eyes that seemed ready to laugh at anyone's joke, whether it was funny or not.

Didn't seem the type to slit a man's throat, drain his blood, then nail his body to a wall. Then again, no one had ever looked at my previous waiflike build and thought I could snap their neck with very little effort.

"The great Evangeline Stone," Walter Thackery said, a touch of humor in his voice. "The teleporting trick is quite impressive. Bravo."

"Show me the crystal," I said.

He clucked his tongue. "Don't be unpleasant about this. It's a simple business transaction. And so far, you're living up to your end of the bargain."

"I tend to do what I'm told when dipshits like you threaten innocent people." Okay, so not antagonizing the bad guy wasn't an easy skill for me to master.

"We all do what we must to ensure our survival. Now, please, show me my property."

"You going to show me the crystal?"

He lifted his left shoulder in a half shrug, then reached into his coat with his right. Instead of the crystal, he produced a handgun. No . . . I stared at it a little harder as he raised it, pointing the barrel at my heart. It was a tranquilizer gun. At least that meant he didn't want me dead.

I put the bag on the ground and tugged open the zipper. Turned it around so he could see the two glass containers carefully packed into cotton batting. He grinned and did a little two-foot dance that looked ridiculous for a grown man.

"Back away, please," he said.

I acquiesced, putting five long paces between me and the bag. He whistled. Someone new came around the trees just as Thackery had. *Awesome.*

He was thin, blond-haired, and looked barely sixteen. Jeans and a T-shirt seemed to dangle on his wiry frame. He kept his head low and wouldn't look at me directly as he came forward holding what looked like a blue silk scarf. Thackery took the scarf from the boy, then unwrapped it as he approached the bag. I almost wept with relief when he put a pulsing black crystal down in the dirt and picked up the bag. He didn't back off, just stared at the crystal a moment. It seemed alive, something ominous and evil trapped beneath its hard surface, aching to be released.

"That thing should have been better protected," he said.

"You almost let the fucking thing loose on the world, asshole."

"But you came through like a champ and saved us all, didn't you? I feel I should thank you for that."

"Yeah? Thank me by telling me what's so important about those vials."

He fixed the bag so its strap hung off his right hand, which never dropped its aim with the gun. Odd that his henchman wasn't armed with anything other than a sullen expression. Thackery's left hand pulled out the larger of the two containers, full of a gelatinous red substance. "This, Ms. Stone, is my greatest creation to date. Something with which I plan to make a lot of money to further fund my research."

"Your monster-making research?"

"Hardly. They were simply a means to an end. You see, I have managed to isolate the parasite that infests a vampire's saliva and keep it suspended in a bloodlike substance for weaponized use." He wiggled the red jar.

My insides quaked. *OhGodohGodohGodohGodoh God.* . . .

"I needed my second sample back," he continued.

"What happened to your first sample?"

I felt the sting before I heard the shot and looked down. A feather-tipped dart stuck out of my chest, directly above my heart. Boiling water ejected into me. I fell to my knees from the onslaught of pain, gasping, too stunned to think.

"My first sample," Thackery said, darkness replacing the sunshine in his voice, "I just shot into you. With these healing abilities you possess, think of yourself as my new guinea pig."

My lungs seized. The raging heat in my chest worked across my abdomen, sending my muscles into spasms of cramps. My arms and legs were shaking, tremors snaking up and down my spine.

The other vial of amber liquid hit the dirt in front of me. "This, on the other hand, is an experimental antibiotic that targets the parasite. Good luck."

I stared at the vial. The heat scorched the tips of my fingers and blasted down to my knees. *Experimental.* Up my throat. *Antibiotic.* It tasted like blood, smelled like bile, ached like a volcano waiting to erupt from the top of my skull.

Fucking hell, is this what Alex felt like when he turned?

I tried to pick it up, but my fingers wouldn't cooperate. I'd never get it open. My throat felt tight, swollen. Couldn't swallow it. I had to try something, dammit.

I smashed my hand onto the vial. Glass shattered, cutting skin and muscle. The liquid was briefly cold, ice water on my palm. Then nothing. I ground down and felt only the pain of torn flesh. Manic laughter choked me. I strained toward the knife at my ankle. Had to get it, slice my throat, fall on it, anything.

Can't turn. Won't be one of them.

"Wyatt!" The shriek ripped from my lungs, torn from a wave of icy fear. Trembling fingers finally grasped the hilt of the knife. Pulled.

Chalice slit her wrists once, killed herself. I can do it, too. Kill the pain before it kills me. It's what she did.

My entire body shuddered, and I fell. The knife bounced away. Agony flared through my guts. I curled inward, afraid I'd explode if I didn't. Splatter my innards all over the dirty train yard. My teeth ached. Eyes burned. Scalp was on fire. I smashed my skull against the ground. The pain was momentary, not nearly enough. I tried again; red lights blinked behind my eyes, but consciousness remained.

I heard voices shouting. Felt footsteps pounding. No,

I have to die before I turn on them. Turn and murder them like Jesse murdered Ash. Won't do it. Can't do it.

I lifted my head, angled my temple, and brought it down with all my might. Beyond the fading light, encroaching darkness, and brain-splitting pain, I heard Wyatt say, "I've got you, Evy."

I smell blood. Fear. Sweat. Mostly blood. All around. Above, below, inside of me, and inside of them. Heated flesh passes close; I snap my teeth, hoping for a bite. A shout.

Hold her down!

No chains. Don't you dare chain her!

Everything aches. My toenails, my hair, my eyeballs, even my sex. Especially there. Above the blood, I smell male. Potency. I throb. Can't move my hands to touch. There's no relief. I howl for freedom.

If you can't do it—

No one puts her down, you fucking hear me?

His voice. It's him I want. I lurch. I cannot move well. Something holds me back, down, away. I jerk my hips, wail, reach for what I can't have. He'll stop the throb if I can get to him.

Blobs of black dance in my empty vision. Taking slow shape. Faces. Alex, Jock Guy, Tattoo Guy, even the nameless Halfie who turned Jesse. Dozens more, leering and licking their fangs and welcoming me home. Inviting me into the darkness. The coolness, empty of pain.

Alex takes my hand, so small in his. Squeezes. Tells me it doesn't have to hurt, baby, we don't feel that sort of pain. Don't fight, be with me. It's time to rest, baby.

I'm not your baby! *I think I scream the words, but I can't be sure. My fist hits flesh. Flesh! I lash again, hoping to grab. Am restrained again. Fuck!*

I'll fuck you, Alex says. If that's what you want. Stop

fighting the darkness. Embrace it, and you'll be able to join me. We can be together. Love each other. Chalice, please.

I shake my head, try to rub my ears and can't. I'm not Chalice. He wants Chalice, not me. I don't want to fuck Alex. I want someone else. And he won't want to fuck me if I'm in the dark.

Alex weeps. Chalice!

Get out of my fucking head!

The faces melt into black blobs. Blobs that shrink, fall back into one another like drops of mercury. One blob now, dark as midnight, scary as hell. It is Hell, beckoning with a frigid finger. Opening its gaping maw, welcoming me in. Warmth and darkness—so easy.

Pain and light and him. *Not so easy. I want* him. Need.

Wyatt!

The voices return. I strain to hear, to push toward them, away from the black blob. It blocks my path, mumbling their words. It's a net, straining, holding, not letting me pass.

. . . much longer do we wait?

As long as it takes. She'll come back.

You don't know that.

Yes I do.

He's still here. Holding on, holding out, not letting me go. I reach for the black net, curl my fingers around its tempting warmth. Peace floods me. Power energizes me. I scent blood and sweat and sex. I want these things, all of them. The black net promises them, if I let go.

It begins to curl around me like a grandmother's shawl. So sweet, so loving. Embracing me like a lover.

Not my lover. He won't want me in the dark, no matter how warm and powerful I am. He just won't. He'd rather die than live here in the warm dark with me. I don't want to be here without him.

The shawl closes, cocooning me. I draw in deep, look-ing for strength. Encouragement. Anything to break this cocoon. Break out of the darkness I've let myself slip into.

Look at her hair.

No.

Face facts, Wyatt, she's gone!

I'm not, I'm here! Get me out of here, please! Too many smells. Too much fear. It hurts.

The dark shawl shudders. It doesn't like the fear. It de-stroys fear, covers it, buries it. I fall deeper into myself, looking for fear. Memories. Anything to wrench this from my body.

Down, down into the past. An erect goblin male sinks onto the mattress on which I lie, waiting to die. Wyatt falls in the midst of battle, bleeding to death for half an hour. Living with so much loneliness and rage that I'd rather slit my own wrist than bear another day. Becom-ing one of the monsters I hate so much.

The black cocoon shudders, trembles, weakens.

Keep him back, dammit!

No, Gina! Stop! Please!

They're hurting you, Wyatt. Why?

I see it—living without him, the rest of my days alone.

NO! *My shout is like a sonic boom. The cocoon shatters. Warmth drops away in shrieking pieces, smok-ing out of existence as they fall. I race toward the light, toward the chilling cold and pain and throbbing. Toward a body on fire with fever, wracked with chills, wrapped so tightly in sheets and blankets it can barely wiggle. Hands that can't protect. Legs that can't kick.*

My mouth. I can work my mouth. Through the ache and scorching dryness in my throat, I force words. Stop, please.

Gina, listen to her!

Hands on my face, not his. Someone else's. Forcing

my eyelids open. The light blinds me. I hold still. Let them look. Just don't kill me. My eyes are released. I close them gladly. Words become a rumble of noise. It hurts too much to listen. Everything fades away.

I fall into the good kind of darkness, and let sleep come.

Awareness stole in on tiny feet, adding increments of consciousness to the cold blanket of blackness I was stuck in. Not a deep, dreamless sleep, but also not restless. Stuck somewhere between awake and asleep, where the sharp odors of blood and desire lingered on the edges of thought. As awareness overtook unconsciousness, I was more alert to my body.

More specifically, to the fact that I could no longer move it. I tested my arms and legs to no avail. They felt squeezed, legs flat together and arms at my sides. Like a mummy. I forced bleary eyes open—an unfamiliar ceiling of dark, rough-cut wood. Unfamiliar smells of pine and earth and burning wood permeated the dark-paneled room with its antique dresser, sunset watercolor, and single door. Serenity was in that room, just not in me. Not while my entire body was wrapped up in a damned sheet, some ass-backward method of straitjacketing me.

What the hell—? Oh, right. I'd almost become a half-Blood.

A choked sob caught in my throat, followed by a high-pitched keen. It wasn't the time for a mental breakdown, but I was alone and in a strange place and my emotions had other plans. My body trembled and shuddered. The keen upgraded to a wail.

Then Wyatt was there, hands framing my face, looking down at me. His eyes were bloodshot, red-rimmed and puffy, smudged with dark circles. He hadn't shaved in a while. He was breathing hard through his mouth. I tried to quiet my cries and merely succeeded in changing the wails to silent sobs.

He didn't hold me, and I wanted him to. Instead, the pressure around my body loosened. The makeshift wrap fell away, releasing arms I could barely work. It didn't matter. He gathered me up, held me close, and I sobbed into his neck. Sobbed for what I'd almost become, and for the fear Chalice had once felt at the prospect of living when the last thing I wanted to do was die. Wyatt stroked my back and arms, cooed soft words, coaxed it all out.

I cried myself back to sleep, because when I woke next, we were side by side in bed, my back pressed to his chest. I was free of the restricting sheet, carefully spooned beneath a heavy blanket instead. Naked except for a long T-shirt and panties. Safe with Wyatt, and very much still human.

Laughter gurgled in my throat.

"Evy?" The arms around my waist tightened.

"Glad to be alive," I forced out between loose giggles. My voice was hoarse, throat dry and tight. From one extreme to the other—maybe I had lost it after all.

"Me, too."

The momentary hysteria subsided after a few minutes. I rolled around to face him, moving easily in the large bed. His onyx eyes seemed to pin me to the bed and never let me go. It wasn't a horrible idea. Every last muscle ached with exhaustion, like I'd been smashed beneath a steamroller and allowed to slowly reinflate.

"I almost didn't come back," I said.

He went stone-faced. "I know."

"How long?"

"You fought it for six days."

My mouth fell open. I didn't believe him. Six days drifting in and out of Hell. Battling to retain control of my body and mind. His expression never changed. Six days. "Where are we?"

"A hunting cabin north of the city. Tybalt knows a guy who comes up here in the fall, and Gina said she stayed here before. We needed someplace safe, away from people. You wouldn't stop yelling, fighting us. . . ." His jaw clenched, loosened. "At first, she wanted to chain you."

I shuddered. "You came up with the sheet trick?"

"Yeah, and it barely kept you down. Every time one of us got too close, you'd try to bite us. You bucked me off a few times. David, too. Phineas was the only one strong enough to hold you down. Your hair changed a little, but it's gone back. You'd fight and scream the most awful things, then cry and shriek, then go quiet, and then start all over again."

"For six days." I could only imagine the things I'd said out loud in that time, especially stoned out of my gourd on vampire saliva. "I remember some voices, I think. You told Gina to stop once."

Fury lit a fire beneath his stone-faced demeanor; I couldn't imagine how hard he was battling to keep his temper under control. "There at the end, your eyes changed. It was enough for her. She . . . She said I could do it, or she would do it."

I swallowed against nausea. This was the second time she'd tried to kill me. "And?"

"I told her to go fuck herself, that no one was killing you unless they killed me first. We had a bit of a scuffle."

"You and Kismet got into a fight?"

He touched the corner of his right eye. When I looked closer, the bruising was distinctly darker than the other eye. "Yeah. She came toward you with a knife, then you just up and screamed *no* like you knew. But it was you, Evy, not the person who'd been screaming at us all week. You."

"Good timing."

"You think?" He stroked my cheek, featherlight. "Your eyes had changed back. Gina finally left on my promise not to unroll you until you'd woken up and verified you were normal."

"Relatively speaking. Wait, you said Phineas?"

"Yeah, he was here for most of the week. When you woke yesterday, I sent him home for a shower and some sleep. He should be coming back later today."

Knowing that Phineas el Chimal, one of the last surviving Coni shape-shifters in the city, had been here all week surprised me. And in some ways, it didn't. His loyalty was unwavering, his heart true. "Was Kismet here the whole time?"

"A lot of it. She rotated in and out with her team when they weren't active, so we were never alone. David and Tybalt were here a lot, too. We kept it quiet. So far, no one outside our group knows about this."

The effort they'd gone through astounded me. Six days of waiting for me to either change or die, coming to a cabin in the woods like conspirators planning their destructive legacy. Keeping a deadly secret. "How long was I out this time?"

"About a day since you first woke up, so in total it's been a week."

"Holy hell." I brushed the thick stubble on his cheeks. "You need a shave."

"You don't like the mountain man look?"

I quirked one eyebrow. "I think it's going to burn when I kiss you."

He leaned over and pressed his forehead to mine. Our noses touched. "Don't tempt me."

"Why?"

Perfect question. His mouth slanted over mine. It was a chaste kiss, though I longed to deepen it. I was just out of a week-long coma—my breath couldn't be all that amazing. As expected, his whiskers grazed my cheeks, a delicious friction on my skin.

"Still want me to shave?" he asked as he pulled back.

"Definitely, Mountain Man." I cleared my throat, desperate for a glass of water. "Have we heard from Thackery since he shot me?"

"No." He practically growled the word.

That surprised me. "He wasn't alone. He had some teenager with him. Hard to tell who he was, and, no, Thackery didn't introduce us. But he did say he had more of what he shot me with, this parasite gel, and that he was going to use it to get what he wanted. I was a test to prove he was serious."

Wyatt propped up on his elbow, thinking cap on. "He's made a weapon out of vampire parasites?"

"Yeah, that's what he said. He also said that the second vial, the one I cut my hand on, was some kind of antivenin."

"It wasn't an antivenin or any sort of antidote. We had a sample of it checked by Erickson's men. It's a tracking dye similar to what we use, but the range is much smaller. He estimated a distance of maybe five hundred feet for it to be traceable."

And I'd put my hand down right on top of it. Brilliant. "Could Thackery have used it to track me here?"

"Unlikely. You'd have needed a higher dose than what little might have entered through your cut hand. We were also on the move for a while before we brought you here, and Phineas did a few flyovers of the mountains to make sure no one was watching."

I felt only a tiny bit better about that. "So Thackery had no reason to think I'd survive being turned, other than my healing ability."

"He took a big gamble on it, yeah."

"He was taking a big gamble on every— The crystal!"

I jackknifed to a sitting position, nearly cracking my skull off Wyatt's chin. "Shit, did we get it?"

"We have it, Evy. He didn't back out of that part of the deal."

"Where?"

"It's at Boot Camp, in a lead-lined box, three sublevels down in R&D, locked far away from people."

Weariness mixed with relief, and I flopped back down against the pillow. Wyatt stayed upright, a looming presence. "Amalie is okay with that?" I asked.

He shifted. "We told her Thackery never gave it up."

"You what?" I gaped at him in amazement, unsure if he was being smart or suicidal.

"Gina and I made the decision. A few hours after you were shot, Deaem called on Amalie's behalf to find out our status. We told her what Thackery did to you, and that we never recovered the crystal."

"But why?"

"Amalie doesn't know how to destroy it, she won't keep it at First Break, we still don't know who Jaron said betrayed who, and the last place Amalie said was perfectly safe was robbed. Do *you* think I should have given it back?"

"Not when you put it that way. I guess the gnomes didn't have a magic crystal that heals vampire infection, huh?" It was a tease that came out a serious question.

Wyatt's expression got impossibly darker. "She never offered to help, and we haven't heard from her since."

Nice to know where I rated with the Fair Ones nowadays. "Anything else happening I should know about?"

"Nothing that can't wait until you're back on your feet."

"Okay." I'd been asleep for a whole damned week, but weariness settled over my limbs like a wet afghan. My body had been through more than just broken bones this time. I'd battled and expelled a parasite intent on changing not only my physical functions but also my brain chemistry. I'd fought for my soul and won.

Yeah, more sleep was allowed. My eyes drooped shut. Wyatt's weight left the bed, and I snapped awake again.

"I'll be in the other room for a while," he said. "I've got some things to do, then I'll be back. Promise."

" 'Kay."

I slept, knowing full well things weren't settled yet. Thackery had issued a threat in the train yard, one he'd not yet put into motion. Better to rest while I could, because sooner or later—as it always did—the shit was going to hit the fan.

Chapter Nine

I woke the next morning alone. The bedroom door was shut. Beams of golden light hit the floor in thin strips, cast through the room's only window, announcing it was still daytime. It took a few tries to get my engines going fast enough to throw off the covers and haul my ass out of bed. I was awake and ready to get back into things, and I didn't fall over when I took a few steps toward the door. Good news for me. I padded across the chilly wood floor on bare feet.

The brass knob turned, and the door opened as I reached for it. Wyatt stepped back, eyebrows arching. "Hey, morning," he said, surprise melting into a grin. "You look rested."

"I would hope so." I ran my hand through my tangled, somewhat greasy hair. Gross. "I'm also desperately in need of a shower. Can't imagine I smell that great."

He chuckled. "You smell fine, but you'll probably feel better. Bathroom's over on the right."

"Clean clothes?"

"Dresser drawers. Listen, I need to run into the city for a bit—"

"So go. I don't need a babysitter." The way his mouth twitched alarmed me to a small degree. "What?"

"Just think of David as a silent guest, then."

"David?" I peered past Wyatt's shoulder into a wide wood-paneled living room. A fire crackled somewhere out of sight—the source of the burnt-wood odor—and an actual deer's head was mounted on the wall by the front door. I spotted a familiar mound of black hair above the back of an ancient, sagging sofa.

"He and Kismet's group are the only people who know you're not dead, so she brought him into her Triad to replace Tybalt. It's temporary, though, as far I know. Sooner or later, David will be assigned to a new Handler."

I blinked. A week was a long time to be out of things. "Replace Tybalt?"

"They won't make allowances at Boot Camp for his condition." Wyatt practically spat the words, as though simply speaking them disgusted him. "Gina can't keep him in her Triad, but she's also not going to just turn him out on the street. They've been together too damned long."

"Fuck."

"Yeah."

I hated it. Fucking hated everything about it. Tybalt was a Hunter. The people he'd fought for, bled for, and sacrificed half an arm for had turned against him. Just like they'd done to me.

"Go run your errand," I said, finished with the depressing conversation. "I really need that shower now."

I slipped past him, waved hello at David, and locked myself in the bathroom. It was small, with an old-fashioned claw-foot tub and single tiny window. After seven days of wrestling with my inner demons and sleeping, I got my first glimpse in the mirror. My hair lay flat as I'd ever seen it, shiny on top and tangled at the ends. My skin was dull, a little too pale, lips dry and cracked. I yanked off the long T-shirt. I'd lost weight, leaving both hip bones more pronounced than they used to be. Ribs, too.

My fingers absently stroked the spot above my left

breast where the dart had struck, sure I could still feel its sting.

I stayed in the shower until the hot water turned luke-warm, taking time to untangle my hair, wash it thoroughly, then scrub every inch of skin twice. I also used Wyatt's disposable razor to feel female again. The mirror was so steamed up I didn't bother using it. The only items on the sink's narrow ledge were a toothbrush, toothpaste, and men's deodorant. Since it was that or BO, I used the sport stick, wrung my hair and blotted out what water I could, then wrapped another thick, fuzzy towel around my body.

David's head was barely visible over the arm of the couch. Looked like my babysitter was taking a nap. Not that I could blame him. The cabin didn't have a television, or any books that I could spot, so his entertainment choices were limited. I crept back into the bedroom and shut the door.

A startled cry stuck in my throat. Wyatt was sitting on the foot of the bed, silent as a statue, hands folded in his lap, watching me. Intently. While my pulse returned to normal, I put my hands on my hips and said, "I guess David had a long night. He fell asleep out there."

He nodded, never breaking that stare. My stomach quivered. I knew that look. I'd seen it several times in the past, usually about ten minutes before I left him high and dry, and myself equally frustrated.

"How'd your errand go?" I asked. Had I been in there an hour? "Don't suppose you bought me my own de-odorant?"

Slowly, he drew to his feet, hands falling to his sides. He closed the small distance between us in long, paced strides. Butterflies erupted in my stomach.

"Wyatt—" He silenced me with a finger to my mouth, his skin cool. The finger traced around the edges of my lips and across my cheek, until his right hand cupped my jaw. I leaned into his touch, usually so warm, now strangely cool and smooth. He was close, barely a pocket of air between us, and me in a damned towel.

I cleared my throat and tried again: "David's outside."

He nodded, silent, and dipped his head. I accepted him without protest. His right hand tightened as his mouth descended. My eyes started to close, then snapped open at the oddness of the kiss. There was no heat, no spark. I was kissing a stranger, and when he parted his lips to deepen the kiss, I flinched. He tasted wrong. Almost sour, nothing like Wyatt. The scent was wrong. Everything was wrong.

I yanked back. Something stung my neck.

The desire in his smile morphed into a sneer as the lights went out.

Cold fear snapped me awake. I tried to strike out, but nothing happened. I flexed fingers that didn't move. My entire body was numb from the neck down, not responding to desperate attempts to sit up, reach out, do something. I couldn't even turn my head. Couldn't feel anything beneath me, but the angle of the ceiling suggested I was in bed.

What the fuck's going on? The words rang in my head and couldn't make it past my lips.

The mattress sank nearby, then Wyatt appeared in my line of sight. My heart hammered and my stomach churned. Sweat broke out on my forehead. What was wrong with him? He gazed down at me as though he'd never seen me before. Up and down the length of my— oh no. I struggled to tilt my head down and managed enough angle to realize one horrifying reality—my towel was open, and I was naked.

Terror seized my chest and squeezed. This wasn't Wyatt; it couldn't be. He'd never do something like this to me, not even as the most horrible, sinister April Fools' prank in history. But my eyes told me he was. He was swabbing at my hip with something chilly.

"No." The sound was garbled, barely a word. He looked at me and smiled, lips curling back from his teeth. Horrible intent was in that smile. I shuddered. Two of my fingers twitched, and my heart leapt. Was the sedative wearing off?

He reached out of sight and drew back with a long-needled, wide-body syringe. I stared, dumbfounded, as he shifted back and lowered the syringe. Pierced my hip. White-hot spikes shot through my abdomen and leg, and a garbled scream erupted from my throat. Down it went. Pressure against my hip, all the way to the bone. Pained, confused tears sparked in my eyes. The strangest pulling sensation accompanied the agony in my hip.

I closed my eyes, breathing deeply, staving off full-blown panic. This wasn't happening; it was another hallucination. Maybe I hadn't actually survived the vampire parasite. Maybe I was a Halfie and this was Hell. I was in Hell, that's it. No way Wyatt was doing this.

Wake up, Stone, please! Somebody, wake me up!

The wail caught in my throat and choked me. I coughed and curled my toes. The numbness had become a strange tingle. I flexed the muscle in my right thigh, felt it respond.

Wyatt reached past me to put the syringe—now full of something dark red from my body—on the bedside table. Came back with a second syringe, just as big as the first. *Please, not again. Don't take any more.*

As the numbness wore off and I caught hold of my initial panic, I felt my tap to the Break return. It snapped into place like a rubber band. I tried to picture the living room, someplace where David would see me and wake the fuck up. I found a few tendrils of loneliness and grasped them. The second syringe broke skin. I closed my eyes, pulled on everything I had, and slipped into the Break.

A scratchy wool rug burned into my naked back. The mounted deer's head loomed above me. I wrenched my head toward the sofa. David lay flat on his back, staring up at the ceiling. Probably drugged with whatever I'd been given. Shit.

The bedroom door squealed open.

I twisted onto my stomach, my limbs still not quite co-operating, like rolling through syrup. My legs were heavy, dead weights. I reached out with both hands, grabbed a handful of the faded area rug, and tried to pull. A foot pressed down on the small of my back. I screamed, although there was no one to hear me. We were in the middle of nowhere.

He kicked. Pain flared in my left side, and it knocked the wind out of me. I felt sick as I gasped. Struggled as he flipped me over on my back and straddled my thighs. I kicked and bucked to little effect, terror overtaking good sense, still lacking full control of my body.

Not him, not him, not him, not him—

The first blow filled my mouth with blood. The second bounced my skull off the floor, and I saw stars. He repeated this one just as I got a good inhale back, and I spun around inside my own brain. My eyesight blurred. Everything was muddled.

Agony in my other hip, just like before. That strange sucking sensation. Maybe he'd take whatever he wanted from my bones and just leave. Leave and never come back, or I'd kill him. Rip his head off his shoulders and use it for volleyball. The syringe came out, but he didn't get up. I clung to consciousness, pulling desperately on my tap to the Break. Loneliness was hard to find, buried under so much rage and fear and pain.

Just one more transport, please!

My entire body screamed as I slipped in and out once more, landing some distance away in the kitchen, on cracked and stained linoleum. I flailed for a weapon, even as heavy footsteps thundered toward me. Got my right hand into a cabinet and around the handle of a pot. His weight was on me, pushing me to the floor. One hand circled my throat. I swung the pot with all my available strength and was rewarded with a dull crack. He howled, released my throat, and punched me in the stomach.

I curled forward, agony flaring in my guts. My lungs seized. I swung feebly with the pot. He caught my wrist. Snapped it. I shrieked, my brain starting to short-circuit. He caught my other wrist and pinned them both above my head. Agony lanced up and down my arm from my broken wrist. I don't know when I'd started crying, but with my torso stretched and my lungs gasping, I began to choke.

He laughed, and in that horrifying, deep-chested, in-human sound, I understood what my heart had kept trying to tell me—the thing holding me down was not my Wyatt. It was something else.

"Help!" I didn't manage many decibels, but I repeated my plea as I sought my tap. Couldn't find it. I couldn't drum up the correct emotional cocktail of loneliness to make my Gift work. Rage rioted in my pain-addled brain.

His weight shifted. I wept, furious at my weakness, disgusted at my inability to protect myself. He leaned down. I could smell his sour breath puffing near my face.

Not again. My eyes snapped open. I saw his neck.

I reared up and sank my teeth into his throat. Fucking hard. I locked my jaw and skin broke. Blood filled my mouth, thick and oily. He bucked, hands beating my hips and chest, but I didn't let go. I clamped down harder, digging into his neck like a stray dog who'd finally found a meal.

I didn't see the pot until it smashed into my temple. Lights flashed in my eyes. Something buzzed in my ears. My jaws relaxed. He rolled away, gasping. His blood was on my face, my tongue, everywhere. I rolled and spit and retched. Then the most beautiful sound in the world made it through the buzz—voices. Not the scary, no-one-hears-them-but-me voices—real ones, on the other side of the cabin door.

Confused, cold, and in desperate agony, I did the only thing I could think of—I took a deep breath and screamed as loudly as I could.

Not-Wyatt backhanded me. The world blurred. Fists were beating on the door. Two male voices shouted. Familiar voices. My attacker had a dish towel pressed to his throat. He made a dive for his abandoned syringe.

Over the din, I recognized one voice screaming my name. Relief only made my tears surge, and I returned the call with everything I had left. "Phineas!"

Syringe in hand, not-Wyatt hauled ass to his feet. The door rattled. He was caught. With primal rage in his eyes, he turned on me. Fire exploded in my ribs, compounding the throbbing in my head. The front door broke open with a dull crash.

"Fucking hell—"

"What the—?"

The activity around me was a blur. I cradled my wrist to my chest, pulled my legs up, and curled in as tight as I could manage, shivering, aching. Heard grunts and slaps of flesh on flesh. Someone hollered. A thud. Footsteps. A hand on my shoulder.

"Evy?"

I cracked one eye open, saw his face so full of rage and concern, and the irrational side of my brain took over. I yelped and scrambled away, backing up until I hit the kitchen cabinets and rattled the things above. New bruises throbbed, and my wrist felt numb, ready to fall off.

Wyatt was frozen so perfectly where he'd knelt that he could have been a statue. Same size as the other one, same face, same every-damn-thing.

No, not the same. This one had talked. He'd said my name.

"Evy, it's me," he said again, desperate.

Nothing. I couldn't move. Couldn't speak. Only my throbbing body kept me from pitching into the haze that had crept around the edges of my vision.

Phineas el Chimal appeared behind him. His narrow face was stony, predatory blue eyes full of cold fury and bloodlust. Our eyes met, and those emotions shifted immediately into something softer. Protective. He stepped out of sight, then was back with a folded blanket. He approached cautiously. I hated that I didn't pull from him as I'd pulled from Wyatt. Hated that I let Phin wrap me in the scratchy blanket and wipe my face with a damp rag. He was my friend, a were-osprey and one of the last of his Clan, but he wasn't the man I loved.

No, the man I loved was left on the kitchen floor, while Phin cradled me in his arms and carried me back to my room. Phin tucked me into bed and piled on the covers. I couldn't stop shaking. I was starting to shut down, and I fought to keep it together.

"You're safe now," Phin said. He picked up the first syringe, his mouth puckering. "He took this from you?"

From beneath my cocoon of blankets, all I could manage was a nod. His eyes flickered to me, so many mixed emotions in them.

"David?" I croaked, teeth chattering.

"Alive, but unable to move."

"Him?"

Phin inclined his head toward the door, listening.

"Being tied up as we speak, and none too gently. The resemblance is remarkable."

I grunted, wanting to cry again for no good reason.

He crouched until we were eye level. I wanted to hide from the ferocity in his gaze and was glad that his anger wasn't directed at me. "Evangeline, I must ask—"

"He didn't." I swallowed, a fresh round of tears clogging my throat. "The drugs wore off."

"He tried to steal from you, and for that he deserves death."

"We need to find out what his game is first," Wyatt said from the doorway. "Then we'll fucking kill him."

Phin shifted so I could see past him. Only my intense shivering prevented me from flinching at the sight of Wyatt. At the misery he exuded in his slumped shoulders and in the downturn of his mouth. He understood what had happened, the perverse way I'd been manipulated, and he was at a loss as to how to fix it. At as much of a loss as I was.

I closed my eyes. Saw Wyatt's face above me, leering down. Felt hands on my skin, pressing roughly. Hitting. I tried to alter that image, change it to a new face. Anyone else's face. It didn't work. A tear trickled down the side of my nose when I opened my eyes again.

"He took blood from my hips," I said. "Deep down, from the bone, I think. He drugged me so I couldn't move, but it wore off."

"Bone marrow?" Wyatt said. "Why would someone come here and steal your bone marrow?"

"We shall have to ask the thief," Phin said. "And then we shall ask the person who hired him."

"Has to be Thackery," I said, surprising myself with the lucid connection. "He hits me with the parasite, hoping I'll heal. He's checking my blood so he can make his antidote."

Wyatt's eyebrows arched. "Natural antibodies. Holy shit."

"I'm his own goddamned petri dish." Fury blossomed in my chest.

"Then why the charade?" Phin asked. "Thackery could have sent his people here to overpower your friends and kidnap you, or simply kill you and take your blood. Why this way?"

"To fuck with my head. If his bloodsucker out there hadn't stopped to cop a feel or two, he would have been in and out before I could move again." I couldn't look Wyatt in the eye. Shame heated my cheeks. "My brain would've had a hell of a harder time separating the real Wyatt from the fake one, had that been the case."

The former made a strangled noise. I shut my eyes. The shivering had lessened to an occasional tremble, but my broken wrist shrieked. All I wanted was another shower, so I could scrub the feeling of those unfamiliar hands off my body. Wash every molecule of his thick, in-human blood from my skin.

"Evangeline, do any of your injuries require medical attention?"

There didn't seem to be an inch of skin that did not ache or smart. My ribs were sore, my head throbbed, my mouth hurt—but all were things that would heal on their own. "Bastard broke my wrist. Need to set it."

"Let me see it."

With Phin's help, I got my arm free of the blankets. He cradled my hand as gently as he could, and I tried not to cry out. Failed. Wyatt appeared next to him long enough to hand over a sports bandage, then retreated to the doorway. My heart wept for the distance he was keeping. Phin wrapped his fingers around my wrist. I held my breath.

"This will hurt a great deal," he said.

"No shit. Do it."

He did. It did. I was crying again by the time he'd firmly wrapped my wrist in the bandage and secured the ends, tight enough to allow the bones to mend. I collapsed back under the covers, exhausted, and closed my eyes, willing the tears to stop. I had to get hold of myself, calm down, and think rationally about this.

Clothing shifted, and I felt Phin move away. "The bastard will be unconscious for a bit longer," he said, not to me. "I'll sit with your other friend until he's properly revived."

I almost shouted for Phin to stay. Leaving meant I'd be alone with Wyatt, and I didn't want that. Didn't want to talk about what had happened, because it would hurt him. Didn't want to flinch if he tried to touch me, because it would hurt him even more. He hadn't attacked me. He didn't deserve that hurt.

The door hinges creaked. No snap to indicate it had closed completely. Silence. Maybe he'd left after all. I hazarded a peek with one eye. No, Wyatt still stood near the door, hands shoved deep in the pockets of his jeans, shoulders hunched. A stance of uncertainty. Attention firmly fixed on the floor by his feet.

"May I stay, Evy?" he asked the floor, and I wanted to cry all over again.

"You've never had to ask before," I replied, opening the other eye.

"You've never been nearly raped by me before."

The bleakness of his tone frightened me. That wasn't what had happened. Was it? I shoved at the fog invading my brain, telling me to give up and just sleep the pain away. "It wasn't you, Wyatt."

He finally looked at me. Hurt and confusion warred with rage, all three compounded by whatever he saw in my face. "That's not what your eyes say when they look at me. You know I'd never do that to you, right? You believe me?"

"Of course." I untangled from the pile of blankets atop me so I could sit up, keeping one around my shoulders. My ribs protested the movement. I ignored the ache and tucked my legs so I was kneeling on the bed, a thin blue blanket folded around me like a cape. All I wanted was time alone to process this, but I couldn't send him away. Not now. "Wyatt, please come here."

He didn't move, coiled so tight I thought he'd shatter. Even from a distance, I saw the faint vibrations in his arms and chest. He was shaking. "I'm sorry I wasn't here again, that I didn't protect you."

He'd walked into a situation so similar to the way I'd died, and all my fear and anger were reflecting back from him tenfold. In his mind, he'd failed to save me once from misery and death. Now he'd decided he had almost failed me a second time. If the drug had worn off just a few seconds later, if I hadn't moved as fast as I had—

No. No what-ifs about this one. I was fine. Shaken up and hell-bent on carving answers out of the thing in the other room, but fine. My broken wrist and bruised ribs and aching head would heal. The real Wyatt was standing nearby, proving to my trauma-addled brain that he hadn't been the one to hurt me. We had survived our deaths; we could survive this, too.

"Wyatt, it wasn't your f—"

He took two sudden steps toward me. I flinched away, heart racing. He froze, and I wanted to weep when I realized what I'd done. Grim acceptance pulled his mouth into a straight line, and, with curt precision, he pivoted and left the room.

I collapsed against the mound of blankets, too stunned to do anything but stare at the hewn door for a while, silent tears leaving hot trails down my cheeks.

Chapter Ten

The longer I lay in bed, the more rage overtook my anxiety. Rage at the stolen blood, at the assault, at the seeds of doubt the attacker had planted in me simply by wearing Wyatt's face. I had to fix this, so I forewent a second shower in favor of acquiring information.

Two pairs of jeans, three of my solid-colored T-shirts, underwear, and a bra were neatly folded in one of the dresser's top drawers—Wyatt must have gone back to the apartment. Curled on one of the shirts was my cross necklace, safe and sound. After struggling one-handed with the bra, jeans, and a T-shirt, and earning a few painful jostles to my wrist, I tried to smooth my damp hair into submission. The shorter locks around my face were stiff in places, darkened with blobs of dried blood.

Gross.

I couldn't manage the necklace with one hand, so I tucked it into my front pocket, just grateful to have it near.

Three familiar faces and one agonizing copy greeted me when I entered the living room. David was sitting up on the sofa, flexing his hands and arms as the numbing agent wore off. He blushed and ducked his head. I wouldn't patronize him; we'd both been fooled. End of story.

Wyatt was barely visible through the kitchen doorway, fiddling with something on the counter. His doppelgänger was tied to a wooden chair with bungee cords, a length of nylon rope, and a twisted bedsheet. The man (or whatever) was bleeding through the bandage on his neck. He had a knot on one cheek, likely from my whack with the pot, a bloody nose, and more blood splattered on his clothes. Most of the blood was a dark shade of red, and I recalled the bitter, oily taste of it. Our prisoner was definitely not human.

Phin had a second chair placed an arm's reach away, and he sat there like a sentinel, shoulders stiff and back straight, full attention on his quarry.

"What is he?" I asked, stopping behind Phin.

"I believe he is a pùca, although he will not speak."

"What the hell's a pùca?" I cast a searching look at Wyatt, who shook his head. This one was new to both of us.

"A rare and distant cousin of Therians. Few are known or recorded in our history, as they are an antisocial sort. They prefer playing tricks and starting trouble to productively living in man's world. I've never met one before, but it does explain his shape-changing ability."

"He's a trickster," Wyatt said, joining us with a paring knife, a serrated bread knife, and a barbecue lighter. "That's what you're saying?"

Phin tilted his head, considering the word. "Yes, from your mythological texts, 'trickster' describes him well."

"Not to me," I said. "They didn't teach this one at Boot Camp, and I didn't pay a lot of attention in school." After three full minutes of explanation from Phin that included names I didn't know—Coyote of the Southwest, Loki in the Norse, Kokopelli and Zuñi, and a lot of others that blended together—I waved my good hand in surrender. "Information overload."

"Apologies."

"So why now?" My question was half directed at the silent doppelgänger, who hadn't looked up from his lap since I'd entered the room. "Why would something that's been unseen and unrecorded for decades suddenly show up, track me down, and suck marrow out of me?"

"Let's ask the fucker." The coldness in Wyatt's voice was almost a physical presence. He switched places with Phin and was now directly across from the man wearing his face. The reflection was eerie in its sameness and in the differences. Wyatt exuded hate in a way I'd never seen and prayed to never, ever be on the receiving end of. The doppelgänger—pùca, trickster, whatever—still stared at his own lap, face bruised and bleeding, resigned.

"You should know up front that you're going to die," Wyatt said to his reflection. "The only thing you get to decide is if you die fast, or piece by piece until you're begging me to end it."

I shuddered.

"Who are you working for?"

The doppelgänger looked up. A crystal shard hung around his neck, swirling a lazy purple, tied with some sort of thin brown leather. "You know who," he replied, and I understood why he had never spoken. His voice was like nails on a chalkboard, high and screechy and teeth-chattering.

"Say it anyway," I said.

He didn't look at me. Wyatt was questioning him, so his attention remained there. "A human male. His given name is Thackery."

"Why?" Wyatt asked.

A blink. "Because it is the name given to him."

"Be literal with your questions," Phin said. "He'll take them that way."

Wyatt nodded. "Why did you accept this job?"

"It was required."

"By what requirement?"

"No."

Wyatt flicked on the barbecue lighter and held the

paring knife blade in the orange flame. Silent seconds passed. "By what requirement?" he asked again, turning the blade handle around. The trickster didn't reply. Wyatt buried the blade in the other man's thigh.

The gasping wail shattered a glass somewhere in the kitchen. Wyatt removed the blade, coated with very little blood. The odor of singed flesh tickled my nostrils. *Cauterize the wounds as you make them to maximize pain and minimize blood loss*—words he'd spoken once upon a time while teaching me new methods for questioning suspects.

"By what requirement?"

Four more times, Wyatt repeated the question and the action, but we didn't get an answer. Finally, sick of the hair-raising squeals and stink of burned meat, I said, "Why do you wear that crystal?"

"Focus," the trickster said, apparently able to answer that particular query. "Longevity. Location."

"Explain those words to me."

"No."

Contrary little prick.

"I have a theory," Phin said. "According to legend, pùcas are able to maintain alternate forms for only brief periods of time. It's possible the crystal allows him to maintain focus on this form for longer periods."

I chewed on that. "So if we take the crystal off?"

"You remove his face."

"Fan-fucking-tastic." I stepped around Wyatt's chair, grabbed the crystal, and yanked. A jolt of energy ran up my hand the instant the leather cord broke. Like candle wax, the fake face swam and ran, melting away. The body shape changed, thinning out and shortening.

Phin was behind the chair before I could register the slipping bonds, and he worked to secure them tightly as our prisoner's form stopped shifting. He had shrunk to two-thirds his previous size, closer to child proportions than adult. The face left behind was half-formed and inhuman—lashless eyes the yellow green of baby poop, a small hump and two small holes instead of a nose, and a lipless, tiny mouth. His ears were holes on the sides of his head, waxy-white skin completely hairless. He looked like a creature that had dwelled in a dark cave too long.

"Hello, gorgeous," I said. The crystal was warm in my palm. "How the hell did this clown track us down in the middle of the woods?"

"Magic, perhaps," Phin said.

Wyatt frowned. "Thackery's human, and, as far as we know, he's not Gifted. How the hell did he manage to charm that crystal? It takes a damned strong magic user to manage a spell, and the only people who use crystals—" He stopped, the sentence dying on his lips. A queer look crossed his face, not quite a flinch, but nothing remotely pleasant.

"What?" I asked. "Crystals what?"

"The Fey," Phin said. "You were going to say the Fey, weren't you?"

Wyatt nodded.

"That's not possible," I said, my insides quivering. "The Fey Council is on our side. They couldn't be working with Thackery."

"Like all large organizations, the Fey are as likely to have dissenters as any other race," Phin said. "It's possible, Evangeline, that whoever is assisting Thackery is doing so without the approval or knowledge of the Council."

Phin knew better than any of us. Some of his own people, other Therians, were working with the dark races to raise an army against the Triads in an effort to overthrow humanity's control of the city. We hadn't squashed their efforts completely, only maimed them momentarily. It shouldn't have been so hard to swallow the idea of Fey following a similar path of vigilantism. But it was.

"Jaron knew," Wyatt said. "She knew someone was being betrayed. If not someone in the Council, then someone close to them. Why else come to us first, instead of directly to Amalie?"

Politics made my head hurt. Beyond Amalie, I didn't know the names or faces, or specific races, of the other members of the Council. She was our only direct link to them, so everything we knew was filtered through her. "So our theory," I said, "is Thackery had the crystal cast for him by a Fey powerful enough to manage the spell, then gave it over to our trickster friend so he could track me down and take my blood?"

"Basically."

Okay, fine, I could accept that. It made all kinds of sense, in a bad-vibe, Fey-betrayal-in-aisle-three kind of way. "So why steal blood samples?" I asked the trickster. "Why didn't he just have you kidnap me, or kill me outright?"

"Did not need to know," he replied, voice even more inhuman with his smaller mouth.

"And he probably wouldn't have bothered asking," Phin said. "Whatever compelled him to take this job also compelled him to do as he's told without question. The only person who knows the whys of this conversation is Thackery."

"Not all the whys," I said. Phin's explanation made sense up to a point. If the only thing Thackery wanted was my blood, why take the time to feel me up? The improvisation of the plan demanded answers. "Phin, do pùcas have anatomy similar to humans?"

"Basic humanoid shape, yes, as well as brain stem functions and— Oh." He got it a few seconds too late.

"No, they do not reproduce sexually or maintain organs for a similar function."

So it hadn't been horniness. That didn't leave a lot of other options. I snatched the serrated bread knife from Wyatt's hand with my left and crouched in front of the trickster. With the crystal gone, that same sour smell I'd detected earlier was wafting off him. "I'm guessing you were warned about my healing ability," I said, running the tip of the knife across his abdomen, scoring the shirt. "Which means you had to be very careful about dosing me. Too much and I'd probably go into cardiac arrest or something, too little and I'd do what I did, which is snap out of it and get away. Stop me if I'm wrong."

He said nothing, horrid eyes fixed on me. I skimmed the same trail a second time, hard enough to slice the shirt and reveal pasty, translucent skin. I flicked my wrist, and dark blood welled up from an inch-long cut. "So consider your answer to this question carefully, because if I don't like it, I'm going to see if you have kidneys in the same place as humans. Understand?"

A nod.

"Why did you try to rape me?" I felt, rather than saw, Wyatt start at the blunt question. He still sat behind me. Phin stood behind the trickster. All attention was on the interviewee.

"For pleasure."

I dragged the blade across pale skin, deep enough to create a steady flow of blood and a high-pitched shriek. More glass shattered. My legs started to tremble, but I kept the knife steady. "What kind of pleasure can a dickless Dreg like you get?"

His puke-yellow eyes swirled as I stared into them. A soft nudge in my mind startled me, like a tiny hand knocking on the inside of my skull. His eyes flashed briefly black and red, before changing back. I blinked hard—those had been goblin eyes.

"Pleasure in mayhem," he said. "Pleasure in chaos. Opportunity presents itself, I am compelled to take it. It is in me."

"Phin, can you translate that for me?"

"It's in a pùca's basic nature to create havoc, to play tricks on others and manipulate them. It's what he is and how he finds pleasure. It wasn't enough to simply betray your emotions by posing as Truman when he stole your blood." Phin's voice was ice-cold. "He knew how to take it further."

A tremor stole up my spine, and I contemplated my earlier threat to go excavating for kidneys.

"The desire to inflict mayhem and play tricks is infused in his being," Phin continued. "In the same manner gremlins sneak around and steal, or goblins crave havoc, he sensed an opportunity and had to seize it."

I shot Phin a withering glare, in no mood for one of his civics lessons. "I don't need a conscience, Phin, and I really don't fucking need you defending him. He made a choice."

"I don't believe he did."

A flare of frustration lit in my belly. I stood up, left hand on my hip, knife tucked sideways so I didn't stab myself. "So what you're saying, Phin, is since he was already impersonating Wyatt in order to sedate me and get my marrow, he saw an opportunity to get his nonexistent pùca rocks off and had to do it, because it's what he is? He had absolutely no choice in the matter? He had to attack me with Wyatt's face on because of the orgasmic pleasure he'd get in screwing with my head? He had to?"

He didn't flinch away from my anger or my sarcasm. "It was instinct."

"Yeah?" Heat rose in my cheeks. "Well, my instinct is to kill the piece of shit, so he can't run around inflicting his practical jokes on anyone else. What happened to 'He tried to steal from you, and for that he deserves death'? You taking that back?"

His head cocked sideways in that perfect down-my-beak-at-you look he seemed to use only when really frustrated. I brought that out in him a lot. "The sentiment stands, Evangeline. I don't take it back. If I believed he had tried to steal from you out of calculated malice, I would tear his neck from his shoulders for you."

"You just don't believe it."

"No, now that I understand what he is, I no longer believe it. However, he isn't my prisoner to punish. He's yours."

Irritation prompted an instinctive reaction, and I clenched both fists. White-hot needles shot up my right wrist. I stumbled away from the interrogation scene, tears sparking again, trying to relax my hand and ease the hurt. *Stupid, stupid, stupid.* I dropped the knife on a small handmade side table and held my bandaged wrist up, closer to my chest.

"Evy?" Wyatt asked.

"I'm fine," I snapped, harsher than I'd intended.

I pivoted toward Phin, my mind churning with indecision. Since I'd first met him, he had made a point of challenging all my preconceived and training-ingrained notions about the nonhumans in the city—and the rest of the world, by extension. My prejudices had kept me alive for a long time in a profession that left good people dead in a matter of years, sometimes months. Dregs were bad, so if they stepped out of line, they died. No jail, no reformation, no penitence—just death.

He'd shown me layers of a world I'd always viewed as flat, and in that cabin in the middle of the forest, when the irrational, passionate side of my brain was screaming at me to kill the thing that had hurt me while wearing Wyatt's face, I hesitated. Because I saw the damned layers, and all I really wanted to see was the pùca's blood splattered across the floor.

Goddamn Phineas for doing this to me.

"Okay, new deal," I said, moving back to my previous position. The pùca watched me carefully, less tense now that I was without the knife. "You've got one minute to convince me you're worth saving. Tell me why I shouldn't kill you."

"I failed," he replied. "I will die for this. At your hands or at his."

"You seem pretty capable. If you escape us, what's to stop you from running from Thackery?"

"Compelled to return."

There was that damned word again. "What compels you?"

"Failure brings death to my *enisi*."

"Phin?"

"The closest human translation," Phin said, "is 'grandfather.' "

My mouth fell open. A human was blackmailing a Dreg by threatening a family member—and here I'd thought nothing else could surprise me today.

Chapter Eleven

An hour's discussion around the sofa kept leading us in frustrating circles. The trickster, whose preferred name was Axon, had met Thackery in a neutral location to receive the syringes, instructions, and verification of his *enisi*'s capture. Axon had been unable to "taste" Thackery during the meeting—his word for how he knew if someone was ripe for tricking—and that was unusual. His people had targeted humans throughout history because we were so "delicious." His word.

As my adrenaline rush cut off and my body settled in to heal itself, I'd curled up on one corner of the sofa with a mug of instant soup and tried to be useful in the discussion. Mostly I listened to Wyatt and Phin bat around ideas on how to find Thackery, ways to use Axon against him, the merits of letting Axon help us versus locking him up good and tight, and who we should include in the current problem.

The latter interested me the most. Kismet hadn't reported me as alive, so her original report on the factory fire and my demise stood on record. Her Hunters were sworn to secrecy. If we needed backup muscle, her team was the only real recourse. Willemy's murder was unsolved. For now. The theory that a powerful Fey was helping Thackery created a good argument against involving Amalie yet—if we could even reach her to do so.

The only thing we knew for certain was that Thackery

wanted my blood, and he was going through a hell of a lot of trouble not to kill me for it.

"The Assembly will assist if you ask them," Phin said, nearest me on the sofa. "They have great respect for Evangeline, and I can curry much support from the Clans."

"It wouldn't hurt to have more than just humans on the lookout for him," I said. "But I don't want to see more innocents dragged into this, and he's been off the grid for this long. I can't see him slipping up and getting randomly spotted on the street."

"And when Axon doesn't return on time with your blood, Thackery will send someone else to find you. Perhaps we should use that to our advantage and try trapping him?"

"The trouble with sitting around and waiting is that the *enisi* dies. If he's just as irritating as his grandson, I can't say I care much in the long run, but I'm not fond of letting hostages get killed."

"Which gives us about three hours to devise an alternate solution."

I glanced at the only clock in the room—an old cast-iron skillet modified with clockworks and numbers—and verified Phin's time frame. Axon had been told to return to a specific phone booth at three o'clock today in order to verify he had my blood and receive further instructions. We'd already shot down David's suggestion to use Axon as bait and coax Thackery out of hiding. Axon was intellectually incapable of participating in subterfuge on the level required to pull that off.

Fucking literalism.

"I just can't believe Kismet hasn't turned anything up," I said, more to myself than the others, since we'd already covered the topic forty minutes ago. "How has Thackery managed these experiments for years without leaving a paper trail for us to follow?"

Phin shook his head. David huffed from his spot on the far end of the sofa.

Wyatt had settled in one of the chairs, legs stretched out and crossed at the ankles, hands folded in his lap. His eyebrows were scrunched, and he worried his lower lip with his teeth. Thinking hard about something. Our only direct conversation outside of the current topic had been me thanking him for preparing the mug of instant soup. Not a word about the elephant in the room.

"If you've got money, you can buy secrecy," David said, "but someone always slips up. We just haven't found the crack yet."

My gaze slid past Phin to David, who I'd guess to be around twenty. Young, but not without experience. Yet he also seemed nervous enough to jump out of his own skin. This mysterious, conspiracy-minded side of things wasn't within his comfort zone, yet he was doing his best to contribute.

"You've been looking for cracks for over a week," I said. "If there was a trail to be followed, you'd—"

"Token," Wyatt said, jackknifing up from the chair. He almost tumbled right out, eyebrows arching into his hairline.

"Did you just sneeze?" Phin asked, confused.

Wyatt shook his head. "Token is the human-goblin hybrid who killed Jaron last week. He was taken to Boot Camp with the other science projects until we could figure out what to do with him."

"I thought Token gave up everything," I said.

"Not everything." Determination blazed in his eyes. "Thackery created Token, and when he was questioned, Token couldn't tell us where. He didn't understand. All we got were vague descriptions of gray walls, metal, and wind."

"Wind?"

"Wind in the walls is how he described where he lived.

He was taken from there blindfolded, driven for a little while, then released to hunt in Grove Park, about a mile from Jaron's avatar's apartment."

I tilted my head to the side and frowned, not following his train of thought on this. "But if he was blindfolded—"

"What's a goblin's most heightened sense?"

"Smell."

"And how do their tiny, illogical minds find their way back to their queen's nest?"

It clicked. "Token would have left his scent behind wherever he was made and kept. He could theoretically still follow his own scent trail back to that source, like a warrior returning to its nest."

"Exactly." His smile was guarded but genuine, and I found myself returning it.

"How do you know you can trust this creature?" Phin asked.

"We don't," I replied. "But he was human before he became a monster, and it may be our best option. Plan B consists of us sitting on our asses until Thackery sends another blood collector after me. And this time, he might not be so generous about letting me live."

If my answer didn't please Phin, he kept it to himself. "To avoid detection, I can track him from the sky. You can then track me with whatever electronic means you have at your disposal."

"Okay, good. That's doable. Next problem is gaining access to Token and getting him out of Boot Camp." To Wyatt, I asked, "You think Kismet will pull some strings for this?"

Wyatt's mouth twisted. "I'll ask, but considering the fight Erickson put up about handing over those two vials, it may take more than the two of us to get Token released."

"Like what? It's not as if we can just break into Boot Camp and spring him. Security's too good."

"Only if we try walking through the front door."

"What—?" Oh. Oh! "You want me to teleport in and out."

"I don't want, but I am asking."

All eyes were on me. I shifted, uncomfortable teleporting before my wrist was fully healed but unable to offer an alternate solution. "If you can get me on the grounds again and provide an extremely detailed visual of the interior so I don't land in a wall or desk or something, I'll do it."

Wyatt smiled, a hint of pride in the turn of his lips. Meant just for me. Any other day, that would have warmed me and gotten a smile in return. But still stinging from his earlier reaction in the bedroom, I just stared. His smile dimmed.

"Driving back in will be hard," he said. "I can't go in, park for five minutes, and then drive out again without someone getting suspicious. Especially when I've been off the radar for a week."

"You mentioned ground security measures," Phin said. "Do they watch the sky for attack as well?"

"There are four watchtowers around the perimeter that monitor the surrounding forest and mountains. If someone came in low enough to the treetops, they might not be noticed right away."

I looked from one man to the other, then stopped on Wyatt. "So you're saying Phin should fly me as close to the perimeter as possible so I can attempt transport into a building I've never been inside of before. Then after I locate Token and convince him to come with me without biting or slashing, transport back out to . . . where? Is teleporting into midair and hoping Phin catches me your escape plan?"

"Of course not," Wyatt replied tartly. "We're discussing options, Evy."

"Teleporting with a broken wrist will be painful enough, and doing it again while carrying someone's going to really hurt. I might be able to get us outside the wall, but don't count on any farther than that."

"Query," Phin said. "If I did fly Evangeline in close, would I be teleported inside as well due to proximity?"

I opened my mouth to reply, but my mind was blank. Not a clue. I'd once teleported out from beneath Wyatt without taking him with me. That was also before I'd fully come into my Gift. Minutes after that fateful moment, I'd teleported myself and two others fifty yards through a magical force field and into a building. Axon had been kneeling over me when I got out from under him—not quite as close contact as I'd be with Phin. We needed to know for sure.

"Stand up," I said. Phin did as asked, and so did I, turning around and crossing my arms over my breasts. His long arms snaked around my waist, and I was again struck by the strange dichotomy of his touch—at once muscular and soft, hollow power. I caught a flash of the two-inch scars on the interior of both wrists—faint reminders of what had happened the last time he volunteered to help me. He pressed his hands flat against my belly; I shivered, and he tensed.

"Are you sure you want to try this?" he asked, breath feathering across my ear.

"If I don't, we'll never know."

"It will hurt?"

"Only me. Now shut up so I can concentrate."

It took great effort to close my eyes without looking at Wyatt. I could guess what I'd see—apprehension at what I was doing, jealousy at Phin's proximity, maybe a scowl tossed in for good measure.

My tap into the Break tickled the edge of my senses. I

used the memory of Wyatt walking away from me in the bedroom to draw on enough loneliness to pour power through me. Snapping and crackling, I focused on the bedroom and on taking only myself there, ignoring the warm body pressed to my back. Imagined us separated, two individual bodies rather than one locked in an embrace.

Now or never.

I slipped in and my wrist shrieked, needles racing up and down my arm as I moved through a solid wall. The hateful throbbing continued even after I materialized in the bedroom. Very much not alone.

"Well, hell," I said. Phin loosened his arms and I spun to face him, cradling my wrist to my chest. "I suppose you could always drop me at the very last second."

His nostrils flared. "Never."

The bedroom door swung open. "Now what?" Wyatt asked.

I exhaled hard. "I guess my workload just doubled. Phin will have to come in with me."

Phin looked ill. "I can't wait."

The rare bit of sarcasm from him made me smile. "Hey, I'm the one doing all the heavy lifting. If you volunteered to fly me and Wyatt together when we first met, you shouldn't have trouble with me and someone half his size."

"I admit," he said, seeming mollified, "I have always wanted to see your Boot Camp up close."

"Well, now's your chance."

A throat cleared. David lingered in the doorway, just behind Wyatt's shoulder. He was looking at us like we'd all grown extra heads. "Um, maybe this is a stupid question, but he's a were-osprey, right? How's he going to fly you anywhere?"

Hell, I'd forgotten that David didn't know Phin's secret. Bi-shifting was something only the oldest, most protected Clans could manage, and Phin was one of the last survivors of his people. He was able to sprout wings with a span of twice his own height while the rest of him remained human. The ability was carefully guarded by the Clan Assembly, and Wyatt and I were privileged to know about it.

Behind me, Phin chuckled. Fabric rustled, followed by a faint breeze. Then twin shadows fell across the floor, cast from the lamp behind him. David's face went slack. I didn't have to turn around but did anyway. A gibbering, terrified half-Blood had seen Phin like that once and asked if Phin was an angel. And standing with hands on hips, bare chest rippling with corded muscle, handsome face smiling benevolently, mottled brown-and-white wings expanded as far as they could go, he looked just like one.

"Whoa," David said.

"Your word you tell no one of this ability," Phin said, tone sharp as a blade.

"Swear."

"Thank you." His wings retracted as quickly as they'd appeared, and his shirt was back on by the time we reassembled in the living room.

"So what do we do with him?" David asked, jacking his thumb at Axon's quiet shape, still tucked in the far corner by the kitchen.

"Put him on ice for now," I said. "It will take Phin, Wyatt, and me at least an hour to get to Boot Camp—"

Phin interrupted. "It'll be faster if I fly us."

I shook my head. "We can't risk it in broad daylight. David, I need you to stay here. After an hour, call Kismet and tell her everything except what we're planning with Token."

"I can't lie to her," David said, eyes narrowing. "I may not be officially assigned, but she's my temporary Handler."

"You're telling me you never lied to Willemy about anything?"

"Not Triad-related. You make it a habit of lying to your Handler?"

"Not a habit, no."

Wyatt made a soft noise. I wanted to roll my eyes and didn't. Sure, I'd embellished and obfuscated and stretched the truth when necessary to get the damned job done. It shouldn't seem so strange.

"We could render him unconscious," Phin said. "That will solve the—"

"Okay, fine." David glared at me. "I'll do it, all right? If she reams me a new asshole when she finds out I lied—"

"Tell her to put it on my tab," I said. "In the meantime, get rid of those syringes and keep Axon secure until Kismet can get here and pick him up. Don't talk to him, don't go near him. Understand?"

"Yeah, I got it." Got it and wasn't happy about it, from the look on his face.

I took a few minutes in front of the bathroom mirror to get my looks in order. The cuts and bruises had healed. With a rough washcloth and aloe-scented soap, I finished washing my face and neck, removing the last remnants of my and Axon's blood. I picked at the dried bits in my hair and wished for a rubber band to pull the thick waves back from my face, not for the first time considering just taking a pair of scissors to it.

Wyatt was already behind the wheel of a black two-door clunker with Phin tucked uncomfortably in the small backseat. I slid into the front and got my first good look at the cabin as we drove down a potholed dirt track that masqueraded as a driveway. The cabin's exterior was constructed of hewn logs, cut to fit at the corners and chinked with clay. It looked ancient tucked among tall oaks and loblolly pines, like the woodsman's cabin in a bleak fairy tale. Two other cars were parked outside. I recognized Phin's but not the second one.

The tire trail dumped into a dirt road, and Wyatt made a right. After a few more miles of winding down from the mountains, he made another right onto a two-lane paved road, heading south toward the city. We really had been in the middle of nowhere.

"Did you leave earlier to meet up with Phin?" I asked after we'd passed the first twenty minutes of the trip in complete silence.

"I hadn't intended to," Wyatt said. He spoke to the road in front of him. "He called my cell while I was in the city. I said you were up and around. I met him, and he followed me back."

"Oh." I skated my fingertip across the dash, leaving a dark trail behind on the dusty molded plastic. Gross. "You left to run an errand."

The steering wheel cracked under his hands. "Yep."

"Which was what?"

"Are you interrogating me now, Evy?"

"You left and he came, Wyatt. I think I'm entitled to ask where you went."

His profile looked pained, then angry. I expected to see a cartoon thundercloud hovering above his head. "There's a bag under your seat." Clipped. "That's what I went out for."

I bent and retrieved a paper sack. The top of the bag was rolled closed, its bulky shape awkward. "Easterbrook Pharmacy" was printed on the side in blue letters. I opened it without ceremony and peered inside.

And almost burst into tears.

A toothbrush, ladies deodorant, a hairbrush, cherry-vanilla body wash and a mesh sponge, a pack of pink disposable razors, aloe-infused shaving lotion, and vanilla lip gloss were jumbled together in the bag. I stared at them, struck dumb. He'd gone out for a bag of female items that had probably embarrassed the hell out of him to purchase. The gesture was so sweet, so simple, it made my heart soar.

"I . . . This is . . . Thank you."

He nodded, never looking away from the road, but his expression had softened. "You're welcome. It seems kind of dumb now."

The only dumbness about it was my questioning him. I tucked the bag back under my seat for safekeeping. Once we reached the highway bypass and crossed the northern branch of the Anjean River, going south by way of East Side, Wyatt started talking. He described each of the three upper floors of R&D in detail—hallways and rooms and blind corners. The first sublevel was as far down as he'd ever gone. It was all laboratories and storage lockers and closets. Those closets would be my best bet for a landing zone. I pictured it all in my head without much trouble, since the details he remembered were amazing—as long as they proved accurate. He wouldn't guess, though; guessing only meant we could transport into a wall or, worse, a person.

Soon we'd left the city behind and, minutes later, the bypass. Two miles past the road that wound its way to Boot Camp, Wyatt turned down a badly paved access road marked with a faded sign. "Reservoir" was the only word still legible. Half a mile down, the road opened into a small gravel lot, bordered on one side by a metal shack the size of a trailer and on the other by water.

"I didn't know this was here," I said, climbing out after we parked. A thick, musty odor mingled with the scents of earth and pine and made me want to sneeze.

"It's not used anymore as a water source," Wyatt said. "It was contaminated about fifteen years ago, so they cut off the pipes and forgot about it." He pointed opposite us, near the start of the tree line. "Kids come up here sometimes and have bonfires, but mostly they're smart enough not to swim."

Bright orange signs were posted near the concrete water barrier, the words too small to read from my position. Probably things like "caution" or "biohazard area."

"Too bad. It's kind of lovely here."

"How far are we from Boot Camp?" Phin asked, joining us by the trunk of the car. He'd left his shirt in the backseat, wings already out and tucked close to his back.

"You need to fly about a mile northeast," Wyatt said. "That will put you within a half mile. You should be able to see the valley from that distance."

"And when we do, that's my cue," I said. "Barring any unexpected resistance, we should be back in thirty minutes, max."

"Speaking of which . . ." Wyatt popped the trunk of his car, opened a small black suitcase, and removed a GLOCK .22 pistol. He checked the magazine and the chamber, then held it toward me, butt first. "In case of unexpected resistance."

I hesitated, understanding the reasons and hating the implications. "What kind of rounds?"

"Something new that Morgan's and Sharpe's teams are field-testing to use on civilians who get in the way. Rubber bullet with a tiny shatter-tip that injects victims with a sedative capable of knocking them out and impairing their memory of the incident."

"Impairing memory," I repeated, and took the gun. I hated guns, but the new rounds were impressive. As impressive as our a-c rounds and their ability to make a flesh wound fatal through the injection of an anticoagulant. "It's a roofie bullet?"

Wyatt snickered. "Yeah, basically. Like I said, it's being field-tested, but I'd rather send you in with that than with something that could kill." They were still our allies.

I tucked the gun into the front of my jeans and covered it with the hem of my T-shirt. "Guess we should do this thing. Time's wasting."

"Be careful."

"You know me."

"Be careful anyway."

Familiar banter that should have been easy was slightly strained by what had happened at the cabin. I shook it off and assumed the position. Phin drew up behind me, his warm chest to my back. Locked arms around my waist and held me closer. His heartbeat thrummed, faster than mine.

A cyclone of air swirled dust and grit, and then we were shooting up, rocketed by the strength of Phin's wings. My legs dangled, helpless, and I struggled to keep from kicking. The parking area disappeared, replaced by the low tops of trees. Very low tops. Leaves and pine needles rustled beneath us as Phin flew hard and fast toward our destination. The wind beat against my face, cool and crisp here in the mountains.

It was nothing like the other two times I'd been flown by a Coni. This time I felt free, as if I were soaring through the air on my own wings, heedless of the world and its stresses. Was this what it felt like when Phin flew as an osprey? Was he going anywhere close to his maximum speed? I wanted to ask, but sound roared in my ears and would have stolen my voice.

Up and down, cresting one peak and swooping down the other side, he flew us onward. I imagined unsuspecting campers below suddenly looking up and seeing two people coasting above the treetops. I laughed. Phin made an indeterminate sound that rumbled from his chest into my back.

"It's coming," he said all too soon, mouth very close to my ear. "Prepare yourself, and I will say when."

I closed my eyes and tugged on a visual of the first sublevel. The carefully described storage closet at the south end of the corridor. Two rows of metal shelving inside, full of supplies. An empty area near the door, kept clear so carts could be brought in to load supplies. Pale yellow tiled floor, gray walls, plaster ceiling. I held on to that, then cast my line for loneliness. With the tension still palpable between me and Wyatt, it was easy to find. My tap to the Break sparked and fizzled, ready. And still we flew.

"Now," Phin said.

I pushed my energy toward him deliberately this time, caught it around him like a net, and pulled us both into the Break. Behind my eyes, a steady throbbing began, the lightest start of a headache. We shattered apart like a shotgun pellet, invisible pieces hurtling toward the image in my mind. Faster, faster. The throb increased to a slight pounding as we moved through solid walls. Almost there.

A tang of astringent cleaning products announced our expulsion from the Break. My knees wobbled, and I would have fallen without Phin. Warmth trickled down to my lip from my nose. The pounding remained, flashing colorful lights behind my eyelids. I shuddered; Phin pulled me tighter to him.

"Are you all right?" he asked.

"Woozy. I just need a second." Two deep breaths later, I blinked my eyes open. The room didn't tilt. Nausea was ebbing again. My wrist-ache was tolerable. I tapped Phin's arm and he let go. The nosebleed had already stopped, and I swiped at the remnants. The occasional tiny tremor still stole through my guts, but for the most part, I was fine. Not too bad for my first long-distance transport.

We'd landed exactly in front of the storage room door. It had a simple aluminum knob. Yellow light spilled through beneath in a narrow line. I pressed my ear against the smooth metal.

"The hallway is empty," Phin whispered. Excellent hearing was a species perk. "I hear muffled voices to our left, about twenty feet away, behind a door. Unless the rooms are soundproof, no one else is on this level."

"Terrific." I turned the knob, grateful it didn't squeal. Neither did the hinges. With my heart in my throat, I led Phin along our predetermined path. Right and down three doors to the stairwell. Each step seemed to ring loudly, even though my sneakers were mostly silent on the clean linoleum. The astringent odor followed us into the stairwell, its door as squeak-free as the other.

We descended past sublevel 1—marked by a simple white plaque next to the landing door—and made our way to sublevel 2. Same plaque, new problem.

"Shit," I muttered. A numbered keypad was fixed below the plaque, and the door looked mechanized. Tighter security around the beasties. "I don't suppose you know how to override one of these?"

"I'm sorry, I don't."

"Then let's hope no one's standing on the other side of the door." I grabbed his right hand with my left; he gave the gentlest squeeze and said, "I hear no one close by."

Good enough. I oriented, then dragged us both into the Break, through the door, and back out the other side. The throb became a relentless pounding, a single hammer knocking at the front of my skull. But Phin was right—the room in front of us was empty of human beings. The same couldn't be said for other things.

It looked like a dog pound from Hell. Cell after cell lined the walls both left and right. Cement blocks made up the floors, ceilings, and partitions, with thick iron bars for doors. The things inside them snuffled, shifted, snorted, and growled. A maelstrom of odors wafted toward us, cloying and intoxicating and thick. Phin made a soft gagging sound. I gave the hand I was still holding a gentle squeeze. I didn't envy him his sense of smell.

Four metal gurneys, each one bolted to the floor, took up the majority of the room's center. Each one had overhead lights, rolling trays full of equipment, and individual drains in the floor. I stared, struck by just how similar it was to the morgue in which I'd first woken up, three weeks ago. Really similar, because one of the gurneys wasn't empty. A white sheet covered a lone figure, its actual shape or species impossible to guess.

"Should we check each cage?" Phin asked.

"Only if you want to have nightmares tonight."

I'd seen some of the abominations Thackery had created—a small child with oily black skin and a prickly dorsal fin down its spine; the living corpse of a house cat with fangs longer than my thumb. I'd heard wings flapping, animals growling, monsters hissing, and skin squelching.

Near us, something gurgled. I glanced at a cage and just as quickly looked away. All I'd seen were its snakelike yellow eyes, swimming in madness.

I approached the gurney, drawn by morbid fascination, and lifted the sheet. A familiar face lay beneath it— one I'd seen many weeks ago in Tovin's underground lab. Once a teenage boy, half his body had been turned to stone, rendering it immobile and useless. Seeing him there, dead, his human side cold and gray, churned my insides into a mass of quivering anger. We hadn't been able to save him.

"Fucking hell," I said, then spun in a complete circle. "Token?" My voice bounced. Something growled, while another something made a high-pitched hissing noise. "Token?"

"Master?"

I cringed, then followed the sound of the call. All the way to the last cage, past glimpses of red skin, scales, shiny teeth, and swiping claws. Token bounced to the front of his cage and wrapped bandaged hands around the bars. His face was a puzzle of cuts and bruises, a horrible reflection of the patterns on his bare chest and arms. I knew they'd torture him for information, but for some reason I couldn't understand, seeing it made me sick.

"You came," he said. "Knew you would, knew it."

He was getting loud. I shushed him. "I need to ask you an important question. Will you answer me?"

"Token answer, yes."

"Do you remember the place you used to live? With your old master, the human man named Thackery?"

"Yes. Took me away, told me to hunt and kill."

Yeah, I remembered that part. "Token, if I take you to the place where he left you, do you think you can find your way back? Can you smell a path to your old home?"

His brown, too-human eyes widened. Narrowed as his brow furrowed. "Can try, yes. For new master, yes." He shifted his attention behind me, and those haunting eyes widened to comical proportions. "Angel."

Phin made a rude noise.

"He's a friend," I said. "Promise me, Token. Promise me if I let you out, you won't hurt anyone. You will do as I say and find your old home for me."

"Token promises. Will do anything for master."

"Good."

It took several minutes to find the collection of flat plastic key cards that opened the cells, and another to sift through them for the correct one. The lock light finally flashed green, and the mechanism released. Token limped out in a cloud of urine-scented air. I swallowed hard.

"We should go," Phin said. "I hear voices."

I folded my arms into position. Phin wrapped himself around me. Token stared.

"Token," I said, "I need you to listen. We are going to get out of here, but you have to hold on to me." Every muscle in my body rebelled at the idea of the human-goblin half-breed clutching me. "Hold on to my legs with both arms, tight, and do not let go. Don't let go until I tell you. Understand?"

Facial muscles twitched as Token struggled with my request. He looked at my legs, my face, legs again.

"Evangeline," Phin said.

"Token, you must. Your master commands it."

His small body flinched. "Token understands." He did me one better by sitting on my feet and wrapping his legs around my ankles. Arms locked around my knees, he held so tightly I feared loss of circulation.

"Ready to fly?" I asked.

Phin grunted. "We cannot fly if you don't transp—"

"Brace yourself."

He did. So did I, and away we went.

Chapter Twelve

The furious pounding in my head, coupled with the cool stream of air against my face, woke me. I was still in Phin's arms, high above the trees, with the reservoir looming in the distance. I didn't look down, but the heavy weight dragging on my legs told me Token hadn't panicked and let go. Cold wetness covered my upper lip, and some had dribbled onto my chin.

Final transport was a blur, but it was obviously a successful blur.

My stomach flipped. I groaned.

"You're awake," Phin said in my ear.

"Gonna hurl. Fly faster."

We were at his maximum speed with two passengers. I breathed deeply, concentrating on the persistent spear of pain between my eyes as the parking lot appeared over the tree line. Wyatt was sitting on the hood of his car, and he launched to his feet when he saw us. Phin set down with an unsettling thud, not his usual graceful stop, and let me go, anticipating the regurgitation. Token, however, didn't uncurl from my legs.

I toppled sideways and skinned my palms on the gravel even as I puked all over it. I barely felt the shock of jarring my wrapped wrist. Token released me and scrambled away. Not much came out, but it left my stomach sore and ribs aching. I spat out the taste of bile. My arms trembled, and I nearly collapsed into my own vomit.

Strong arms slid around my waist and hauled me back to safety. I let him pull me against his chest, nearly cradled in his lap, and it took several deep breaths to realize it wasn't Phin. "I've got you," Wyatt said. "Phin, there's bottled water in the backseat."

I closed my eyes, drawing on the familiar heat of Wyatt's chest, the steady thu-dump of his heartbeat, for strength. The nausea was gone, but the headache hadn't dimmed. Something cold and wet dabbed at my lips and chin, then hard plastic pressed to my mouth. I drank a few sips.

"She passed out during the final teleport," Phin said.

"Lotta walls," I said. "Fucking walls hurt."

"Did anyone see you?" Wyatt asked.

"I don't believe so," Phin replied. "I heard no alarms raised. The mission, it seems, was successful."

I peeled my eyelids open and winced against the sunlight. Phin was crouched next to us, Token shadowing him on the right. Wyatt's hold was loose, and he didn't protest when I sat up. It felt good—*more than good; right*—being in his arms like that.

"We shouldn't hang around," I said. "Phin heard voices coming toward the lab, so they might realize Token's gone and start looking."

Gravel crunched as Wyatt stood. He circled around and offered me his hand. I took it, grateful, and used his support to pull unsteadily to my feet. The ground tilted a bit. I squeezed his hand until the dizziness subsided, then let go. We took our previous places in the car, with Token tucked into the backseat with Phin. Good thing Token was the size of a fifth grader or they wouldn't have had much room back there.

I relaxed against the seat, eyes closed, willing away the headache. It would take time. It always did when I teleported too much at once. Even with my healing ability, it took its toll, and I couldn't image how much damage the teleporting would cause if I couldn't heal quickly. Then again, without the healing, I'd have been dead long ago.

The road smoothed out, and we began a steady descent out of the mountains, back toward the city. I listened to the hum of the engine and tried to ignore the new, itchy pressure in my right wrist. Finally the bones were starting to mend.

"Let's assume that Token successfully leads us to Thackery's location," Phin said sometime into the trip. "Do you have a plan in mind?"

"Surveillance," Wyatt replied. "We can't go in until we know what to expect. Who's there, who's not, and where the trickster's *enisi* is being held."

"And once we know these things?"

Silence. I listed my head to the side and squinted at Wyatt through half-closed lids. He chewed on his lower lip, brow furrowed. Thinking. I asked, "Your first response wasn't calling in the Triads, so what's up? Having trust issues again?"

"Bringing them in to clean this up exposes you."

He wasn't wrong. Even if I hid during whatever operation breached the hideout and apprehended Thackery and his latest menagerie of monsters, there was nothing to stop Thackery from flapping his yap about me. He wanted my blood. Would the Triads turn down a deal from Thackery? Me for whatever new weapons or defenses he'd devised against the Dregs? Hell, what if he offered them a vaccine against vampire bites? The idea of such a thing, its base components likely coursing through my veins, horrified me as much as it thrilled me. No more Hunters lost to accidental bites.

Was Thackery good enough to develop a cure for existing Halfies as well?

"What about the Bloods?" I asked.

"They're just as risky, Evy. They're a very logical

species and will likely see the potential in the science Thackery has to offer in exchange for his life. I don't know if I trust them not to turn on us if a reason presents itself."

Good point. Vampires preferred logic to emotions and had no apparent qualms about sacrificing their own in order to achieve a greater goal. Their MO of late was to observe and lend a hand when necessary. I'd received help from Isleen, a daughter of the royal family of Bloods, and I trusted her with my life. (Easy to do when she'd saved it once.) I didn't trust any of the others. Not as far as I could throw their skinny, pale, white-haired asses.

"Well, the three of us aren't going to be much good on our own," I said. "We know Thackery's not working alone. He at least has that blond kid, and who knows how many other people?"

"You have a point, and the fewer people we tell about this little operation, the fewer birdies can fly over and warn him."

"Still doesn't mean we don't need backup."

"Makes quite the predicament."

"I admit," Phin said, "this conversation surprises me."

I twisted around in my seat. He was behind Wyatt, hands folded in his lap, pensive. "What do you mean?"

"You can imagine the benefits of Thackery's work for your people, and yet you hesitate to allow the Triads access to it?"

"I can't say I automatically trust it in their hands, no."

"Would you risk it falling into the hands of another race? My people, for example? The vampires? Or, worse, the goblins?"

My stomach clenched. "The goblins haven't been much of a threat since Olsmill. They aren't exactly known for their higher thinking skills, so they'd have little use for vaccines and hybrids."

"And yet the risk remains. Will the technology fall into the hands of humans or Dregs?" His use of the derogatory word—one he'd made no bones about hating—was deliberate. It drove his point home good and hard.

I glanced at Token, curled up in the far corner of the seat. His brown eyes watched me intently from behind crossed arms. I thought of the stone boy in that lab, dead on a gurney, and Token's words. Had the stone boy been subjected to terrible torture at the hands of Erickson's science team? Probably. The hybrids were new to all of us—none had existed in our lifetimes, and in the course of a month, we'd seen a dozen different kinds. Thackery had created the hounds that had nearly killed me—all claws and teeth and long, muscled torsos. What if he was making more? And this time it wasn't just a power-crazed elf who set them loose on the city?

No matter what it meant for my future and the weird new blood pumping through my veins, I couldn't let nonhumans have Thackery's research. Even the ones I considered allies.

"Once we know it's not a trap, we call in the Triads," I said, speaking with confidence I didn't feel. I turned back around. "They're best equipped to go in and clean up the place. We've been cleaning up Dreg messes for years. This shouldn't be that hard."

Phin made an indeterminate noise. Less than a growl, more than a grunt.

I ignored Phin's annoyance. "We'll tell Kismet first, so she can put her game face on and act surprised when she sees me. Then report it to Baylor or Morgan."

Wyatt nodded.

I watched the city streets course by, bringing us closer to the park. The whole plan hinged on Token actually finding his old nesting grounds, as promised—a result I started doubting when I looked up. The western sky was darkening on the horizon, thick with navy clouds. An early-summer storm was coming, and if it hit before Token reached his destination, we were screwed.

Despite its name, Grove Park wasn't very green. A few years ago, a team of kids from the local university branch came up with a community outreach program that involved bringing the joy of gardening to the poorer folk of Mercy's Lot. Someone donated an empty lot sandwiched among several blocks of crumbling, run-down brick row houses, and those students worked over a weekend. The trees they planted had died and been replaced several times, and spring flowers managed to bloom in the tended beds on the north border, but the rest of it had been overtaken by the local kids.

Grass was beaten down to packed earth around a makeshift basketball hoop, at least two feet lower than regulation. Two wooden benches sat near an old bird-bath someone had filled with fake flowers, now faded with age and weather. A dirt pit had been dug out and lined with cement blocks—the poor man's version of a sandbox.

We parked a block away on the south-bordering street. Without immediate access to—and with no real time to locate—any sort of tracking device, we'd agreed to follow Phin visually as best we could. If we lost him, we'd hang back and wait for a phone call.

Residents strolled down the uneven sidewalks but paid us little attention. It was easy to be anonymous in the Lot. No one minded your business until you tried minding theirs. Dregs loved it for that simple reason.

"Don't go inside when you get there," I said to Token, repeating myself for at least the third time in as many minutes. "Just wait for us."

"Token understands," he replied. He nodded sagely,

but his small frame trembled like an autumn leaf on a dying branch.

"We should begin," Phin said. "The storm is approaching quickly."

He wasn't kidding. In the last ten minutes of our trip, it had crept across a quarter of the western sky, hiding the sun and casting a murky shadow over the city. The energy in the storm made the air around us heavy, thick—like nothing I'd ever felt before. Wyatt had always seemed restless during thunderstorms, and he'd once told me it messed with control of his Gift. Now that I felt it, too, I understood why.

"Get going, then," I said.

Phin nodded. He'd left his shirt off and had already removed his shoes. When he unzipped his jeans, I turned back around to face front. Seconds later came a familiar sound, not unlike Velcro when it's pulled apart slowly. Then the flap of wings and his osprey form jumped into the front seat between us. He ruffled his brown-and-white feathers and waited.

I opened my door and climbed out. Phin flew up and over to the roof of a neighboring house. Token came next, slower, still trembling. He'd be hard to disguise, with his strange skin and fangs, but most folks wouldn't look. Or they'd convince themselves they hadn't seen him.

Token scampered across the street and ducked behind a parked car. I caught glimpses as he raced down the sidewalk toward Grove Park, intent on his new task. Or eager to escape and be free. With Phin watching, we'd know soon if Token intended to betray us.

I slid back into my seat and slammed the door, antsy now, static tickling the deep corners of my mind. Even parked in the middle of an urban street, it occurred to me that I was alone with Wyatt for the first time since the bedroom. Not that it was the time or place for any real conversation, so I leaned forward, elbows on knees, and watched the sky near the park.

"How do you feel?" Wyatt asked.

"Fine. The headache's mostly gone, and my wrist is definitely on the mend. Probably take a few hours to fully heal, though."

"I knew those teleports would be hard on you—"

"Can we not talk about it? It hurt like a fucking bitch, but I did it. Moving on."

"Fine." He should have just said, "I'm letting this go for now, but we're talking about it later." "I admit, Evy, I didn't think you'd want the Triads involved in this."

Still no movement above the park. "I don't, but they're really the lesser of all evils, aren't they?"

"I don't mean about Thackery. I mean you. Let's look past the fact that you're supposed to be twice-dead. What if Thackery tells them what he did to you? They may want to turn you over to Erickson."

"As if I'd let them. I'd rather die a third death than become anyone's guinea pig, and you can quote me."

He didn't reply. Several minutes had passed without our seeing Phin in the ever-darkening sky. Either Token had been unable to pick up his own scent, or something was wrong. Neither possibility thrilled me.

"Storm's close. Do you feel it, Evy? Like a live current running along your tap to the Break?"

"Yeah, I do. I don't suppose this means our Gifts will work extra good during the storm?"

"The storm can give you more power, but it also messes like hell with your control. You may accidentally use your Gift without tapping into your emotional trigger."

"Good to know."

Another minute and nothing. A young couple scurried down the street on the opposite side, holding hands and laughing. Probably trying to get home before the bottom fell out. Even the few robins I'd seen earlier were gone, hiding from what was coming. My anxiety level tipped the scales, souring my stomach and ratcheting up my heart rate.

"It's going to rain soon," Wyatt said. "It'll wash away any trail left."

Come on, Phin, where are you? "I'm going to check out the roof nearest the park."

"Evy—"

"Save it. I'm going."

His hand circled my left wrist, a gentle pressure. The touch sent my pulse racing, spurred as much by him as the storm. "I was going to say concentrate. The storm's going to play with your Gift. Don't let the power unfocus you."

"I won't."

He let go. I pulled the roofie-ammo gun out of my jeans with my left hand. The steady ache-itch in my right was a frustrating distraction, but one I could live with for now. I eyed the farthest house on the block, trying to recall anything I knew about the roofs of these houses. Usually flat, some with access from below.

I closed my eyes. My tap into the Break flared like a lighthouse beacon, flashing through my mind and body in a current of live energy. I flew apart faster than ever and zinged toward the roof. My direction shifted, spinning toward the west, drawn by the power of the thunderstorm. I yanked away from it. Grasped for the roof. Back again, then forward. Pulled in one direction but desperate to go in the other.

No! Another mental jerk got me over the house, and I let go of my tap. I spilled onto the tarred roof in a tumble of limbs, banging my wounded wrist hard enough to send flares of white-hot pain through my arm and shoulder. Not my most graceful landing ever.

I scrambled to my feet, heedless of the new headache

pounding behind my eyes. It would go away, just like the others. A quick scan of the rooftop revealed no one, osprey or otherwise. I crabbed toward the edge of the roof overlooking the park and peered down. Four teens were gathering their shirts, done with their basketball game, but that was it. No Token, and no Phin.

Spinning around, I sat hard on the tar-paper roof, back to the short wall, gun loose in my hand. A light splattering of raindrops plinked off the roof and left dark spots on my jeans. Could I have missed seeing Phin fly off? No, he would have made sure we'd spotted him before tailing Token.

Music tinkled nearby, a muffled orchestral tune I didn't know. I stuffed the gun into the back of my jeans and crept down the length of the roof, toward the northern end of the house, until I found the source. A black case blended into the ground, the perfect size for a pair of glasses. I picked up the case and pried it open.

It wasn't the ringing cell phone—identical to the phone we'd found with Willemy's body—that made my stomach wrench. It was the careless wad of brown-and-white feathers stuffed into the case next to it.

Chapter Thirteen

I plucked out the phone, snapped the case shut, and slipped it into my back pocket, determined to shove the whole thing right up Thackery's ass the next time we met.

Secured line, private number, just like before. "Are the chicken feathers supposed to scare me?" I snarled into the phone.

Thackery's deep, rumbling laugh made me want to reach through the line and throttle him. "You know whose feathers they are, Ms. Stone. Don't play dumb. It doesn't suit you."

"Why don't you come out so we can chat in person?"

"I don't like the rain and despise getting wet."

The rain was growing heavier, a steady drizzle that soaked my thin T-shirt and weighed down my jeans. I shielded the phone with my bandaged hand. "So what? You just wanted your hybrid back and thought you'd kidnap a member of the Assembly of Clan Elders while you were at it?"

"That particular hybrid is of no use to me. He's yours to do with as you wish."

Telling him that I didn't have Token seemed kind of stupid, so I kept it to myself. Token was probably wandering the streets in the rain, hoping to sniff his way back home, with no idea we'd lost him. Shit.

"As for the shape-shifter," Thackery continued, "his

position as an Elder is an unfortunate circumstance. I'm more interested in the fact that he's a friend of yours."

"Fuck you" died on my lips. I had to keep calm, even though my temper had reached its boiling point. Thackery knew we'd be here. He knew we'd be tracking Token somehow, and he'd taken Phin to use against me. "I don't respond well to threats."

"So I've heard. Think of this as a negotiation, then, not a threat, because you have a decision to make."

"Let me guess? Me and my special blood for Phin's life?"

"Among other things, yes."

"Which means what?"

"Very soon your loyalties will be put to the ultimate test, and you will have to make a decision about where you stand."

I snorted. "Like I haven't heard that before. I don't suppose you want to save me a little time and effort and tell me who betrayed me to you?"

" 'Betrayed' is such a strong word in this particular case, as their loyalty was never to you."

Not helpful. Thunder rumbled loudly overhead, reminding me I hadn't seen the start of the real storm. My insides vibrated with its power. "When do we do this?"

"Are you injured?"

"What does it matter?" If my betrayer was as close as I assumed, Thackery should know I was hurt.

"It matters to Phineas."

Bastard. "I have a broken wrist."

"How long will it take to heal?"

"Completely heal?"

"Yes."

"Maybe twelve hours."

"Are you lying?"

"Do you want it partially healed or completely? And why the hell do you care if I'm injured?"

"Because I prefer my test subjects to be in the best possible shape when they come to me. I had only intended to take samples of your blood, Ms. Stone, but you couldn't let it happen, so now this has to. I need those samples."

"I couldn't let it happen?" I was on my feet pacing, sneakers slapping against the wet roof with each step. Rage tore through me like an electric shock. "Do you have any fucking clue what that trickster you sent did to me?"

Something I said surprised him, because several long beats preceded his reply. "I underestimated the trickster's need to follow its instincts. For whatever it did to you, I am sorry."

"Shove it up your ass, Thackery! You aren't worried about what I'll do in the next twelve hours? That I could still find you? Maybe even get myself killed before you get your precious blood?"

"I think you'll take care not to do anything that will force me to kill your shape-shifting friend. I have no qualms about angering the Assembly, so please do not assume my threat is empty."

The image of Rhys Willemy, bled dry and impaled on a wall, flashed in my brain. "Trust me, I'm done assuming things about you."

"Good. We'll speak again in twelve hours."

I fought hard for control as I put the phone in the pocket opposite the case. The rain beat down harder, ice-cold, stinging the bare skin on my arms and face. I shivered, gooseflesh breaking out over my neck and down the backs of my legs. I'd been played for a fucking fool by someone today, and I was determined to have that person's head on a pike before the end of my twelve hours.

*   *   *

Wyatt practically flew out of the car when he spotted me jogging down the street toward him. I'd found a fire escape on the back of the building and saved myself another topsy-turvy teleporting trip. He stopped a few steps in front of the car, alert, probably checking to see if I was being followed. I waved him back into the car and piled in moments later, panting and dripping rainwater.

"Christ, Evy, you were gone so long—what's wrong?" He saw it in my face and went very still.

"Thackery knew we'd be here. He has Phin." I used his stunned silence to elaborate on the phone conversation, Token's MIA status, and Thackery's demands. By the time I finished, my anger had tempered into determination: find the person who'd betrayed me and rip their goddamned head off. After I got every possible answer that head had to offer, of course.

"Twelve hours," Wyatt whispered. "That's not a lot of time."

"It's what we've got. Thackery knows I'll try to find him before the time is up, and he also knows I won't let Phin die if I can stop it."

"If you trade yourself for Phin, you give Thackery exactly what he wants. He'll have the components of a biological weapon capable of devastating this city. Hell, the world if he wants."

"So what do you expect me to do, Wyatt? Tell Thackery to go fuck himself when he calls back? Let him murder Phin, probably after he tortures him for fun?"

His silence was my answer.

"Screw that, Truman. Phin's my friend, and I'm supposed to be the good guy here. The good guy doesn't sacrifice her friends."

"She does when she's protecting the greater good."

I snorted. "Don't feed me that clichéd bull—"

"Thackery's a pragmatist, Evy. He won't use his weapon until he's got his antidote, and he doesn't have that yet. We can keep him from getting it, which means keeping you away from him." He inhaled, held it, exhaled. "Phineas cares about you. He'd understand."

An angry bark—not a sob, not a growl—tore from my throat. "Why not? Everyone I care about eventually gets taken away. I guess it's just Phin's turn, right?"

Wyatt flinched back as if struck. I didn't care. Time hadn't run out yet. The clock had only just been set. I still had options, and until the clock ticked down to its final seconds, sacrificing Phin's life wasn't one of them.

"We need to find David and Kismet," I said, done with the argument. Wyatt fumbled for his cell as I continued. "David is the only person not in this car or being held hostage who knew the plan."

"You think David's playing the other side?"

"It was either him or Kismet, if he gave her the details when I asked him not to, or anyone she—"

"This entire fiasco with Thackery's been off the books. I can't imagine she's brought any other teams in."

"But you don't know." The glare I shot in his general direction went unnoticed—he was concentrating on his phone. Waiting for the call to connect.

He frowned, cleared it, then tried another number. The frown deepened. "She's not answering her cell." He snapped his phone shut. It fell into his lap as he turned the key, revving the engine. "The landline at the cabin is disconnected. Keep trying her cell."

I plucked the phone from between his legs and hit Redial every couple of minutes. It rang and rang, then jumped to voice mail. The phone wasn't off, so she was either ignoring our call or out of cell range. The latter meant she was at the cabin, which had lost its phone connection.

The city passed in a silent blur. A dozen different scenarios played out in my head—what we might find at the cabin, who might have ratted us out and why, and what I'd do to that person when I got a confession out of him or her. It had been close to two hours since we left David at the cabin, but only one hour since we told him to call Kismet. One hour or two, it was enough time to set us up.

We turned onto the two-track driveway with the full force of the storm beating down on us. Rain swept through the trees, driving water, leaves, and small branches against the car like shrapnel. Thunder and lightning came almost simultaneously, brightening the twilight sky every few seconds. Even with the headlights and the wipers on high, navigation was slow.

I gave up on the phone and leaned forward, squinting through the maelstrom, ready to jump out of my skin. Each lightning crack snapped in my mind, urging me to use the Break. Slip in, shatter, and let it take me away. My mouth was dry, my breathing erratic.

"Do you always feel like this?" I asked. "Ready to fly apart at any moment?"

"It never gets easier," he replied.

Terrific.

Another flash illuminated the cabin. No lights shone in the windows, casting it back into darkness in between bolts of lightning. We rounded a bend and thumped through a rut in the road. I leaned so far my nose was nearly pressed against the windshield, trying to make out a twisted shape ahead. Rain roared against the car. Lightning broke across the sky and showed me the shape. Four tires were all that identified the skeleton of someone's vehicle.

"Wyatt—"

Glass exploded as my door caved in. I cracked my chin off the dashboard and flew sideways, hitting Wyatt and the steering wheel with equal force. The car spun, fishtailed, then slammed trunk-first into something hard. The rear windshield spiderwebbed. We stopped. The engine sputtered.

Rain poured through my broken window, twisted like a gaping mouth, jagged teeth of glass sticking up from the bottom. A shadow moved in the darkness. I shivered. My chin stung. Blood dripped down my neck.

"Evy?" Wyatt's hand was on my shoulder, skating down my arm.

"I'm okay. We need to get out of here."

"Right."

The entire car shook as something large and heavy slammed down on the center of the hood, sending cracks through the windshield. The engine died with a wheezing gasp. Through the pouring rain, a hulking, horrifyingly familiar shape was lit up by the raging storm—a hound. A beast of Hell genetically created to house a demon—part human, part goblin, part vampire. They ran on rage and bloodlust, and were damned hard to kill.

Somewhere behind us, one of them howled.

"Oh my God," Wyatt said.

I reached behind me without looking, unable to tear my gaze away from the open door. I expected snapping jaws to lunge for my throat at any moment. "Take my hand."

He did. I let the power of the storm drag us into the Break, and it took all of me to hold on to Wyatt. Buffeted by power from two sources, I grasped at the thin strings of the Break, desperate not to lose us both to nothingness. I felt trees and leaves and rain and knew we couldn't be out here when we materialized. We needed the shelter of the cabin.

I tugged us there, drumming up an image of the main room's interior. The far corner, away from the kitchen and bedroom. No windows that I recalled, less likely for someone to be standing watch. Or standing at all. I saw it. I felt it. But I couldn't get there.

The hand clasping Wyatt's tingled—power surged through me from that single point of contact, as though someone had turned on a second tap into the Break. I didn't ponder it, didn't question the reason, just tugged on that extension cord and used the energy to focus on the cabin. Through the solid walls, out of the fury of the storm, I dragged us indoors. My body shrieked as we passed. I saw our destination in my mind and fled for it.

The Break didn't want to let us go. I fought against the storm. Pushed, pulled, kicked, and screamed my way free. Pressure closed around me like a fist, trying to squeeze me into nothing. My body was on fire. Letting go seemed easier. Simpler and less painful. Except I wasn't alone. Wyatt's tap flooded me, tinged with aftershocks of arrogance—his emotional trigger.

I battled the agony and hit the hardwood floor in a wet, tangled heap, with Wyatt on top of me. Tremors raced up and down my body. I coughed and cried out when it sent daggers of pain through my head. Wyatt rolled away. I curled in tight, arms around my knees, eyes shut, desperate to balance myself again. Just focused on breathing steadily and staying whole when my entire body wanted to shatter.

Wyatt's soothing voice was in my ear, his hand pressed between my shoulder blades. I let his touch center me and draw me away from the fury of the storm. A clap of thunder broke directly over the house. I jumped, then slowly sat up.

We were about where I'd expected, in the corner of a room that had changed drastically since we'd left. The couch was on its side, shoved lengthwise against the front door. The bedroom dresser created a similar barrier over one of the windows. Deep scores in the wood floor marked the path of the refrigerator from kitchen to living room, and it stood against the other window. A blanket-covered lump was by the couch. The bedroom mattress was laid out against the wall by the open bedroom door and held a second blanket-covered lump, and two blood-covered people bore down on us.

"Not that I'm ungrateful for the rescue attempt," Kismet said, a deep bruise coloring her left temple and both eyes red, swollen, "but I'm guessing your car is in as great a shape as mine?" She looked weary, strained, ready to be bowled over by the gentlest breeze.

"Engine's crushed," Wyatt replied. "What the hell happened?"

She offered her hand; he took it and was pulled to his feet. Milo offered me his, face pinched and pale, right forearm patched with a red-stained dish towel. I accepted his help, struggling to stand. My vision darkened briefly, and I blinked it away. Brown hair poked out of the blanket lump tucked onto the mattress—Felix. My attention flickered to the other lump and the dark stains soaking through the blanket. My stomach roiled at the strong odor of blood.

"We got here about forty-five minutes ago, right before the rain started," Kismet said. "David explained what was going on, where you three had gone— Wait." She looked around. "He said the shape-shifter was with you."

"He was," I said. So David had told her the details of our plan. Just great.

She nodded as though my two words explained everything. "We got the trickster secured in my vehicle. Milo was closing up the cabin. The rest of us were in the yard. The hounds attacked out of nowhere. We didn't know they were there until one jumped on Felix." She cast a look over her shoulder, at her wounded Hunter. "Our bullets didn't affect them much, so we retreated to the cabin. David covered us while Milo and I dragged Felix inside. . . ."

Milo took over the story where she fumbled for words, fuming as he relived the incident. "The hounds were going after the cars, so we thought we'd have time. I could hear the trickster screaming in the SUV, but we couldn't get to him."

The trickster was dead, which meant his *enisi* was no longer a useful hostage.

"The hounds each took David by a leg. We got half of him inside." Milo blanched. "He died pretty fast."

A thick lump stuck in my throat. "Felix?"

"He's hurt bad. They shredded his back all to hell, and he's lost a lot of blood." Milo inhaled sharply, his eyes gleaming. "The hounds were breaking the windows and trying the door. The bastards knew what they were doing, too, because we spent all our ammunition missing them. Gina and I barricaded ourselves as best we could."

"No cell service," Kismet said. "The landline is out, too. Every once in a while, they'll hit a wall to remind us they're outside."

"They destroyed all the cars," Wyatt said. "They knocked ours into a tree."

Milo gave me a pensive look. "Good thing you've got your little teleporting trick, huh?"

I didn't feel so lucky. Another Hunter was dead—worse still, he'd been my number one suspect. "Kismet, did you report the apprehension of the trickster before the attack?"

"No."

"You didn't test the landline?"

"No."

David had to have used it to call Kismet, so it must have been tampered with afterward. Were the hounds that smart? Or had David really been playing us, setting

Kismet's team up to die, giving Axon to the hounds on a platter? Had the hounds turned on him by accident?

Was I grasping at fucking straws?

"So no one else knew you were coming up here?" I asked. "And no one except David knew about the trickster?"

"Tybalt knew we were coming here, but not about the trickster."

Tybalt knew. . . . Nope. I derailed that line of doubt before it even began. No fucking way. "How long do you think it'll take him to worry?"

"Morning, maybe. He'll probably call in and see if my location is on the books. When it's not, he might alert someone."

"Might." Less than twelve hours to find Thackery. "I can't sit here overnight and hope on might."

"No shit," Milo snapped. "Felix needs a hospital, or he's going to die."

Shame silenced me. Two lives hinged on a very small time frame.

"How are you for weapons?" Wyatt asked.

My hands flew to my waist. At some point, I'd lost the roofie gun. Perfect.

"We have three guns but no ammo," Kismet said. "Two hunting knives of ours, plus a few different knives from the kitchen. I found a shotgun in the closet, no shells. Everything else is in what's left of the car." And every Handler's official vehicle had a hidden cache of weapons. A cache we needed—and soon.

"Is it just the two hounds?" Wyatt asked.

"From what we can tell, yes."

As if they knew we were discussing them, a heavy body slammed against the front door, shuddering the sofa. Kismet jumped, as on-edge as I've ever seen her. A groan rang out over the steady pounding of rain on the roof. Milo bolted to the mattress. He crouched next to his friend and took his hand, speaking too softly to hear. I didn't envy him the fear and anguish of watching a beloved partner die—emotions with which I was all too familiar.

"There's no attic in this place?" I asked. "Nowhere else useful things could be stored?"

Wyatt shook his head. "It's an out-of-season hunting cabin that was closed up until fall when we brought you here."

I clenched my fists, then winced as the healing bones in my right wrist protested the action with white-hot shrieks. The bandage was soaked, my clothes were soaked, Wyatt was soaked, and we were all royally screwed.

"What happened to you two?" Kismet asked.

Wyatt fielded the question, filling her in loudly enough for Milo to hear. I knelt next to him. Felix's eyes were closed, but he wasn't asleep. His lips were pressed so hard they were white. Pain creased his forehead and furrowed his brow, and he squeezed Milo's hand so tight I expected to hear bones snap. Above the pallor, two roses had sprouted on his cheeks. Sweat beaded on his skin. I gently pressed the back of my left hand to one of those roses of color—hot. Not good.

"Guess if that was you, you'd be healing by now," Milo whispered. The words would have stung had there been any ire in his voice, but I heard only sorrow and didn't reply.

"Wait a minute," Kismet said once Wyatt reached the part where we'd fled the city. "You think David Moreau, who found his Handler's dead body a week ago and who is lying on the floor in pieces right now, set you up?"

"It's a theory, Gina," Wyatt replied. "You said you didn't find out about our plan until David told you, and you didn't call anyone to inform them, and I believe you. He's the only person—"

"No." Milo's bark attracted everyone's attention. He looked up at Kismet, his face a queer mix of dread and fascination. "David wasn't the only person who knew about you guys stealing the goblin-hybrid. You're all missing the obvious."

I stared, not following his train of thought at all, and willing him to just say it and end the suspense. It was Wyatt who supplied the answer. "Boot Camp," he said, gazing down at me. I met his onyx eyes, cowed by the sudden fury I saw in them. "Erickson, or someone at R&D. You said you heard somebody coming right before you teleported out. They knew almost immediately that Token was gone."

"Yeah, okay," I said. Putting the pieces together still wasn't my strongest suit. "And?"

Kismet made a choking sound, obviously coming to the same conclusion as the men in the room. "You think someone in R&D told Thackery you stole Token, and Thackery guessed at what you wanted him for, don't you?"

My insides quivered, and I felt faint. Absolutely impossible. Accepting their theory meant accepting that someone inside Boot Camp was a traitor. Or playing both sides, which amounted to the same damned thing. I couldn't look away from the blazing fury in Wyatt's eyes.

"Yeah," he said. "That's exactly what I think."

Chapter Fourteen

I pulled a bottle of water from the fridge, cracked the top off, and gulped down half of it before taking a breath. The cold liquid spilled into my empty, roiling stomach and did little to calm it. But my mouth was soothed, my lips less parched. My brain more able to correctly process thoughts and participate in planning our escape.

Priority one was killing the hounds and getting the hell out of Dodge. All other discussion of traitors and backstabbing had ceased in favor of pondering that particular problem. The simplest fact remained unchanged, taunting us: all the weapons we needed were outside, at least twenty feet from the cabin, trapped in the twisted remains of Kismet's SUV. Anyone who tried going outside would be attacked. I'd briefly entertained the notion of teleporting to the car and testing my luck, but I didn't dare broach the idea. The storm continued raging, screwing with my control, and even if I did manage to materialize in the correct place, I'd have to somehow get to the weapons before the Hounds got me.

No, no one was going outside.

A warm hand pushed a lock of damp hair off my shoulder. I offered Wyatt the water. He finished off the bottle and cringed, probably as seasick as me.

"I wanted to ask," he said, keeping his voice low. "When we teleported in, did you feel . . . ? I don't know, could you tap into . . . ? How did . . . ?" He couldn't quite figure out the question he wanted to ask.

"I think we shared our taps," I said, turning to face him. For the first time, I noticed a darkening bruise on his cheek, probably from the crash into the tree. "When I was struggling to get us into the cabin, I felt your power. It gave me what I needed to get us here."

Curiosity changed to wonder. "I didn't know Gifted could do that."

"Maybe no one's ever tried."

"Or tried during a thunderstorm when our energy is amped up."

I nodded, then froze as an impossible scenario became suddenly less so.

Wyatt took a step closer. "Evy, what?"

"I just had the wildest idea to get the weapons cache in here with us. You can use the power of the storm, have me as a backup battery, and summon it right into the cabin."

His eyes unfocused as he considered my suggestion. I could almost see the hamster wheel going. He smiled proudly. "I think that just might work. But it's risky."

"So's sitting around all night hoping to be rescued."

"I've noticed." He spun around. Kismet and Milo were still sitting with Felix, giving us room. She looked up when Wyatt walked toward them. "Which window's got the best view of your car?"

Kismet pointed at the refrigerator. "There. Why?"

"We've got an idea, so just bear with us a minute. And you might want to take Felix into the bedroom."

She seemed poised to question him. Instead, she stood up, and she and Milo began dragging the bloody mattress and its burden into the other room.

Wyatt and I pushed the fridge a few inches to the right, just enough to give him a peek outside. Two of the panes were broken, the rest cracked, but the frame was intact. Rain blew inside, peppering his cheek. He peered out, then jumped when something roared. We shoved the fridge back into place.

"Okay, I can see where it is," he said, wiping the water from his face. "Are you sure—"

"Yes, I want to do this." I squeezed his arm. "Phin and Felix are counting on us."

"Guys?" Kismet asked from the bedroom doorway. "What exactly are you up to?"

"We're getting those weapons," Wyatt said. "Close the door."

She acquiesced without argument. I shoved the coffee table into the corner, giving us a completely open space. We went to stand by the cold fireplace.

"I'll need my hands free," he said. "Maybe if you're behind me?"

I circled to his back and looped my arms beneath his, up and around to clasp his shoulders. My breasts pressed hard into his back, and our heartbeats hammered together, speeding faster with the strength of the storm.

"Tell me when to tap in," I said, resting my chin on his shoulder. Power crackled through him, and I felt his tap as keenly as I'd felt it before, energized by the electrical output of the thunderstorm. Wild and unpredictable and laced with the scent of ozone. My nose tingled.

"Now, Evy."

My emotional trigger was easy to find, and the input from the Break surged through me like a lightning strike. The hairs on my arms and neck stood straight. Faint tremors traveled between our bodies, tiny sparks of power being shared through our connection. I pushed that power forward, feeding everything I could into Wyatt's Gift.

He made a noise—not quite a groan, but nothing pleasant. I held on, fighting my own Gift's attempts to break us apart and send us flying elsewhere. I concentrated on the wood floor beneath me, the walls around us, the exact spot on which we stood. We weren't leaving; we were bringing something to us.

The air snap-crackled. Thunder broke overhead, and the rumble seemed to last forever. Over and over, growing louder, until it broke again in a deafening clap. I squeezed Wyatt tighter, pressing my face into his shoulder. Just held on as raw power coursed through me and into him. My throat hurt, and I realized too late that I was screaming.

So was he.

A sound like a cannon shot rattled the walls, and the pressure in the room changed as air displaced. Wyatt collapsed, and I fell with him, afraid to let go until I was certain it was finished. His tap was gone. I no longer felt power from him. I let my tap go, and the surge of storm energy ceased, leaving me shivering and cold. Drained like a wrung-out sponge.

I opened my eyes and blinked away the dryness. Stared over Wyatt's shoulder. The entire rear half of Kismet's SUV was in the middle of the cabin, dripping with rainwater, a twisted hunk of metal and tires and broken glass. The stink of motor oil joined the already rank smells inside the cabin.

"Holy fuck," Kismet said from the bedroom door. "You did it."

"We did it," I said. "Wyatt?"

Nothing.

I pulled out from beneath him and gently rolled him onto his back. His chest rose and fell. Blood trickled from both nostrils and stained his upper lip and chin. He was paler than his complexion had any right to be. I checked his pulse with trembling fingers—weak, but steady.

"Is he okay?" Kismet squatted on his other side, her green eyes wide.

"He just needs to rest."

She left and returned with a spare blanket and pillow. It wasn't an ideal spot, but I tucked the pillow under his head, careful not to jostle. He'd have a big enough headache when he woke up. My own head was throbbing steadily, but I ignored it in favor of seeing to him. He'd always taken care of me. I wiped his face with a corner of the blanket, kissed his cheek, and stood.

Dizziness nearly toppled me, so I stood still, trying to get my bearings.

Kismet and Milo were attacking the remains of her car, attempting to get at the rear compartment. I wandered into the bathroom and shivered as I remembered the last time I'd walked out of it. Had it been only that morning? It felt like a lifetime ago.

I rummaged in the medicine cabinet and found a bottle of ibuprofen. I dry-swallowed three. As I closed the cabinet, I caught my reflection—dark circles stood out beneath both eyes like identical shiners. The cuts from the glass had healed, but my healing power couldn't seem to stay on top of the wear and tear of using my Gift. Unless it was from something else—something like the petri dish my body had become for Thackery's benefit.

My blood had the potential to fight off vampiric parasites. Too bad it couldn't heal the wounds of others. I'd have gladly offered a pint to Felix if it meant saving his life. I didn't want any more Hunters dying because of their association with me.

In the main room, they'd managed to clear a path wide enough for Kismet to climb into the wreckage; sometimes being five foot two and gymnast-fit had advantages. She was passing weapons out to Milo, who dutifully piled them on the floor. Guns, clips, knives, a short sword, throwing stars, silver spikes, a few grenades—we might just have a chance at killing those hounds.

"That's all I can reach," Kismet said. She wiggled her way back out of the wreck, clothes damp, and ran a hand through her short, red hair. "Now we just need an attack plan."

"We can't fight them hand to hand," I said. "Our best bet is the guns."

"Agreed. We've got frag and a-c clips, plus three flash grenades."

"Flash won't do much in this weather. We may want to wait a little longer for the storm to move out. The wind and rain will make it too difficult to aim."

"We don't have a lot of time."

"I know, but we've seen the heart of the storm. I can feel the change. Give it half an hour to die down."

She nodded, then started arranging the weapons. I'd expected more of a fight.

Wyatt was still out cold. His pulse beat a little stronger, and his color was better. I sat with him for a few minutes, watching him sleep. How I'd ever believed the trickster had been this man next to me, I didn't know. The visual had been perfect, but even shape-shifters can't replicate a person's heart and soul. Can't replicate a smell or taste. I pressed my lips to his forehead and inhaled. So familiar, so completely him.

"Wake up for me," I whispered.

He didn't.

"Do you really think someone at Boot Camp is responsible for this?" Kismet asked.

"I don't want to," I replied, "even though it makes sense. Look at the hounds outside. Someone had enough time to warn Thackery that we had Token, and I'm positive Thackery's smart enough to have anticipated how we'd use him."

"Why work with someone like Thackery? His research is unnatural."

"Roofie rounds."

"What?"

I gazed up at her from my crouched position. "We do research similar to it at R&D, don't we? We have frag bullets that can pierce gargoyle hide and a-c's that make even the strongest vampires bleed out. Could you imagine the power we'd have if we could inoculate humans against a vampire's bite? Eradicating the Halfie problem would make our jobs so much easier, and no one else would have to suffer like Alex did."

Kismet looked at the ammunition box in her hands.

I dropped my forehead onto my palm. The power to save other people from Halfie infection could be coursing through my veins, hiding in my blood. Or Thackery's theory was full of shit, and I was getting my hopes way up.

"So you . . . what?" Kismet asked. "You agree with this possible traitor?"

My head snapped up, cheeks blazing. "Not even a little fucking bit. The research could be helpful, but it's no excuse for turning on us."

"Doing what you think is right isn't reason enough to turn against the people you work with?"

I started to blast off a retort, then snapped my mouth shut. She wasn't talking about this mystery person at Boot Camp. Her intense green eyes gazed at me, hard and piercing, daring me to answer. Goading me into denying I'd done the exact same thing.

Dammit, I hated being called on my own mistakes.

A groan saved me from answering. Wyatt was blinking at the ceiling with bloodshot eyes and trying to sit up. I pushed him back down.

"Did it work?" he asked.

"It worked." I placed a palm flat on his chest, rubbing gentle circles. "You did good. We've got weapons."

"I think . . ." He swallowed hard. "I think I'm going to be sick."

I helped him half run, half crawl into the bathroom, and I rubbed his back while he threw up. When retching turned to dry heaves, I soaked a rag in warm water and wiped his face. The pallor was back, and his entire body trembled. I sat down with my back to the wall and pulled him into my arms, holding him against my chest like he'd done so many times for me.

"I feel so weird," he said.

"You channeled a lot of power through your body. Just relax." I didn't have a lot of practice in offering comfort. Even when Jesse and Ash were injured, I'd let them tend to each other. They'd tended to me on occasion, but some invisible thing kept me from returning the favor. From showing without words how much I cared.

Wyatt's head rested in the crook of my shoulder. I pressed my cheek to his temple, tightened my arms around him, and tried to do just that—show it without words. "I love you," I whispered.

One of his hands found mine, and our fingers threaded together, palm to palm. He kissed my knuckles, and I felt the smile on his lips.

Another hour passed before the storm showed signs of calming. The worst of it had moved beyond us, but the air remained thick with residual energy. After I forced some crackers and half a can of soup down Wyatt's throat, he seemed coherent enough to join me, Kismet, and Milo at the table.

"His fever's up," Milo said, referencing Felix without saying so. "We can't wait much longer."

"Even if we kill the hounds," Wyatt said, "how do we get off the mountain? All our cars are smashed to shit."

"Someone will have to get down where there's a signal," Kismet said. "Make a call and get some backup."

I grunted. "That could take another hour to get someone up here, and then get Felix back down." She shot me a look that asked if I had a better idea. I hated to admit I did, mostly because it was going to hurt like hell. "I can teleport him closer to the road. I'll have more control now that the storm's moving—"

"But less power," Wyatt said.

"Yes, but with the condition he's in, I need control more."

"Is that even wise?" Kismet asked. "You've been through two huge power surges, or whatever you call them, already today. Can you manage one more, and with a wounded person?"

"I can try."

"No." Milo surprised me with his sharp delivery, and even more with the cold glare he leveled in my direction.

"Milo—"

"No fucking way, Evy. You don't know these roads. You can't tell me you know exactly where to teleport so you don't land both of you inside a damned tree. You're not going to *try* with Felix's life."

"I've been up here before," Kismet said. "It's not as fast, but I can run the mountain, and I know a shortcut to the road. I'll go until I can get a signal."

"You can make it in the dark?" Wyatt asked.

"Yes." No hesitation. To me, she said, "You can't do everything, Stone. Even you have limits."

And I had no business testing those limits with someone else's life. She was right. I could get us farther down the mountain in seconds, but given the dense foliage and unfamiliar terrain, I was more likely to materialize with my legs in a boulder.

"First things first, though," Milo said. "Gina can't get help until we take care of the hounds outside."

"Back at Olsmill we hit them with a mix of frags and a-c's," Kismet said. "Underbelly is the softest hit when they're standing. But they're strong and they're fast."

Wyatt nodded. "We also can't just open the door and rush outside shooting, because they could get in here."

With Felix, who couldn't defend himself.

"So we need to ambush them," Kismet said. "Or at least distract them enough so I can slip out and get help."

"Without being followed," Milo added.

"Right."

As I gazed at our stock of weapons, an idea began to coalesce. My right hand still wasn't healed enough to hold a gun and aim properly. That left the men to handle the heavy offensive. And it left me as bait.

Kismet had one of the guns in her hand, her cell phone tucked into her pocket, and she bounced on her heels by the front door, ready to make a run for it. We'd closed Felix into the bedroom and blocked it with the dining table for good measure. Milo and Wyatt had their guns locked and loaded, and they flanked either side of the front door.

I'd tucked a hunting knife into my shoe and another into the back of my jeans for good measure. In my hands I held one of the flash grenades, a second in my front pocket. Rain still pattered gently outside, but the thunder was soft and far away. The raw electricity was barely there—a gentle caress across my skin that was easy to ignore.

Next thunderstorm, I was hiding under my bed for the duration.

"We're sure there are just two of them?" I asked.

"Pretty positive," Kismet replied, as though I hadn't asked the same question four times since we'd agreed to my plan.

On impulse, I took a step closer, lowering my voice. "You know, I never did thank you."

"Thank me? For what? After everything that's happened these last few weeks, I figure you'd rather punch me in the head than thank me."

My mouth twitched. "Thank you for bringing me here to fight off the infection."

"You're welcome."

"You could have killed me and gotten me out of everyone's hair."

She pinched the bridge of her nose with her free hand. "I don't think my friendship with Wyatt could have survived killing you twice. Even if the first time didn't take." Her voice held a hint of teasing, but nothing in her expression was amused.

"You did it for him?"

"Yes." Her gaze flickered over my shoulder. "I've known Wyatt for a long time, Stone, and I was trying to protect what he'd helped build for ten years. Bringing you here last week? That was for him, because he believed you could fight it. He never stopped believing you'd win, and he believes you'll win again now. So let's use his faith and do this."

I nodded and faced the door, adrenaline surging through me. My heart sped up and a metallic taste filled my mouth. I clenched my fist around the grenade. Bounced on my tiptoes. "Here we go," I said.

Milo and Wyatt took new positions by the sofa, prepared to shove it out of the way as soon as I disappeared. I closed my eyes and felt the spark of the Break. It was fainter than it should have been, and harder to grab. I struggled for my emotional tap, but loneliness wasn't coming easily.

I thought back to earlier in the day—a lifetime ago in some ways—that moment in the bedroom when I'd flinched and Wyatt had walked away. I tried to imagine if he'd kept going, driven out of my life by guilt. My guts clenched. Tears stung my eyes, and the power of the Break flooded through me on a sea of loneliness. I was moving, willing myself out of the cabin, to a spot ten feet from the front door. An open area of mud, according to Wyatt, and my best destination.

Rain passed through me with the oddest tickling sensation, then spattered on my skin as I materialized. Mud squished around my shoes. I immediately pulled the pin on the grenade and spun in a careful circle, looking. Waiting. Tiny shafts of light spilled from the blocked windows and closed door, barely enough to see.

A roar rattled the quiet, a terrible bass rumbling in my chest, followed by an answering growl. One on either side of me, closing in. Footsteps smacked the soaked ground. I held on to my tap. Listened. A flash of black in my peripheral vision was enough. I dropped the grenade and fell into the Break. Heard a snap, then cries of pain.

I hit the cabin floor on my knees, disoriented by something—had I been caught in the blast? I shook my head, blinking hard, aware of rapid gunfire ahead of me. Cool air wafted inside from the open cabin door. Kismet was gone. Something inhuman shrieked in agony. Wyatt shouted.

I rushed outside, into the chilly rain. One of the hounds was dead, its hulking form limp on the ground by the front half of Kismet's car, bleeding from a dozen holes. Even above the odors of wet earth and ozone, I could smell the stink of its blood.

The second was trying to crawl away with one clawed hand. Its legs dragged behind it, covered in blood from two wounds in the center of its back. It gurgled and growled, leaving a trail of brackish blood in the mud as it slithered. Milo and Wyatt trailed behind it for a few feet, fascinated by the thing's attempt to escape.

Milo circled in front of the wounded hound and stopped. It raised its head and growled. Milo squeezed off a round that shattered the hound's face. It fell, dead. His hand was shaking as he lowered his arm to his side. Rain slicked his face and hair.

"That was for Felix," he said, almost too softly to hear. He looked up, first at me, then past me. Up. His eyes bugged out.

I didn't ask, just pulled the knife from the back of my pants and started to pivot. The mud made my move awkward, and the undetected third hound slammed into my left side.

Chapter Fifteen

The hound and I toppled to the ground and skidded a few feet, my knife buried in its guts. Claws slashed at my back. Teeth snapped at my face. I thrashed like a beached fish, desperately wrenching at the knife, trying to inflict maximum damage.

Gunshots popped. The hound screamed, deafening my right ear and numbing my senses. Silver flashed above us and sliced downward. Its weight collapsed on top of me, smashing me into wet earth. The hilt of the knife jammed under my ribs so hard I expected one or two to break.

"Come on, pull!" Wyatt's voice was muffled, but no less welcome.

The body was lifted enough for me to scramble out and, finally free, collapse on the ground, breathing hard. Noxious blood coated my skin. My ribs were on fire from my left breast to the small of my back, and I could imagine the furrows that thing's claws had left behind.

"Dammit," I said. "Should've expected that."

"Can you move?" Wyatt asked, kneeling beside me in the mud.

"Yeah. Any others?"

"None so far. Milo's scouting around."

Wyatt tried to be gentle about helping me stand, but there was no way not to disturb my new wounds. We limped into the cabin. He steered me straight to the bathroom, leaving a blotchy trail of mud, rainwater, and gore behind. The hound's blood felt like acid in my open gashes. I clenched my fists, grateful for the ache in my still-healing right wrist. It gave me something to concentrate on while Wyatt turned on the shower. He helped me undress with the clinical detachment of the Handler he'd once been, and then he left and pulled the bathroom door shut behind him.

I unwound the soaked and stained bandage from my wrist. The bone was tender and the skin angry-red, but the worst of the break had healed. It could bear weight. I let myself cry through the pain as the hot shower sluiced away the hound's blood. Brown and red swirled down the drain together, and eventually the water ran clear.

Clean clothes waited for me on the back of the toilet. Underwear and bra went on first and with extra care. I twisted to look at my back in the mirror and wished I hadn't. Four long scores went from just below my breast down across my left side and stopped at the small of my back. The gashes still wept blood, the edges jagged and swollen. Just great.

I opened the door and peered out. Wyatt stopped in the middle of what appeared to be impatient pacing. "I need your hands," I said. Off his startled look, I added, "Not for that. Come here."

He came in and closed the door. I presented my back, and he hissed. "Damn, Evy, those look bad."

"No shit. Can you put some gauze on them so they don't bleed through the last of my clean clothes?"

"Yeah . . . okay." Wyatt opened the first-aid kit. "Hold your left arm up."

I did, locking it across my sternum with my right. The healing ache was still present. How close to twelve hours had it been since my phone chat with Thackery? Maybe five hours? I'd lost track of time long ago and—"Shit!"

He'd pressed too hard on a tender spot in the small of my back, igniting spikes of fire that shot all the way through me. I inhaled between gritted teeth.

"Sorry." He ripped strips of medical tape and applied them to my right shoulder for safekeeping. They tickled.

In the mirror, I watched his black hair appear and disappear behind me as he reached for bandages and tossed their wrappers. I hated how much practice he had at patching wounds. His fingers were warm, tickling in places, a little too hard in others. Each time he pulled a strip of tape off my shoulder, my skin tingled. The pain of that first touch had settled deep in my gut, where it was slowly tightening into something that squirmed at his touch.

I just closed my eyes and tried to ignore the rest of the process. The gentle presses of his fingers, the way they brushed over my bare skin as he covered my wounds. He traced lines across my ribs, testing the tape's hold. Gooseflesh prickled my shoulders.

His hand paused in the center of my back, just below my bra clasp, then withdrew. "I'm finished, Evy."

I let my left arm down, and sensation ran back into the starving muscles. Eyes still closed, I braced both hands on the edge of the sink and leaned forward. Just enough pressure to concentrate on. My left arm tingled; my right arm ached sweetly. My stomach quivered, fed by indecision and anxiety.

"Do you want me to leave, Evy?"

"No. Wyatt, I'm sorry I flinched." The words flew out before I thought about them, and it was too late to take them back.

I felt air movement. Oh no, he wasn't leaving. I turned and took a long step sideways, positioning myself in front of the door. He stopped short, hands clenched. Tension bracketed his eyes and etched fine lines around his mouth. His clothes were rain-damp, streaked with drying blood and mud, both eyes still bloodshot. Behind his front of annoyance wafted a soft breath of fear.

"I'm. Sorry. I. Flinched. I hurt you, and I didn't mean to."

Surprise widened his eyes. "That son of a bitch used my appearance to attack you, used your trust of me to get close to you, and *you're* apologizing to *me?*"

He was not getting to play the self-pity card this time around. No way in hell. "Screw that, Truman, and stop fucking blaming yourself. I know you, and I know you'd never hurt me like that."

He didn't move, didn't speak. Just stared at me from an arm's reach away, emotions warring behind his black eyes.

"Come here," I said firmly. He hesitated, then slid a half step closer. I glared. He moved again until a thin cushion of air separated us. I felt the heat of his body, the gentle puff of his breath on my cheeks. My heart fluttered. "Now hold still."

I leaned forward and pressed my forehead to his, nose to nose. His breath dusted across my lips. I inhaled. No sour smell, no unfamiliarity. Just Wyatt—heady maleness, with the barest hint of cinnamon and tomato soup. "I can smell you," I whispered, allowing my fingertips to skim his chest. "I can feel you. Not the trickster. You, Wyatt Truman."

He shuddered, his breath hitching, catching. His eyes were closed.

"You can't blame yourself every time someone tries to hurt me. You're one man. I have enemies, and I always will. You cannot always be there to save me from them. Hell, you won't always be able to save me from myself."

He choked through a bark of laughter. No, not laughter. Something else, sadder. More desperate.

I flung my arms around his shoulders and pressed my face into his neck. He pulled me close, tight to his shuddering chest, and I just held on, keenly aware of my near-nudity and how perfectly our bodies locked together. I pressed my lips to the pulse in his throat, parted them just enough to stroke it with the tip of my tongue. Tasting him. He shivered, his skin prickling.

"I don't know what I did to deserve you, Evy."

"Under different circumstances," I said, "that could be construed as an insult."

"It's definitely a compliment. You've been my life for four years."

I skimmed a fingertip down his throat to his collarbone. "I haven't given up on that happy-ending thing, you know. We just seem to have more dragons to slay than most."

"Dragons?" His lips quirked.

"Metaphorically speaking. If dragons ever start spewing across the Break, I'm moving to Antarctica, I swear to God."

He chuckled. "Not without me."

Our mouths came together with a clashing of teeth and wrestling of tongues. His taste flooded my senses, so familiar and wonderful and *him*. His cheeks were rough, unshaven since the day before, a delicious abrasion on my skin. My hands locked at the nape of his neck. The towel around my hair was loosened, and the damp locks tumbled down around us. His body pressed against me, hard in all the right places, holding me against the bathroom door.

My wounded back hissed and sputtered, and I didn't care. All I felt was him—a man who would give (and had given) up everything for me. He'd follow me anywhere and—I hoped—stay put and let me go ahead when I asked. And with Thackery's deadline looming, I knew I'd be putting that dedication to the test. Wyatt would have to let me go alone.

He pulled back, eyebrows slanted curiously. "You tensed up."

One of these days I'd learn how to control my body's reactions a little better. Instead of telling him the truth and sharing my thoughts, I lied. "Back hurts."

Worked better than a cooler of ice water. He backed off and reached for my clothes. I cleaned up a few smears of gore that had transferred from his shirt to my chest—a perfect reminder of just how fucked-up our lives were, in that his blood-smeared clothes hadn't even fazed me. He helped me into my jeans, and as he tugged my shirt down over my head, I felt my wounds start their familiar healing itch-ache. I ignored my damp hair in favor of allowing it to air-dry in whatever wavy, tangled mess it chose. Wyatt helped me put on the cross necklace, and I was grateful for its familiar weight.

The living room was empty when we emerged. The cooler air chilled my skin and sent prickles across the back of my neck. The half car sitting in a dripping heap in the center of the room still impressed me. We'd done that—together.

I checked the clock on the wall—about forty minutes since Kismet raced down the mountain. Backup should be arriving any time now. Not that we really needed backup as much as transportation. And answers. Goddamn did we need answers.

We separated then, our individual actions needing no explanation—a testament to years of working together. Wyatt went to the front door, probably to check and see if anyone was coming. I wandered into the back bedroom, amazingly wide-awake, given the hour. Milo sat cross-legged on the floor with a bowl of melting ice cubes and a pile of dish towels. He folded a dozen cubes into one of the towels, then tucked it beneath the blanket, close to Felix's body. Two similar ice packs bracketed Felix's flushed face.

"It was the only thing I could think to do," Milo said without looking up. His voice was tight, strained.

"It was a good call."

"How do you do it?"

"Do what?" I circled around and crouched next to Milo. A soft twinge wormed through my back.

He looked at me, face clouded. "Cope with losing people you love?"

His question threw me. Milo and I had been very similar in team status—the newest members of our respective Triads. While Tybalt and I had left Boot Camp within weeks of each other four years ago, Milo had been a Hunter for just over a year. Felix and Tybalt had always been there with him, and now the future looked bleak for both men.

"You haven't lost anyone yet," I said. "Maybe Tybalt won't be a Hunter anymore, but he's alive. He's strong. So's Felix."

Milo took Felix's right hand in his and squeezed tight, a gesture of solidarity and comfort. My heart ached. I'd never offered that sort of support to my former partners when they were injured. Doing so felt like exposing my own weakness to them, and I hated appearing weak—to anyone.

My years in Juvie and hard training at Boot Camp had beaten weakness out of me and replaced it with hardness. Coldness. My survival instincts were slowly crumbling now under Wyatt's persistent love and support—more powerful than the unwavering friendship I'd gotten from Jesse and Ash.

I let my gaze linger on Milo's hand and the strong, anchoring grip he had on Felix's. On the strain and barely contained grief bracketing Milo's eyes—hooded eyes that gazed at his wounded partner with a scary intensity not dissimilar to the way Wyatt sometimes looked at me. I blinked.

The new observation only reinforced how little I knew about any Hunters outside my former Triad. Hell, how little I knew about *anyone* outside my narrow little world.

"So what's our next step?" Milo asked after a few minutes of silence. "Break into Boot Camp and torture answers out of the people at R&D?"

"Nah. I plan to storm the front entrance."

His mouth quirked. "You want backup for that?"

"I'll take all the help I can get."

Then the most beautiful sound I'd heard all day rumbled in the distance—engines. I scrambled outside to stand with Wyatt and was greeted by the glare of headlights. Three sets, all from Triad Jeeps. The first stopped just behind the half SUV, and Kismet tumbled out of the passenger door with a first-aid bag in her hand.

"His fever's worse," I said before she could ask.

She nodded and bolted into the cabin. Conrad Morgan climbed out of the first Jeep with his three Hunters in tow. One of the men I knew by face only—he'd been at Olsmill, battled alongside us to defeat the combined goblin/Halfie forces. The other male Hunter I glared at, and he wouldn't look at me. Paul Ryan was a rookie, skittish, and had accidentally shot Wyatt once. I hated the kid on general principle. The third, Claudia Burke, a tall brunette Hunter with a scar that ran beneath her chin from ear to ear, was one of the only three Gifted Hunters in the Triads—not counting me—and was a limited telepath.

The other two Jeeps spilled out Adrian Baylor and his two Hunters. Baylor had lost one at Olsmill, then lost the replacement at Parker's Palace. Either he'd run out of rookies or had refused to take another so soon.

Everyone who exited those Jeeps, save Kismet, stopped to stare at me and Wyatt, but mostly at me. While Kismet had probably told them I was still alive (there had really been no way around it), seeing is usually believing. Baylor seemed amused. Paul Ryan looked ready to barf all over his shoes.

"The perimeter's clear," Wyatt said. "A third hound surprised us. All three have been neutralized."

Baylor nodded. "Paul, Oliver, go help them get Felix into the Jeep." The two Hunters trotted past us without comment. "Gina mentioned something called a pùca?"

"It's dead. Milo found a couple of pieces a few yards into the woods. Did Gina fill you in on everything?"

"Everything Tybalt didn't know. He called about fifteen minutes before she did. Told me what he knew and that he couldn't get anyone's cell or the cabin's landline. We were already mobilizing when I got word from Gina."

Note to self: Tybalt deserves a big, sloppy kiss.

Muscled arms crossed over his chest, Baylor fixed me with a curious stare. "So once again things come down to someone wanting you."

Internally, I flinched. Externally, I quirked an eyebrow and lifted my shoulder in a casual shrug. "Well, when you're popular . . ."

"Claudia, open the back!"

Four people shuffled out the front door of the cabin, using a sheet as a quasi stretcher-hammock to support Felix. Claudia opened the rear of the last Jeep, then helped the carriers deliver their burden.

When Felix was tucked neatly inside and the rear door shut, Kismet turned to Milo and started to say, "Go with—"

"I'm staying to help." His tone left no room for argument.

She frowned.

"I'll take him," said Baylor's female Hunter. She was my height, with bowl-cut black hair and eyebrows so thin they looked drawn in marker. On the approving nod from her Handler, she climbed into the Jeep and started to turn it around.

"Tybalt's meeting them at the hospital," Kismet said to no one in particular. Her way of reassuring herself that the injured Hunter wouldn't be alone. Milo touched her elbow, and Hunter and Handler shared their worry in a brief, pained exchange.

Silent up until now, Conrad Morgan seemed to creep out of the shadows to glare right at me. Unlike Baylor, this Handler wasn't a large man. White-blond hair and sharp features made up for his average height and build. His ski-slope nose, pointed chin, and hollow cheekbones were attractive from one angle and terrifying from another. In the strange shadows cast by the headlights of the Jeeps, he looked like an angry corpse.

He said, "Excellent work getting an Assembly Elder kidnapped. Well done."

I bristled, hands clenching into tight fists. Only Wyatt's hand on my arm kept a bright flare of anger from propelling me across the muddy yard, fist-first into Morgan's too-sharp face. "Phineas understood the risks," I said darkly, "but Thackery will not hesitate to kill him if I don't do what he wants."

"Which is turn yourself over?"

"Yup. Me and my potentially very special blood."

"Your what?"

Morgan's confusion was reflected in Baylor, and in their Hunters. Shit. I cast Kismet a curious look. She gave a slight shake of her head. So they'd gotten only the condensed version of the day's events. I fed them the details of the last week, from the crystal theft to the pùca's motivation for attacking, up to their arrival. Half a dozen pairs of eyebrows arched to the heavens and several mouths were hanging open as my audience grasped the extent of what Thackery had done.

"And if anyone here," I concluded with a growl, "even

ponders the idea of tying me up and hand-delivering me to R&D for their personal research, know right now you will have to kill me first. I am fucking done being a guinea pig."

Baylor was eyeing the closest hound corpse, one hand stroking his chin in a gesture of thought more suited to a college professor than a hard-hitting Handler. "Those look like the same hounds we confiscated from Olsmill," he said.

"Might just be," I said.

He snapped his head in my direction, eyes narrowing. "Meaning what? They escaped their cages, made it out of a second-level basement facility, and then got past the perimeter fence?"

"No." Time to put these particular cards on the table. "Not if they were let out."

"Impossible," Morgan said.

"Fine, then let's go to R&D, check out sublevel 3, and make sure there are still six hounds in captivity. Because if even one of them is missing, every person who works in that building is on my goddamned suspect list."

"What the hell is it with you and seeing traitors everywhere you look, Stone?"

Instead of infuriating me, Morgan's question made me laugh. Actual, amused laughter. "Are you kidding? After what happened last month with my Triad, you have the balls to ask me that?"

After my Triad had been set up by a group of Halfies, my partners Jesse and Ash killed, and me blamed for their deaths, I hadn't known who to trust. Maybe I still hadn't gotten past that initial betrayal, and maybe I'd let it color my judgment last week when I'd wanted to expose the brass and make them take responsibility for the massacre of a were-Clan, but not now. This time all evidence pointed at a traitor.

Morgan's jaw twitched. "You really think someone at Boot Camp is working with Thackery?"

"Yes," I said, in stereo with Wyatt and Kismet.

"They're not lying," Claudia said. Her voice was lighter than I'd have guessed, almost breathy in a stage whisper sort of way.

Limited telepath, huh? "You're reading our minds?" I asked, bristling at the idea of such an intrusion.

"Not exactly," she said. "More like reading the emotion in the words as they're linked to your subconscious mind. Truth sounds different from lies." She shrugged, and I noticed the pinched lines around her eyes and the crease in her forehead.

"You have a hard time during the storm, too?"

She blinked, seeming startled by the question.

"Who do you think is working against us?" Morgan asked, steering the conversation back on course.

"There's only one way to find out," I replied. A way that may or may not involve my fists and someone else's kidneys.

"You want back into Boot Camp?" Baylor asked.

I decided not to inform him I'd already been there twice in the very recent past. "I need to see for myself that the six hounds are still there. So, yes, I want back in."

Baylor's left eye twitched. Even though Wyatt had seniority, and Kismet second after him, everyone seemed to defer to Baylor on this decision. Probably because he had seniority over Morgan and was less personally invested in this than the other two Handlers. Adrian Baylor had been a huge asset at Olsmill, and I found myself silently pleading for him to be on my side. I couldn't keep doing this with the Triads as my enemies—not with the odds we were facing.

"Morgan," he finally said, "your team is on cleanup. Get the bodies together for collection. The hounds have to go back to Boot Camp." There was no need to ask where David's body was going. We had disposal locations for slain Hunters.

Morgan scowled, then started barking orders to his Hunters.

"Everyone else," Baylor said, "in the front Jeep."

Five bodies went in one direction; I went in the other. Wyatt called out, but I dashed back into the cabin. No way was I walking into semi-enemy territory empty-handed. I shuffled through the cache of weapons on the floor, choosing a small knife, which I tucked into my shoe, and a .38 with regular rounds. With the gun in the back waistband of my jeans, I left the cabin without a backward glance.

One more location on my list of places I hoped never to see again.

Chapter Sixteen

For the third time in one week, I was back on Boot Camp grounds. Only this trip, I wasn't hiding in the back of an SUV and I wasn't breaking in. I was being escorted into a building I'd never had access to by three Handlers to whom I'd trust my life. Okay, Baylor wasn't quite on that list yet, but he was damned close. Research and Development was restricted to Handlers only, so taking me inside was a huge risk.

Milo and Oliver waited in the Jeep. Kismet used her password to gain entry, then led the way with Baylor and Wyatt watching my back. It was the middle of the night, and the lobby was empty. Small, like a doctor's waiting room, it had two leather couches flanking the entry and framed watercolors hanging on the walls. Opposite the entrance was an elevator and two heavy gray doors. All three exits had keypads. Next to the center door was a black wall-mounted telephone. The room reeked of furniture polish and bleach.

Kismet strode to the phone, picked up the handset, and pressed one of the four multicolored keys. Waited, then said, "Gina Kismet, Triad Three, requesting sublevel escort." She waited a beat, then hung up.

"An escort?" I asked.

"Our passwords won't get us into the sublevels," she said.

"What about those doors?"

"We can get into those. It's mostly offices and low-level research behind one of them. The other houses the entire history of the Triads."

"Ever been in there?"

"Once or twice."

I glanced at Wyatt. "You?"

He nodded but didn't elaborate. His lips were pressed thin, his cheeks pallid. I wasn't used to seeing Wyatt Truman nervous. For someone who'd helped create the program and place we were in, he didn't seem very sure of his position. Not that I begrudged him a little anxiety. His rank hadn't helped save me from a Neutralize order the first time around.

The center door swung open, and a too-familiar striking face stepped into the lobby. White-blond hair, still model-handsome, dressed in the same black slacks and white tieless dress shirt I'd always seen Bastian wear.

What the hell was the Triad recruiter doing here at the ass crack of dawn?

Bastian froze when he saw me, his face going absolutely still. Unreadable. His eyes flickered to my left, where Wyatt stood, then back to me. "I don't believe we've had the pleasure," he said, each word clipped and carefully chosen.

Don't be so sure.

Kismet surprised me by saying, "Call her Chalice. She used to know Evy Stone."

He turned that even gaze on Kismet. He seemed uncertain how to react to her proclamation. Like everyone else in the Triads, he'd have heard about my resurrection three weeks ago. And like everyone else who paid attention, he'd have heard Kismet's report of my death at the potato chip factory a week after that. Even though he'd never met me in my present body, he *knew*. I could see it in the slant of one eyebrow and the thin line of his lips.

"I hope she has a damned good reason for being here,"

Bastian finally said, radiating familiar calm. "Otherwise, she may not be allowed to leave."

I nearly snorted in his face. Unless they kept some sort of Break-blocking magic crystal handy—I mentally shuddered, remembering that damned thing—there wasn't a holding cell in Boot Camp that could keep me against my will.

"One of your Hunters was killed tonight," I said before anyone could stop me, "and another seriously wounded by hounds that are exact replicas of the six you supposedly have locked up in this building."

His lips parted, that steady calm starting to crack. "The hounds from Olsmill are still locked up. The only nonhuman who's left this building in the last four days is the goblin-hybrid who was mysteriously ghosted away yesterday."

"Let's pretend I'm very cynical and will believe only what I see for myself."

"You shouldn't have gotten into this building, much less be getting past this lobby, *Chalice*."

I threw out a name. "Walter Thackery."

Another crack in the form of furrowed eyebrows. "What about him?"

Not *"Who is he?"*

"He created the hounds and all the other hybrids locked down in your sublevels. I have information that can help you catch him, but first I need to see those hounds."

His eyes narrowed. Bastian seemed to weigh my words, in no hurry, unaware I was on a big damned deadline. He finally broke the hold on my gaze and looked at the trio of Handlers. "Who's responsible for her?"

"I am," all three replied in chorus. I would have laughed if it hadn't been so generous.

Bastian blinked. "Adrian comes with us. You two stay."

Wyatt made a startled grunt. I squeezed his arm just above the elbow, then winked when he caught my eye.

"Weapons stay here," Bastian said.

"Not a fucking chance in hell," I replied, as nonchalant as if he'd asked whether I wanted cream in my coffee.

He scowled, then walked over to the elevator and entered a code. A little yellow light flashed green, and the doors slid open. I followed him and Baylor into the wide polished-metal interior, turned, and held Wyatt's gaze until the doors closed. My stomach flipped as the elevator dropped. I hated elevators, had for most of my life. Felt too much like free-falling.

Bastian flanked my right side, and, this close, I smelled oranges and patchouli—an odd mix of scents that mingled with memory. If not for Bastian, my life would have been completely different. Maybe I'd have died long ago on the streets, another victim of random violence—Dreg or otherwise. Maybe I'd have fallen in love with a handsome older man who would have taken me away from this damned city, to a life of luxury and pleasure. And maybe rainbows would've shot out of my ass. For better or worse or something in between, Bastian had gotten me here.

I was tempted to punch him in the eye for it. Fortunately for his good looks, the elevator dinged on level S-3. Another keypad lit up by the door, and Bastian typed in another code. The security in the place impressed me. It meant everyone who went in and out was recorded and logged somewhere—information that would make discovering the traitor much easier.

The doors opened on a long, well-lit corridor that stretched a good twenty yards before ending in a T junction. Every few yards a stark gray metal door presented itself. Each had a fist-size door at eye level, with a slot to slide it back and see what was inside. At waist level on the left side of each door was a keypad and a card slider—double security on these doors.

As we exited the elevator, my nose was assaulted by the rank odors of urine, blood, sweat, wet dog, and something I couldn't identify. Sweet like honey, but with an undercurrent of tang. The strength of the smells made my eyes water. Even Baylor looked queasy.

Bastian strolled down the corridor, past a dozen doors, and turned right at the T junction. More doors, these a bit closer together. He stopped at the first on our left and pulled back the slot guard. He moved to the next and repeated it with six doors, not even bothering to look inside, so confident the hounds were there.

I glanced at Baylor, who quirked an eyebrow. "Your show, Stone," he seemed to say.

The slot window was protected by thick (and hopefully shatterproof) glass. I peered through, into a room roughly six-by-six feet, dimly lit by an overhead, inset light source. A hulking shadow crouched in the corner of the room, its dark brown pelt glimmering, back to me. But I knew that shape—long limbs and human torso, roped with deadly muscles, hands that sported razor claws. My stomach knotted fiercely.

"One down," I said, then moved to the next door. Each presented a repeat of the last—a hound huddled in one of the corners, facing away, subdued and very much not dead. All six hounds present and accounted for. "Hell."

"You genuinely suspected someone here released those monsters?" Bastian asked.

"No reason not to, since someone here tipped off Thackery about Token's removal."

Bastian's face drew in on itself, like the man had just sucked on a lemon. "That's a serious charge."

"You didn't deny it."

"No, I didn't."

A chill spread through my chest. Behind me, Baylor drew to his full height, tense, watching. I instinctively felt for my tap to the Break and grasped the fine edges of power with my mind. Just in case I needed to get us out in a hurry.

"I don't speak for the scientists who work here," Bastian said. "So I don't dare speak for or against their possible actions regarding this man Thackery. You came to see the hounds, and as you can see, they're tucked in nice and secure."

"The hounds are here, fine," I snapped, "but that doesn't mean someone in R&D isn't responsible for the other hounds being turned loose, or for getting Phineas el Chimal, a member of the Assembly of Clan Elders, fucking kidnapped."

Bastian cocked his head to the side. "Is he the same Elder who demanded the execution of one of our Handlers less than two weeks ago?"

"So? Phin pardoned Rufus and rescinded his demand of execution. You know that."

"Yes, but how do *you* know that, *Chalice*?"

I had not for a single second thought Bastian a fool. There was no sense in bothering with the charade. "I know because I was the one who protected the last three—four if you count the infant—living members of the Coni Clan. I caught Snow, one of the perpetrators of the Parker's Palace massacre, and I'm the one who actually put Leonard Call into a coma by jumping out a window with him."

Annoyance and awe warred on Bastian's face, skewing his mouth into an uneven line and creasing his forehead. "So," he said slowly, "we meet again, Evangeline. It's been quite a few years, and—"

"Oh my, how I've changed? Save it. I've heard it before."

"I can imagine. It's not every Hunter who has two death certificates in her file."

"Can we pretend the one at the factory stuck?"

"I'm still working off the premise that the one at the train station stuck. It's difficult to accept the notion that someone was actually raised from the dead and put into another person's body."

"Tell me about it."

Baylor cleared his throat. "Do we really have time for this?" he asked.

"Explain to me again why you believe someone at R&D betrayed you," Bastian asked. I did, and he nodded along, either accepting or simply absorbing. No idea which until he spoke. "It's a logical assumption, based on evidence presented."

"But?" I asked.

"But no one will admit to it, Evangeline. And given your deadline, you don't have time to sift through telephone records and individually question everyone who works in this building."

"The only people I need to question are the ones who were on duty yesterday when Token went missing. Where do I find that roster of names?"

"I can get it from my office upstairs. Everyone who comes and goes uses an individual key code to enter and exit the building."

"Good. Were you here?"

His eyebrows slanted in a deep V. "Yes. As I said, my office is upstairs. Are you going to accuse me of being the traitor now?"

"Depends."

"On?"

I swallowed, my heart beating just a little faster. "Did you call Thackery to tell him that Token was missing?"

"No."

Phew. Scratch one name off the immediate list. He'd

come off the Official List as soon as someone checked his cell phone—

"I didn't call Thackery," Bastian said wearily, "because he called me first."

Sound roared in my ears. I didn't register Baylor pulling his gun, only him stepping around in front of me, pistol leveled on Bastian's throat. I couldn't seem to pick my jaw up off the floor. Had Bastian seriously just confessed his compliance with the Bad Guy?

He seemed unconcerned that Baylor was holding a cocked gun on him, his eyes never wavering from my face. He didn't even look upset, like what he'd just said had absolutely nothing to do with our current problem. It was . . . strange.

"Why?" I asked, my voice shaky. "Why did Thackery call you?"

"Not while there's a gun in my face," Bastian said calmly.

Baylor took two steps back but didn't change his aim. "Gun's out of your face," Baylor growled. "Now talk." God bless big men and their guns.

"I've known Walter Thackery for twelve years," Bastian said. "I met him at the university when I was an undergrad on a student visa and he was working on his doctoral thesis in molecular biology. He was a brilliant man, with his theories on interspecies breeding. Mostly plants back then, of course. He didn't learn of the existence of Dregs until his wife was turned into one."

"Five years ago," I said. Memory circled back to my apartment right after the earthquake. "His wife was bitten by a vampire, and six months later a Triad team neutralized her."

Bastian nodded, not a trace of emotion leaking through. "Thackery was broken when he lost Anne, but he was shattered the following year when he lost his son."

"Son?"

"Anne was four months pregnant when she was infected. Thackery cashed in his life insurance, his stocks, sold everything he owned to find a way to cure her. Somehow the baby was born, and, at first, he didn't seem infected. Anne escaped and was later killed. But the baby—" Bastian's voice cracked. "The baby wasn't normal."

I wanted to tell him to stop, that I didn't give a flying fuck about any of this. The gory details of Walter Thackery's life didn't excuse his actions, and Bastian should just shut his mouth. Instead, I asked, "He tried to cure his son?"

"Tried and failed. After that, he became obsessed with the eradication of the vampire race. He wanted to study them, to discover a vaccine against their salivary parasite, anything to stop the spread of their infection and halt the creation of half-Bloods."

Little worms wriggled up the backs of my legs. "What about the other things in his lab at Olsmill? What about the hounds and Token and all the other half-breeds he created?"

"I don't know."

"Bullshit."

"I don't know." More force in his words that time, a spark of fury. "Thackery didn't tell me anything he didn't want to tell me. I had no idea he was involved in Tovin's plans at Olsmill. We had very little contact these last two years, maybe a phone call once a month. I understood what he was trying to do, and, until Olsmill, he never interfered with Triad business. He was off everyone's radar, except mine."

I fisted my hands to keep them from shaking, rage bubbling up, staining my cheeks with a hot flush. "And after Olsmill? After we recovered his projects and brought them here?"

He looked at the floor, finally—fucking finally!—

showing some semblance of shame. "Thackery called the day after," he said to the floor. "He knew we employed our own scientists here and wanted to make sure they were receiving proper care."

Cartilage broke beneath my knuckles and blood spurted hot across my skin before I realized I'd hit him. Bastian stumbled into the wall, his once perfect nose gushing blood and oddly angled. He stared at me, wide eyes glazed with pain, not even trying to staunch the flow.

"Motherfucker," I snarled, fist drawn back and ready to strike again. "You knew Thackery had been working with Tovin and you didn't fucking say anything? Didn't turn him in? Tell me why I shouldn't break your balls next!"

"He said he was close to a vaccine for the vampire parasite, and that he only needed two more months to find it. He swore to me he'd share it when he had it, that the Triads could use it to inoculate ourselves. The payoff was an acceptable risk, so I said nothing."

Slivers of pain laced across the palm of my hand—I'd clenched my fist so hard I'd broken skin, created tiny, bloody half-moon indents. Hysteria was gnawing at the corners of my conscious mind, threatening to overthrow my rage. I wanted to beat Bastian senseless for his part in what Thackery had done to me, because intentionally or not, he'd been a willing accomplice to the research. A willing participant in the way my body had been used to incubate a potential antidote to a parasite that had ruined hundreds, if not thousands, of lives. That had killed people important to me. People I loved.

"The timing of yesterday's call, then," Baylor said. "You want us to believe it was a coincidence?"

"It was his weekly check-in on his projects. I got the report of Token's removal while we were talking, and

Thackery overheard. He cut off the conversation, and we haven't spoken since."

"And you never said a damned word to anyone?" Baylor's finger twitched on the trigger, fury coloring his face. "Thackery murdered Rhys Willemy. His hounds killed David Moreau tonight, and Felix Diggory is hanging on by a thread. Not to mention the living hell he's put Stone through this last week."

Each of the names spat at him seemed to affect Bastian in some way—little tics of his eyes, a flare of nostrils, hints of pain and regret. My name, however, brought on something different. With blood oozing down his chin and staining the crisp white collar of his shirt, Bastian looked genuinely confused.

"Thackery may have finally stumbled onto his promised vaccine," I said. "The trade is Phineas for the antibody carrier. Under other circumstances, I'd have no qualms about making the trade, but Thackery isn't being a philanthropist here. He's weaponized the parasite, but without the cure he won't use his weapon, and I've got only about four hours left to come up with a Plan B before he kills Phin."

"You'll never find Thackery before the clock runs out," Bastian said. "He's stayed hidden for this long. He won't make a stupid mistake so close to the end."

"I have to try."

"Why—?" He stopped, realization dawning. I could almost see a cartoon lightbulb blink on above his head. "You're the carrier."

"Give that man a fucking prize."

"Do you realize what a gift you could have?"

I groaned. "For all I know, I'm lugging around ten pints of regular old O positive. Right now the only thing I'm thinking about is how to save Phin's life and prevent Thackery from using his weapon against us in some sort of power play."

"You can't trade for Phineas."

Good lord, he was starting to sound like Wyatt. Everyone wanted to protect me, but no one else saw it was the only solution. How could I not trade myself for Phin? "I won't let Thackery kill him," I said. "Period."

Was that panic flittering across Bastian's face? "He's one man, Evangeline."

"He's my friend."

He went to pinch the bridge of his nose—a universal gesture of annoyance, I supposed, since it got directed at me a lot—then stopped before he made the break worse. "Thackery will bleed you dry if it means developing the cure he wants."

I lifted one shoulder in a nonchalant shrug, even though my insides were quaking at the idea of being Thackery's lab rat. My mouth was dry when I said, "Maybe, but I've been the cause of a lot of friends' deaths lately, and I will not leave Phineas on the chopping block. I will get him out."

"And give up the cure?"

"There may not be a fucking cure!" I threw my hands in the air. "Maybe the only reason I fought off the parasite is because I was gifted healing powers by a gnome. Maybe Thackery will stick me, test me, and realize I don't have anything useful for him."

"Then let *us* test your blood."

I stared at him. "Are you serious?"

His expression left little doubt. "Perfectly serious."

Chapter Seventeen

"Hell no, you're not testing my blood," I said.

"Just a sample, please." A spark of excitement was back in his voice, and, combined with the blood on his face, it made him look downright terrifying.

Another denial hung on my lips. I could give Erickson's team a sample, just to test and see if there really was anything unusual. Not that it would change my mind about trading for Phineas, but knowing for sure I didn't have any sort of antibody might change Thackery's demands. Might make him realize he didn't need me and just let Phin go.

Yeah, right.

If nothing else, I'd get the peace of mind of knowing I was going to my potential death because I had value.

I glanced at Baylor. He'd lowered his gun and was watching me with rapt attention. He made a face that seemed to say, "Sorry. You're on your own with this one."

"Just a sample," I said to Bastian. "So we can know for sure."

"Agreed. The lab is upstairs on sublevel 1."

As we retraced our steps to the elevator, I studied Bastian's back. Straight posture, no shoulder slump, no falter in his steps. He walked as he had before—confident in his position within the hierarchy. Somewhere below the brass but above the Handlers.

"Even after Olsmill," I said, "you never said anything.

You knew Thackery had helped Tovin create those abominations, but you didn't turn him in."

"No," he said, punching in his elevator code.

"Why?"

"You said it a few moments ago. He was my friend."

Sublevel 1 was another labyrinth of corridors that honey-combed around dozens of doors and oddly shaped rooms. The doors had alphanumeric designations that gave no hint as to their purpose or contents. Mixed with lemon disinfectant and chemicals was the sharper scent of a recently fired gun. Or many recently fired guns. Underground shooting range for bullet development, most likely. It was kind of cool.

And nerve-racking. Even with Baylor watching my back, I didn't trust Bastian. Not only for what he'd told me about his history with Thackery but because, as our recruiter, Bastian had the ear of the brass. He had influence. He knew how important a vaccine could be. He couldn't possibly agree with my decision to trade myself for Phineas.

Which meant he might try to keep me here.

Bastian slid a plastic key card through the lock of a plain white door. I followed him, Baylor behind me, into a room that looked like every stereotypical biology lab I'd ever seen. I didn't know the names of the machines or what they did. There were no chairs, no exam tables—just equipment—and the odor of blood made my stomach churn.

"What are you doing?" I asked when Bastian reached for a phone.

"Calling a lab assistant. Unless you know how to draw your own blood?"

I shook my head. He made the call and we waited. Bastian took some gauze out of a drawer, pressed it to his nose, and then stared at me until I couldn't stand it anymore.

"What?"

"Just trying to remember the fragile blond girl I first met almost five years ago," he said.

Fragile? "And?"

"And I'm a bit disappointed we never managed to locate Chalice Frost and train her. This teleporting ability of hers would have been a terrific advantage."

I blinked. I hadn't expected that. "I think this teleporting ability of *mine* has been a great advantage."

"An advantage you're giving away to Thackery."

"Dude, even if I weren't between a rock and a fucking hard place with Thackery, it's not an advantage you'd get to use anytime soon. I'm not a Hunter anymore."

"Perhaps not in occupation, but you'll always be a Hunter in spirit. I've never chosen unwisely, Evangeline."

The lab assistant arrived, a flighty, overcaffeinated young woman with boy-cut brown hair and black-rimmed glasses. She took one look at Baylor, who hadn't put his gun away, and shrank back.

"Marie," Bastian said, "Ms. Stone here needs a blood sample drawn."

Marie nodded vigorously, those thick glasses slipping down her long nose. She filled two vials with my blood—such normal-looking blood. And maybe it was. Part of me hoped it was. "Do you need this tested?" she asked.

"Yes," Bastian said. "Priority scan for absolutely anything abnormal, no matter how small."

"Okay." She took the vials to one of the other counters and put them in a rack for safekeeping.

"If you're determined to do this," Bastian said to me, "then may I request one further precaution?"

"Request away," I said.

"Let Marie inject you with the internal tracking dye."

I'd been injected with the radioactive dye a few times in the past without ill effects. Still, everything that had ever come out of R&D was now suspect. "Thackery's probably the one who told Erickson how to develop ours and knows how to find it, so no thanks."

"This is a new varietal that's improved upon the old formula. It allows us to track you within a half-mile radius now. Thackery shouldn't be able to scan you for it."

"Is it detectable?"

"You mean when he tests your blood? No, it shouldn't be."

"Shouldn't be." I hated words like that. And yet, for all my suspicions, it was actually a damned good backup plan. As long as he wasn't lying to me. "Okay, then."

Bastian smiled. "Marie, can you fetch the D-34 solution?"

The lab assistant produced a bottle of blue liquid from a locked cabinet. I watched her insert a syringe, suck out a small amount, and flick it with her finger. She stepped toward me, and I held up my hand in a warning gesture. "Nuh-uh, him first."

"We don't need to track me," Bastian said.

"True, but I don't know what's really in that bottle, or if D-34 is code for a sedative. You stay on your feet, then she can hit me with it."

A flicker of respect passed across Bastian's face. He unbuttoned his shirt sleeve and rolled it to just above the elbow. "Okay, then. Go ahead, Marie."

She swabbed the inside of his elbow and made the injection. We stood there for a full minute afterward, everyone deferring to me. When Bastian remained upright, bemused, without showing any sign of passing out, I presented my arm to Marie. She prepped a new syringe. Heat flared outward from the injection site, dissipating seconds later. No dizziness, no nausea. So far, so good.

"You been here a while?" I asked Marie.

She nodded, wary of being addressed directly. "Yes."

"A week ago, Gina Kismet sent a sample of liquid here. She was told it was an experimental antidote. Did you test it?"

She glanced at Bastian first, then shook her head at me. "I didn't test it, but I saw the file. It was a deteriorating tracking liquid, meant to last about seventy-two hours. Its tracking range isn't impressive."

Damn. We still didn't know how the pùca found the cabin, or how Thackery knew I'd survived the infection.

"I'll get the computer you'll need to track her," Bastian said to Baylor. "Meet me back at the elevator."

Baylor seemed poised to argue, but Bastian slid out of the room like a vapor. Marie discarded the used needles and went back to her blood work.

"How long will your testing take?" I asked.

"A couple of hours," she replied, not looking at me.

Baylor and I retreated to the corridor. The networking hallways made navigating back to the elevator difficult, but Baylor seemed to remember the way, so I let him lead. We arrived first and waited. He'd finally reholstered his gun and stood there like a statue, the modern model of a dedicated bodyguard. We'd interacted quite a bit in the last month, but I really knew next to nothing about him. Nothing except his dedication to the Triads and his bullheaded integrity.

"Do me a favor?" I asked before I could talk myself out of it.

"Within my power," he replied, a curious slant to his mouth.

"Don't let Wyatt do anything stupid. He won't like me going to Thackery willingly—hell, I don't like me going willingly—but right now, I don't see any other way to save Phineas. Thackery's got the cards, and he knows how to play them. If things go badly and I . . ." My stomach clenched. "Just don't let him do anything stupid, okay?"

"Like try to mount an ill-advised rescue and get himself killed?"

"Basically. Or, you know, hunt down another crazy elf and try to resurrect me again."

Baylor smiled warmly. "I'll do my best. Sure you wouldn't rather ask Gina?"

"I think she could talk him down, but you're more likely to actually knock him down, if it comes to that."

"Understood."

Bastian joined us a minute later, a laptop case dangling from one shoulder. "What are you going to tell the others about me?" he asked.

"You mean the lying-by-omission thing?" Baylor took a menacing step forward. "Nothing. But you've got one hour to come clean about it to the brass. One hour." He didn't have to make a threat—the violence was implied.

Bravo.

We went back up to the lobby; Bastian stayed below. Wyatt was stalking the elevator doors, looking ready to burst out of his skin. Kismet stood from the chair she'd folded herself into. Both were studies of anxiety and nerves.

"They're all down there," I said before he could ask. "All six."

"What took so long?" His dark gaze roved over me.

"Little preemptive planning." I told him about the tracking dye and my blood donation, but left out the details of Bastian's confession. The latter because I didn't need the headache of prying Wyatt's hands from Bastian's throat. I almost didn't mention the blood—telling Wyatt I'd left a sample behind seemed like saying I didn't think I'd be back. "It's being tested downstairs, but I don't know if they'll have results before game time."

"That's good, though," Kismet said. "The blood gives our side a chance to look for antibodies, and if the dye isn't something Thackery can identify, it'll go a long way toward finding out where he's set up his little laboratory."

"Exactly," I said. And if Marie happened to learn that I wasn't carrying anything extraordinary in my veins, so much the better. It meant I wasn't giving Thackery anything useful, and I'd beaten the infection through good, old-fashioned gnome healing magic.

A newly familiar clanging bell broke from Wyatt's hip. He pulled Thackery's cell phone out and held it to me.

I stared at it, wide-eyed. "He's early." I took it, flipped it open. Hit Speaker. "Stone."

"Ah, excellent," Thackery said. "When I heard about your presence at the cabin, I feared for your safety."

"Fuck you."

He chuckled, and I wanted to reach through the phone and strangle him. "No sense in being vulgar, my dear."

"Why are you calling? Our agreement was twelve hours, and it's been only eight. You reneging?"

"Not exactly. The deadline stands, but I've decided to alter the price of your friend's freedom."

"And if I don't feel like negotiating?"

Thackery sighed. Then a scream erupted on his end of the call, long and loud and agonized. I nearly dropped the phone. I knew that voice. Wyatt held my gaze, steely determination in his black eyes, and I didn't look away.

"You were saying about not wishing to negotiate?" Thackery asked.

It took several tries to get my voice steady enough to answer. "What do you want?"

"Two hundred thousand dollars wired to the overseas account of my choice."

I barked laughter, stung by the absurdity of his request. Had I left my life behind and landed in the middle of a police television drama? "How the hell am I supposed to get my hands on two hundred grand, not to mention have a clue as to how to wire it somewhere?"

"Your friends will help you. Have it ready to go when I call at the end of our deadline. And just in case you're planning on double-crossing me in some way, I think I've proved I'll not hesitate to take it out on the shapeshifter. But if you need further incentive, I have two hounds left at my disposal."

My heart sank.

"Cross me," he said, "and I'll release them in a populated area. Perhaps a park or inside the mall. A good place for them to hunt. Talk to you soon." He hung up with an audible click.

Motherfucker! The sound of Phin's agonized scream haunted me as I tucked the phone away with trembling hands. I couldn't stop imagining what Thackery had done to make him shriek like that. Wyatt slipped his arm around my waist, and I sagged against him, eyes closed, trying to collect my racing thoughts. Any plans I'd had to get Phin free and make a run for it were gone. I would never risk Thackery loosing those hounds on the public. The casualties would be catastrophic. Thackery had played every card right, and I had nothing to challenge his hand.

As though sensing my defeat, Wyatt held me tighter.

"Where are we going to get that kind of money?" I asked, focusing on the problem I could fix.

"We'll ask the Assembly," he said, voice rumbling through his chest.

"What if they pull some sort of nonnegotiation policy on us?"

"Doubtful." His hand stroked my arm in comforting lines. "Phin's an Elder, Evy, and he's one of the last of his kind. Something tells me the Assembly will pay. I'm almost surprised Thackery didn't demand more."

I snorted and stood up straighter. He'd demanded plenty. In fact, his demand had cemented my course of action in a way nothing else had. Wyatt's hand stayed on my hip, and I threaded my fingers through his, holding it there. "I'll call Michael Jenner. He'll be able to help."

Jenner was the official representative of the Assembly of Clan Elders, speaking publicly for them in matters involving the Triads and most other species. He was Therian, like Phin, but he'd never verified from which Clan. He was also a public defender. He'd helped save my life twice, and here I was about to ask him for another favor.

The call went well, considering it was almost five in the morning and the first Jenner was hearing about Phin's abduction. I gave him the condensed version of events and promised details later. He said to give him two hours to alert the Assembly Elders and collect the money in a transferable account. I didn't know how he'd manage it before any banks actually opened but trusted him to get it done.

I didn't have a choice, really, and I despised being left without choices. With a promise to get every available Therian on the streets looking for Phin and inspecting potential hound hunting grounds, he hung up. I gave Kismet's cell back to her and gazed at the faces around me. No one had left the lobby during the call, not even Bastian. He'd come upstairs, nose bandaged, and had been showing Baylor and Kismet how to use the laptop for tracking me. He got looks, but no one asked about his fresh injury.

"So you're really going through with this?" Baylor asked as they tucked the laptop back into its case.

"I don't have a choice," I said. "Let's pretend I could actually justify allowing Phin to be tortured and murdered in order to protect what may or may not be in my blood. Even if I could manage that, I cannot justify the dozens, if not hundreds, of people who will be killed, hurt, or maimed when Thackery releases those hounds in public. You know he wasn't bluffing. We've been lucky with them so far, because they've been sent after specific targets"—usually me—"but when they're let out to kill indiscriminately? No, and if we weren't so unsure about my blood, none of us would consider any other course of action beyond trading me."

"But this isn't just any other demand," Kismet said. "If he gets his antidote, he has an effective weapon—"

"And you'll deal with it, if it comes to that. Just like we always deal with everything that gets thrown at us. One step at a time. We can only battle what's in front of us." *They* can only battle what's in front of *them*. I had to stop thinking in terms of "we." A chill skated up my spine as the reality of what was happening truly set in. I was going to willingly turn myself over to Thackery, and all signs pointed toward a very slow death at his hands.

God, not again . . .

"I'll call Morgan and Nevada," Baylor said. "Start the phone chain. We need every team we have out there scouting potential attack zones. It's likely Thackery hasn't placed the hounds yet, so someone may get lucky. I'm going to stay here for now and coordinate things."

"I'll take the Hunters off base," Kismet said, accepting his plan with a curt nod. "Where do you want—?"

"Can you take Oliver to the hospital to meet up with Carly?"

Ah, so Baylor's female Hunter had a name. Good to know.

"Yeah, I'll do that. I wanted to swing by and check on Felix anyway." She looked at me, her expression warring between sympathy and grim determination. "You want a lift?"

"I don't have anywhere to go," I said, which was true enough. Our old apartment wasn't the best spot, even though I hadn't been back since the morning of the earthquake. Too many people knew where it was.

Kismet considered it a moment. "How about I drop you both at the boys' apartment? No one's there, and no offense, Wyatt, but you're covered in mud, streaked with blood, and you kind of stink. Use their shower. Milo's clothes should fit you."

Wyatt blinked, and I couldn't help but smile. It was the not-oft-seen mother hen side of her peeking through. It seemed that rumpled and worn fellow Handlers also rated high on her sympathy meter. And it gave Wyatt and me some time alone before . . . well, everything.

"Okay," I said, then gave Bastian a fierce glare. "As soon as Marie or whoever knows something?"

"We'll call," he replied. "My word."

I wanted to tell him just what I thought his word was worth. "Call Wyatt. I might not be able to answer."

"Of course."

"Kis, I'll let you know when I've got things squared here," Baylor said.

We left R&D, still the dead of night—well, morning, technically. Crickets were actually chirping somewhere nearby, and overhead a sky full of stars winked down at us. As beautiful as the mountains were, I didn't stop to admire them. Wyatt, Kismet, and I crowded into the already stuffed Jeep. The Hunters waiting in the backseat were subdued, and Kismet filled them in on the way back to the city, giving them all the details she had. I just held Wyatt's hand and tried not to panic.

Half an hour later, she dropped us off in front of the

apartment with a key and promise to return in about an hour and a quarter. As Wyatt and I walked inside and veered toward the elevator, those seventy-five minutes loomed. It wasn't nearly enough time.

But if Thackery had his way, it was all the time we had left together to explore the intense, if somewhat peculiar, relationship we'd begun so many months ago. Long before I truly realized anything had changed.

Chapter Eighteen

Four Weeks Predeath

An hour-long soak in the tub has relieved the majority of my aches and pains. My own stupidity brought them on, and, for once, they aren't the result of a fistfight or brawl with bloodthirsty Dregs. Our Triad isn't even on rotation again until tomorrow evening. Nope, the bruises and scrapes on my back and shoulders are my own fucking fault.

No pun intended, however apropos.

I watch the bathwater swirl down the drain in a mini-cyclone of bubbles and soap, and hope Ash is still having a good time. I hated ditching her at the club but was in no mood to continue our usual barhopping extravaganza. The cab driver I flagged down took one look at me, muttered something that sounded like "hooker," and drove me home.

Bastard didn't get a tip. He was lucky I didn't plant my heel in the back of his head.

After I'm thoroughly towel-dried, I check the scrapes in the bathroom mirror. A few along my shoulder blades are still oozing clear liquid. Most are surface abrasions—they'll itch like crazy later. The backs of my thighs have smatterings of blue bruises, perfectly oval and fingertip-size. They'll keep darkening, I bet. Good thing I prefer jeans.

In my line of work, dating is out of the question, but

I'm a woman with needs, dammit, which is why Ash and I troll the bars on our nights off. Once in a while, one of us will find someone to hook up with for a little . . . activity. Location is rarely important, as long as I get my itch scratched.

Only tonight's selection had been a little rougher than usual, and doing it up against a brick wall, in a storage room at the club, hadn't been exactly comfortable. Oh, I got off all right, but my back regrets it with a vengeance.

I slip into clean sweats and pad into the kitchen for a snack. It's been a week since I shook off a horrid bout of the flu, and my appetite has finally returned. I settle on a bologna sandwich with mustard and steal one of Jesse's lagers. He likes the dark brown sludge that tastes like rat piss, but it's that or water.

We need to go shopping.

Sandwich and beer in hand, I retreat to the living room and curl up on the sofa. A gentle ache between my legs reminds me my back isn't the only thing regretting tonight's interlude. What was it Wyatt used to tell me? Sometimes I don't have the good sense God gave goats. I shoulda said no.

I didn't, though.

The apartment phone's shrill chime makes me jump. We keep the landline for emergencies and in case "real people" need to contact us; everything else is handled over our Triad-issued cells. I stare at the telephone, an old rotary Ash picked up at a yard sale eons ago, and debate answering it. On the fifth ring, I do.

"Hello?"

"Yeah, this is the super," a deep baritone says, not happy about making this call. "One of your neighbors called and complained about a drunk man sitting in front of your door."

"I— What?" I sit up straighter and peer at the metal door, as if I can see right through it.

"Drunk man in front of your door. People are tripping over him. If he's a friend, take him inside. If he's a vagrant, call the cops. I just don't want no more of these damned calls at three A.M." With that, he slams his phone down.

Okaaay.

On the way to the door, I snag one of my favorite serrated knives from the weapons trunk behind the couch, just in case. I press one ear to the door and listen— nothing. Try the peephole. All I see are a pair of black sneakers sticking out from jeans-clad legs that disappear beneath my line of sight. Confident in my ability to subdue a regular human male if the need arises, I turn the various door locks, grasp the knob, and pull.

Wyatt tumbles through the open door and lands on his back, cracking his head on the cement floor. He blinks up at me with bleary, bloodshot eyes. He hasn't shaved recently, and a black beard creeps along his jaw and chin, spilling down his neck. A brown paper bag is clutched in one hand, obscuring my view of the bottle's label.

"What the fuck, Truman?" I toss my knife on a nearby side table and glare down at him. "Don't you have a home?"

"Sure," he says. "Few blocks from here. Why?"

Oh boy, he's three sheets to the fucking wind. In the four years I've worked for Wyatt Truman, I've seen him run the gamut from cool and collected to wholly enraged, but I've never before seen him utterly shitfaced.

"Because you're loitering in front of my home instead of sleeping this off in yours," I finally say. Lame.

"My apartment's empty." His tone is solemn, as if the statement alone explained everything. It's also sort of loud, and the hall door is still open. The last thing I want is another call from the building super.

"Think you can crawl to the couch?"

He frowns, which looks like a smile upside down. "Nope. Can walk."

Uh-huh.

He ends up half crawling ten feet to the stained, beaten sofa, and curls up on one end, head on the arm-rest. He still hasn't let go of that bottle, but the smell hints at whiskey. Yuck. I relock the door, then move to stand in front of him, arms crossed over my chest. He swigs from the neck of the bottle and winces as he swallows.

"Where's everyone?" he asks.

"Out."

"Duh."

I can't help smiling. I think it's quite possibly the first time in our entire history he's ever said that. "Jesse's up north, picking up a new ax from that blacksmith friend of his," I say. "Ash is still out having a good time."

"Why didn't you go?" he asks my midsection.

"I did. Now I'm home."

He manages to raise his gaze so our eyes meet. Something like confusion or concern flickers there but is beaten back by liquor. He struggles to sit up straighter. I make it easier on him by sitting down on the opposite end of the sofa. He squirms until he can face me, half his body braced on the back of the couch.

"Didn't have a good time?" he asks.

I lift one shoulder. "Ended on a sore note."

He frowns. "Sour note?"

"No, sore note."

More of that indeterminate emotion creeps into his eyes. What the hell? He gets drunk and suddenly gives two shits about my social life? I'm off duty and off Triad rotation, which means I can do whatever the fuck I want as long as it doesn't draw attention to us.

"So what's got you out at three A.M., drinking straight from the bottle on a school night?"

"Celebrating."

"Yeah? You look like you're about to celebrate yourself right into alcohol poisoning."

He snorts, then hiccups. I lean across the sofa and snatch the bottle from him. He reacts several seconds too late, which only shows me how gone he is. I swig from the bottle, and the bourbon sears down my throat to settle hot in my belly. My eyes water. Coughing, I hand it back. He stares at the bag-covered bottle as though he isn't sure what he is holding.

"So what are we celebrating?" I ask.

"Anniversary."

He doesn't elaborate, and the one-word answers are getting boring. I search my memory for anything important about today, or April in general. I was assigned to him in July, and even though I admit to being a pain in the ass, I'm not worth a drunk like this one. Must be personal.

I can count on the fingers of one hand the personal things I know about Wyatt. If he discusses his personal life with anyone else, it's when I'm not around. He and Ash have been together for almost eight years, so she makes sense as a confidante. Jesse has the male camaraderie thing going.

Wyatt's so sloshed it would take only a few well-formed questions to learn everything I want to know. But I'm not sure if he's a blackout drunk, and the last thing I need is him sobering up tomorrow and getting pissed because he remembers everything. No, it's safer to let it lie. Especially since he's been riding me so hard this last month or so.

He's watching me intently, if a little unfocused . . . no, a little too focused.

"So why'd you bring your anniversary party here?" I ask.

"My apartment's empty."

"Yeah, that happens when you leave it and stumble across town to someone else's."

"Didn't want to be alone."

Okay, this is definitely a personal anniversary. I know the Triads kicked off roughly ten years ago. Could this be it? If so, why the drunken stupor? He should be proud of what he's accomplished, not pickling his liver like he's ashamed to be in the same room with himself.

His stare is making me uncomfortable.

"Want a bologna sandwich?" I ask.

"Mustard?"

I hand him my uneaten sandwich, then get up to fetch a bottle of water and two aspirin. He probably deserves to stew in hangover hell tomorrow for how hard he's been on me lately, but I can't bring myself to let him suffer.

He pops the aspirin with a swig of bourbon, which makes me chuckle. I settle back down and channel surf while he eats. All I really want now is to go to bed, but my internal clock is set for nocturnal hours—the curse of a Hunter whose prey mostly comes out after dark.

His plate and abandoned liquor bottle both end up on the coffee table, and he nurses the water for a few minutes. I flip channels to some historical movie in which a cowboy is struggling to undo the many buttons and ribbons of his ladylove's fancy dress. He finally gets the frilly thing off and makes contact with skin. The scene changes and they wake in each other's arms, still tangled up in bed together.

I snort. "You know what I hate about basic cable?

They cut out all the good stuff. Especially the nookie scenes."

He makes an indeterminate sound. "Thought you had sex already tonight."

"I did, but doesn't mean I don't like to watch."

"That movie sucks anyway."

I shrug and change channels again.

"Do you want me to leave?" Wyatt asks.

"Did I say I did?"

"No."

"Well?" He doesn't reply. "Besides, if you leave now, in this state, you'll probably end up hit by a car or at the wrong end of a goblin's hunger pang. I won't be responsible for your death, Truman."

"We're all responsible for someone's death." He says it so quietly I almost miss the grief layering each word. He studies the water's generic label, stuck on his own responsibility for something.

It's nearly impossible to stay quiet, and I battle my instinct to ask whose death he's responsible for. I'll question his orders, smart-mouth him when he's not listening, provoke him into fits of anger, and even go against his wishes when the mood suits me. I just can't breach this last line—this invisible barrier of personal information that keeps our roles as Hunter and Handler so perfectly defined.

"God, I'm tired," he says. Three words with a greater weight than just tonight's physical exhaustion. There's a fatigue in him about life in general that makes me sad. He looks beat down, ready to lie there and be trampled. Wyatt's our Handler. He's the boss, the guy in charge who has all the answers. He's always on top of things. He isn't supposed to be like this.

Ash would know what to say.

My gaze flickers to the door, as though she might spontaneously appear. But no such luck.

I slide across the worn sofa to the center cushion, knowing full well offering comfort just isn't my thing. I tend to unwittingly err on the side of pity, which most people hate. If I do this wrong, he's going to get fucking pissed, and I don't know how he'll react if he gets pissed while plastered.

He's slouching with his left leg tucked beneath him, which puts his knee at the closest point to me. I give his thigh a gentle squeeze just above the kneecap. When I look up to offer a friendly smile, I'm startled by the intensity of his stare. His eyes burn with something that takes my breath away and squeezes my heart tight. I can't even pin a name on the emotion.

"I'm glad you were home," he says.

It takes me a minute to find my voice. "I almost wasn't. Guess you have good timing, huh?" Every note of humor falls flat.

"Was it worth it?"

Okay, now he's really not making sense. "Was what worth it?"

He points his water bottle at me, then gestures all around us. "You. It. Going out. Sore note."

It takes a supreme effort not to roll my eyes at his patronizing tone. "Why do you care, Wyatt? Jealous?" His silence sends a niggle of worry worming through my guts. I yank my hand off his leg, embarrassed that I left it there. He's probably just feeling some Handler-produced overprotective instinct because I was so sick last week. Sick enough for him to sit by my bed and nurse me through the worst of the fever. Surely I can nurse him through this.

Or at least make it so he doesn't hurt himself until he's over it. "Look, why don't you go sleep it off in my room?"

I offer only because I have the private, closet-sized bedroom. Ash and Jesse share the cramped apartment's other room. Triads live together, always within close proximity to their Handlers and assigned hunting grounds. Makes life easier. Except on nights like this when your drunk Handler shows up at your doorstep acting completely out of character, and you have to battle the urge to drop-kick his plastered ass to the curb.

My question finally seems to penetrate the fog in his brain. He nods, then sucks down the remaining water in his bottle. It misses the coffee table when he tries to put it down, and the bottle skitters to the floor. We reach for it at the same time. Our heads actually collide with a dull crack that sends white lightning between my eyes.

I give up and let Wyatt snag the bottle. He takes great care to balance it this time, then slithers to the edge of the couch cushion. I scoot closer and drape his arm across my shoulders. "Come on, drunkie. Let's go." I wrap my right arm around his waist. This close, I smell the whiskey on his breath and the faint hint of cinnamon on his skin and, beneath it, something sharper. More masculine.

The oddest thought strikes me: Wyatt smells good.

I bat it away and promise to beat the thought to a bloody pulp later. We get a good swing going, and Wyatt finally lurches to his feet. He's several inches taller than me and a good thirty pounds heavier, but I'm trained to kill goblins and half-Blood vampires in large numbers, and to potentially haul around wounded partners. Supporting him isn't too much trouble.

His feet drag across the floor as if he's not quite in control of them. We get through the bedroom door, and then he stops. Just ceases all forward motion, and I feel the tension creeping into his body and shoulders.

"What?" I ask.

He drops his chin, head turning to gaze down at me with a question in his eyes. His mouth opens, and whatever profound thing he might have been about to say is lost in an eye-watering belch.

I can't help it. I double over laughing, which leaves Wyatt without his crutch. He stumbles sideways until he hits the dresser. I drop to my knees, holding my stomach as deep belly laughs make my ribs ache. It isn't that I've never heard Wyatt burp before, or that I harbor any illusion about his perfect manners. It's seeing him down at my level—drunk, upset, and feeling the effects keenly—that's doing me in.

By the time I sober up, my stomach hurts and my legs are cramping. I use the bed for leverage and manage to stand. Wyatt's staring at me from his perch on top of the dresser—I can't even fathom how he got up there without falling right back off—legs wide apart, with a peculiar expression on his face.

He realizes I'm staring back, and the embarrassment disappears, shut down and glossed over with perfect calm. Perfect calm seasoned with a dash of that same strange intensity.

"I always knew you had more than one Gift," I say.

"What? To make an ass of myself?"

I blink. "Well, I was going to say a Magic Giggle-Inducing Burp, but okay." So he has made a tiny bit of an ass of himself, but I do it on a regular basis. He's due. And if he's feeling it now, he'll definitely be feeling it in the morning. That's just what I need—us regressing to year one, when I couldn't follow his orders for shit, and he threatened more than once to send me back to Boot Camp as a living example of what not to be. I finally found my footing with him, so what does he do? He crashes my place in the middle of the night, stone drunk, and then gets indignant about his own behavior.

"Look." I cross the half-dozen paces to stand in front of him—and right between his parted legs. "Just go to

bed, okay? Get pissy with me when we go back on rotation, but right now, I'm off the clock."

Both eyebrows arch high. His lips part, and he moist-
ens them with his tongue. Prepping an apology, perhaps? Or a simple agreement that, yes, it's time for bed.
I'm certainly ready to crash. Dealing with him lately
has been exhausting. He keeps staring, not talking. I tilt
my head and stick out my chin—something Ash calls my
"Yeah? And?" face. Wyatt finally moves, and it's to do
something I don't expect.

He kisses me full on the mouth. He has to lean out to
reach me, which leaves him teetering on the edge of the
dresser. There's no insistence, no tongue, no touching
anywhere except our mouths. A sweet press of his lips to
mine, offering hints of whiskey and mustard. It's nice. I
haven't had nice in . . . well, ever. Which is likely why
I haven't slapped him yet.

I don't get nice. I don't get sweet. I get fast and rough,
in a storeroom with a stranger. It's easier.

This is fucking complicated.

I pull away and take two steps back, his taste still lingering on my mouth. He blinks at me, owl-eyed, and I
have nothing in my arsenal capable of comprehending
the expression. So stupid me latches onto the first thing
that presents itself—self-deprecating humor.

"I said go to bed, not join me in bed. What do you
want sloppy seconds for anyway?"

A violent thundercloud darkens his expression. "You're
no one's sloppy seconds."

Danger alert. Kiss aside, this entire evening is teetering
on the cusp of becoming a full-blown disaster. "I'm flattered," I say, choosing my words carefully, "but you'll
still be my Handler in the morning—even if you can't
boss me around for two more days."

He nods, blinking hard.

I lift one shoulder in a shrug, hopefully conveying

more nonchalance than I feel. "Besides, we're all some-one's sloppy seconds, Wyatt." I'm done talking to him while he's carrying around so much booze in his blood-stream. I jack my thumb at the bed. "Now, buster."

Miraculously, he slides off the dresser and lands on his feet. I pull back the worn blanket and top sheet. He sits hard, and the mattress gives a few angry squeaks. After a couple of unsuccessful attempts to unlace his own sneakers, I do it for him, aware of his eyes drilling metaphorical holes in my skull.

Task done, he draws up his legs and falls onto his back, the already-beaten pillow puffing air as it's smashed even flatter. I toss the sheet and blanket across his chest—my version of tucking in.

Wyatt came here in some sort of pain, but I'll be damned if I'm going to ask what's got him so turned around. It was a mistake. The kiss was a mistake. It will be better for both of us if we wake up tomorrow and never mention tonight again.

At the door, I pause to hit the light. The door is nearly shut behind me when I hear him say, "I'm sorry."

I don't know if the apology is directed at me or his own disturbed memories, so I don't reply.

Chapter Nineteen

Kismet said to help ourselves to food and clothing, and yet it felt strange to walk into someone else's apartment. Without the boys—even I was starting to think of them that way, even though all three were anything but—the apartment felt empty. Missing the spark of life that made a place a home.

I wandered into the center of the living room, tense. Nervous, too, though I'd never say it out loud. The locks clicking into place did nothing to relax me. Wyatt lingered by the door. I didn't turn around. I wasn't ready to talk. Talking just complicated everything, and my life was complicated enough. My decision was made. Now I had to convince my heart to let go.

"Are you hungry?" Wyatt asked, the suddenness of his voice startling me.

A little. "No."

A pregnant pause. "Thirsty?"

"I'm fine." As if. "You know, Kismet was right about one thing."

"Yeah?"

I one-eightied and smiled. "You do kind of smell."

His face went perfectly still. Then a grin cracked through, and he chuckled. "Guess I should take advantage." With a wicked glint in his eyes, he added, "Of the shower."

"Have at it, Stinky. I'll rummage for clean clothes."

He strolled toward me, needing to pass in order to get

to the bathroom, and my heart leapt. Then fell when he brushed right by. He whipped back a split second later, grabbed me around the waist hard enough to send heated flares up my healing back, and pulled. I tumbled into his chest, pulse racing, with a gasp he swallowed with a kiss. For its sudden buildup, the kiss was surprisingly gentle. His mouth moved softly over mine, tongue tracing gentle lines across my lips. Probing no deeper, even when I opened for him. Thumbs rose to caress the sensitive spots behind my ears. My scalp tingled. The abrasion of his beard scraped my cheeks. If a kiss could be both sensual and chaste, he'd mastered it.

I didn't shake myself out of it until the bathroom door shut with a loud clack. A few more kisses like that and I'd never be able to leave him. Just thinking it made my heart hurt and my stomach ache. My cheeks still burned from the brush of his unshaven skin and a wicked plan formed in my mind.

I kicked off my shoes and socks and, ignoring my promise to find him clean clothes, darted barefoot around the apartment to the background music of running water, collecting a few things in the kitchen as I went. The two most important items, however, were behind the closed bathroom door. I briefly contemplated teleporting inside to get them. The quick shower shutoff decided for me. That had to be a record.

Why not, idiot? Isn't like you have a lot of time to waste.

With one of the items in my hand, I staked out the bathroom door. Heard the clink of the shower curtain rings. Faint ruffling that could only be a towel over skin. The door pulled inward. Wyatt's damp head poked out, searching. He caught me in his peripheral and jumped. Grinned. I smiled back. He glanced down at my hands.

"Am I supposed to wear that?" he asked.

"Yep," I replied, twisting it around my fingers.

"Just that? I don't really think it's decent."

"You got a towel on?"

He stepped out, presenting arms and legs and everything they were attached to, the best parts hidden behind a cinched bath towel. Water trickled from his hair, down his neck, making thin rivulets across his shoulders. Every muscle was perfectly toned, his abs well defined, though he seemed thinner without his clothes on. I guess I wasn't the only one not eating much for the past week.

"I think the color clashes with my towel," he said.

"I won't mind and you won't see it."

His eyebrows arched dramatically. A playful grin quirked the corners of his mouth, showing me a side of him I rarely got to see. The man who knew how to tease and have fun when the world wasn't crashing down around his ears.

"Turn around and close your eyes," I said.

He obeyed without fussing. I stretched the candy cane–speckled necktie—who owned it or why was not something I wanted to contemplate—across his eyes and tied it tight.

"Evy?"

"Trust me."

"You know I do."

"Then hush."

I led him into the kitchen, turned him around, and helped him sit on the dining chair I'd put near the sink. He tilted his head curiously when I tucked another towel around his neck and secured it with a chip clip.

"I'll be right back," I said, and then darted into the bathroom to collect the last two things necessary for this little experiment. I deliberately dragged my feet on the carpet as I returned. No sense in startling him. He was already tense, straight-backed, hands picking at the towel covering his lap. His head turned toward me with a question on his lips and in the slant of his eyebrows.

I placed one of the objects on the counter and shook the other a few times, then swirled an apple-sized amount onto my palm. The sudsy scent of shaving cream made his nostrils flare. I smoothed it across his cheeks and chin, over his upper lip, and as far down his throat as his prickly dark hair went, covering it all in a marshmallow of white.

"Tilt your head back." I rinsed my hand in the sink and let the water run until it warmed, then held the razor under it.

"Do you know what you're doing?"

I laughed. "Nope. Want me to stop?"

"No." If his quiet tone didn't convince me, the slight tenting of his towel did.

I pressed the razor to his throat, struck by the sheer power of it. Wyatt had nothing to fear, no reason to think I'd use this submissive position against him. I'd die for him, and in some ways, it's what I was preparing to do. For him and Phin and Kismet and Tybalt, and for all the innocent people in my city that Thackery had threatened.

My hand started shaking. I pulled the razor away, held a deep breath, then exhaled.

"Evy?"

"I'm fine. Just relax."

The gurgle of running water and scrape of the razor over skin was all I heard until the unmistakable raspy sound of his increased breathing overtook them. I ignored it, as well as the tenting towel and the growing ache in my abdomen, and continued the intimate act.

His upper lip was last, the cream falling away to reveal clean skin that would be shadowed again in a few hours. I rinsed the razor, patted it dry, and used the towel around his neck to wipe away any excess cream.

A dollop tried to hide behind his left ear. Leaning close, back aching, I inhaled the clean scent. Exhaled. Wyatt made a soft noise in his throat, recognizing the nearness of me. I pressed my cheek to his—first one, then the other.

"Close enough?" he asked.

"Definitely."

Strong arms circled my waist and pulled me onto his lap. Instead of removing the blindfold, he traced the shape of my face with featherlight touches, the pads of his fingertips blazing a hot path on my cool skin. Over my cheeks, across my chin, down the slope of my nose. The seam of my lips. I flicked out my tongue and tasted his finger—the barest hint of soap still lingered. He shuddered. His erection strained hot and hard, even beneath layers of terry and denim.

I remembered the first and only time we'd made love—literally a lifetime ago—but the memories were faint. Like watching an old movie slightly out of focus. It was all there—his gentle, questing hands and possessive kisses, the strong slide of him in and out of my body—distanced and unclear, marred by my new body's lack of physical memory. Knowledge without experience.

I hated it and loved it, because I got to try something no one else could—two first times with the same man.

I pulled off his blindfold and let it flutter to the floor. He blinked hard, eyes readjusting to the harsh kitchen light, and settled his hands on my hips. My fingers grazed his chest, the pads of my thumbs brushing over his nipples. He made a sound deep in his throat—something caught between a growl and a groan.

His right hand tangled in my hair and drew me down, and finally we kissed. Our mouths moved, lips parting, and I drank in the taste of him. His tongue darted into my mouth, stroked across my teeth, until it was met by mine. A delicate dance began as flesh teased flesh. I dragged my fingers down his bare arms and earned a soft moan. His free hand drifted from my hip to my butt and squeezed, sending a shock of heat searing straight to my core.

Wyatt's mouth left gentle, tasting kisses across my cheeks to my neck. I breathed him in, holding firmly to the knowledge that this was *Wyatt*. I shifted on his lap, unsure what to do with my hands. So I directed his instead. I untangled his hand from my hair and slid it down to the hem of my T-shirt, pressing it against my stomach.

The rough pads of his fingers tickled my bare skin, but he didn't take the hint. I helped him out by yanking the shirt up and off, my hair tumbling back down around my shoulders in thick waves. Much like our positions a week ago on our apartment sofa, and I actually froze.

"What?" he asked, a tiny sparkle of panic in his expression.

"Just waiting for the Earth to move."

He blinked, and I could see the retort forming in his mind. Then he smiled warmly. "For a second, I thought—"

"I was having a flashback?"

"Yeah." He swirled his finger in my belly button. "Or you'd just remembered you forgot to lock the door."

"You locked the door, dummy. Besides, even if it wasn't, after the pointed look Kismet gave me in the car when she dropped us off, I think she'd recognize the necktie on the doorknob as the universal sign to keep out."

Wyatt blanched. "You didn't."

"No, I didn't, but I won't let myself regret not being with you while I have the chance."

Grief flickered across his face, there and gone so quickly I might not have noticed it if I weren't staring right at him. I knew him, could practically hear his thoughts, begging me not to think of this as our last time together. To think of it as the first of many, and to continue believing we'd find another way.

His fingers skated across my ribs to my back, pausing where the bandages started. The itch-ache of healing was persistent and constant. The wounds would be gone soon. "They won't bother me," I said, answering his unasked question.

"I don't want to hurt you."

"Then don't say no."

"I'm not." His voice was so quiet, almost a hoarse whisper. "This just feels like some cruel déjà vu, that's all. Making love to you hours before you leave and don't come back."

A lump clogged my throat. I wrapped my arms around his shoulders and hugged him tight, even as he enveloped me in his. He wasn't wrong, and that scared me. A month ago, still Original Recipe Evy, we'd been together in a cheap motel, and then I'd gone off to chase a lead, only to end up kidnapped, tortured, and eventually dead. Now we weren't in a motel, and I wasn't the woman I'd been, but his emotions hadn't changed. He'd loved me then, and he loved me now.

I hated how heartlessly life seemed to be repeating itself.

"The future isn't guaranteed, Wyatt, we both know that better than most. So let's stop living in the past and dreaming of the future. Let's just enjoy the now. Please?" My voice cracked on the final word.

He pushed against me, and I slid off his lap, sure I was in for either a fight or a rejection. I wasn't prepared for him to stand and scoop me up. I wrapped my arms around his neck and snuggled against his shoulder, inhaling him as he walked us across the living room, toward the bedrooms, his answer given without words.

The first bedroom had a single twin-sized bed. Not completely ideal, but better than a sofa or the floor. Wyatt lowered me to my feet, and I didn't have time to wonder whose room we were in before he seared me with a kiss. His tongue dove into my mouth, and I surged against him, his arousal pressing hot against my belly. When had he lost the towel?

Well, that wasn't quite fair. Reeling with the intensity of his kiss, I reached around and fumbled with my bra clasp, desperate for more skin on skin. It snapped open. The straps slid down my shoulders and arms, and then it was on the floor. He kissed each breast with butterfly touches. I gasped, twining my fingers in his hair, holding him there unnecessarily, because he seemed in no hurry to stop.

Heat and desire made my legs tremble. I finally pulled him away, and he grunted a halfhearted protest. I silenced him with a finger to his lips. He kissed the tip of it, his eyes half-lidded and flaming with want.

Aware of the silver cross dangling between my naked breasts, I unfastened the necklace and tucked it into my pocket. I undid my jeans and pushed them down, slapping his hands when he tried to help. I kicked the jeans and underwear away.

"God, Evy," he whispered, staring hungrily at my naked body. My hips jutted too sharply; my stomach was too concave. He didn't seem to notice the flaws, the reminders of the hell I'd survived. Part of me was embarrassed by his appraisal—a small bit of Chalice rebelling against my nudity.

I took a step forward and kissed him with featherlightness. Just a reminder of who he was. I ached for him in a way I'd never ached for anyone. I wanted gentle; I wanted nice; I wanted both with him. I needed them with him, even if only once.

I cupped his cheeks in my palms, then slid them down

his neck to his shoulders, across his pecs. Just feeling and memorizing the way smooth skin stretched over taut muscle. Watching his chest rise and fall. I circled behind him, hands skating across his ribs, then up each ridge of his spine. Gooseflesh prickled the back of his neck. I traced them again, down to the thin scar in the middle of his back. He inhaled sharply.

So many different adjectives to describe him perched on my tongue without falling. In the past, sex was about getting off quickly. I'd never taken the time to truly appreciate a man's naked body—especially one as toned and well proportioned as Wyatt's. It had never seemed important, until now. Everything about him was stunning—and I had to let it all go.

Grief tightened my throat. I pressed my forehead to his shoulder. Somehow his hands found mine, pulled them to his hips and squeezed.

"Evy?"

I couldn't speak, certain I'd burst into tears if I opened my mouth and verbalized my thoughts. I had to be strong for both of us. Being left behind a second time would be ten times harder for Wyatt than leaving was for me. Right?

Yeah, and there's this bridge for sale. . . .

Wyatt released my hands and turned to face me. I didn't look up, even when he cupped my cheek and tried to lift my head. He stroked my hair, his thoughts hidden, but affection clear in his gentle touches. "Talk to me, Evy, please?"

"I'm scared." I breathed the words, unsure if they had enough volume to even be counted as spoken.

He must have heard me, because he tensed. "Of me?"

The question pierced my heart like a needle. "God no. Not of you, Wyatt."

Only a fraction of tension lifted. "Of sex?"

Yes. No. A little of both. "Of after." My eyes stung and my throat closed. No, dammit, I was not going to cry. His earlier words about a cruel déjà vu came back to me like a splash of cold water. Could I do this to him again? To us?

"Come here." He pulled me close. I wrapped my arms around his shoulders and melted against his warm skin, face pressed to the crook of his neck. His hands rubbed up and down my back. The embrace should have been awkward, given our nudity, but it wasn't. I found an unexpected strength in it—in him.

God, I hated losing this. I hated not having an actual choice about giving him up. I hated Thackery for taking Phin, and myself for not being smart enough to find another solution. Any other solution.

Dammit all.

A soft sheet caressed my skin. I hadn't noticed us moving or curling up together on the bed, or Wyatt pulling the blankets up over us. I snuggled close to his chest, our legs twined together, and tucked my head beneath his chin. I wanted to climb inside of him and stay there, embraced by his strength and love. I inhaled him, safe in his arms. Temporarily.

I shoved away my macabre thoughts and self-loathing— nothing I could do about any of it at this late hour. I concentrated on feeling Wyatt all around me. Just us.

Our combined breathing was the only sound for a while.

"I'll get you back, Evy," he whispered.

I nodded, the only response I could muster for his impossible-to-keep promise. My heart was tearing in two. One half was desperate to make love to him, to feel him in my body, to see his face when he climaxed—to give him this final gift. The other half was terrified it meant I wasn't coming back. As a Hunter, my life was about dying to protect others; as supercombo Evy, my life was about so much more. I had something to lose.

I loved Wyatt. Whether I wanted to or not, I loved him. It didn't matter anymore if it had started with Chalice's attraction, or if it had started that night in my old apartment when he kissed me for the first time. Hers or mine, I no longer cared, because we were me. And both parts were vital to my survival in the here and now. More than anything else, I needed to love Wyatt. I needed to live for him.

Yes, I could give him this. Give *us* this.

I trailed my fingers down Wyatt's abs, through the coarse hair below his belly button, and wrapped gentle fingers around his erection. He trembled, and I reveled in the power of such a simple thing. I stroked my hand up and down, working a light, steady rhythm, encouraged by the soft sounds coming from his throat. His half-lidded eyes and loving smile made my heart flutter.

"You keep doing that, and I'm going to come," he gasped.

"Better not."

"Is that a challenge?"

I grinned. "Maybe."

With a soft growl, he shifted us in the small bed so that I was on my back with him settled nicely between my legs. He captured my mouth in a bruising kiss that meant business. His right hand tickled down to cup my breast, tweaking the nipple into hardness and sending liquid heat straight to my core. I arched up, wanting more, and his erection rubbed hot against my belly.

A wicked gleam sparked in his eyes. Fingers skated across my hip, down my leg to my kneecap, caressing the skin and tickling. He kissed me again, his tongue licking into my mouth, as those questing fingers drew circles back up my leg. So close to where I wanted his touch. I made a soft, begging sound—not a whimper but damned close.

Please, Wyatt, oh please . . .

Finally, he slipped a single digit down, down, then into the very center of me. I cried out against his lips and clenched around him, amazed and alarmed at how full I felt. In and out, over and over—his finger worked me, hitting all the right places. A second finger joined the first, and my hips thrust against his hand, eager for the ache to be replaced by something else. My belly tightened in anticipation. Then he moved his thumb up to press against my clitoris, and lights winked behind my eyes.

It hadn't felt like this before, had it? No, it had never felt like this before.

I didn't think it would happen so soon, but it did—I came hard, gasping nonsense, and he didn't relent. He nibbled my throat, my cheeks, my mouth, drawing out the orgasm until I cried for him to stop.

He did. Using his elbows for leverage, he smiled at me. I could only grin lazily, still a bit breathless. Tiny aftershocks made my stomach quiver. God, but I wanted this always. The thought hitched the air in my lungs.

He kissed me, his tongue stabbing into my mouth, and I welcomed it greedily. I traced circles on his back, over each lump of his spine, across the scar I hated so much, down to his ass and squeezed.

With a soft growl, he tore his mouth from mine. His hips jerked and pressed his length closer. I saw how hard it was for him to take it slow and savor each moment. Saw it in the tight pull of his mouth, the lines of concentration around his eyes, the beads of sweat on his forehead.

"Make love to me, Wyatt. Please."

My encouragement broke the last of his restraint. He raised his hips. I slid one hand around to grasp him and guide him to my entrance. With agonizing slowness, he slid inside. Filled me, stretched me achingly far, made my body weep with discomfort and pleasure. Chalice . . . we . . . *I* hadn't been a virgin. No, just inexperienced— so the opposite of what I'd once been.

But oh, how I wanted this.

Our hips finally met, and Wyatt could go no farther. A sense of completion washed over me, tinged with something else that clambered in the far reaches of my mind. I shoved away the memories that threatened to surface and destroy everything, and concentrated solely on him. On us, finally together.

"God, Evy."

I thrust my hips just a bit, reveling in the exquisite fullness of having him inside me. "Love me."

He groaned. "I don't want to hurt you."

"You won't."

He was hesitant at first, his thrusts shallow and gentle, allowing me to adjust, but it was not what I wanted. I encouraged him with upward thrusts of my own, and his hesitation crumbled. I wrapped my legs around his waist and locked my ankles. He slid in and out, his hard, burning thrusts timed with his labored breathing. I rose to meet him, my own pleasure building again over the persistent throb in my back and the exquisite ache of his length stretching me. Loving me. I tried to ignore the wounds and concentrate wholly on Wyatt.

Not on my position beneath him.

On the way my insides quivered, and on the thick slide of him in my body, the scent of his sweat, the heat of his breath on my face.

Not on the way he pressed me down, held me hard to the mattress.

On Wyatt.

No one else. Nowhere else. Here and now.

Breath on my face . . . sweet and heady and human breath.

Holding me down . . . pleasuring me, driving me to orgasm.

Pressing me into the mattress . . . making love to me.

Making love.

His pace slowed; a thumb brushed my cheek. "Evy?"

I met his concerned gaze but couldn't force out words. My mind and body were consumed by conflicting emotions as old memories scratched just below the surface. I didn't want them but couldn't seem to turn them off.

Somehow Wyatt knew, or he simply guessed my back was bothering me. He rolled us until Wyatt was beneath me, me straddling his waist, hands on his chest.

In control.

Just us.

I didn't think I could love him more if I tried.

I set the pace, starting slow, a gentle glide up and down, and nothing else existed. The memories stayed away, beaten into the recesses of my mind by the pleasure coiling in my abdomen. I leaned down, thrusting my tongue into his mouth to taste him, and once again, we shared a breath. He squeezed my hips, and I rocked faster, harder. Our labored breathing melted into a dull roar that blocked out everything except the pounding of my heart and the joining of our bodies. Faster. Harder still, unrelenting. I closed my eyes and held on, his thrusts matching mine, as a second orgasm washed over me, fast and blinding. Pleasure rippled from head to toes, trembling my limbs and seizing my heart. I shouted, hearing only Wyatt's voice as he roared his climax and spilled into me.

We melted together, a tangle of arms and legs and sweat and sex. I felt his lips on my face and throat. After a bit—seconds? hours?—he slipped out, and we rolled onto our sides. I snuggled close, nearly bursting with satisfaction.

Wyatt grinned at me with swollen lips and rosy cheeks. "You continue to amaze me, Evangeline Stone." The awe in his voice threatened to turn me into a puddle of goo.

I kissed the center of his chest, tasting the salt of his sweat. "You're not so bad yourself."

Laughter rumbled through his chest. His hands stroked my arms and shoulders. "Careful, or you may inflate my ego."

"Arrogance is your emotional tap, right? Just doing my duty as your partner."

Partner. It was an odd word to use for a man who'd been my boss for the four years I'd known him—save the last month or so of our lives as we'd first become allied fugitives, and then so much more. All in such a short amount of time. Triumph and defeat. Love and loss. Joy and fear. We'd defied death, defeated a demon-possessed elf, protected the future of a were-Clan, saved the lives of countless innocents, and summoned half a truck into a log cabin—not too bad, really.

Wyatt folded me against his chest, and I could have stayed like that forever. Or until restlessness drove me back out into the world, ready to hunt and fight. Knowing I'd be able to return to his arms at the end of the day and be loved and protected all over again.

But I wasn't able to.

Lips brushed my forehead. "Think we should change the bedding?"

"Be my guest."

He chuckled. "We should probably get up, though."

I lifted my head and peered over him. Groaned. The blue neon numbers on the bedside clock announced ten minutes until company arrived. "You're right."

"Go clean up. I'll find some clothes and tidy up in here."

I gifted him with a soft kiss, which he returned with enthusiasm, then reluctantly climbed out of bed, chilly from the loss of physical contact. I gathered my scattered clothes and went across the hall.

In the bathroom, I washed as best I could, then scrubbed my face and brushed my hair. No time for a proper shower. Everything ached deliciously and for all the right reasons this time. My cheeks were flushed and my eyes bright, and for the first time since waking from that damned coma, I looked somewhat healthy.

I returned to the living area. Wyatt was dressed in someone's dark blue jeans and a hunter-green polo, not his usual color combo. "What, no black?" I teased.

"Not that looked clean." He closed the distance between us and settled his hands on my hips. He didn't have to ask the question lurking in his mind.

"I'm fine. Better than fine, actually. Kind of amazing." I drew him into a gentle kiss, just enough to put the taste of him back on my lips.

The doorbell rang. I jumped, both of us startled by the unfamiliar chime.

"Gina wouldn't ring," Wyatt said.

A second chime, followed by a fist rapping on the door. "Mr. Truman?" a muffled male voice said, oddly familiar.

"Who the hell knows you're here?" I whispered.

He crossed to the door on silent feet and peered through the peephole. His shoulders tensed. Not good.

"Mr. Truman, I need to speak with you."

Wyatt turned his head toward me and mouthed two words I didn't understand at first: "James Reilly." I stared. Mouthed back: "Who?" Then the penny dropped. The private investigator who'd cornered him at Alex's memorial last week. Fucking hell. Wyatt waved at me. I bolted into the bathroom (apparently my new favorite hiding place) and closed the door nearly all the way.

The front door creaked open. "What can I do for you, Mr. Reilly?" Wyatt's voice was icy.

"I was hoping for a few moments of your time," Reilly said. That same conversational tone, designed to set his interviewee at ease.

"I really don't have a few minutes today. I'm about to head out on business."

"Of course, and I apologize for—"

"How did you know I was here?"

The silence was deafening. I craned to see. They hadn't moved from the front door. Still out of my line of sight.

"I'm an investigator, Mr. Truman. It's my job to find people."

"Have you been following me?" We both knew that wasn't possible.

"No, I've been following a red-haired young woman who's come to this apartment several times over the last week."

Bastard was following Kismet? Why? Reilly said he was looking into the fire at Rufus's old apartment building, and Kismet wasn't involved in— Shit. If she'd gone to visit Rufus recently—

"So you were watching the apartment," Wyatt said, "and you saw me come inside."

"Yes, with a rather pretty brunette, as a matter of fact."

I didn't have to see Wyatt to know he'd tensed up, even if he'd somehow managed to keep his expression neutral. This Reilly was a major pain in the ass.

"Mr. Truman, may I come inside?"

"No. Like I said, I'm leaving very soon."

"Of course."

"I still have your business card, so why don't I call you—"

"May I speak with Chalice Frost please?" Reilly's tone had changed completely. Gone was the genial fellow asking harmless questions, replaced with cold determination. "Because unless she has an unrecorded twin roaming the city, she was the brunette I saw come inside with you. So where is she?"

Crap.

Chapter Twenty

"I really think you should leave," Wyatt said.

"Why?" Reilly asked. "Because you have a dead woman hiding in this apartment? Or because the red-head I've been following has fingerprints that match those of a young woman named Virginia O'Malley who died seven years ago?"

Seven years ago—the time Kismet joined the Triads. It shouldn't have surprised me that she'd changed her name, but it did. This guy was learning too much. There were always detectives or self-important P.I.'s who poked into Triad business, hoping to make a name for themselves or discover some huge cover-up. We had always dealt with them the same way—by making an offer they couldn't refuse. Reilly was teetering very close to the tipping point.

"Fine," Wyatt said. "Come in."

Uh-oh.

The door clicked shut. Shoes shuffled across carpet.

"Might as well come out and show him."

Trusting Wyatt to have a plan, I emerged from the bathroom and presented myself. Reilly stared wide-eyed, lips parted, as though he hadn't quite believed his own bluff. He took a step toward me. Wyatt slipped behind him and got the older man in a choke hold. Reilly wheezed, fingers clawing at Wyatt's forearm, face turning red. He was unconscious in moments, and Wyatt let his body slump to the floor.

"Now what?" I asked.

"He becomes someone else's problem." He crouched and searched Reilly's pockets, producing a small notepad, which he flipped open. It looked nearly full of cramped, precise printing. Wyatt's eyebrows shot into his hairline.

"Do I want to know?" He continued flipping pages as though he hadn't heard me. "Hello?"

"Audaìn."

My stomach knotted. "What?"

"It's the name of—"

"Of a Blood Family. I know." Or more precisely, of Isleen's family. Isleen was as close to a friend among the vampires as I'd ever admit to having. She'd saved my life once by fishing me out of a sunbaked trash bin after I'd been stabbed and tossed into it. We were tentative allies. "Why does he have that name in his notebook?"

"Don't know, but something tells me he's not as disinterested in the paranormal side of this city as he seems." Wyatt put the notebook aside and emptied Reilly's pockets—wallet, handgun, car keys, an envelope of photographs.

I flipped through the pictures. They were impersonal shots, probably from surveillance. Photos of Kismet and her Hunters outside this building, Phineas outside his apartment building, various people I didn't know at all, Wyatt at the cemetery with Leo Forrester, Wyatt exiting our old building. Near the end was one that startled me into nearly dropping the entire stack—long white hair, willowy build so slim as to appear sexless, eyes hidden behind sunglasses, pale skin shimmering in what was obviously daylight.

"Holy fuck," I said, showing the photo to Wyatt. "This is Istral. It's Isleen's sister."

"The one Kelsa killed?"

"Yes." The night old-me was captured by the goblins,

I'd gone to see Max, a gargoyle informant, and was blindsided. Max had been arguing with Istral about rising hostilities among the various races. Perhaps to prove she was serious, Kelsa—the goblin Queen who tortured me to death—shot Istral with an anticoagulant round that killed her within seconds. That was a month ago.

So much for Reilly investigating the apartment fire, which had happened over a week later. Four more photos of different Bloods I didn't recognize followed, the last pictures in the stack. No names, no dates. The backgrounds had no discernible buildings.

"He knew a hell of a lot more than he was letting on," I said.

I rummaged around in the kitchen until I found a couple of zip ties to secure Reilly. Wyatt's cell rang. He flipped it open with a terse "Yeah?" A pause. "We have a problem upstairs that needs to be babysat." He explained briefly, then listened, and I shifted impatiently. "Okay."

"Kismet?" I asked when he hung up.

"Yeah. She and Milo are on their way up."

"Nice of her to call first."

A smile ghosted his face, pinched off by worry. We maneuvered the unconscious Reilly into a dining chair, zipped him, tied him with a length of nylon rope from under the kitchen sink, and gagged him with a stretched T-shirt. Not bad for two minutes' work. Then we collected the few weapons we'd had on us when we entered.

Wyatt's phone rang a second time right as the front door opened. He checked the display, then handed it to me and went to shush the new arrivals.

"Stone," I said.

"It's Jenner. The money is ready to be transferred. I'll text the account number to this phone."

"Thank you, Mr. Jenner."

"The Assembly will not forget this debt, Ms. Stone."
For a second, I thought he meant the money. Then he
said, "You honor your species with your sacrifice, and
that will be long remembered." The vehemence in his
words made me want to cry.

"Are your people—?"

"Searching, yes, but the city is vast and he is not likely
to be kept in plain sight."

"Well, with any luck, he'll be home in a couple of
hours."

"Yes. Good-bye, Evangeline Stone."

"Yeah." I closed the phone, and a few seconds later,
the account number was saved in the phone's memory.
One hour until we'd need to use it.

Kismet was already poring over Reilly's photos and
notebook. She didn't try to hide her anger at the surveillance pictures, or the fact that she hadn't noticed a tail.
"Too bad the asshole didn't follow me up to the cabin.
We'd have been saved the problem of dealing with him
ourselves."

I snorted. "He said he was new to the city."

"He could have been lying."

"Does it even matter?" Milo asked. "He knows a lot
more than is healthy for him, which makes him not our
problem. He's Nevada's problem now."

"Nevada?"

"Yeah," Kismet said without looking up from the
notebook. "He'll be here with his team in twenty minutes to pick up the prisoner and take him to a holding
facility for questioning."

Terrific. Nice to be told pertinent details like that.
Only she probably assumed I wasn't in the need-to-
know circle anymore, and she was right. "How's Felix?"
I asked suddenly. How selfish was I that it took me so
long?

"Critical, but alive." This time she looked up, her

green eyes cold. "He's had transfusions, but he also has a raging infection the doctors have never seen before. Tybalt's staying with him."

"Anyone want breakfast?" Milo asked as he wandered into the kitchen.

"Whatever you can knock out," Kismet said. "Coffee, too."

I stared. She wanted breakfast? The idea of eating anything made my stomach churn in an unpleasant way. Even though it was probably nerves, I wasn't about to tempt fate. I shook my head at Milo.

"You should eat, Evy," Wyatt said.

"I'll have coffee." It was my compromise. We'd been up all night, hadn't slept, hadn't eaten much, and had used our Gifts to their limits and beyond. At least the caffeine would keep me conscious for a few more hours. "When's Baylor coming back with the computer?"

"Around the same time as Nevada," Kismet replied.

"Okay." Time was ticking away loudly inside my head. I hadn't felt it so keenly since the battle at Olsmill, and, while the end results wouldn't be quite as spectacular as unleashing demons on the world, I was still preparing to sacrifice myself to protect others. Protect the city from the whims of a madman, and all I wanted to do was hide in the other room until the problem went away.

But I just couldn't live with myself if I did that. It would have been so much easier to fall on my sword when all I had in my life were people I'd willingly die for. Because now I had someone in my life I'd not only die for but I wanted desperately to *live* for.

The freshly deodorized scent of the bedroom surrounded me. I didn't close the door, just wandered inside and sat down on the neatly made bed. Smoothed my hand across the damp blanket where I'd made love to Wyatt not a quarter hour ago. The pillows had lost their scent of us, and I longed for it. Just a small whiff as I pressed one pillow to my face. Held it tight to my chest. I shifted until my back rested against the wall and drew my knees up, locking the pillow in my lap.

The clock didn't stop ticking.

"Coffee's ready."

I snapped my head up, unsure when I'd rested my forehead on the pillow and shut my eyes. Kismet stood just inside the bedroom. She'd traded her bloodstained shirt for something that belonged to one of her Hunters, judging by the bagginess on her slim frame. Her stance screamed of repressed frustration and the need to go a couple rounds with a heavy bag.

"Thanks," I said.

"For what it's worth, I admire you. I don't know if I could do what you're doing."

I couldn't have been more shocked if she'd said she was actually a vampire, had sucked everyone dry in the other room, and was about to eat me for dessert. It took several tries to find my voice. "What is it I'm doing?"

"Willingly giving yourself to who knows what fate at Thackery's hands, even after everything you've already been through."

My lips curled in a sneer. "You mean I'm letting myself be potentially tortured to death twice?"

"Yes."

"Nothing Thackery could physically cook up will ever come close to what Kelsa did to me." The only true torture he could possibly inflict was leaving Wyatt behind to wonder, and to hope for my rescue, knowing Wyatt would never rest until he saw proof of my life or death. Knowing that finding my broken, disposed-of body for a second time might destroy him.

"We'll be tracking you," she said, stepping into the room and pushing the door to within an inch of being shut. She fished into her jeans pocket and pulled out a small box, the size of a tin of mints. Matte black, with a single red dot on the center of the lid. She didn't have to tell me what was inside; they'd been explained to us in Boot Camp. "We'll do everything we can to keep tabs and bring you back, Stone, but you may want this, too."

I took the tin, unable to keep my fingers from shaking, and tucked it into my rear pocket. As far as backup plans went, swallowing a suicide pill wasn't my style. "Yeah, thanks."

"Wyatt would kill me if he knew I gave that to you."

I snickered at her poor choice of words. "We have them available for a reason, right?"

"Right."

More and more, against my better judgment, I was starting to like Gina Kismet. I was also starting to get very curious about her. Perhaps because I really knew so little, and every tidbit I learned contradicted the one before. It drew me back to a conversation that seemed like years ago and a comment I hadn't been able to shake.

"Who was he?"

Kismet frowned, her slim eyebrows furrowing. "Who was who?"

I hesitated. She could tell me to shut up, mind my own business, or quite possibly shoot me between the eyes for my impudence. But I'd asked the question, and it was time to shit or get off the metaphorical pot.

"Who was the Hunter you weren't supposed to fall in love with?"

Kismet went perfectly still. Not a muscle twitched, not a wisp of hair moved. Even her eyes seemed flat, lifeless. Fascinating, if it weren't so damned scary. Then she blinked and the spell was broken. I resigned myself to getting no answers and watching her storm back out of the bedroom.

Instead, she plunked down next to me, slid back until she hit the wall, and sat cross-legged, as if we were girlfriends sharing a weekly gabfest. "His name was Lucas Moore."

I knew the name, and if I recalled my history correctly, Milo had been his replacement in the Triad. She'd been in love with her own Hunter. Hypocrite didn't begin to describe what she was, and yet I couldn't drum up any anger or indignation. Just pity. And I knew she'd hate pity.

I covered with a stupid question, because I already knew the answer. "When did he die?"

"One year, two months, twelve days ago." Her perfectly trimmed fingernails picked at an imaginary snag on her jeans leg. "He was my Hunter for almost two years, and I . . . we felt something from the first day. Denied it, of course, for as long as we could, and then we hid it for over a year. I always told myself it didn't affect my leadership decisions, but I don't really know. It's hard to judge actions when your mind is clouded by emotion."

"It's not easy staying behind."

"No." If she understood how much more was implied in my statement beyond simply her duties as a Handler, she gave no indication. "When Lucas died, I thought I would die, too. I'd never loved someone with my whole heart, and it broke me, Evy."

Her use of my nickname didn't go unnoticed. I couldn't picture the strong, vital, persistent redhead next to me as a crying, shattered emotional wreck. Couldn't picture her as anything except what I'd always seen, even with the tremor in her voice and glimmer in her eyes.

Our history was tangential, our paths barely crossing in four years—Kismet and I hadn't directly interacted in any meaningful way until Olsmill, even though our Triads had. And gossip never really died. People talked, especially when teams went out of rotation for Hunter injury or loss, and Gina's Triad had seen more than its fair share of bad luck and loss—four deaths in four years. The Handler herself had barely survived a brutal attack the night Felix was assigned.

The only thing I really remembered about the time around Lucas's death was Wyatt. He'd seemed distracted, around less than he should have been. Guess he'd been helping out a grieving friend.

"Wyatt loved you for a long time," she said, switching conversational tracks. "He never said anything, but if you've lived it, you can spot it. Then you died and he went apeshit. After seeing what I'd . . . I was furious at him for a lot of reasons, and now I think it was because I was jealous."

I gaped at her, flabbergasted. "Jealous?"

She tilted her head, never breaking eye contact. "Jealous that he loved you so much he was willing to trade everything to bring you back. And he did. It made what I'd felt for Lucas seem very small."

"Wyatt was manipulated by Tovin into agreeing to that deal. Tovin made him believe that if I was brought back, we'd both live and have a future together. Wyatt never would have done it without that promise."

"True, but I asked myself not long after Olsmill if I'd do what Wyatt did, had our situations been reversed. If I would trade my free will for the tiniest hope of Lucas and me being together again."

Don't ask, don't ask, don't ask! "And?"

"I couldn't say yes."

"That doesn't mean anything, Kismet. People feel differently, they love differently, but it doesn't . . ." Emotional soul-baring was not my forte, and I hadn't had this sort of girl talk in . . . well, ever. I'd never had a best friend. While Ash had been the closest thing I'd had to a girlfriend, we'd never discussed love or boyfriends or anything similar. Our jobs had always canceled out the odds of a healthy long-term relationship, so why bother?

"Would you have died in Lucas's place?" I asked.

She nodded.

"So you and Wyatt really aren't that different."

"Yet he got his love back."

"Only because a gnome happened to give me a magic healing crystal." The crystal had been a lucky gift, given by an elderly gnome named Horzt in an effort to atone for his part in my resurrection. He'd both blessed and cursed me with my healing ability, and without that crystal, everything would be different now. Wyatt would have stayed dead, having bled out from friendly fire; I'd be dead for all intents and purposes, seeing as a demon had been hell-bent on having his demon wife possess my body for a fiendish reunion. The city would be in ruins.

Yeah, lucky preempt, that crystal.

Kismet made a sound—louder than a sigh and softer than a grunt. "After this little chat, you probably think trying to kill you at the factory was personal."

"No, I don't." I didn't have to think about my answer. Gina Kismet was the consummate professional—duty above self.

"Thanks."

And since we were on the topic of unusual Hunter romances . . . "Can I ask you a question about Milo?"

"If you have questions about Milo, you should ask Milo." It came out as a friendly suggestion, but I also heard the hidden warning in her tone.

The doorbell chimed. Kismet climbed off the bed and went out, leaving the door half-open. Muffled voices filtered down the hall and into the bedroom. I stayed put through questions about Reilly and what was going on. I'd never met Seth Nevada but guessed his voice was the deep, grating one doing most of the asking. It seemed none of the Handlers who patrolled outside of Mercy's

Lot were in on our little operation, and Nevada didn't seem happy about being left out of the loop.

Too fucking bad. The fewer people who knew about this trade with Thackery, the fewer would blame us if Thackery managed to develop and use his weapon. When the number of voices in the other room dwindled and the front door shut with a resounding bang, I rejoined the others.

Paul, Oliver, and Carly were there, sitting restlessly in the living room with Milo. Kismet and Baylor were at the dining room table with the laptop, going over basic functions. Without a word, Wyatt handed me a mug of steaming coffee. I carried it with me to the table. On the laptop's screen, a steady beep on top of a city map said that the dye was still working perfectly.

"Bastian talk to anyone after we left?" I asked.

Baylor nodded. "Exactly who he said he'd talk to."

When we didn't elaborate, Kismet asked, "And that means what, precisely?"

I deferred to my sort-of-superior and drank my coffee while Baylor expounded on Bastian's duplicity, his voice barely above a whisper so only Wyatt and Kismet could hear. The fury of their combined tempers was palpable. I grabbed Wyatt's hand and squeezed. The tension was vibrating off him. He held tight in return. A little too tight, but I didn't protest.

"This is insane," Kismet said.

No one argued with her.

"How much time before Thackery calls?" Baylor asked.

Wyatt replied before I could look for a clock. "Less than ten minutes."

Fucking hell. My stomach twisted into tiny, frozen knots. I put the half-finished coffee on the table and pulled Wyatt back down the hall to the bedroom. I didn't care what they thought. I wanted a few more minutes.

Once inside, Wyatt swept me into his arms, his mouth finding mine in a bruising kiss. I held him around the waist, molding my body to his, kissing him so hard our teeth scraped. Imprinting his taste on my tongue, his smell in my nose, his touch all over my skin. We held each other a while, until my arms trembled and some internal chronometer told me our time was almost up.

I pulled back, cold everywhere we no longer touched, and fished my necklace out of my pocket. It had become a part of me since I'd first found it. The silver cross glittered in the light. I opened Wyatt's palm, coiled it there, then curled his fingers back to hold it, and kissed his fist.

"I gave this to you once before for safekeeping," I said, my voice tight. "Hold it for me again?"

His eyes glittered. "Only if that means you're coming back for it."

"You know I'll do everything in my power, Wyatt. Me and Defeat aren't exactly pals."

"Yeah. It's one of the things I love about you, Evy."

I smiled. "I love you, too."

And that was when my ass rang.

"Fuck," he muttered.

"Yeah." I fished out the phone as we walked back to the living room, hand in hand, and had it on speaker by the time we got there. Instead of opening with my usual terse "Stone," I said, "The money's ready."

"Cutting to the chase, Ms. Stone? I like that." The calm lilt of Thackery's voice made my toes curl—and not in a good way. "Tell whoever else is listening to send it to this account."

He rattled off a number that Kismet typed into the laptop. I let her do her thing, having no earthly idea how money transfers worked. Two hundred grand was more cash than I'd see in a lifetime, and it was all going to this bastard via Blackmail Express. A full minute passed in silence. Even the other Hunters had gone completely still.

"Excellent," Thackery finally said. "I don't suppose, after our first meeting, I need remind you that you're to be alone and unarmed?"

"You don't."

"Keep this phone with you and go back to Grove Park. You have fifteen minutes."

"That's cutting it close from my current location."

"Then I suggest you get started." And he hung up.

Baylor closed the laptop. Everyone began moving without a single order being barked. Those cold knots continued twisting my stomach, unaffected by the scorching coffee I'd gulped.

I climbed into one Jeep with Wyatt, Kismet, and Milo. Baylor's crew piled into the second Jeep. Kismet drove. Wyatt and I sat in the back, clutching hands, just existing for a few more minutes. I couldn't think of anything else to say. He didn't try to offer platitudes or reiterate his unerring promise to find me and get me back alive. It was implied. Expected.

Six blocks from Grove Park, Kismet pulled to the curb. My heart hammered so hard I thought it might beat out of my chest. I started to stand. Wyatt pulled me down for one more kiss. A gentle promise in the brush of his lips. On any other day, I might have been embarrassed by the PDA. But today, I didn't give a shit.

His expression was carefully schooled into intense calm, but he couldn't keep the fear out of his eyes. Eyes that begged me to stay even as he silently watched me go.

"See you later," I said, and he nodded. Replied, "See you."

I didn't look back as I walked. If I had, the tightness in my chest and throat would have turned into wrenching sobs. Crying where they could see me would only make this harder. And walking away now was hard enough.

Chapter Twenty-one

It was just past sunrise, the north-south streets still cast in shadows. Halfway to the park, in the gloom between two streetlamps, I pulled the little tin box out of my back pocket. Flipped the lid and looked at the two white capsules nestled in a bit of cotton. Enough poison lurked in one of those to kill a three-hundred-pound man in under ten seconds. I took the pills and tossed the tin into a garbage can. Held the milky capsules in my palm a moment, contemplating how benign they looked.

I had told Wyatt I would rather die again than be anyone's guinea pig. I had meant it then, and still did now. But staying alive meant a continued chance of rescue or escape. Killing myself precluded those possibilities. Precluded him.

I dropped the pills and crushed them beneath my heel, grinding the poisonous contents into the sidewalk. Even as I'd suffered at Kelsa's hands, I'd stayed sane with thoughts of rescue. Thoughts of Wyatt looking for me, doing everything in his power to find me. No matter what Thackery had in mind, I wasn't going down without a fight.

The park was empty, silent as a grave. The neighborhood around it would be waking up soon; for now, not even birds occupied the stubbly trees. The ground was soaked and muddy in places from last night's rainstorm, and the odor of wet earth was cloying. Almost suffocating.

I tested my tap to the Break and found its familiar, buzzing power quickly. Just in case. The utter silence unnerved me. Then the phone rang, and I had it open and to my ear before it could chime a second time. "Where's Phineas?"

"The trade isn't happening at the park. It's too public."

"Where, then?"

"I'm sending a courier to get you, Ms. Stone. And, please, try to keep an open mind about your transportation."

"I don't—"

He hung up and I grunted, sick of him doing that. I pocketed the phone. I didn't have to wait long, though, to see just what he meant by transportation. I sensed movement behind me and pivoted, dropping my weight back to my right foot, ready for a fight.

I wasn't ready for the sight of a two-hundred-pound gray wolf standing on the sidewalk, less than twenty feet from me. Streetlight glistened off its long canines, glinted across the sleek gray pelt that covered its heavily muscled body, and sparkled in its intelligent silver eyes. It drew back black lips and snarled.

My stomach hit the dirt. What the fuck was a wolf doing in the middle of the city? I had no weapons, and no way to defend myself short of teleporting onto the roof of the next building. I stared, waiting for its muscles to tense, for any sign of impending attack. It didn't. It actually turned and hunched sideways, offering its back, then swiveled its head around to stare at me again. I gaped.

Try to keep an open mind about your transportation.

"You have got to be shitting me!"

It was actually kind of brilliant, as long as the wolf

didn't get hungry and decide to make a snack of me on the way to our destination. Wolves were fast—much faster than any human being—and had the agility and grace of natural predators. It could carry me on a zigzagging course through Mercy's Lot that would leave my trackers in the dust, rendering the dye useless as a means to follow me.

Fucking genius.

I took two tentative steps forward. "Nice doggie," I said softly.

The wolf remained still. More steps, a few at a time, until I was nearly at its back. I longed for one of my knives. Something to plunge into the animal's hide and rip through muscle and flesh. The odor of it roiled my stomach—sweat and meat and something musky, almost sinister—both familiar and completely foreign. I touched its shoulder. Coarse fur and hot skin rippled under my touch. A low, almost inaudible growl rumbled in its chest. Orders warring with its killer instinct to rend rather than carry.

The growl grew louder, and I swore it was from impatience. I took a deep breath, summoned up my courage, and climbed on like it was a pony ride. My arms tightened around its neck, fingers finding purchase in unexpectedly soft fur, my legs clamped firmly around its hard, muscled waist. It paused only a moment to let me get a grip, then bolted. I pressed my cheek into its neck and held on for the horseback ride from Hell.

The city sped past—alleys and streets and sidewalks, everything mixing together in a blur. Steel muscles rippled beneath me as it moved seemingly without effort. I saw very few cars, fewer people. Oddly, we passed what I guessed was a small group of gremlins conferring in an alley behind a bakery. Gremlins, of all damned things.

The wolf made several more sharp turns, keeping to side streets for a while, and then raced into a condemned public parking garage. It leapt over the white-and-black-painted pole permanently dropped into place across the entrance, and I nearly fell off. Not just from the momentum but also from the sparkle of orange light that flashed through my brain and body as we passed. Protection barrier. Figured.

I barely hung on as the wolf continued its breakneck pace. Up to the center level. Dirt and grime and a few abandoned cars marked our path, as well as something else—fresh tire tracks and footprints.

I tried to drum up a location and could think of only one condemned parking garage in Mercy's Lot, as far south as you could get on the peninsula without crossing one of the rivers. Based on the length of time we'd been traveling—and the fact that we hadn't crossed either of the rivers—it had to be where we were. Outside the half-mile limit of the tracking dye.

On the third level, the wolf came to an abrupt stop and crouched. The sudden forward momentum pitched me over its head. I hit the cement on my back, blasting the air from my lungs in a pained *whoosh*, sending bolts of agony up my backside. I gasped, seeing stars and winking lights in my vision. I felt, more than saw, the wolf circling me. Watching me.

"Ms. Stone?"

I bolted upright, sending more spasms through my lower back, which had tears stinging my eyes. Walter Thackery stood ten feet from me, dressed exactly as before in a long coat and snazzy suit. Behind him was a long black vehicle, and I had to blink several times to make sure I wasn't seeing things. He'd driven up here in a hearse.

The irony of it made me snort.

"Not a terribly polite greeting," Thackery said. "But that doesn't surprise me, given your abrupt unseating. I apologize for the mode of transportation. It seemed the

most effective method of preventing you from being followed."

"Forgive me for not bowing to your evil genius," I
said bitterly.

"What you see as evil, I see as the preservation of the
human race."

"At the expense of what?"

"Whatever it takes."

"Even your friends? We know about Bastian."

Something akin to annoyance flickered across his face.
"Did you kill him?"

I kept my expression neutral—at least, I tried to while
I continued getting my breathing under control. He
didn't like my silence. Anger tightened his shoulders and
clenched his fists. I ignored it as I stood up, a little wob-
bly, back shrieking in protest.

"Where's Phineas?" I asked.

"Did you kill Bastian?"

Part of me wanted to say yes, just to see his face. To
cause him a fraction of the pain he'd already caused me.
Only I feared his temper if he decided to retaliate. He'd
use Phin as a punching bag, not me. "No, I didn't, and I
doubt anyone else will."

"I believe you. I admit, I'm a little surprised you aren't
trying to use him against me."

"You wouldn't trade your science project for his life,
so why bother?"

"You're correct, Ms. Stone. The applications of my research are worth far more than one man's life."

"Really? More than the lives of your wife and son?"

A thundercloud stole across his expression. I'd hit a
nerve. Good.

Thackery waved me toward the rear of the hearse. I
kept a good-sized pocket of air between us. The wolf
stayed close to me, canines still bared, probably hungry
and ready to chew on my hand with one order from his

master. Thackery opened the back of the hearse. I stifled a startled cry at the sight of an actual coffin.

He grabbed a handle and pulled. The coffin glided halfway out on a metal track. With a key I didn't see him produce, he unsealed the front half of the coffin. Air hissed. I took another step forward, my entire body trembling. *God help you, Thackery, if you went back on your word....*

He lifted the lid. I choked.

Phin's skin was ghastly white, almost gray, against the coffin's cream lining. He was bare-chested, his eyes shut, an oxygen mask over nose and chapped lips with a tube leading somewhere down and out of sight. His chest rose and fell sporadically, almost impossible to see. It wasn't those things, though, that made tears sting my eyes.

It was the long, Y-shaped scar running lengthwise from chest to belly, sewn up with neat black stitches. Just like incisions made during autopsies. I stared, cold even as two hot tears streaked down my cheeks, remembering how Phin had screamed over the phone. Had he been conscious while Thackery cut him open?

"I've always wanted the chance to study a were's anatomy."

My fist connected with Thackery's jaw with a solid crack. Even as he reeled, the wolf tackled me from behind. It didn't bite or rend, just held me down, suffocating me with its bulk. I bucked and screamed, unable to dislodge the damned thing. I couldn't even teleport out from under it with that protection spell blocking my tap. Rage crept over me.

"Let her up!"

The wolf moved, taking its musky smell with it, and after another command from Thackery, retreated to the other side of the hearse. I rolled onto my knees and pulled into a crouch, only to come face to muzzle with

Thackery's gun. This time it didn't look like a dart gun. He glared down at me over the length of it.

"Make another move like that, Ms. Stone, and I will kill the shape-shifter. Don't mistake my allowing him to live for kindness."

"I wouldn't dream of it."

A car door opened, then shut seconds later. Someone else from the hearse joined Thackery. It was the blond teenager from the train yards, same loose clothes, head bowed in the same submissive stance as before. Our eyes met briefly, and I flinched at the predatory hate in his—so much hate for someone so young.

Between Thackery and the boy, they lifted the coffin out of the hearse and put it on the concrete, shocking me with their combined strength. Thackery opened the bottom half, confirming my suspicion that Phin was hooked up to an oxygen tank. He'd been left in a pair of gray briefs and nothing else. Thackery removed the oxygen mask, and the pair lifted Phin out and deposited him on the chilly ground in an undignified heap.

I scooted forward and, when Thackery didn't warn me to stay away, crouched at Phin's side. His skin was cold and clammy, his breathing shallow. All I wanted was for my friend to open his eyes and look at me, to tell me he'd be okay. He was deeply unconscious, and it was probably for the best. I pressed a soft kiss to his cheek.

"Time is wasting, Ms. Stone. Into the coffin, if you don't mind."

A startled cry choked me, and I looked up. "Into the coffin?"

"The oxygen will keep you from suffocating until we reach our intended destination."

Oxygen or not, the idea of being locked into a box for the next however many hours terrified me. *Stall, stall, stall.* "Why did you send those hounds after us at the cabin?"

"The pùca failed me. I was simply tying up loose ends. He knew too much to allow him to stay in your hands for long."

"Did you kill his *enisi*, too?"

"Of course not. He was returned to the desert from which he was taken."

The nearest desert was hundreds of miles away, across several states. "By who?"

A muscle twitched in Thackery's jaw. "Who, indeed?"

"Token's still out there, you know. You keep losing your science projects, Thackery. That's pretty careless."

He quirked his eyebrow, but my words produced no other reaction. Still, I had only one more bluff up my sleeve. "They tested my blood at R&D before I left. Hate to see you going through all this trouble when there's nothing useful to be found."

"Your scientists have no idea what to look for."

"You feel confident of that?"

"Yes."

Shit.

"Get in the coffin, Ms. Stone."

I hesitated. Not good. Thackery barked something at the boy, who immediately pounced on me. I wriggled and kicked, surprised by his steel grip on my arms. Something stung my shoulder, spreading warmth beneath my skin. Then the strange musk of the boy's scent faded, my muscles grew too heavy to move, and I passed out.

Chapter Twenty-two

The first thing clueing me in to impending consciousness was the gentle rumble of movement. Not me moving, exactly—an encompassing sensation of motion. Vibrations beneath me and around me, like I'd fallen asleep in a car.

I lurched toward a sitting position and didn't even get my head up. I was strapped down to something moderately padded, secured at every joint from my ankles to my wrists, across my stomach, and even one strap over my forehead. Sleep and tears had sealed my eyes shut. I worked them open, aware of a barrage of new smells—disinfectant, motor oil, bleach, blood, sweat—among other, unidentifiable odors.

My eyes focused on a ceiling of sheet metal, dull and unpolished, reflecting light from elsewhere in the room. It wasn't very wide, maybe ten feet. The length was impossible to tell without turning my head, which I couldn't. Panic splashed across me like ice water. Where the hell was I? Why was I moving? Where was Thackery? Had Phin been found?

On my right was an IV stand with a single bag and tube attached. A bag slowly filling up with blood. I flexed my right arm, felt the prick of the needle in my vein. He'd already started collecting his samples. Bastard. I tested my other limbs. Nothing could move, but nothing else felt poked, pricked, or cut. Just held down and a little numb—especially my ass. I'd been lying there a while.

My tongue was dry and did little to wet my parched lips. My brain was muddled, almost lethargic. Side effects of whatever he'd knocked me out with, I'd bet. My eyelids kept drifting shut, ready to sleep again.

No, not yet.

A door opened and closed, and shoes squeaked across the floor. Thackery stepped up on my left side, smiling like a doctor welcoming his favorite patient back to life. "Didn't expect to see you awake," he said. "Not after drawing nearly six pints of your blood."

Shit, so that's why I was so sleepy. He really was going to drain me dry. Still, this allayed my fears of him performing exploratory surgery on me. You can't torture someone if they've bled to death first. But the thought gave me little comfort. Fast or slow, dead was dead.

"Why . . . moving?" Both words took a concentrated effort that left me panting.

"Staying on the move makes it harder for my enemies to track me."

Good point. I poked around for my tap. Felt nothing. Was I too weak? Were we so far out of the city that the Break's power had disappeared? Had he enchanted this mobile lab with protection like he had the parking garage? All three thoughts made my heart ache. No, I wouldn't let Thackery see me cry. I closed my eyes and allowed fatigue to overtake me. I'd rather die in my sleep than give him the satisfaction.

I drifted for a while, thinking of my morning in bed with Wyatt, holding him, being held by him, and let those precious memories carry me into blackness.

Bleach . . . urine . . . car exhaust. I had to be in Hell; no way heaven smelled this bad. Ugh. I always thought Hell would smell more like brimstone—not that I knew exactly what brimstone smelled like. Rotten eggs or something. And shouldn't it be hotter in here? I wasn't cold. I just couldn't feel anything below my neck.

What the—?

That subliminal sense of motion was still there. Getting my eyes open took a concentrated effort. Glued together from sleep and tears, I probably tore out a couple of eyelashes forcing them apart. A silver blur greeted me. Even out of focus, I knew it was the same roof. The same table, the same straps, the same damned place. I wasn't dead. So what the fuck was Thackery playing at?

My head wasn't strapped down as before, giving me a bit more freedom to look around. The IV stand was still there. Instead of a bag sucking out blood, a clear bag hung from it, dripping something into me. Gee, so nice to offer an intravenous snack in between drainings.

The thought seized my heart. Was that his game? Drain me as dry as he could, then let me rest and refuel for a while before round two? Or three, or ten? I had no idea how long I'd been unconscious. Hours? Days? My numb body was cause for concern. I'd been lying here for too damned long. I tried testing my extremities again. Wiggled my fingers and toes, flexed one knee. Nothing else. Just an odd pressure between my legs that didn't make— Son of a bitch! I'd been hospitalized with traumatic injuries enough times to recognize the feel of a catheter. He'd also removed my clothes and put me into a plain cotton gown, not unlike a hospital drape.

Asshole had seen me naked!

"Welcome back."

A low growl rumbled out of my throat in response to the strange voice. It warbled in that odd middle between adolescence and maturity. The blond teen shifted into my line of sight, that same blazing hatred in eyes I now saw were a deep, glinting silver. The coloring was familiar somehow. I licked my parched lips with a still-dry tongue, then rasped out, "Fuck you." It wasn't poetry, but it would do.

Bastard laughed at me. "No thank you, you're not my type."

Grrrr. "Why?"

"Why are you not my type? Because you're a filthy, fucking human."

Which meant he wasn't. "No, why am I alive?" God, my throat was on fire.

"Because you're of less value to the master dead." Spoken as though his reply should have been painfully obvious. Maybe it was, and I just didn't want to admit it.

"Leverage?"

"Goodness no," Thackery said, stepping up behind the teen. "I think I gave away my best leverage yesterday. You, Ms. Stone, intrigue me."

Yesterday. It had been a whole day since the trade. Wyatt must be going out of his mind.

"Point of fact, you were dead," Thackery continued. "For precisely forty-three seconds, your heart stopped beating from the blood loss. After I unhooked the drain, your body recovered on its own. I was, as you can imagine, fascinated. No matter what my other experiment yields, I couldn't pass up this chance to study you."

I had a sudden, terror-inducing vision of a high school–level science video I'd watched once upon a time, in which some man in glasses and a loud bow tie had expounded on a lizard's ability to regenerate its own tail.

"In the interest of full disclosure, this is the third time I've had to reinsert your IV needle. Over the course of about three hours, your body pushes out the foreign object and then heals the tiny wound."

A small, fascinated part of my mind wondered if that meant my body would expel a bullet on its own, given enough time. Not that I was about to give Thackery any ideas.

As he spoke, I tried to get a look around. The room was wider than I expected, the walls lined with locked cabinets and drawers. One counter was empty, save for a few racks that seemed bolted down. Coupled with the sense of motion and the odors of fuel, I was willing to bet anything we were on a train, or maybe even in the trailer of a big rig. I tested my Break tap and, as before, found nothing. Unlike before, I felt the orange haze blocking me. Shit.

"You don't seem interested." He sounded disappointed.

"Science wasn't my . . . best subject."

"No doubt."

Had I just been insulted by the guy preparing to torture me?

He said something to the boy—did they have a secret language for just the two of them?—who strode to one of the cabinets and removed a metal case the size of a credit card. Returning to Thackery's side, he snapped it open and removed a thin sliver of silver, much like a thick sewing needle. My stomach spasmed as he passed it to Thackery.

"Healing is gnome magic, not biology," I said, ignoring the parched heat of my throat. God I wanted a drink of water.

"What is magic, Ms. Stone, if not the manipulation of matter and energy?" Thackery asked. "You manipulate your matter and the energy around you when you teleport. Mr. Truman manipulates the matter of solid objects when he summons them. Your Hunter colleague, Ms. Burke, manipulates the energy from your mind when she senses your truth and lies."

I could get him knowing about Wyatt's Gift, but his "Ms. Burke" had to be Claudia. How did he know about her? Did he know all the Gifted who worked for the Triads? What else had Bastian told him about us, the little fucker?

"No, I have a theory," Thackery continued, "that whatever gift the gnomes bestowed upon you is less intangible than you think. It is part of you physically now, not something to be removed. Anything that is a physical manifestation can likewise be studied. And potentially duplicated."

It sounded like a horrible joke, but he was completely serious. He wanted to study the way I healed and somehow use that to fight the vampire parasite.

"I also regret to inform you that I'll be unable to administer an anesthetic during this process. I can't risk its use tainting my results." He wasn't patronizing me, either—it was clear in his voice and his somber expression.

His sincerity made me hate him even more.

A lump formed in my throat as a chill tore down my spine. He might call it studying. I called it torture. And I didn't think I could survive another round of torture. Physically, maybe—but not mentally. Not again. I'd survived with sanity intact because I'd been handed a new body—a body that didn't come with sensory experience of those events. It had made recovery simpler and the physical healing process moot. I had memories of activity without the accompanying pain.

This time, I wouldn't be so lucky. If I survived this, I wouldn't be the woman Wyatt had loved. Would I even be myself anymore? I'd been Evy Stone once. I'd become a combination of Evy and Chalice Frost, rolled up into one. Who would be left behind when Thackery was finished? And did I want to be her?

"Make a deal with you?" I asked.

His slim eyebrows arched. "I admit, I am intrigued. What do you propose?"

"I won't fight you . . . whatever you do to me." I swallowed and it did nothing for my throat. I had to say it, though. I couldn't live that way, not again. A tiny part of me regretted smashing those suicide pills, even though Thackery would have found and taken them away hours ago. "Just promise you'll kill me when you're done."

He leaned down, placing one palm on either side of my shoulders, looming over me like a lover might. "You know I'm a man of my word, Ms. Stone. If you ask this of me, I will do it."

I'd done enough self-sacrificing for one lifetime. I wasn't strong enough to do this again. I didn't think I wanted to try. I couldn't put Wyatt through it. I couldn't put myself through it. It was time to be selfish.

I'm sorry, Wyatt. "Yes. It's what I want."

It might have been admiration in his gaze, but I doubted it. "All right, then, you have my word. As soon as I have acquired all the knowledge I desire, I will kill you."

Tears pricked my eyes, but I blinked them away. Nope, not crying in front of this asshole or his accomplice. He moved away and returned moments later with a plastic cup and spoon. He scooped out a spoonful of ice chips and offered them to me. I wanted to refuse.

But who the hell was I being brave for? The ice felt heavenly against my parched throat, bringing some measure of relief—short-lived though it was.

"Now, then, let's get started." He shifted down the bed. The hem of my gown was lifted to the top of my thigh, high enough to send a shard of fear into my heart. My fingers curled into the thin pad on which I lay. He held one of the gleaming needles up to the light, as though contemplating its shape and width.

"Again, I do apologize for this," he said. And then I felt the first sting in my thigh.

Followed, soon after, by five more.

* * *

I received more ice chips before each round began. I couldn't guess at the passage of time—hours? days?—only that the size of the needles kept growing. Five different sizes, from pinpricks to wood nails, were shoved into my legs and eventually pushed back out.

I'd fallen asleep while my left thigh expelled the last of the wood nails and woke to the familiar shuffle of Thackery's feet. The metallic taste of blood was still in my mouth from biting my tongue during their insertion. I hadn't cried. I hadn't screamed. Yet.

The boy had disappeared a while ago. Thackery was typing notes into a PDA—he didn't seem to use normal clipboards like other doctors I'd seen—his mouth puckered into a grimace. As though sensing my curiosity, he said, "I calculated four and a half hours for these to eject, based on the times of the other instruments. It's been six, and while the instruments are out, the wounds have yet to heal properly."

Instruments. I grunted.

"Perhaps you've had too much stimulation for such a brief period of time. I have other things to attend to, so I'll let you rest."

Other things. Other patients? Other torture victims?

He left without a word, shutting off the last of the lights, bathing the room in complete darkness. In the pitch black, I was aware of something else—the constant motion had ceased. We'd reached a destination of some sort. Would I be moved out of this lab-on-wheels? Relocated to a lab with even more horrific methods of testing my body's ability to heal?

Waning ability, it seemed. I flexed my thigh muscles and was rewarded with tiny shocks of pain, one from each of the six wounds. I'd had a snapped wrist heal in less than twelve hours. Half a dozen holes shouldn't still be there after six.

My scalp itched just behind my right ear. I reached automatically, and my wrist slammed hard against the strap holding it down. The itch intensified, taunting me to scratch it. I pulled against the strap, twisted, yanked until my wrist was raw. No luck. The restraint held.

My fucking scalp itched all night long.

A sudden glare of light shrieked through my brain, and I squeezed my eyes shut as hard as I could. It wasn't enough to block out the onslaught and, after being in pitch darkness for what felt like days, the light fried my senses. I shrieked and yanked at the restraints on my wrists, desperate to cover my eyes. Nuggets of fear blossomed into full-on panic.

With the light came pain; with darkness came throbbing relief.

God, what was Kelsa going to do to me today?

No, not Kelsa. Thackery.

Shit. I was already losing it.

"My apologies," Thackery said. The level of glare seemed to dim, but my headache did not relent. "I thought you'd be pleased to know your shape-shifter friend, Phineas, is well on his way to a full recovery."

My eyelids popped open, glare be damned. He was grinning at me, and oh how I longed to break those perfect white teeth. "You saw him?"

"Oh no, but I still have sources in the city. He's been kept quite protected, not only by his people but also yours."

"Mine?"

"Specifically, Mr. Truman."

My heart soared. Wyatt was keeping company with Phin. It was an idea I loved and hated in equal measure.

Loved, because the pair were not terribly fond of each other, and I was glad Wyatt wasn't alone. Hated, because it meant Wyatt wasn't looking for me. Had he given up? How long had I been gone?

Thackery held a bendy straw up to my mouth. "Drink a few swallows of this."

"What is it?"

"A protein shake. It's likely you aren't healing as you should because your body has been deprived of basic nutrients since you came into my care. I was foolish for neglecting those needs."

Good point. My mind rebelled against doing anything to help him, even as my empty stomach and trembling limbs craved sustenance. I took three hard pulls on the straw. Something cool and thick and lemon-flavored oozed down my throat. It settled heavily in my stomach, which threatened to expel it as quickly as I swallowed.

Ugh. I was never fond of lemon, but this made me absolutely despise the flavor. Before I could suck down any more and see if I could manage to projectile-vomit onto Thackery, he removed the temptation and backed out of sight.

"I'll give you more in fifteen minutes," he said, returning. "Too much at once is dangerous to your system. I don't want to shock you."

"Just torture me," I said.

"Study you."

"Fuck off."

He smiled, and almost seemed . . . sad? Nah.

"So what now? Bamboo shoots up my fingernails?"

"I told you—"

"Yeah, right, not torture." Something occurred to me. "You find that thing in my blood you were looking for?"

"Yes and no." My face must have flashed a "What the

fuck does that mean?" at him. "I didn't find what I expected; however, results were not a complete loss."

"Can't cure a vampire infection, huh?"

His mouth pressed into a thin line. "No, not yet. I do have my most encouraging results thus far, and discovering the secret of your regenerative abilities may be the final piece of the puzzle I'm lacking."

"You can't re-create magic."

"It's physical." Something cold stole across his face, cutting hard lines in his otherwise handsome features. "The vampire infection is physical, and you physically repelled it from your body."

"With a magic healing—"

"No!" It was the first outburst I'd ever seen from him, and it was truly a terrifying sight. Cracks of madness peeked through his carefully erected exterior and proper manner. The madness of a man whose entire world had been devoted to one singular goal, and who wouldn't let anyone tell him his goal was unattainable. He'd lost his family to an infection he was now determined to eradicate, no matter the cost. And it was a cost that had slowly eaten away at his soul.

Definitely his sanity.

He closed his eyes and inhaled deeply, held it, then exhaled. Repeated the action several times. Calm centeredness reigned when he looked at me again, the raging storm quieted. For now. "How many Hunters have you lost to this battle? How many half-Bloods have you killed who were once innocents, whose minds were ravaged by the disease and turned into raving murderers? Wouldn't you pay any price to stop it from happening to others?"

Images of Jesse and Alex haunted me, both of them torn apart by the bloodlust and hate in their newly altered DNA, thrown into turmoil by the residual memories of their old lives. Both of them infected because of me, and both of them dead by my hands.

Thackery stepped away. Drawers opened and shut. He arranged instruments on a tray and brought it back to the bedside.

Here we go again.

"What if you can't?" I asked. "What if you can't find a cure, no matter what you do?"

His mouth twisted into a contemplative expression. He plucked a scalpel off his tray and held it up, light glinting off its mirrored surface. My insides clenched. "I believe I will cure it, Ms. Stone, I sincerely do. But you are correct. One should always have a Plan B." He studied his scalpel, offering no more.

"And?"

"And my Plan B is quite simple. If you can't fight an infection, you remove the damaged limb."

The hair on my scalp prickled. He pushed the gown up my arm to expose my right shoulder. The tip of the scalpel dragged over my bicep, not quite cutting.

"You mean destroy the vampire race," I said.

"Precisely."

He cut deeply, and I gasped. Swallowed a shriek. Deeper, the blade ate into my skin and muscle. Tears welled and spilled, and I couldn't stop them. I didn't scream, though, not even when he held up a chunk of my flesh the size of a thumb, oozing blood and quivering like skin-coated gelatin.

I did manage to turn my head and vomit onto his shoes.

Suck through a straw—check.

Crunch some ice—check.

Scream for a while—double check.

Occasionally the sense of movement would return. Or

it was always there, and I just didn't notice. Time blurred in a manner that made higher thought difficult. Thackery no longer talked to me. The kid was there a few times. I rarely had enough energy to rasp out a couple of cuss words. I tried, determined not to show that Thackery was starting to break me.

He seemed to like his scalpels best. I tried to stay asleep and ignore it whenever possible, but Thackery knew anatomy. He knew the nerves and tendons to cut. I was in a constant state of healing, leaving my body throbbing and itching like mad. All the damned time. Couldn't stop it. Just had to endure a while longer. He had to be nearing his research limit. Death was coming for me soon.

Right?

We were moving again when he came. I listened to him shuffle around, my eyelids too damned heavy to lift. Everything hurt; even my insides ached. My kidneys throbbed, and I wondered if the catheter had shifted. My throat was raw from screaming, the insides of my cheeks still bleeding from having bitten through them at some point.

Please, God, if you're listening, let him be here to end this.

But God wasn't listening.

"I have one last experiment for you, Ms. Stone, and then I believe we'll be through." Thackery's voice was like sandpaper in my head, grating and painful. "I've seen your torn flesh and muscles regenerate, and I know from your own word that repaired bones have mended within a day of their breaking. I simply cannot isolate the physical process that causes it to happen."

"Magic." Somehow I got that single word out.

"No, I'll find it. I simply haven't taken you far enough."

We've gone plenty far, thanks. No more on a first date.

"The answer is here, in how your body regenerates from its wounds. It must be here. We've tested so many things, but I wonder how far your regeneration ability extends."

I forced my eyelids apart and sought him out with bleary vision. He stood on my left side with something in his hand. I stared, not quite comprehending the object. His expression was contemplative, neutral. It horrified me. A high-pitched keen tore from my damaged throat. Even before he switched the object on and grabbed my left hand, I understood what the cordless carving knife was for.

. . . not healing . . .
  . . . not regrowing . . .
  . . . don't understand . . .
  . . . no, can't be magical . . .
  . . . dammit to hell . . .
  . . . so sorry, Anne . . .

Unceasing agony beckoned to me from the source of that damned voice, and I shied away. Tried to stay locked firmly into my own mind. To ignore Thackery's ranting. He was angry. I was glad. We'd completed his last experiment. Time for him to uphold his end of the deal and kill me.

Please, just let me go.
  . . . can't do that yet . . .
No, no, no, you promised.
  . . . can't kill you yet . . .
Son of a goblin's bitch! I wanted to wake up and attack him. Stab his eyes out with the scalpel. Cut a few small appendages off with that electric knife. Pay him back for what he'd done to me. For taking back his

promise. I just can't move. Won't stretch toward consciousness, not now. It hurts, and it'll hurt worse if I wake up. I can't scream for him again.

What was that noise? Cell phone?

. . . *us out of here!*

The world around me shuddered. Pitched. Rolled.

I slammed against my restraints as everything turned upside down.

Chapter Twenty-three

I jackknifed into a sitting position, screaming to wake the dead. Or the supposed-to-be-dead. My body was on fire, burning with every muscle I clenched or patch of skin that rubbed against fabric. Each scream was torture to my damaged throat—scorching shocks that put the taste of blood and bile on my tongue.

No. Either I'd gone deaf or the screaming was just in my head. The only sounds coming from my throat were tiny squeaks and squeals. I caught hold of myself and realized two things. First, I was sitting up, which seemed wrong. Second, I was in a dusty, dim room with a single newspaper-covered window that hid any hint of day or night, and no furniture. Just the pile of blankets on which I sat.

Where the hell was I?

My nose twitched, and I forced back a sneeze. Black dots danced in my vision. The pained muscles in my back gave out, and I flopped onto the hard floor again, energy spent. I felt the sticky pull of bandages on my arms, legs, and stomach. My left hand was wrapped tight in gauze, and as I lifted it above my head to really look, agony speared me all the way to the shoulder. Blood splattered the cotton gauze above my left pinkie joint—the source of that awful shock of pain.

What happened to my hand? What happened to the rest of me?

I closed my eyes and tried to think. Push past the cocoon of pain that kept my brain muddled and my thoughts mushy. This wasn't my room, of that I was positive. Being able to move had surprised me, but I didn't know why. I was wounded and didn't know how I'd been hurt, or by whom. I couldn't even shout for help, because my throat was damaged. This was so fucked-up.

Think, girl. Think.

An image formed in my mind's eye. A man with black hair and dark eyes, a shadow on his chin and cheeks. He was smiling at me, laughing. I knew him, didn't I? What was his name?

Hell, what was *my* name?

Footsteps thundered toward me from elsewhere in the house. I stared at the warped, faded door, my heart pounding in my ears. The steps seemed heavier than any man should make, like bricks falling on wood. The stamps stopped at the door. My right hand fumbled for a weapon and found only scratchy blankets.

The knob twisted, and the door squealed open on rusty hinges. A large figure towered in the doorway, so tall he actually ducked to step inside. I sucked in a startled shriek, positive I'd lost my mind. It couldn't be a man, this seven-foot-tall giant with his hard-looking gray skin and figure that seemed hewn from stone. His face was squared off, his head flat and hairless. Eyes gleamed predator-like, and I suddenly knew what a cornered mouse felt like as the cat approached.

"You are awake," the thing said, his voice grating like sandpaper on metal. "This pleases me."

I couldn't come up with a reply. Did he prefer his meals awake before he consumed them? He took another shambling step forward, and I hunched lower under the blankets. Instinct screamed at me to flee or attack, but my body hadn't the strength to do either. Just lie there and let it kill me, like someone else should already have done. . . .

The creature regarded me for a moment, head tilted to one side, his chiseled face blank. "Evangeline, do you not remember me?"

He knew my name. "Evangeline" sounded correct, even though something else lingered in the recesses of memory. A name that sounded like "Alice." I studied him, repeated the way his gravelly voice had said my name, so foreign and familiar at the same time. It seemed impossible to be both. My head hurt from trying to decipher it all.

"You have suffered recently," he said. "It is not uncommon for memory loss to occur."

"I know you?" I whispered, barely able to hear the words.

He didn't seem to have trouble. "Yes, for many years. You called me Max."

"Max."

The name fell easily from my lips. Shadowed images swirled in my mind. A large library in the middle of a city. Neat piles of gleaming bird bones, picked clean and set aside. Standing with him on a ledge high above that same city, gazing down at its nighttime colors. Sneaking into his lair. Hit from behind. A woman with white hair bleeding to death while Max stood by and watched. The handsome man with black hair threatening Max with a ball of sunlight.

A ball of sunlight. Max. Gargoyle. I did know him.

"You left," I wheezed. "Left the city."

"I did, and have not returned since our last encounter."

Memories were coming back in snips and bits—Max saying his race would not choose sides in the upcoming war; realizing he'd been responsible for my kidnapping once before; racing to stop an elf mage from raising a demon. It played out like a video on fast-forward, flashing faces and events without any real clarity. Most of their names hovered on the edge of conscious thought, just out of reach.

"Where?"

"In a small rural town sixty miles south of the city," he said. "This house is secluded, and it serves our need for protection during daylight. We have been searching for one of our coven these past five weeks. We found him the day before yesterday, his body taken apart, the remnants turned to stone. He had likely been dead for several days."

I thought of a young boy, half his body stone, the other half barely human, dead on an operating table. Only gargoyles turned completely to stone in sunlight. Their cousin race, vampires, scorched and burned. Vampires . . . A shiver tore up my spine. *Gargoyles, vampires, and half-breeds, oh my!*

"We were not far behind the man who disposed of our coven member so carelessly." A biting edge crept into Max's voice, making it even more inhuman than usual. "We attacked only moments before dawn, sending the tractor-trailer and its inhabitants off a high mountain road to the gorge below. We were not able to search the wreckage until the sun set again."

Tractor-trailer. My stomach gurgled at a dimly recalled sense of motion, of constant movement rocking me in and out of consciousness. I'd been on that trailer, strapped to a table. Someone had held me there. The same person who'd held and tortured Max's friend. Someone named—

"Thackery," I squeaked. "Alive?"

"I believe he is." My heart howled in agony. "His body was not found in the wreckage. We discovered footprints leading off, back to the road, but they were not human. They were animal, some sort of dog."

"The driver?" Someone had to drive the tractor-trailer. Had it been that blond kid? No, he'd been inside with us a few times.

"We found no one in the cab. We discovered two other bodies near the wreckage," he continued. "One vampire and one half-Blood vampire. Both were dead when we discovered them. I was . . . surprised to discover you there. Your wounds are . . . unforgivable."

You forgot painful. Also not healing. I'd been away from the Break for too long. I had told Thackery that my healing Gift was more magic than physical. All that I'd endured, just for Thackery to get away. "Did you save . . . anything?"

"I saved you, Evangeline."

Not what I meant. I swallowed, ignoring the fire in my throat. "Recover research? Computers? Information?"

"One of my brethren searched the wreckage. He is more familiar with human technology than I. He retrieved one item. I shall fetch it for you."

He left the room with those same thundering stone steps. I'd never noticed before how heavily he walked. He returned moments later with something that made me want to hug him—Thackery's PDA. The one he'd used to record every minute of our time together. Bingo.

"It is damaged, but my brother is certain it can be repaired."

I needed to get it to the city, into the hands of people who could decipher the scientist-speak and tell me what Thackery had learned about my blood. Any leaps he'd made in his plans to eradicate vampires. I had to tell people, too, that I wasn't dead. Someone in particular would be worried about me. Someone I cared about a great deal. Who? The broader strokes were filling in, but I was still missing details. The things closest to my heart weren't there, and I needed to find them.

"Phone?"

"I am sorry, I do not possess a telephone. Nor have we contacted anyone else about your recovery. I wished to know your mind before I did so."

It was kind of thoughtful, really, to make sure he didn't accidentally tell an enemy I'd been found. If I couldn't call anyone—and several phone numbers rattled through my head, just no names to go with them—I'd have to go to them. "Home, please."

"The sun will set in two hours. We shall return to the city at that time."

I nodded. I didn't want to wait but had no choice. Not when my only means of transportation would crisp in the sun.

"Do you require anything?"

I required a whole hell of a lot but said no. Mostly I just needed to get closer to the Break so I could start to heal. I'd gotten used to it. Thackery had taken advantage of it. And until I returned, I was helpless to do anything except wallow in every ache and pain.

True to his word, Max and I were in the sky moments after sunset. Stars were just peeking through the cloud cover, winking in a purple and navy sky. Two other gargoyles flew with us in flanking positions, each as tall and hewn as Max. I'd never seen three at once and guessed several more had stayed behind in the house.

The town was tiny—just a few houses around a blinker-light intersection, a market, and a church. It seemed like the kind of village where no one could keep a secret for long, and yet a coven of gargoyles was hiding out a few miles down the road.

I was wrapped up in three blankets, tight like a body cast, and Max held me to his hard chest as though I were his child. Each movement sent shocks of pain through me. I closed my eyes and tried to block it out until we arrived, to ignore everything except the brush of humid night air on my face. I'd always wondered how gargoyles' small wings—maybe four feet of thin skin stretched across a batlike frame—kept their huge forms in the air. And somehow Max was managing it with me as added weight, and with no apparent hindrance.

On the edge of sleep, it occurred to me I hadn't asked how long I'd been with Thackery. Max wouldn't know, even if I told him the date I'd turned myself over. Gargoyles didn't have calendars, didn't follow time the way humans did. I'd have to ask my friends.

Friends. I had friends waiting for me, worrying about me. Had they been searching for me? Surely yes. The man with the black hair wouldn't have stopped as long as he knew I was alive. I was certain of it. Secure in his love for me. He'd do anything to find me.

Wyatt.

I choked on a gasp, and the sound made Max turn his head. "Are you all right?"

"Fine." I shouted to be heard over the roar of the wind.

With that one name, dozens more slammed home and restored my memory completely. Wyatt. Phineas. Kismet. Tybalt. Milo. Felix. Baylor. Amalie. Rufus. Bastian. Each slid into place like a perfectly cut puzzle piece, re-creating the picture of my life.

My heart ached for Wyatt. For leaving him behind with the uncertainty of my future. For how much I loved him and wanted him to hold me in his arms until the hurt went away. I recalled his cell number and wished for a phone so desperately my body trembled. Just to hear his voice and let him hear mine. Put his fears to rest.

"We are over the city," Max said at some point.

I hazarded one eye open and saw the high-rises and gleaming buildings of Uptown passing by beneath us.

Headlights and street signs and business billboards glared up from the ground, lighting the sky with their particular type of pollution. The cathedral spire of the Fourth Street Library loomed, and the three gargoyles swooped down. They alighted on the library roof—a narrow strip of gravel that surrounded a hollow building in which Max had once nested.

The familiarity warmed me. Max crawled through the passageway that led inside. The heated interior sent a flush across my cheeks. He put me down in a corner and loosened the blankets. Tears threatened, teased out by all the movement. I didn't let them fall. I curled onto my side, uncomfortable on the stone floor, with humid summer air all around me.

But I was home. I searched with my mind and felt the sudden, electrical spark of the Break. Its energy flooded my mind, tingling through my very core. Enveloping me like a warm sweater I'd almost forgotten I had once owned and loved. I snuggled into it and let it carry me into unconsciousness, this time sure I'd wake feeling better.

And I did. Daylight shone through the tunnel leading outside, adding to the stifling heat inside. I stretched and rolled onto my back, tired muscles protesting their stiffness. My left hand still hurt with the constant itch-ache of my healing Gift. My head throbbed from exhaustion, heat, and lack of food and water. Everything else seemed healed.

I sat up. Max was huddled in the corner, far from the reach of the sunlight, wings folded over his face. Asleep for the day. His companions were gone. Guess they'd only been traveling bodyguards. I started to stand, then thought better of it. I was still dressed in the same cotton gown Thackery had put me in, stained with blood and vomit, and torn in immodest places. It also didn't tie in the back.

I wanted something to drink badly. I also wanted a cheeseburger and fries, with ketchup and onions, but the idea of nourishment made my stomach roll. Those lemon-flavored shakes had been my only food for a long time, and if I hadn't hated lemons before . . .

Max stirred. His wing curled back, and he raised his head, looking directly at the passageway. I followed his gaze. Two shadows moved in the light, then footsteps scuffled toward us. I scooted back, closer to the wall, drawing one of the blankets up around my waist. Two familiar figures stepped into the room.

"Holy shit, you really are alive," Gina Kismet said. Her eyes were wide, her mouth open.

Milo Gant stepped toward me first, smiling warmly, his eyes sparkling. He squatted down, and for a brief moment, I panicked. Then I threw my arms around his shoulders and hugged him, overjoyed just to feel the comforting embrace of another human being. A friend. He held me close. I didn't realize I'd started crying until he leaned back and wiped an errant spot of moisture off my cheek.

"How many lives are you down to now?" he asked. "Six?"

"More like four," I replied. My mouth was dry, but talking no longer felt like gargling razor blades.

Kismet crouched next to us and offered me an open bottle of water. I took a few sips, eager to guzzle the entire thing, holding back only because I wanted to keep it down. It moistened my mouth and cooled me a little. I handed it back and licked my lips.

"Where's Wyatt?" I asked.

Milo looked away, and Kismet couldn't hide a flash of guilt. My heart thundered in my chest. Blood roared in my ears. I grabbed Kismet's wrist and squeezed.

"Where?"

"We don't know, Evy," she said. "No one's heard

from him in three days." She cringed, and I loosened my grip on her arm.

"How long have I been gone?"

She chewed on her lower lip. "Twenty days."

Everything tilted. I'd expected to hear a week, ten days max. Not twenty days. Almost three weeks. Wyatt must have gone out of his mind. Or accepted I was dead and moved on. Or accepted I was dead and— No, no more "ors." Not going there.

She didn't need prompting from me to start filling in the gaps. "We lost track of you at the park that day. You moved so damned fast the tracking dye was useless before we could get on the road. It was two hours before we got a call telling us where to find Phineas."

He'd laid on that cold cement for two hours, alone. "Is he okay?"

"Almost one hundred percent again, last I heard. Therians not only grow faster than humans, they also heal much more quickly." She cleared her throat. "He was taken to the hospital while we searched the parking garage. We didn't find anything except tire tracks, footprints, and some odd paw prints. Any trail we might have followed was cold. We drove around all day and half the night with that computer, until long after Bastian said the effects of the dye would wear off."

Bastian—*grrrr*.

"I finally dragged Wyatt to my place and made him sleep for a few hours. We all looked for you, Evy, as often as we could, even after the brass forbade it. Whenever Wyatt wasn't in the field searching, he was at the hospital with Phineas. Both of them felt so guilty. Wyatt went back to your apartment once, I think. After Phineas was released, he stayed with them. Rufus is still wheelchair-bound, and I'm sure he convinced Wyatt that the two invalids needed him, but I—"

"Rufus wanted to keep an eye on Wyatt," I said.

"Yeah. He's been so cold, Evy."

I closed my eyes, fighting back tears. I blinked away a film when I opened them again. "Amalie couldn't sense that I was still alive?"

Another uncomfortable look. "As far as I know, no one has had contact with Amalie since the day Thackery shot you and we told her we didn't recover the Tainted crystal."

Shit. "No one?"

Kismet shook her head. "There was another disturbance—Break-quake, Wyatt called it—about a week ago, and another one yesterday, according to Claudia. There's been no contact with any of the Fey for more than three weeks, not to the brass or the Assembly."

"That's . . ." I didn't know what it was, but "bad," "screwed-up," "fucked-up," and a number of other things raced through my addled mind. "And you haven't seen Wyatt for three days?"

"No. Rufus said Wyatt got a phone call on Wednesday, talked to whoever it was in private for nearly half an hour, then just left." She sucked in her lower lip and looked away, hiding something. Some detail she didn't want to share.

"For fuck's sake, what?"

"Phineas is gone, too. He's been missing the same amount of time. Rufus hasn't talked to or seen either of them, and Michael Jenner isn't returning my calls. I've tried to get the brass involved, but they no longer consider Wyatt an active Handler, so they won't interfere." The sneer in her voice was striking. "I even called Aurora yesterday, and she said she hasn't heard from either of them in days."

Poor Aurora. The gentle were-kestrel was one of Phin's last living Clans-people, and he had already gone to great lengths to protect her and her daughter, Ava. Being abandoned by him had to hurt like hell.

"You tried his phone?" I asked stupidly. "The apartment again?"

"Went straight to voice mail, and now the damned box is full, so I can't even tell him you're alive and hope he hears it. We bugged the old apartment, but no one's gone in or out. We're trying, Evy, but Wyatt knows how to disappear if he wants to."

"But he can't." It came out as a wail, and the sound shamed me. I could not lose it now, not in front of Max and Kismet and Milo. I found moderate comfort in the fact that Phin and Wyatt were probably together, wherever they were. It meant Wyatt hadn't done something really stupid, like fling himself off the Wharton Street Bridge.

"Thackery's still out there," I said. I had to focus on business or I'd fall apart. "It sounds like he lost most of his research, so he's going to get desperate."

"Desperate people make mistakes," Milo said. "And then we catch them."

"Bastian?"

"He was interrogated, with both Claudia Burke and a freelance telepath present," Kismet replied. "They believed him when he said he never shared our information with Thackery. He accepted information from him only regarding certain scientific applications of his research. He said Erickson's team never knew where the information came from, so they were cleared, too."

"Bastian was cleared?" I gaped at her.

She frowned. "Pretty much. He got a wrist slap for not passing along what he knew about Thackery after Olsmill went down. The brass is of the opinion that the Hunter known as Evangeline Stone died on May seventeenth, so nothing that happened to you afterward is their problem."

My shoulders were shaking as I tried to rein in my fury. "That's what they've declared, huh? Thackery slips

Bastian info that helps us build a better bullet, so he gets a free fucking pass?"

"They still want Thackery caught, but, yeah, Bastian remains on the payroll. I guess they think they're hemorrhaging Handlers and Hunters so fast they can't afford to lose any more people." Her voice was bitter enough to make a lemon pucker.

I studied her face—the lines of grief bracketing her eyes and the dullness of her skin. Milo had the same basic look, down to the red veins spiderwebbing his eyes. They both seemed overstressed, sleep-deprived, and ready to shatter. Twenty days later and their lives had descended into Hell. Unless it was . . . Damn.

"Felix?"

Milo flinched and his brown eyes went dull, cold. My heart ached.

Kismet said, "The infection kept him in ICU for days. It weakened his heart. A severed nerve in his back has pretty much left him in serious pain all the time. He can walk, but I don't—" She paused.

"He'll probably never hunt again, just like Tybalt," Milo said, so quietly I almost didn't hear him. I squeezed his hand, not bothering with placating words, and he squeezed back—a gesture of comfort for another hurting soul, small comfort though it was. His tentative smile never reached his eyes.

"Anything else happen while I was out of town?" I asked, exhausted and emotionally torn—a dish towel wrung out hard and left to slowly untwist. "Token? Was he found?"

"No, he wasn't," Kismet said. "There's been no sign, but all active Triads have a description. So far no one's seen him. He's either dead or hiding."

I was impressed something as unusual as Token had remained hidden for so long. Unless we just hadn't yet tripped over his body.

Someone else was still unaccounted for. "Reilly?" I asked. "The guy looking for Chalice? Where'd he end up?"

"He has a pretty interesting story, actually," she replied.

"Yeah, well, I didn't think he took pictures of vampire royalty for shits and giggles."

"Not exactly. He really is a P.I., though, with some pretty impressive police assists on the West Coast. He stumbled onto some vampires out there while working on a case, and a few months ago his investigation led him here."

"What's he want?"

"The truth, mostly. And he's gotten a heaping helping of it lately, but I can give you those details later. It can wait until you're back on your feet. You feel up to changing your clothes? Walking out of the library like that's going to be kind of conspicuous."

I snorted. She retrieved a bag from the mouth of the passage. Everyone, Max included, turned their backs while I slipped into jeans that gapped around my waist and a shirt that, when tucked in, helped keep the jeans up. I was dangerously thin and needed to put some weight on before a strong wind blew me to Oz.

I tucked the PDA into my back pocket, keeping its existence a secret for now. When I tried to thank Max, he held up a stony hand and shook his massive head. "I have been in your debt from the moment of your capture by the goblins, Evangeline. I have repaid it."

"Are you leaving the city again?" I asked.

"For now. Nothing is as it was. Good journey to you."

"And you."

The sun beat down on us from the midday sky, hot and oppressive. Summer was upon us, and it was only going to get hotter. Terrific. The three of us made our way through the library without incident or strange looks. The last time I left here, I'd been accosted in the street by an old friend of Chalice's. No such distraction met us on our way to Kismet's Jeep. I settled into the backseat and let the city go by in a blur.

Kismet insisted on walking me up while Milo waited with the Jeep. I didn't have the energy to protest. I realized halfway up the narrow stairway that led to an equally narrow hallway of tiny apartments that I didn't have a key. It was an absurd thought, really. We had a spare hidden beneath a loose piece of the doorframe. I pried it out, unlocked the deadbolt and knob, and let us in.

The apartment was spotless. The old rug had been replaced by a new one, deep blue and thick-pile. The cement floor was scrubbed clean and still smelled of bleach. Even the walls were freshly painted, erasing all signs of what had occurred my last day here—Jaron's death, Token's capture and interrogation, and all the blood spilled. Even the hole where Wyatt had knifed Token's hand to the wall was filled in, as if it had never existed.

Everything was straight, clean, in its place. Not a sign that anyone had lived here in quite a while. The sterility of it squeezed my heart. A place that had once felt so cozy, so much like home, felt about as welcoming as a motel room.

How did I get here?

Oh yeah, a psychopath and my not-so-special blood. Speaking of which . . . "The blood tests."

"The what?" Kismet asked.

"The blood tests they ran at R&D. They should have had the results the day I left."

Her expression softened into understanding. "They didn't find anything. Whatever your body did to heal from the vampire parasite, it's not something modern science can trace. Guess magic wins this one."

I could have told everyone that weeks ago and saved myself a crapload of agony and heartache. Oh, wait, I did tell everyone that.

"You don't have to stay here alone," Kismet said.

"Yes, I do need to be alone." Even if only for a while.

"Take this, then." She pushed a disposable cell phone at me. "Call me if you need anything. Actually, call me later tonight just to check in."

It looked like her mothering was starting to broaden its horizons. I may have been much closer to her in age now, but she still had nearly a decade of life experience on me. It would be nice to have a female friend again. I took the phone.

"If I hear anything from Wyatt, I'll call," she said, turning to go. "I'll talk to you later."

"Yeah."

She lingered in the doorway, as if waiting for me to vanish in a puff of smoke, and finally left. I turned the locks, dumped the phone on the coffee table, then wandered into the kitchen. The fridge was empty, which was probably good. I didn't want to have to clean out green-and-gray goop that had once been food. I found some bottled water in a cupboard and swigged it warm, then put a few bottles into the fridge to chill. I still had meals in the freezer, plus cans of soup and boxes of pasta in the cupboards. It was something.

I took my water into the bedroom, and grief nearly bowled me over. The bed on which Wyatt and I had shared a handful of chaste nights was neatly made, the blanket smooth and unruffled. Swept, dusted, and as sterile as the rest of the apartment. My clothes—the few tops and single pair of jeans that hadn't been stained or torn beyond usefulness yet—were there. Even the laptop and photo he'd brought to the cabin, assuming we'd never be back here, were on the dresser. I gazed at the photo of Chalice and Alex, taken before all three of us died and our lives became inexplicably tangled, and my vision blurred.

Hot tears scorched paths down my cheeks. I fell to my knees, rocking back and forth with my arms tight around my stomach, and sobbed. I cried until my head ached and I had nothing left in me. Then I crawled onto the bed and, exhausted, fell asleep.

Thankfully, I didn't dream.

Chapter Twenty-four

Kismet called at some point during the night to check in. I remembered muttering about needing my sleep, then hanging up and sleeping until morning. Getting up took a lot of effort, and I had to think hard to remember why it was worth bothering—Wyatt. He was out there, somewhere. And I needed to find him so he'd know I was alive.

It motivated me into the shower. The water sluiced off weeks of sweat and other things and helped me finally feel healed. I also got my first look at my left hand and almost started crying again. My pinkie was gone, severed below the knuckle, the skin healed over and the tendons repaired. A vivid reminder of Thackery's daft theory that I'd regenerate body parts. He'd taken a piece of me, and I needed to return the favor.

I slipped into a pair of ill-fitting jeans and layered on a second T-shirt to help hold them up. I brushed my hair into a neat ponytail, then wandered into the kitchen. The apartment was still empty. It was silly to hope Wyatt would have come home during the night, and I felt the crushing weight of his absence in every inch of space.

Pasta wasn't the breakfast of champions, but it was my only option unless I wanted a can of tomato soup. I boiled some macaroni. The carbs made me feel a little better. A little more human.

A cab took me across town. I'd found some emergency cash in Wyatt's favorite hiding place—a sealed plastic bag inside the toilet tank, for grossness' sake—to pay the fare, unsure of my destination until I gave the driver the address. It seemed the best first place to look for Wyatt.

Rufus St. James welcomed me at the condo's front door, and I bent down to give him an awkward hug.

We hadn't seen each other since his release from the hospital, and I'd never been to the place he shared with Phin. It was gorgeous, with dark wood floors and high ceilings. The furniture was mostly chocolate leather, and the wood mahogany and simply carved. All of the goodies I expected of a bachelor pad were there—minibar, stereo and gaming systems, wide-screen television.

Everything was spaced apart at perfect intervals to allow Rufus access with his wheelchair. His curly strawberry blond hair had grown out and tousled around his forehead. A few burn scars peeked out from behind his shirt collar, and his left hand was badly scarred. He looked otherwise healthy—color in his cheeks, a sparkle in hazel-green eyes also bracketed with worry.

"Can I get you anything?" he asked as he motored down the short hall to the living room.

I followed, taking in the carefully arranged décor as I went. "You can get me Wyatt on the phone."

He snorted softly. "I would if I could, Evy. How about in the realm of breakfast foods or coffee?"

"No, I'm fine."

"You don't look fine." He circled around and indicated the sofa.

Look who's talking. I slid into its plush upholstery with a grunt. "How'd you look if you'd been held captive and tortured for twenty days?" He flinched, and I sighed. "You really don't know where Wyatt went?"

"I'm sorry, I don't. He or Phineas, as a matter of fact. Wyatt's gone off on his own for a day or so before, but he always came back. He's working on four days now without a word, and that's just—"

"That's what?"

Rufus shook his head. "I was going to say it's just not like him, but he wasn't himself the whole time you were gone. I think if he'd had proof you were dead, instead of uncertainty eating him up . . . He drank a lot but wouldn't talk to anyone, not even Gina. We tried to get him to accept you were gone, and I think near the end he did, but he was just so—"

"Cold?" I offered the word Kismet had used.

"Yeah. So is that why you came over this morning? To make sure I wasn't in cahoots and hiding it from Gina?"

"Kind of." It was also better than hanging around the apartment alone, slowly going crazy.

"His room is down the hall, first door on the right."

I nodded my thanks.

The door was shut. I turned the brass knob and pushed. The furniture in the bedroom was the same carved mahogany as in the rest of the house—a headboard, nightstand, and dresser, and thick navy area rug over more wood flooring. It was impersonal, except for the small pile of laundry by the corner of the made bed. I snagged a black short-sleeved polo, held it to my face, and inhaled the rich, familiar scent that was Wyatt.

I could almost imagine him standing in front of me wearing that shirt, his heart thrumming steadily against my breast as he held me tightly in his arms. *You son of a bitch, if you're out there doing something stupid . . .*

A quick search led to nothing of note. Rufus had probably searched once. I did it for personal peace of mind. Whatever Wyatt had been planning, wherever he and Phin had gone, they'd been careful to leave no trace behind.

Rufus was in the kitchen watching coffee brew. Two mugs were on the counter, next to an assortment of sweetener packets. I sat on one of the stools and fiddled with the red ceramic mug nearest me.

"Didn't find anything either, huh?" he asked.

"No."

The pot gurgled the last of its water through the grounds. "What are your plans now?"

Plans? "Get back into fighting form, mostly," I said. "I need to gain weight, rebuild my muscle mass. Frankly, I've needed to train since I got this body, only I haven't had the chance." It had been almost two months since my resurrection—a difficult concept to swallow, since I'd spent half of it unconscious for various reasons.

"You know, Gina said Tybalt made a similar comment to her the other week, about staying in fighting shape."

I met Rufus's hazel gaze. "Did he?"

"She says he's found something to keep himself occupied but won't tell her what. She got stuck with three rookies last week anyway, so she doesn't see much of him."

"Three?"

"Yeah, they're graduating rookies earlier and without the usual pomp and circumstance." Read: without fights to the death. "Because they're several Handlers down, the working Triads are all getting extra team members."

No wonder Gina and Milo both looked so stressed. I was glad for Tybalt, but also a little sad for Gina. She and Tybalt had been together for four years. In just a few weeks, she'd lost two of her longtime Hunters and had them replaced by green newbies. "Are you lending your sage wisdom to the rookies, too?" I asked, unsure just how to continue the conversation.

"I'm not a Handler anymore, Evy. And I never will be."

"What?" I hadn't expected that. Yes, he was recovering, but it was supposed to be a temporary setback.

"I'll never walk normally again, so I can't be out in the

field," he said with no ire in his voice. Just bland acceptance.

Christ on a cracker. "But you were a Handler for ten years. You and Wyatt were two of the first Hunters in the Triads and founding Handlers. You're good at your job, Rufus. You can train—"

"No, I can't." He grabbed the pot and whirred over to the counter to pour. "Brass won't let me. But it's kind of weird to think that Wyatt and I are no longer part of something we helped create."

"Weird?"

"Okay, fucked-up."

I blew across the top of my steaming coffee, then inhaled its rich aroma. "Things fall apart," I muttered.

"What?"

"Nothing." I pondered that as I sucked down the scorching liquid, grateful for the heat in my stomach and the caffeine jolt that would accompany it. Rufus was out of a job. Tybalt and Felix and I were out of jobs. Wyatt and Phin were . . . somewhere.

Phin had come to me once with the very genuine desire to see his people—not just Therians but all Dregs—have a hand in policing themselves. He'd never get his wish of seeing Therians join the Triads, I knew that now. He had to see it, too. But the Triads were rotting from the inside out. Losing members left and right, breaking apart, betraying their own. With the experience Rufus and Wyatt had in training people to hunt, track, fight, and kill, we could be a new force to be reckoned with.

All I had to do was find my fucking boyfriend, tell him I was alive, and lay out the suggestion.

I scratched my fingernail across the smooth granite countertop, once again struck by the condo's class. It wasn't upscale by any means, but it wasn't cheap. And Rufus looked completely out of place in its high level of comfort. The apartment he'd maintained in Mercy's Lot was a hole compared to this (charitably, it had been a hole compared to almost anywhere else) but had somehow seemed more him.

My face must have given me away.

"What?" he asked.

"Just marveling at your new digs. They're nice."

His expression soured. "This is all Phin, trust me. But the wood floors are handy, and so's the elevator. I'd have had a bitch of a time navigating the stairs at my old place in this chair. I only got upstairs that first time because of Nadia."

"After everything you've been through, Rufus, I think you kind of deserve the break."

"That's debatable." He fiddled with his coffee mug, and I wanted to reach out and hit him with it.

I déjà vued back to our conversation in the hospital when he'd thought he deserved execution for his part in the Owlkin massacre. He hadn't wanted me to fight for his life. *I've done some amazingly shitty things in my lifetime, Evy. You'd never believe it. Feels like it's finally my time to pay up, is all.*

He was stuck in a wheelchair, scarred for life, and unable to go back to his old job with the Triads—and the idiot still thought he had more than he deserved? What. The. Hell? "Well, I guess you've still got the market cornered on self-pity," I said.

His glare didn't dissuade me, either. I was tired, hurt, mentally wrung out, and bordering on a nervous breakdown. I was so sick of bullshit I could scream. "Look, whatever the hell you did that was so awful? Get the fuck over it, Rufus. Most of us don't get forgiveness, and we don't get punished by the people who deserve a shot at us. Life's unfair, but we keep going. There's no other choice."

He managed to keep his expression neutral, but his voice dripped with sadness as he replied, "Evy, you have survived more hurt and pain in the last two months than any of your crimes could ever demand, and you haven't stopped fighting. I admire that, and I admit that it shames me, too."

"So do something about it."

"Easier said than done, believe me. I joined the Triads to give my life purpose and focus, and I've tried to atone for my mistakes." He tapped his fingers on the arm of his wheelchair and heaved a deep, resigned sigh. "But even if I found a way to forgive myself, he'd never forgive me."

"He who?"

"Wyatt."

If I hadn't already put my mug down, I would have dropped it. He looked away, and I studied his profile, as if the slope of his nose and jut of his jaw would tell me everything I needed to know. It didn't. Maybe if I weren't coming off a three-week torture binge, half-starved and emotionally crushed, I'd be able to figure out the reference on my own. It couldn't have been recent, and except for our mutual outpourings of pain in a motel room last month, Wyatt didn't talk about the early days of the Triads.

"Rufus, you've known Wyatt for ten years," I said. "What unforgiveable thing could you possibly have done?"

Rufus snapped his head up, hazel eyes lit with a fire I'd never seen before—more emotion than he'd ever displayed in my presence. For an instant, I expected him to leap from his chair and attack. Then the fire flickered out, replaced by the familiar hardness he'd had in place since his Triad died. His eyebrows furrowed together, and he seemed torn between a desire to shut up and to finally get something off his chest.

I didn't want him to tell me, but I also couldn't let him not. Not if it was about Wyatt.

"He told you how his family died."

It wasn't a question, and my mind flashed to Wyatt's brother. Nicky and Wyatt had been two of the first Hunters trained by the Fey. Nicky's death had been an accident, but I knew it still haunted Wyatt. He felt responsible, and he'd said nothing about Rufus being present during the fight that led to Nicky's death. Wyatt pushed, Nicky tripped, end of sad story.

No, not that family. Their parents and sister died months before that incident, when a group of half-Bloods invaded their family-owned restaurant and proceeded to torture and kill everyone there. Two out-of-state bounty hunters had come in, killed the Halfies, then killed everyone else to eliminate witnesses. Wyatt said he'd caught and killed one of the bounty hunters.

Cold fingers raked down my spine. Acid churned in my stomach. My mouth dried out, and it took several tries to get my tongue moist enough to speak. "You know who the second bounty hunter is, don't you?"

He flinched. Nodded. Misery and relief made a peculiar combination on his face as he prepared to hoist a years-old burden onto someone else. I wanted to flee the room before he could say anything else. One of Wyatt's biggest regrets was never learning who that second bounty hunter was—a regret that still gnawed at him a decade later.

Indignation and anger on his behalf began to heat my chest. "How the hell could you keep this from him, Rufus? You have to tell him who."

Another nod, this one resigned. "He'll kill me."

"He might beat you up, but he won't kill—" Holy. Fucking. Shit. My brain stuttered and my vision grayed.

Rufus never looked away, and the depth of misery in his gaze reached into my chest and squeezed my heart into bloody pulp. "I couldn't possibly tell him, Evy," he said. "At first it was survival. Then over the years we actually became friends. After that it was impossible. How do I tell him the second bounty hunter was me?"

A dull roar in my ears blocked out all sound. The words I hadn't wanted to hear rocketed through my mind and heart, and I was crushed under the weight of the secret I'd just been handed. Did I tell Wyatt when I finally saw him again? Did I force Rufus to? Did I keep it a secret, even though lying to Wyatt was the last thing on Earth I ever wanted to do?

God*damm*it!

The front doorbell rang with a deep chime. I jumped, sloshing my coffee. Rufus frowned. He didn't ask me not to tell, didn't make me promise him anything about his confession. He just motored out of the kitchen to the front door. It creaked open. The voices were muffled.

I stared at my spilled coffee, willing my brain to function. I hadn't wanted to know this, but it was too damned late to take it back. It certainly explained Rufus's tendency toward self-loathing and punishing himself by pushing away external comforts. He said he didn't deserve the luxury of this apartment, and the petty, vindictive side of my mind agreed with him. The rest of me didn't know what the hell to think.

Moments later, Rufus returned with Kismet in tow.

"You're up and about early," she said to me as she put a box of bakery doughnuts on the counter.

"I've spent the better part of a month sleeping, so I'm not very tired," I said.

"Touché." She poured herself a mug of coffee and added milk from the fridge, seeming very at home here. Rufus helped himself to a glazed doughnut. He offered one to me. The sugary, fried ring made my stomach gurgle unpleasantly.

"You need to eat, Evy," he said.

"Yeah, but I'm not eating that. You eat those every morning?"

"Just Sunday."

It was Sunday? Good to know. I sipped at my coffee, keenly aware of how strange my situation was—having Sunday-morning coffee and doughnuts with two Handlers who had each, in their own way and for their own reasons, tried to kill me in the not-so-distant past. And now they were among the people I trusted most with my life. They'd also both recently experienced tremendous loss. Rufus's entire Triad had been killed. Kismet had lost two long-term Hunters to crippling injuries. Add Wyatt's losses to the list, and they were the Three Musketeers of Grief.

I stayed quiet while they ate their doughnuts and chatted about nonsensical things. Nothing work-related or even borderline important. A song she'd heard on the radio that made her laugh. The television movie he'd watched last night and made fun of out loud. It was so normal I wanted to scream.

"What are the Triads doing to find Thackery?" I asked when I couldn't stand it anymore.

Kismet put her half-eaten doughnut down and steepled her fingertips, elbows on the counter. "His photo is out to the Metro Police. He's regarded as a dangerous suspect, wanted for kidnapping and attempted murder. From what I hear, the Clans are still looking, and I'm going to assume so are the gargoyles. Everyone's doing what they can."

The response should have placated me. Instead, I got angry. "Doing what they can like before, when he had me?"

She bristled. "He was keeping you on the move outside the city, Evy. We did what we could. We can't search the entire world. Thackery made it impossible to find you, and now that his mobile laboratory is destroyed, he'll probably lie low for a long time."

"Don't count on it. Thackery's entire life for the last five years has been dedicated to curing vampire infection in humans. It's his driving force, and he won't just curl up and hibernate until it's safe to start over. He'll resume as soon as he's able."

She stared, but my gaze never wavered.

"What do you suggest?" she asked.

"Don't underestimate him."

An awkward silence stretched out over the next few minutes as we sipped our coffee and avoided looking at one another. Until I couldn't stand it anymore. "So tell me more about James Reilly," I said. "You said he got a heaping helping of truth. Does that mean he's working with us now?"

"Pretty much," she replied. "We haven't gotten an official okay from the brass yet, but most of the other Handlers are on board. We can't keep Reilly quiet unless we kill him, which we aren't going to do, so—"

"If you can't kill them, recruit them?"

Her lips quirked. Rufus chuckled.

Kismet's cell phone rang. She checked the I.D., then snapped it open. "Kismet." Her eyebrows puckered. "Adrian, slow down, I—" She went perfectly still, her already pale skin taking on a frightening pallor. Her mouth slowly fell open.

I exchanged a look with Rufus, whose face reflected the concern and confusion that was ripping through my body.

"I'll be there as soon as I can," she said, and hung up. "Fucking hell."

"What?" I asked.

"Boot Camp is being attacked."

"Attacked?" Rufus and I squawked in stereo. Again?

"I'll call you with details," she said, already on her way to the door.

Hell no.

I chased after her.

No way was I sitting this out.

Chapter Twenty-five

She didn't protest, and I waited until we were in her Jeep and on the road before demanding to know what the fuck was going on.

"Adrian got a call from one of the trainers," she said, voice shaking. "She said the creatures we'd collected from Olsmill started going berserk. They were enraged like nothing she'd ever seen before, some of them bursting out of their cages. The six hounds got loose, too. No one realized it until they got out of R&D and started tearing through the compound."

I bit my lower lip hard. Six hounds, plus fourteen other inhuman beasts, loose in an enclosed compound full of trainers and half-skilled rookie Hunters. It would be a slaughter.

"Thackery," I said. "He created those things; it makes sense he'd have some method of controlling them. Some switch we couldn't see to set them off. A fail-safe."

As far-fetched as it sounded, given what I now knew about Thackery, it also seemed perfectly reasonable. He could control his newest breed of hounds. He had a trained fucking wolf. Who was to say he couldn't also control the other creatures in his menagerie? We'd taken them into our most protected, private facility, and now he was attacking our heart.

Bastard!

Kismet tossed her phone at me. "Call the apartment.

Tell Milo and the rookies to get weapons and be ready for us to pick them up in five minutes."

I did, not even bothering to explain, and points to Milo for not asking. At Kismet's direction, I called four other Handlers and repeated an emergency code. Two teams were remaining in the city, just in case. Everyone else was scrambling to Boot Camp. She repeated the message to her team after we picked them up. Her rookies were all teen boys, fresh-faced and completely forgettable, and probably about to become cannon fodder.

God, did I ever look that young?

They passed out weapons. Apparently, Milo remembered my fondness for knives, because I was given three—one for my ankle and one on each hip, plus a gun loaded with frag rounds and two extra clips. Kismet's gun and various rounds went on the seat between us.

No one talked, each of us absorbed in our own thoughts. I kept imagining the trainees being cornered and slaughtered by those creatures. Being hunted in their own safe haven by monsters that shouldn't exist. As a trainee, I'd been able to reconcile the existence of vampires and shape-shifters and Fey because they'd been here long before humans. But the hounds? That thing with the fish fin? The skeleton cat? Nature had been raped and abused to create them, and now we were paying the price.

The city fell away, and a black sedan appeared behind us on the dirt road that wound up to Boot Camp. Kismet raced along the bumpy path, and I swear I heard a tire pop. At a bend, the road was blocked by a second Jeep. She slammed on the brakes. I braced against the dash, my seat belt snapping me back. Tires squealed behind us. Just beyond the first vehicle was the gate.

We tumbled out, joined from the rear sedan by Morgan's team. Four figures had gathered next to the front

Jeep—a Triad I didn't know. They waved at us to take cover, and I finally realized why.

Three creatures prowled the front gate, on our side of the barrier. The familiar hulking shapes of two hounds walked on their hind legs, darting in and out of the decimated guard hut, daring us to try and get inside. Both of them were bleeding in half a dozen places, but seemingly unfazed by the wounds. The third shape was the oversized gray wolf—Thackery's wolf, with the intelligent silver eyes. Silver eyes seemed to be a theme with his sidekicks.

The wolf watched me from the safety of the hounds' shadows, ears perked. Surprised to see me alive, maybe?

None of them were attacking. Shit. They were stalling us. Keeping us out. I said as much to Kismet.

"Kis, Morgan," the oldest of the unfamiliar foursome said. Had to be their Handler. "How much firepower do you have?"

"Plenty," Morgan said. He and Paul were lugging a trunk forward.

"Mix up the frags and a-c's," Kismet said. "It kills them faster."

"We don't have time for this," I said, and gave her a hard look. "There's no barrier spell that I can sense, so I could try three."

"Take Milo." To the Handler, she said, "Sharpe, I need two of yours."

Sharpe shot her a sour look. His close-cropped brown hair and deep-set eyes gave him an Italian mobster air that wasn't dispelled by the way he drew out some of his vowels. "Greg and Scott, do what she tells you. Everyone else, switch out your ammo."

I rolled my eyes. Fools must have been using regular rounds. Then I surveyed my temporary partners.

Greg and Scott were perfect opposites as Hunters. The former was short and stocky, with the bulk of a midget wrestler, while the latter was tall and lean and tight sinew. They were also armed to the teeth. Scott even had a short sword in a sheath across his back. Nice.

Only Milo seemed to have some inkling of what we were about to do. I grabbed his hand, then took Greg's. Milo reached for Scott's. The other two men frowned.

"Take his fucking hand," Kismet snapped before I had to.

"Don't break the circle," I said when they finally got over holding a man's hand. "No matter what, because this is going to feel weird."

I closed my eyes and ignored the sounds of clips sliding into place and Handlers shouting orders. I reached out to find my tap, then sought loneliness. With Wyatt gone, unreachable, untouchable, it wasn't hard. The emotion flooded me, bordering on grief, and the Break snapped all around me. Around us. Someone shouted as we dissolved. I guided us through the familiar crackle of energy, toward the road just past the gate. A sharp stab of pain hit between my eyes. Warm wetness stained my upper lip.

And then we were out. Milo caught me before I fell, and I sagged against his chest, dizzy and nauseated.

"Holy shit, that was awesome," either Greg or Scott said. The other asked, "She okay?"

A high-pitched shriek bounced off the trees from the direction of Boot Camp. "Go!" I said, and pushed Milo away.

The three took off down the road and disappeared around the first bend. I stumbled after them. Wouldn't be very good in the battle today, but at least I'd gotten a few extra hands into the fray sooner.

An out-of-place whirring sound approached from the west, high above the trees. I gazed up at the sky as I half walked, half ran. A helicopter buzzed aloft, heading toward the heart of the compound. Airborne backup—

that made me smile. Behind me, an eruption of gunfire added to the cacophony.

The trees parted. The smoking ruins of R&D lay straight ahead, burning from the inside out. Smoke stung my eyes. Two twisted, bloodied bodies decorated the sidewalk. Gunfire and screams still echoed from the rear, closer to the recruit barracks and training facilities. The helicopter was gone, and I hoped it had at least dumped a couple of capable bodies before flying away.

I dug up some energy reserves and ran. Rounded past R&D and tripped over another body, scraping my palms on the ground as I ate dirt. In times past, I would have used the momentum to tuck into a roll and come up gracefully on my knees. Instead, I belly flopped and looked back.

The girl was probably just eighteen. Her blond hair was streaked crimson, blue eyes wide and unseeing above a gaping throat. Her chest was likewise torn open, one of her arms missing. Strike that, not missing— lying a few feet away. She could have been me four years ago.

People were still screaming. Engines roared as the rest of our backup made entry. I hauled myself up and ran toward the gymnasium a dozen yards away. The doors were gone, and the bulk of the screams were coming from inside.

The interior of the gym was the size of a pro-football arena, divided up into smaller sections designated for specific activities. The largest of these was an obstacle course, and I turned in that direction. Past two more ripped-apart bodies of young trainees. Kids who'd come here for a chance at a meaningful (albeit brief) future and had died gruesome deaths.

Grief for them hardened into anger, and I latched onto it for fuel. It was all I had. Someone darted out of an intersecting corridor and slammed into me. Milo and I went tumbling to the ground. His shirt was coated in blood, but he didn't seem wounded.

"I think we're too late," he said, panting, as we helped each other stand.

"No."

He followed me into the obstacle arena. We were on a balcony overlooking the course, where our instructors had watched as we failed test after test. Below and half-way across the stretch of space, three battered trainees were high up on the climbing ropes. A single hound stalked them from the ground, swatting at the ropes, seeming not to know how to climb them.

Small favors.

Milo and I pulled our guns at the same time. "Frags," I said, to which he answered, "A-c's."

Good. We opened fire on the hound. Its inhuman howl sliced through my eardrums. Four shots hit home before it dove for cover, but none on its soft underbelly. I bolted for the ladder that led down. The trainees had seen us and were shouting for help. I wanted to scream back to shut up, it's what we're doing.

At the ladder, I paused and scanned. A flash of black was moving toward us. I took aim at where I thought it was likely to dart next and waited.

Milo screamed as he pitched past me and to the floor below, a wriggling, snarling creature the size of a cat attached to his back. Skele-kitty, one of the first hy-brids I'd seen in the Olsmill lab. Milo hit and rolled. I braced my wrist and aimed. He rolled again, shouting. I squeezed the trigger. The thing's bald head exploded green gore all over Milo's back. He looked up, panting, nose bleeding, and gave me a thumbs-up.

"The hound!" I said.

He understood and scrambled for the ladder. The hound blurred toward him. He spun and we both fired, me from above, him from below. Blood gushed. My frags tore chunks of flesh away. It collapsed inches from Milo and lay still.

"Hell yeah," Milo said.

"Stay up there as long as you can," I shouted to the trainees. "It's not safe for you yet!"

Milo stumbled to his feet and started climbing back up. More shouts and gunfire erupted around us, muffled by walls in all directions, intermixed with unidentifiable noises—things breaking, being shoved, shattered, I wasn't certain. Milo's head cleared the balcony.

One of the dangling trainees screeched: "Look out!"

How come they never yelled a split second faster and gave us enough reaction time?

A moving body slammed into me, and I pitched forward. Startled by the sudden spur into motion, I lost my grip on the damned gun. I braced for impact only to scream when four daggers pierced my right ankle and kept me from falling. No, I was moving and it wasn't daggers. Upside down, I thrashed against whatever was holding my leg. Air beat around me, and we were flying above the obstacle course.

Flying?

Shit.

I plucked a knife from one of the sheaths in my belt and slashed at the winged monstrosity hauling me around. Dark-skinned, mottled with patches of black feathers, its wings were long and stretched like a bat's. Or a gargoyle's, only I'd never seen gargoyle wings that long—a full ten-foot wingspan—or one that had feathers. Good God, what had Thackery created?

My blade bounced off the thing's thickly hided feet, and its talons tightened. Blood oozed from the small wounds in my ankle. I was getting light-headed from hanging ass over teakettle. Milo was shouting about not having a clean shot, and I'd lost my gun. The gar-bat-thing zoomed directly toward the far wall, and for one brief moment, I expected it to try to crash straight through. It veered sharply right at the last instant. My head and left shoulder smacked the wall, leaving me reeling.

As it spun me again, I noticed the trainees were off the ropes. Smart move, now that we had airborne enemies. Gar-Bat flew right toward the ropes, heedless of their existence. Or maybe it was having too much fun hauling me around like a bag of flailing potatoes.

I put the blade between my teeth and grabbed the rope with both hands as we passed, holding on with all my might. My palms burned. My ankle lost a little more meat, and I screamed, but Gar-Bat was yanked to a sudden halt. It turned its head and screeched at me—a head-splitting shriek that sounded like tortured baboons. Its face was unidentifiable—hints of different creature-features combined into one squashed maw that was more sea lion–ish than anything else. It was almost absurd.

No, it *was* absurd. A flying sea lion–bat was attacking me. Absurd didn't even begin to cover it.

It beat its wings, trying to yank me off the rope. I waited for an upswing, the slightest drop in pull. Then I held with my left hand, took the knife with my right, and flung it at the creature's chest. It struck center. It screamed and let go so suddenly I didn't have time to grab the rope again. I plummeted to the ground.

There were no mats, just the hard Astroturf surface that covered most of the obstacle course floor. I hit on my back, knocking the wind out of my lungs in a solid, aching *whoosh*. My chest constricted. Tears stung my eyes. Every frail, unexercised bone in my body ached. I lay there, desperate to suck in some air.

I couldn't see the Gar-Bat, but I could hear it, still screeching and wailing. On the other side of the climbing wall, maybe. At least I'd wounded it. It gave me a minute to pull myself together. I inhaled hard. Sweet oxygen filled my straining lungs, and I coughed. Inhaled, coughed out, inhaled again. My head started clearing.

I didn't know of any shortcuts on the obstacle course. My only way out was to go through it to the end. And I was somewhere in the middle, down on the lowest level. During training, this was where each runner climbed the rope to get a flag tacked at the very top and held on to it for the rest of the course. The only way out from here was a rope ladder angled up at forty-five degrees, anchored on hooks so it swiveled with your weight.

I hated this one. Even when I was in peak physical shape and not sporting a chewed-on ankle, I had trouble and had fallen off more than once. I used the anchor post to stand up. My ankle cried at the pressure, and my arms were shaking. My vision blurred. Just terrific.

Claws scrabbled against the wall separating me from Gar-Bat. It was trying to climb. I guess it was too wounded to fly out.

I closed my eyes and felt for the Break. It was there, on the fringes of my mind, taunting me. Too far. And I was too upset. A tremor seized my spine and shook my entire body. Not the shock I got when a blocking spell was being used; this was my body protesting the idea of teleporting. No strength for it. Fuck.

The rope ladder swayed on its own, mocking me. Climb it and escape, or wait and see if Gar-Bat makes it over the wall. Both choices sucked.

I reached as far up the rungs as I could, looped my left ankle around a lower one, and lunged. The ladder swiveled upside down. I clung to the ropes, dangling. Hand over hand, foot over rung, I inched my way up the twenty-foot rope ladder. The floor below was more hardwood. The trainers put down mats the first two times you ran the course. If you fell after that, you ate floor.

Having eaten enough floor for one day, I concentrated

on my ascent and nothing else. Sweat dotted my hairline and upper lip. The rope seared my scraped palms. My ankle was probably leaving lovely little blood smears behind. Up, up, up, until the top anchor post was just one lunge away. Urgency almost made me reach. The unwillingness to fall two stories and start over blocked that urge, and I inched my way up. Grabbed the post with my right hand and the floor with my left and hauled ass up to the platform. I hugged the wood, polished smooth with years of hands and bodies doing just what I'd done.

Gar-Bat screeched. Either he was getting frustrated by his own inability to climb the wall or he didn't like my progress. Maybe both.

I had a better vantage point over the course from here, so I sat up. Heat whizzed by my cheek, slicing the skin. I jerked back. My knife was buried in the anchor post. Hell's bells, the thing had thrown my own knife at me!

The next challenge made my heart sink. Six erratically spaced uneven bars were my only path to the next platform. Some trainees were gymnastically inclined and had excelled at this one. Me? Not so much.

I looked at my palms, both weeping and scraped. Then at the ground below. The air mattresses were deflated. One more time I tested my Gift. That same brittle distance filled me. If I tried, I'd probably end up inside of something or dead from my brain exploding.

"Fuck!" It came out like a plea and bounced around the open gym. Where the hell had Milo gone? He'd better be off saving lives.

Screw this. One wrong move on those bars and I'd break my neck. There had to be another way. I perched my toes on the edge of the platform and leapt for the nearest bar. My grip nearly slipped. I held tight and stiffened, stopping all motion. Inched sideways until I got to the support post, shifted my grip, and shinnied down to the floor.

The court was narrow and long, built up on all sides with two-by-fours nailed into thicker beams. Something slammed against the wall on my left. Gar-Bat was still at it. I worked my way along the opposite wall, checking for any sort of access or hatchway. The trainers had to have some way to get around this course. I just needed to find it.

At the end of the court, hope presented itself in the form of a square sliding door. I pried it up to reveal a crawl space barely large enough for a grown man to slither through. Good thing I was smaller than that.

Gar-Bat shrieked, this time above me. I looked up as a shadow fell. It was perched on the platform, braced to jump. I crawled through the rabbit hole and immediately sneezed. Didn't stop. Seconds later Gar-Bat was scrabbling at the hole, too large to follow me inside.

I crept along the narrow path until it opened up into what looked like the interior of another raised platform. Judging from the wide spaces between the boards, it was another sort of climbing wall. I slipped through one of the wider slats and stumbled. My ankle was numb, making it difficult to walk. No sign yet of Gar-Bat.

I hobbled fast across another open floor, getting much closer to the end of the course. Two, maybe three, challenges lay between me and the end.

My frustration at being stuck doing this was nothing compared to my anger at not being outside, part of the ongoing battle. Had they killed the rest of the hounds? How many of Thackery's projects were loose? How many had been captured or killed? How many of our people were wounded? Dead?

I dropped to my knee when the shadow fell, drawing the knife from my right ankle sheath. Blood dripped from above, viscous and bluish. Gar-Bat dive-bombed me. I pitched sideways at the last moment and thrust up, dragging the blade across its lower belly. More blood splashed on my hands and arms. Its rear legs lashed out and slammed me to the left even as it crashed to the floor. It thrashed and flopped, spreading its blood across the floor like a fresh coat of paint.

The raw-sewage odor turned my stomach. I crawled away, slipped, and finally got to my feet. The stink was on my hands. I wiped them on the seat of my jeans, then repositioned the knife so the handle was clasped between both hands. Gar-Bat's thrashing had slowed. It lay on its stomach, wings folded close to its back, the pool of blood widening around it.

I almost felt sorry for it, whining in pain and paling quickly. It hadn't asked to be created, and now it was paying the price. I thrust my blade down, directly into Gar-Bat's skull. The impact jolted my wrists. Bone cracked. Matter oozed. My enemy lay still.

"Class dismissed," I said.

Chapter Twenty-six

With less haste now that I wasn't being hunted, I limped through two more hidden hatches and crawl spaces—bypassing a grid of dangling chains one had to swing through to pass and a complicated setup of balance beams, tires, and parallel bars—and hit the finale. A mirror maze, not unlike those found at carnivals and fairs, only this one didn't just try to fool you into hitting a dead end. The space between each panel was supernarrow, twenty inches on average, and most of the joints hid a cruel punishment—nearly invisible razors. I'd gotten my fair share of slices in the past.

I remembered one trainee who'd barely passed the obstacle course, getting so tired and beaten up over the run of it that he'd been unsteady going into the maze. He'd stumbled out sobbing, coated in blood, but on his feet. Just barely. Too bad he'd failed the final exam.

Desperate to skip this one, I searched for another way out. A hatch or ladder or means to climb up and over. Screaming in frustration, I sucked in a breath and went in. I hit a wall first thing. Inched through sideways. Nicked my wrist and elbow on one turn. Sliced my other elbow on another. I ignored my reflection, uninterested in how awful I must look coated in blood and gore and sweat. All I wanted was out.

Out so I could finish helping. So I could try to save some lives today. Urgency kept goading me to speed up, but I battled to remain careful, steady. Patience wasn't in my nature; taking it so slowly was torture. Even when the end seemed in sight, I kept up my tentative pace. One sliding step sideways, careful turns. Only a handful of cuts accompanied me outside.

Fucking finally!

I stumbled through the exit, into the narrow strip of open corridor that bordered the wall of the obstacle course and the wall of the gymnasium. It circled the length of it in straight sections of twenty feet or so, then sharply angled into the next. From above, it looked like a giant octagon or something, only with more than eight sides.

I turned and started jogging back toward the ladder, or any other way up that presented itself.

Halfway back I turned a corner and tripped over a headless corpse. Male, standard trainee outfit. I gagged at the heavy odor of blood and stepped around, only to nearly fall over two more. The three kids from the ropes. They'd made it through the obstacle course only to die here, ripped apart. Torn flesh and bits of guts made it hard to navigate without falling. My stomach twisted, and the sight sent a shock of fear through me. Whatever had killed them—likely a hound—was probably still close by, and I was down to one blade.

Something shuffled out of sight, ahead of the turn into the next stretch of corridor. I slunk back around the last corner I'd passed, behind the sprawl of bodies, pressing close to the inner wall. I crouched and palmed my last weapon. Switched it to my right hand, angled so the blade rested on the underside of my wrist, and shifted my weight to my strong ankle. Ready to pounce. The sound drew closer, then stopped near the bodies.

The footsteps were softer, predator-like. Over the stench of blood, I couldn't catch a scent of the thing approaching to determine if it was human, hound, or other. I held my breath, adrenaline taking over. Attack first and ask questions later.

Survive.

Air shifted. A shadow fell. I twisted upward and lunged, knocking the body hard against the wall with my left hand across his chest and my blade against his Adam's apple. Something cold pressed hard against my own neck, just barely slicing skin.

Wide navy-blue eyes stared at me, round with disbelief and shock. My heart jackhammered. I gasped.

"Stone?"

I stepped back, my hands dropping. My neck stung from the new cut. I'd come within a millimeter of slicing Bastian's throat. A small part of me wished I had, the traitorous bastard. He was staring at me like he thought I still might.

"Surprise," I said. "Your pal Thackery didn't get the best of me after all. Disappointed?"

Something like fear flashed across Bastian's face. "Is he dead?"

I wanted to slap him for being so stupid. "No, asshole, who the fuck do you think is responsible for all this?" I waved my hand sideways, toward the sprawled bodies nearby. "Thackery set off his pet projects to tear us apart. And, gee, I wonder how he knew they were here?"

He didn't actually say anything, but he did lose every drop of color in his face. I took a step forward, knife up. He either forgot he had his own weapon, or I was menacing enough to cow him, because he didn't protest. He actually shrank back.

"This is your fault, you—"

"Get down!" he shouted, eyes going wide.

I ducked low, and a bulky form sailed over me. It hit the bloody mess of bodies and skidded into the far wall. Bastian was already moving. I leapt up and pivoted in time to see him pull a GLOCK from a hidden back holster and unload four rounds into the flailing hound's back. It flung itself sideways at him, roaring its anger, and sent Bastian careening into the opposite wall. He hit with a nauseating crunch and crumpled to the floor.

My temper spiked. I scooped up Bastian's dropped knife and, one knife in each fist, whistled at the snarling beast. "Hey, ugly, come and get me!"

With a snarl and a sound eerily close to disdainful laughter, it charged. I raced down the corridor away from Bastian's body, keenly aware of the hound gaining even with its multiple wounds. My ankle was still unsteady. I had one chance at this. The hound howled, and the hairs on my neck stood up straight. Hot breath puffed ripe and too damned close.

As the next corner approached, I measured my steps. I let my wounded ankle slide beneath me and twisted my body so that I ended up on my back. Every bone and joint vibrated. The hound didn't have time to adjust its path for my roadblock and chose to leap over me. Perfect. I slashed up with both knives, and the hound's own momentum ripped its abdomen open from ribs to nuts. Sour, suffocating blood rained down. It crashed to the floor as I rolled sideways to avoid being crushed.

Stop, drop, and roll isn't just for fighting fires anymore.

I wiped my hands and knives on the hound's fur-covered legs, fighting my gag reflex the entire time. I don't know why their blood reeks so badly. Just another of life's unanswerable questions.

The corridor behind me was silent. "Bastian?" My voice bounced and pinged. No one answered. I yelled again, louder.

I backtracked. The four bodies were still there, Bastian included. I checked for a pulse and found it weak, thready. Blood soaked his white-blond hair scarlet, oozing from a head wound I couldn't see. Shit. I didn't have time to wait for help, and some awful corner of my heart didn't really care if the asshole lived or died. My compromise: I cut off a section of his shirt and pressed it against the head wound.

I followed the length of the track past the obstacle course exit I'd come through not ten minutes ago, and beyond. I found another ladder up to the high track. Two small smears of fresh blood marked the rungs at eye level. Someone had come this way recently.

A female scream, muffled and distant, broke the silence. I sheathed one knife, clenched the other in my teeth, and ascended the ladder. A few sprints down the upper track and I shoved through an emergency exit door. It was a different corridor from before. Half the lights were out, bathing it in shadows. There were a handful of doors, spaced pretty far apart.

The scream came again, somewhere down the hall. I ran. The corridor ended abruptly at a T junction. The left branch led to a heavy metal door, reinforced glass, and streaming sunlight. To the right were more doors. Before I could pick a direction, the door nearest me was flung open by a sailing body.

Greg hit the opposite wall with a pained grunt and slumped to the floor. His left thigh was bleeding heavily, as was his right bicep. He struggled to stand and slipped on his own blood. I took two steps forward. Something else flew through the open door and hit the wall above Greg with a disgusting splat, then fell to the floor like a sack of wet laundry. It was a human arm.

I palmed my second knife.

"Careful," Greg said.

The plaque next to the door said Weight Room. Another dismembered limb joined the arm—calf and foot.

A horrible thought assaulted me: what if that was Milo's foot? He was there somewhere, fighting. And while we weren't exactly best buds, we were still friends. I hadn't had real friends since Jesse and Ash died.

Rage and adrenaline drove me through the door. I ducked another flying body part, then tucked and rolled to the right. I came up with knives ready. The room was large, full of dozens of weight machines, benches, racks of free weights, and other equipment I barely remembered using once. In the corner nearest the door, something was huddled over the remains of a body.

Something was all I had. If someone took a gremlin, stuck a hose up its ass, and filled it full of chicken fat until it resembled an obese version of itself, it would look a lot like the thing in the corner—if you added extra fangs and clawed arms long enough to scrape the floor if it tried to stand straight. The fucking thing ripped the other arm off its victim, licked the gore at the shoulder socket, then tossed it out the door.

If I lived to be a hundred years old, that image would still be haunting me on the day I died.

It didn't seem to see me. I saw enough of the victim's torso to know it was female. My tiny flare of relief in knowing my sort-of-friend hadn't become an entrée was squelched by the fact that *someone* had. Someone who was being picked apart by E.T.'s evil spawn.

The layers of fat and skin would make my small knives ineffective. Spawn's claws tore flesh like a hot knife through butter, and its arms were strong enough to rend bone from tendon. I didn't stand a chance up close. I sheathed the knives and crept to the wall where a dozen metal bars were bracketed to a wooden frame, just waiting for someone to attach weights to the ends.

I selected a thick bar and tested it. It should work. I choked my hands around the center like I would a baseball bat, drew it high over my right shoulder, and eyed my target. The rest of the first leg flew out the door. The puddle of blood around Spawn was so wide I'd never be able to avoid it. Just had to watch my footing and hope I didn't splat into the puddle.

Like an Olympic javelin thrower, I raced toward my target. The bar pierced its skin with a squelching pop, driving down through fat, muscle, and other tissue, all the way to my hands. Spawn shrieked, glass-shatteringly high, and didn't stop. It also didn't whip around to try to swat me. Just huddled there over its dinner, squealing to burst my eardrums. Purple blood bubbled up from the wound. I got a higher grip and thrust deeper, until the bar popped out Spawn's front and hit the floor.

I yanked down on the bar and twisted it sideways— anything to kill Spawn faster and shut it up. It didn't like that. I crashed into a bench, and stars exploded behind my eyes. Then I felt throbbing in my ribs from the offensive blow. Damn and hell, that hurt. But at least the shrieking stopped. I sat up and shook off a wave of dizziness.

Spawn was slumped over the remains of its victim, purple blood swirling with human red. Vampires had purple blood, but there wasn't anything vampire-like about that thing. Odd.

Yeah, like anything about today's been normal.

I plucked another bar off the rack and retreated to the hall. Greg was on his feet, sweating heavily, shirt and pant leg soaked with blood.

"Remind me never to piss you off," he said.

"I get that a lot," I said. "Come on."

We searched the rest of the rooms on the corridor and found nothing. No hounds, no hybrids, and no other Hunters. No more screams alerted us to trouble indoors. We backtracked to the exit and burst into the morning sunlight. Humid summer heat pressed down like a damp blanket, instantly stifling, even out here in the mountains. We were behind the gymnasium, facing the single-story dormitory and, beyond it, the Pit.

Windows in the dorm were smashed out. Half a body lay on the ground nearby, a second mangled body not far from the first. A hound's corpse, riddled with bullet holes, was halfway between us and the dorm. The bodies of two hybrids decorated the yard in other places. A spattering of gunfire erupted behind the dorm. Another on the other side of the gym. Were we winning? Losing? Who else was alive?

Greg's cell beeped. He retrieved it with a shaky hand. Scanned the message. "Out front," he said. "Near Admin."

Halfway around the perimeter of the gym, Greg faltered. While my ankle was better and starting the familiar itch-ache, he'd lost a lot of blood. I looped an arm around his waist and used my last real burst of adrenaline to keep us going. I was panting when we got back to the gym's entrance, well within sight of the smoking R&D building.

Two more Jeeps and a sedan had arrived and ejected the last of our forces. Their forces. Whatever. With two teams still in the city, every available body was now on site. Four people stood around a laptop, talking heatedly, practically shouting at one another. Kismet was easy to identify by her build and red hair. Baylor turned his head to say something to Kismet. The third man had to be another Handler, who offered what seemed to be a scathing reply to the man holding the laptop. That man wore black cargo pants with stuffed pockets, a black shirt of some sort, and a pair of twin shoulder holsters. He practically screamed black ops, but that was ridiculous.

I stared at the back of that man's head, and as if sensing me, he turned to look. My mouth fell open. Phineas nearly dropped the laptop, his bright blue eyes going wide. I wanted to be happy to see him alive and well—

since he'd been so close to death the last time—but extreme fatigue was short-circuiting my brain.

Phin was here. Did that mean Wyatt was here? No one had seen either of them in four days. How had they heard about this? I wanted to haul Phin into a bear hug, then throttle him for disappearing in the first place.

Duty first—even if I was technically a civilian. I gave my rod to Greg for a crutch and jogged over to the huddled group. "Two hounds, two hybrids," I reported, staring at Phin the entire time—he seemed pale but otherwise himself. "And at least six dead trainees."

Phin typed the information into his laptop. "That means one hound and three hybrids still unaccounted for," he said.

Joy. "Is he here?" I asked.

He nodded and my heart soared. But before he could answer in detail, Kismet's phone chirped as a text came through. She glanced at the display. "Another hybrid down." Her lips quirked, not quite a smile. "Tybalt's kill."

Tybalt was here, too?

"One hound and two hybrids against the lot of us," Baylor said. "Not good odds for them."

"No, but that damned wolf at the gate got away," Kismet said. "And this is a large complex. It won't be easy tracking them in the woods."

Somehow it didn't surprise me the wolf had escaped. "These things were bred to kill and destroy," I said, finding it difficult to concentrate on tactics right then. Focus now, dammit, meltdown later. "They won't hide for long, if they're hiding at all. Do you know where they're still looking?"

"West of the dorms, near the Pit."

"Thanks." Oh yeah. "Bastian's hurt pretty bad. He's on the lower track around the obstacle course."

"We'll get someone to him," Kismet said. There was a

question in her tone, but I was too wrung out to bother saying I wasn't the one who hurt him.

I turned to go. Phin snagged my wrist and tugged me back. So many thoughts and emotions danced in his eyes, unfiltered and genuine, and I nearly stumbled under the weight of them. Above all was gratitude, and he didn't have to say it. I smiled.

"Glad you're okay," I said, and kissed him on the cheek. "Don't think I'm not yelling at you later for getting kidnapped and then disappearing on everyone, though."

He grinned and released my wrist. "Take one of my guns."

I pulled a pistol out of one shoulder holster. He'd been up to something, and I was damned sure going to find out what—as soon as our last three problems were eating dirt. Weapon in hand, I jogged back in the direction from which I'd come.

Claudia limped past me, her right leg bleeding fiercely. "Pit," she shouted.

On the edges of the forest east and south of the main buildings, four Hunters I didn't recognize patrolled the tree line. Two people in black gear identical to Phin's poked around the exterior of the dorms. Milo and Scott were scouting the opposite tree line. A third Hunter emerged and gave a thumbs-up. Scott immediately texted a message on his cell. Another one bites the dust?

The Pit wasn't a pit, exactly. It was more like an old, Roman-style amphitheater, with a center platform down low and bleacher-style seating on three sides. It descended twelve rows that were never full. The platform was a dirt floor twenty feet squared, stained black from years of fights to the death. It was also empty save for the shriveling remains of a hybrid-vampire-thing.

Someone shouted a warning too late. Weight slammed

into my back, and I tumbled ass over teakettle into the Pit, shoulders and elbows and knees cracking painfully off the metal bleachers. I twisted far enough onto my side to stop forward momentum and lay on my back, stunned and panting. A shadow loomed and I rolled sideways, just fast enough to avoid being smashed by the gray wolf.

I came up on my knees, halfway to the bottom of the Pit. I'd lost my gun on the way down, so I palmed a knife from the sheath at my hip as I pivoted to face . . . a naked teenage boy. Thackery's blond-haired, silver-eyed assistant. Something in my stunned expression must have amused him, because he laughed.

"I thought you'd cut and run at the gate," I said, sizing him up. He was skinny, but I didn't forget the way he'd manhandled me in that parking structure. "Run like a coward back to your master."

"The master keeps his promises, Evangeline," he replied in his ridiculous voice.

"Uh-huh. And what promise was that?"

His scorn was as obvious in his expression as in his next words. "He promised to kill you when the experiment was over."

A promise I'd asked him to make—stupid. "So why isn't he here himself? He get a little banged up in the crash?"

Wolf Boy's response was a low, deep-chested growl that would have put any real wolf to shame. I shifted my stance, ready for attack. Time to put this dog down. Voices shouted above us, around us, but I tuned them out. Let them fucking watch. Maybe I couldn't have the satisfaction of killing Thackery today, but I could sure as hell kill his shape-shifting wolf-minion.

"What's the matter?" I said, giving him all the attitude I had. "Don't eat girls?"

He growled again, and his face changed. The nose and

mouth lengthened, thinned out, speckled with gray hair, and sprouted longer, thicker teeth. His ears grew to points, and lines of fur filled in around both eyes, now perfectly round and shimmering with bloodlust.

Holy hell.

He lunged, human body moving like quicksilver, wolf teeth snapping at my throat. Not trusting my own body to do what my mind told it, I avoided initial contact by dropping to one knee, tucking, and rolling. It successfully caused Wolf Boy to sail over my head; it also made me fall down the rest of the bleachers to the dirt arena.

Thundering footsteps announced his descent, and I had the sense to roll again and avoid another attempt to smash my skull. His hands had transformed into clawed paws, thick with fur and sharp nails eerily similar to the other hounds'. The half morphing scared me. I'd seen it only in one species of Therian, and surely this thing wasn't Therian. It couldn't be. Phin had once told me there were coyotes and other wild dog species in the Clans, but no wolves.

Wolf Boy slammed into me sideways, and we tumbled through the rough sand, wrestling to see who would come out on top. Dirt flew, landing in my ears and nose and mouth. Claws scored my right arm, trying to dislodge the knife. My entire body ached from wounds and exhaustion, but a final surge of adrenaline kept me moving. Kept me fighting. If anyone eventually killed me, it wasn't going to be this mixed-breed bastard.

I jammed my left fist into his throat, and he gasped a wheeze through his half-formed mouth. Perfect target, and I slid the knife home. His teeth cut my knuckles even as the blade sliced meat and muscle, until it could go no farther and the point stuck out the back of Wolf Boy's neck. Blood flowed from his mouth, down over my hand. I shoved as he pitched, and he fell sideways into the dirt, gurgling through his own death until he was still.

A scattering of applause broke out, and I looked up, panting. Half a dozen people ringed the top of the Pit. Some clapped; others still had their guns raised and pointed at the dead boy-monster. I sat there stupidly a moment, unsure if I should be furious they'd stood and watched or grateful to have been given the chance to kill Wolf Boy without interference.

The latter seemed less migraine-inducing, so I went with it.

Footsteps clattered down the bleachers. I hauled ass to my feet, a little dizzy and grossed out by the amount of sand adhering to the new gashes on my arm. I turned around to address whichever audience member had rushed to join me and stood face to face with Wyatt.

I jumped back, startled by his sudden appearance. My heart stuttered. Utter shock and absolute joy choked every word out of my throat. All I could do was gape at him. Fresh blood oozed from a cut on his cheek. His clothes and weapons were almost identical to Phin's, and from the front I saw a thick leather belt dotted with ammo pouches, sheathed knives, and a few throwing stars.

The hell?

He raised a walkie-talkie and pressed a button, his wide eyes never wavering from mine. "Hound dead, hybrid dead," he said.

The frequency crackled, then Phin's voice came back. "That's it. Everything's accounted for. Have you seen—?"

"Seeing her right now."

"Out, then."

Wyatt slipped the walkie-talkie into his belt. His face was a maelstrom of emotions, each so powerful I felt beaten by them. A knot formed in my throat, and I couldn't swallow it away. Couldn't escape the rising tide storming inside me. I stared back, trying to form a coherent reply. A shout of joy, a reassurance that it was me and he wasn't dreaming, even a few tears of happiness wouldn't be so bad.

"Where the fuck have you been?" I snapped instead.

His mouth opened and closed like a fish. The last time I'd seen him so pale was just after he realized a crazy elf had tricked him into, essentially, selling his soul to the devil. Combined with battle stress—evidenced by the splotches of oddly colored blood on his dark clothes and the sheen of sweat already coating his skin—he seemed on the verge of stroking out.

"Working," he said, as if asking a question instead of answering one. "Building up something. We looked for you, but you weren't . . . Phin and I, we . . ." The train of thought moved on without him. "It's all different now."

"Different?" My heart ached. "Different how?"

"You're alive." Wyatt's voice had never sounded so . . . small. "You were dead, but Christ, Evy, you're alive."

He was persuading himself of the complete opposite of something he'd probably convinced himself to be true. A cloud of tension surrounded him, creating an invisible barrier I hesitated to physically cross. He'd accepted my death, that much was becoming clear. And the knowledge that he'd changed so much during my disappearance stabbed me through the heart. Had coming back been a mistake? Was I hurting him more by being here now?

"Max saved me," I said.

He cocked his head, not understanding. Then the name must have clicked. Absolute wonder came over him, softening the lines around his eyes and mouth, and turning his open-mouthed shock into awe. His watering gaze flickered to my various injuries, taking stock of me. I was so close, able to be in his arms in two steps.

Our gazes met, and I nearly fell into the inky blackness of his eyes. He raised his hand. Fingertips hovered near my cheek but didn't touch. I pressed against his hand and felt the instant heat of skin on skin. The spark of life in his touch. He made a soft choking sound in his throat. "I'm really not imagining you?"

"Would you imagine me in torn clothes, covered in blood?" I asked. My voice was thick, clogged. Damned lump.

"You were dead."

"Since when has that stopped me?" I couldn't quite manage flip, and the question came out like a plea.

Moisture pooled in his eyes. His lips worked, straining to create words. What he finally managed was "I love you."

Those final three words broke the last of my restraint, and I launched myself at him, throwing my arms around his neck in a choking hug. His arms snaked around my waist, painfully tight. I pressed my face into his neck, inhaling his scent, feeling his sandpapery skin on my cheek. I wanted to burrow into him and never let go. We were twirling in a circle, and I laughed out loud. I hadn't felt him lift me off the ground.

He set me back down and crushed his lips to mine. I opened for him and groaned under the bruising, possessive force of a kiss tinged with desperation and joy. Tiny shivers sparked through every nerve ending, awakening my sore, abused body in ways I'd forgotten were possible. Reminding me how very alive we both still were and were very likely to remain.

Nothing was settled. Boot Camp burned around us, and our exact casualty numbers were still unknown. The Fey hadn't been seen or heard from in weeks. Thackery's hybrids were dead, the last of his known hounds were dead, and I'd just shoved a knife through his teenage wolf's skull. Yet Thackery remained at large, possibly injured from the tractor-trailer wreck, and certainly about to be in a very bad mood over his latest failure.

I felt no pride in having once again tossed a monkey wrench into one of his carefully laid plans—only weariness at knowing he wasn't finished with us.

If you can't fight an infection, you remove the damaged limb.

Thackery wouldn't quit until he'd either found his elusive cure or eradicated the entire vampire race. And we'd be there to stop him. The Triads were in ruins, but we weren't destroyed. Wyatt and Phin were up to something, and they likely had been for a while. Their assistance today was well timed and raised a lot of questions: Did the brass know? The Assembly? Who else worked with them? Who was in charge?

I'd get the answers soon enough. We'd worry about finally capturing Walter Thackery in a little while. For now, the aftermath of the battle faded into the background, and nothing existed except us, in each other's arms—a place I thought I'd never be again. A place I could stay forever.

Okay, realistically, given battle fatigue and other recent trauma, another ten minutes or so.

Or until we both started to smell.

Whichever came first.

Read on for an excerpt from

WRONG SIDE OF DEAD

by Kelly Meding

Published by Bantam Books

Coming soon!

The rave was already in full swing by the time Phineas and I showed up dressed to blend, even though we weren't there for a party. Illegal raves full of drunk college students and twenty-somethings were the perfect hunting ground for half-Blood vampires, which made the transformed warehouse the perfect place for our little stakeout. But while any Halfie would do, I was hoping to see one particular target show up.

The music vibrated in my chest, loud enough to know my ears would be ringing by the time I left. We paused just inside, and Phineas el Chimal, my squad leader and partner for the night, closed his eyes to orient his more sensitive were-hearing to the din. Ravers jostled past us, ignorant of the partygoers around them, caught up in their own narrow little worlds. They had no clue why we were there, or that death was mingling out there among the kegs, glow sticks, and gyrating bodies.

No clue and no fucking manners. I was ready to turn around and slap the next person who elbowed me.

Phin saved them future bruises by opening his clear blue eyes and smiling. "Ready to have some fun?" he asked.

"Definitely." I draped myself onto his arm like the happy couple we were pretending to be, and his fingers laced through mine. We both knew we'd have to do some acting, and I trusted him to watch my back. He'd been doing it without fail since the day we met.

I stumbled a little in my knee-high boots, not used to the three-inch heels. My default shoes of choice were sneakers or combat boots—better for running and kicking. The black leather boots I had on now matched my black leather miniskirt, and their knee-high length carefully hid a pair of serrated blades. The boots were the only place my skimpy outfit could easily camouflage weapons, so I suffered the indignity of stumbling around in them. It was also a good excuse to lean on Phin and put on a lovey-dovey show.

At least Phin had the benefit of jeans and a black wife-beater, which showed off his toned physique and earned him appreciative smiles from a few female gawkers. I shot them possessive glares as we wove our way into the dancing, gyrating crowd. The air was thick with the distinctive odors of smoke, beer, and sweat.

Phin tilted his head, pretended to nuzzle my neck, and whispered, "Team one, six o'clock."

I spotted them easily, dancing amid a tight cluster near the DJ's stage. Gina Kismet and Marcus Dane were team one to our team two, and even from a distance they made quite the convincing (if mismatched) couple—Gina's five-foot-two, pale-skinned, red-haired goth girl to his six-foot-one, black-haired, copper-eyed pirate.

Okay, so I never actually called him a pirate to his face, but the long hair in a ponytail, the ruddy complexion, and the tendency toward scruffy facial hair gave that impression. Even if I hadn't known the man was actually Felia—a were-jaguar, to be precise—I'd have suspected he wasn't quite what he appeared to be.

They were burning it up on the dance floor, completely into each other—at least to the untrained eye. And besides our two pairs, we had four single plants mingling around the rave, on the lookout for shimmering eyes and silver-streaked hair, or even a set of fangs that hadn't been filed down. Half-blood vampires have certain telltale signs that can be covered up with contacts and hair dye, but the newest crop of Halfies were bolder, smarter, and they weren't as afraid of us as they used to be, back when an organization called the Triads existed and just our name sent them fleeing in fear.

God, I missed those days.

It didn't really help that one of our own was now one of these bolder Halfies and seemed to be using our hard-learned tactics against us.

Phin swept me through the crowd and we ended up near the makeshift bar where two guys with silver rings in their noses were filling cups from dozens of different kegs. He collected a beer for each of us to complete the fitting-in image. Beer wasn't my favorite, but I'd guzzled worse in the line of duty.

At least a hundred people were in the main part of the warehouse, and I imagined dozens more wandered around, getting into any unlocked rooms they could find. Initial surveillance told us the place had a section of offices on the north side of the warehouse, as well as roof access from the main floor.

While I had officially returned to the field last week, after spending almost three weeks training and recovering from being nearly tortured to death (again), this was my first big mission since . . . well, since my time with the Triads.

And a lot was riding on finding the guy we were looking for.

"Time to play," I said.

Phin grinned. The strobe lights lit his angular face in a way that accentuated the fact that he was a were-osprey—a predator in every sense of the word, but also a very loyal ally. Our relationship had its share of ups (me saving his life twice in the first two weeks of knowing each other) and downs (him stabbing me in the stomach the first day of knowing each other), but I wouldn't have wanted anyone else by my side for this little operation.

We moved with the crowd, creating an easy dance of grinding and groping, while carefully observing the other dancers and slowly sipping at our beers. Gina and Marcus had disappeared. I spotted one of our single plants, a full-blood vampire named Quince, dancing it up with a pair of girls in slinky dresses. He'd dyed his white hair dark-blond and wore blue contact lenses to cover his glimmering purple eyes—two very distinctive vampire attributes. The other was his long, lean frame, which he carried like a male model.

Quince had joined our organization two weeks ago and proved, right from the start, to be eager and very trainable. Phin immediately asked to have him assigned to his squad.

Before separating for the night's mission, our working sextet had come up with a handful of signals, since using ear-buds would be useless with the noise levels. Quince caught me looking at him and tugged hard on his left earlobe—shorthand for "I might have something."

I scratched my forehead, along the hairline, motioning that I understood. "Come on," I said to Phineas.

We leaned on each other as we threaded our way to the opposite wall, which was painted with Day-Glo stripes and splatters, both of us pretending to be more tipsy than we were. Quince extricated himself from his dance partners and met us there, slapping Phin on the shoulder as if greeting an old buddy.

"Rumors are circulating about a private party at midnight," Quince said, tone serious even as his expression remained playful. "It promises a narcotic experience that is both mind-altering and life-changing."

It definitely sounded like what happened when a human was infected with the vampiric parasite that turned them into a half-Blood. Vampires are a species unto themselves; they aren't made and they were never human. Their saliva, however, is highly infectious to humans, and a single bite alters a human's brain functions and physical nature. Many infected humans go insane from the change, but some adapt and are able to function with relative ease—relative given that they're still driven by blood-lust and are at risk of infecting more humans. Which is why all Halfies are on our "kill first, don't ask questions" list.

But the functional Halfies were even more dangerous. During the last two weeks, we'd stumbled across several places where a dozen or more Halfie corpses had been dumped after being beheaded. Word on the street said that several functioning Halfies were looking to create an army of similarly functioning Halfies to take us on. And since two in three went bat-shit crazy from the infection, they were building their ranks by trial and error.

Which meant the bodies of the once-innocent were piling up, and their makers had to be stopped. Of all the minor disasters plaguing the city, this was our most pressing. And the most personal, given the former Hunter who was helping to organize it.

"Where's the party?" I asked.

"Meeting on the roof," he replied. "For a brief inspection, I assume, before reporting the location to the chosen candidates."

"Awesome. What time is it?"

Phin checked his cell phone. "Eleven-twenty."

Good, we had a little time. "Quince, I want you and the other plants to stay down here just in case things get rowdy. Phin and I will let team one know, then head up to the roof."

Quince nodded, laughed like I'd just told the funniest joke ever, then melted back into the crowd. He was a damned good actor, for a vampire.

Phin crowded in and pressed his forehead to mine, like a lover going in for a kiss. His familiar scent, wild and clean like a raging mountain river, settled around me. "Think he'll show for the roof meet?" he asked, mouth mere inches from mine.

"Hope so," I replied, keenly aware of his warmth. "But I'm not counting on it."

"I'll go tell Marcus. Meet me by the roof access."

"Okay."

I lingered against the wall for the length of a song. That should be enough time for Phin to track down Marcus and Kismet and let them in on the new plan. The music changed. I eyed a path toward the far end of the warehouse where the stairwell (according to the blueprints) was located, aware of the throng in front of me.

Which was why I didn't notice my shadow until he'd sidled up next to me, leaning casually against the wall like he belonged there. I shifted sideways, prepared to tell him to get lost, and froze. Shit.

"Hey, Evy."

He had taken care to dye his hair back to its natural shade of brown, and donned a pair of lavender-tinted sunglasses to obscure the new shimmer to his eyes, but the face was the same. Felix Diggory, former Hunter and two-week-old half-Blood, grinned at me, his unfiled fangs gleaming brightly under the constantly shifting lights.

I wasn't sure how I'd react when I saw him again. I expected anger, grief, maybe even a little bit of shame, since I was there the night Felix got infected. Instead, all I felt was relief. Relief that he was there and I had the chance to correct my mistake. The mistake that allowed him to run free in the first place.

"Hey, Felix," I said.

"You look good. Been training?"

"Yeah, getting back into fighting form."

He dragged his tongue along the front teeth between his fangs, as if he thought I hadn't noticed them. (Or maybe it was a nervous tick; who knew?) "Saw you with Phineas earlier. You two on a date or are you working?"

I considered lying—for about three seconds. "Working. Looking for you, actually."

"Me?" He tilted his head. "I'm flattered."

"Don't be. You know why we're after you."

His mouth quirked at the corners. "Because I'm a big, bad Halfie now, and therefore must be slaughtered with extreme prejudice?"

"Bingo."

"Good luck with that."

The nonchalance was beginning to grate. I narrowed my eyes. "You don't think I can take you?"

"The last time I saw you, you couldn't take a house cat."

Okay, it was a challenge then. Good. I needed to get him out of the warehouse and away from hundreds of potential human shields—or victims. Rumors were circulating. The newspapers were printing stories full of incomplete information, speculating on mutilated bodies and the extraordinary number of missing persons. People weren't stupid, no matter what we did to try to convince them it was business as usual. I couldn't kill him in front of so many witnesses without causing a huge mess—and not of the spilled-blood variety.

I shifted my stance and pulled back my shoulders. "I might surprise you. I killed three Halfies just last week, all by my little old self."

He chuckled. "Good for you, Evy," he said, then let his gaze scan the crowd. "So who's here with you? I know you and the osprey can't be out hunting by yourselves."

"Marcus and Gina are here, and some new guys you don't know."

His attention snapped back to me. Eyebrows arched and lips slightly parted, he was caught somewhere between surprise and excitement. "She is? Really?"

The eagerness in those words broke my heart a little bit. Gina Kismet had been his boss, his Handler, for a little over two years. Their entire Triad had been very close, and losing Felix to infection had devastated all of them—Gina, Tybalt Monahan, and especially Milo Gant.

"Yeah, she's here somewhere," I said. I didn't bother trying to be casual as I scanned the crowd myself, looking for familiar faces. But we were tucked against a wall with a sea of people in front of us, and the lights made it difficult to see far or well.

"I wish I had time to say hello."

"Someplace else you need to be?"

"Yep."

"Okay, but you do realize that's not going to happen, yeah?"

In an instant, the predatory intensity was back. His nostrils flared, and he parted his lips just enough to let the tips of his fangs show. "You couldn't kill me the last time."

"I wasn't myself the last time."

"Oh?"

"Yeah."

"So what do you propose? We duke it out right here on the dance floor?"

He was playing along nicely. "I was thinking the roof," I said. "You and me."

"Let me guess." Felix cocked his head, clearly amused. "I win, and I get bragging rights on finally killing the unkillable Evy Stone."

I shrugged one shoulder. "As long as you promise to kill me and not infect me."

"I don't know. I think infecting the un-killable Evy

Stone would be a hell of a lot more fun." He frowned. "Then again, you survived infection once before."

Barely. A unique healing ability, gifted to me by a gnome, helped me battle the parasite that infects humans and turns them into Halfies. The ability also helped me survive too many near-fatal wounds in the two months since I died and was magically resurrected into my current body. An ability that part of me wished had been physical—something that could be duplicated and used to help others who were wounded or dying.

Because sometimes being the one who always survived when your friends died all around you really sucked. "Then I guess we're both fighting to kill," I said.

He ran his tongue along his front teeth, between his fangs. "Guess so. And I kind of still owe you."

"For what?"

"Punching me in the head the night before the factory fire."

I snorted. "Somehow I think getting blown up in that fire is payback enough."

"Maybe." He checked his wristwatch. "Well, let's get this over with so I can still make my appointment."

The utter normalcy of the statement took me momentarily aback. For the vast majority of Halfies, the infection makes them go mad. They can't think about anything except blood and death, and they rarely run around making plans and speaking about appointments. The utterly normal conversation (so to speak) I was having with Felix was an anomaly. The insane Halfies were the ones we most often encountered and killed. It made me wonder again just how many other lucid Halfies were out there—and how many more Felix had made in the two weeks since he was infected.

I just nodded.

"Ladies first?"

"You're fucking out of your mind if you think I'm turning my back on you."

Felix laughed. "That's the Evy I remember."

He pushed off the wall and strolled past me. Other partygoers, tired of the grind, slid quickly into our places. I kept my attention on Felix as I followed him through the smoke-and-liquor-scented throng, barely an arm's reach between us. As much as I wanted to look for someone in my group, to signal them about my destination, I couldn't risk Felix disappearing into the crowd. Now that I had him, I wasn't about to let him get away.

His path wound us in and out of clusters of dancers and groups of drinkers, but his goal always seemed to be the roof access doors at the opposite end of the warehouse. Three-quarters of the way there, I spotted Quince. His attention was on Felix, who he knew on sight from photographs. But if Felix sensed the full-Blood vampire nearby, he made no indication. And if Felix was signaling anyone else, I couldn't tell.

I passed into Quince's line of sight and pretended to adjust one of my clip-on earrings—the signal that I had engaged the target.

Felix reached the access door. It was partially hidden behind a stack of old wooden pallets, in what was a pretty lame attempt at keeping people from opening it. The door itself was metal, large, but he opened it easily with one hand and slipped inside. I grabbed the handle before it could slam shut and nearly wrenched my arm from its socket. The fucking thing was heavy.

The stairwell itself was dark and stifling. I stopped inside and let my eyes adjust to the murky shadows. Felix's pale skin came into focus first, several steps up the first flight. He beckoned, and I followed the sound of his echoing footsteps.

He could have attacked at any time, using his extra-sensitive night vision to easily gain the upper hand and kill me. But he didn't. He just kept going until he reached the roof door. It didn't open right away, probably rusted shut from disuse. I waited one step below the landing while he slammed one shoulder into the door.

It squealed open, and he stumbled out onto the roof. I followed, maintaining distance and caution as I stepped into the humid night air. The roof was tar and metal, longer than it was wide, and dotted with dozens of vents. It sagged in places. We'd probably missed a sign warning that it wasn't safe to walk on, but it was too late now.

The noise of the rave was muffled, bass vibrations occasionally dancing up through my feet and ankles. The sounds of the city seemed far away, even though we were still in her midst. Maybe three blocks from here was the old potato chip factory where I'd nearly died.

The rush of air clued me in to duck and I narrowly missed the fist aimed at my skull. I slammed my right shoulder forward and up, hitting muscle and ribs, and ejected an "oof!" of air from Felix. I drove my left fist sideways and landed a perfect kidney shot. A regular human male might have dropped to the roof in pain. Felix stumbled, and then returned the favor by driving his elbow down into the middle of my back.

Bolts of fire blossomed from the point of contact, searing all the way down to my toes. I dropped to my knees, saw his knee coming at my face, and rolled with the blow. It glanced off my cheekbone, a flash of pain, and I tumbled sideways. I used the momentum to keep rolling, and also reach into my boot.

I came up in a crouch a few feet away, one blade curled backward against my wrist, ready to slash at anything that came at me. My cheek smarted, and something warm dripped down my neck.

Felix grinned, fangs gleaming brightly. "First blood," he said, preening like it was some sort of accomplishment. Maybe in his infected deluded mind it was, but far worse (and far better) men had made me bleed.

"Lucky shot," I replied. The open wound concerned me. If he managed to get saliva into the wound (gross, yeah, but possible), it could spread the parasite. Even though the chance of me changing was very, very small, fighting the infection would hurt like hell, and I'd much rather avoid the agony.

"I wish I could make this last, Evy, but we'll be interrupted pretty soon."

I didn't know if he meant by my people, or by his. "Come and get me, big boy," I drawled.

He lunged, and I leapt up to meet him.

I seriously overestimated my leaping abilities.

We slammed together in an awkward tangle and hit the roof with a dull thud, thrashing and seeking purchase. I slashed with my blade, felt it cut skin and cloth. Warm blood slicked my hands, making my grip on the knife less certain. Felix clawed with his hands and kicked with his knees, landing blows on my thighs and upper arms. We probably looked like a pair of angry chicks in a cat fight, for all the grace either of us was showing.

Pretty sad for a pair of former Hunters.

He snapped at my face with his fangs, and I rewarded him with a head butt that cracked his nose. He howled and reeled back, even as his grip on my arms tightened, fingernails digging into skin. It exposed his throat, but I couldn't get my hand up. Couldn't get the blade across his windpipe to put him out of his fucking misery.

I got my right knee up and between us (not a small feat, considering the leather miniskirt), using it as a brace to keep him out of biting distance. My knife hand was stuck making shallow stabs at his ribs, but I was not close enough to cause real damage. We were at an awkward impasse, locked in a clinch that neither one of us was going to win.

Interruption was inevitable. The only question was by his people, or by mine?

It turned out to be both at the same time. An explosion of activity stole Felix's attention first, and it loosened his grip on my arms just enough. I shoved my knee against his chest, broke his hold, and rolled away. Someone slammed into me sideways, and we went tumbling across the tarred roof, my arms and legs scraping against the grit accumulated there over many years. I ended up on top of my attacker, back to chest, and slammed my left elbow backward. Bone connected with bone and sent a jolt through my arm from wrist to shoulder.

Plan B. I lifted my head up and crashed it back down, effectively breaking my second nose of the evening. The person below me—male, from the serious lack of breasts pressing in my shoulders—screeched and shoved. I lunged away and came up in a crouch. He tried to scuttle away. I scrambled up behind him and slit his throat. As he slumped to the ground, gurgling out purplish blood, I checked out the chaos.

Kismet and Phineas were going two against five with some teenage Halfies about fifteen feet away. Neither of them had drawn guns. So close to the rave and hundreds of innocents, gunshots would be too damned loud. They fought with blades, and with as much skill as any Hunter I'd ever seen. Especially Phin. He moved like liquid, dancing out of arm's reach, lunging in to draw blood then back out before the Halfie could bite.

I'd seen him fight before, several times. The very first time, though, he'd been in bi-shift form—still human, but with man-sized osprey wings protruding from his back like a dark-haired angel. He told me once his people had been fierce warriors, and he proved it each time he went into battle.

His wings weren't out this time, but he was no less intense. He caught me watching, gave me a wink, then grinned. Uh-oh.

Phin grabbed a Halfie by the neck and sent him at me like a bowling ball down a lane. I stopped the male Halfie's progress with the sharp heel of my boot, crouched, and cleanly snapped his neck. He thudded to the roof. Kismet and Phin dispatched the other Halfies with only a bit more effort. The front of Kismet's dress was ripped, nearly exposing her breasts, and her skin was spattered with Halfie blood. Phin, meanwhile, barely looked disheveled.

He gave me a wicked grin, battle lust shining in his eyes. Eyes that flickered past me, then blinked. In surprise, not in warning. I turned, curious. My jaw dropped and I nearly burst out laughing.

Marcus had shifted into jaguar form, a big black thing of beauty and power, but that wasn't what was so funny. He was sitting on top of Felix, front paws pinning down the thrashing man's shoulders, like a giant paperweight. The fact that Felix was struggling to remove the two hundred pound immoveable object threatened to give me a bad case of the giggles. It was just so ridiculous.

I stared. Marcus yawned. Behind me, Phin laughed.

Kismet appeared by my shoulder. She hadn't seen Felix since the day he was infected. Her jaw was set, her expression hard. She had mourned him, just as Milo and Tybalt had, but that didn't mean much when the "dead" person was still "alive" and being held down by a werecat.

She looked up at me, and I held her gaze without blinking. I'd been where she was—about to end the suffering of a loved one because of vampire infection. I didn't know exactly what she felt, but I could damned well guess. She blinked, then inhaled a deep breath. Let it out. Palmed a blade.

Felix had stopped struggling. As Kismet walked toward him, he twisted his head around to look at her. Despite his position, he smiled. "Hey, Kis," he said. "We had a good couple years, huh?"

She froze. Even with her back to me, I saw muscles tense and could just imagine her expression—ice and anger flashing in wide green eyes. "No," she said in a voice full of cold fury, "we didn't. You have his memories and body, but you aren't Felix. Felix died the moment he was infected."

"Maybe. Probably. Shit."

He seemed so sane, so completely in his right mind, that my curiosity bubbled over. I closed the distance between me and Kismet. "How did you not go insane from the infection?" I asked before I could censor myself.

His iridescent eyes flickered from her to me. "I can smell your blood, Evy. It smells so good, sweet even. I want to taste it."

Marcus growled.

"It's partially impulse control," Felix said as if he hadn't even mentioned wanting my blood. "I want to hunt and feed, but I don't. Or if I do, I don't let the blood lust control my actions. I don't let it make me crazy."

"You just don't let it?" I asked. "Bullshit."

He shrugged—or at least, he tried to shrug. "It isn't easy. It's like an addiction, a craving. I was a Hunter so I know it's wrong to feed, but I have to. I know I'm a monster, and I don't want to be." He sounded so . . . resigned. Almost sad. With the shimmering eyes and the fangs, it was pretty damned eerie.

Half-Bloods were abominations. They weren't controllable, hence the entire reason for our open execution policy on them. You can feed and tame a wild animal, but you live with the constant risk of being turned on and attacked.

Marcus made a noise not unlike a bored grunt. His bright copper eyes shifted from me to Phin, then down to his trapped prey. He bared long, deadly teeth, silently asking if it was time to end this. Therians were not prone to infection, so he could crush Felix's throat with those powerful jaws and not risk turning. But I knew Kismet wouldn't allow that.

Kismet squatted next to his head.

"Tell Milo and Tybalt I'm sorry," Felix said.

She nodded, turning the blade in her hand . . .